MARCUS EMERSON

RECESS WARRIORS

BAD GUY IS A TWO-WORD WORD

ROARING BROOK PRESS

New York

Published by Roaring Brook Press
Roaring Brook Press is a division of Holtzbrinck Publishing Holdings Limited Partnership
175 Fifth Avenue, New York, NY 10010
mackids.com

Library of Congress Control Number: 2016961552
ISBN: 978-1-62672-709-0

Our books may be purchased in bulk for promotional, educational, or business use.
Please contact your local bookseller or the Macmillan Corporate and Premium Sales Department
at (800) 221-7945 ext. 5442 or by e-mail at MacmillanSpecialMarkets@macmillan.com.

First eedition 2017
Book design by Andrew Arnold
Printed in China by Toppan Leefung Printing Ltd., Dongguan City, Guangdong Province

1 3 5 7 9 10 8 6 4 2

FOR CAMME...

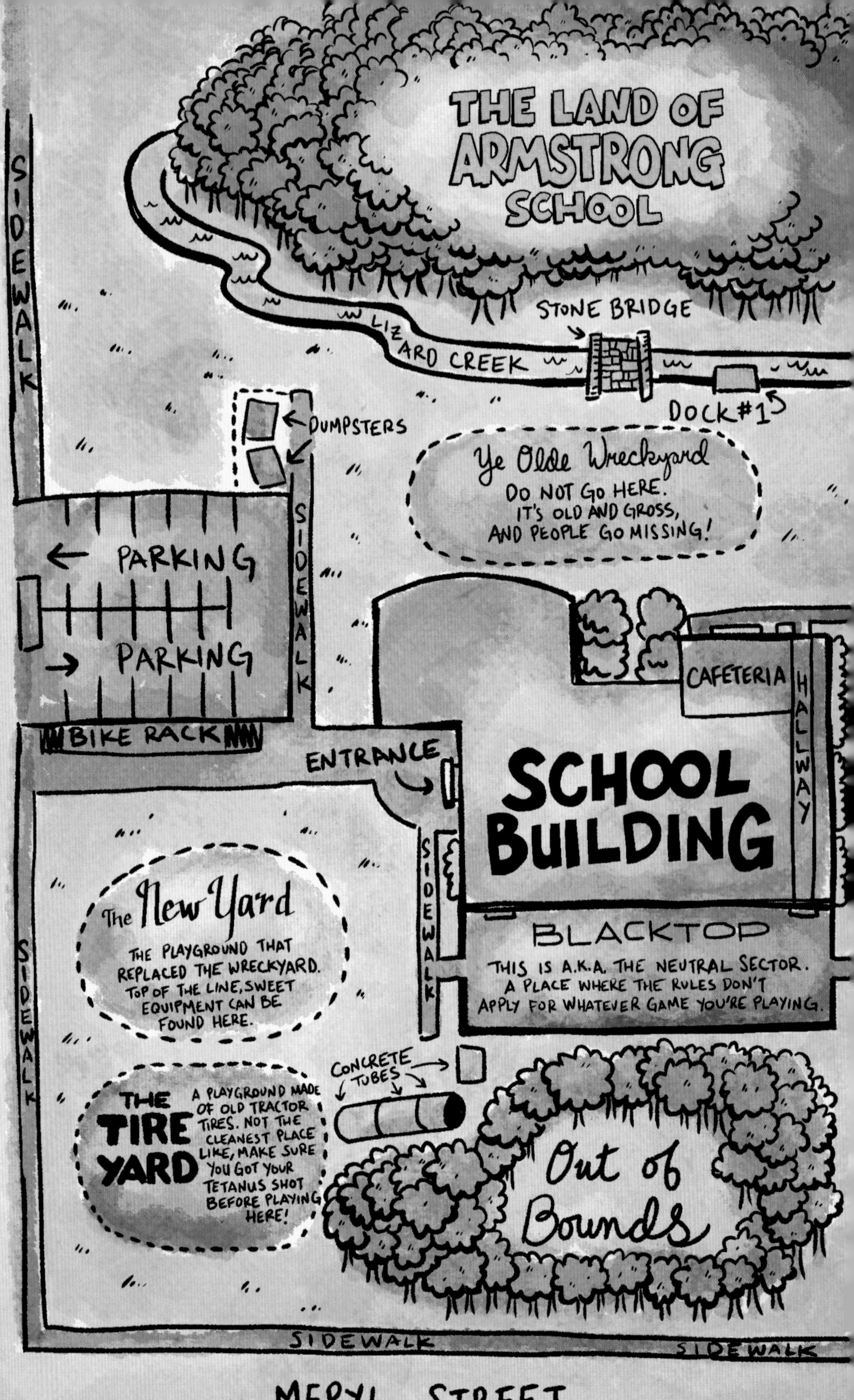
THE LAND OF ARMSTRONG SCHOOL
SIDEWALK
LIZARD CREEK
STONE BRIDGE
DOCK #1
DUMPSTERS
Ye Olde Wreckyard
DO NOT GO HERE. IT'S OLD AND GROSS, AND PEOPLE GO MISSING!
PARKING
PARKING
SIDEWALK
CAFETERIA
HALLWAY
BIKE RACK
ENTRANCE
SCHOOL BUILDING
SIDEWALK
BLACKTOP
THIS IS A.K.A. THE NEUTRAL SECTOR. A PLACE WHERE THE RULES DON'T APPLY FOR WHATEVER GAME YOU'RE PLAYING.
The New Yard
THE PLAYGROUND THAT REPLACED THE WRECKYARD. TOP OF THE LINE, SWEET EQUIPMENT CAN BE FOUND HERE.
SIDEWALK
CONCRETE TUBES
THE TIRE YARD
A PLAYGROUND MADE OF OLD TRACTOR TIRES. NOT THE CLEANEST PLACE LIKE, MAKE SURE YOU GOT YOUR TETANUS SHOT BEFORE PLAYING HERE!
Out of Bounds
SIDEWALK
SIDEWALK
MERYL STREET

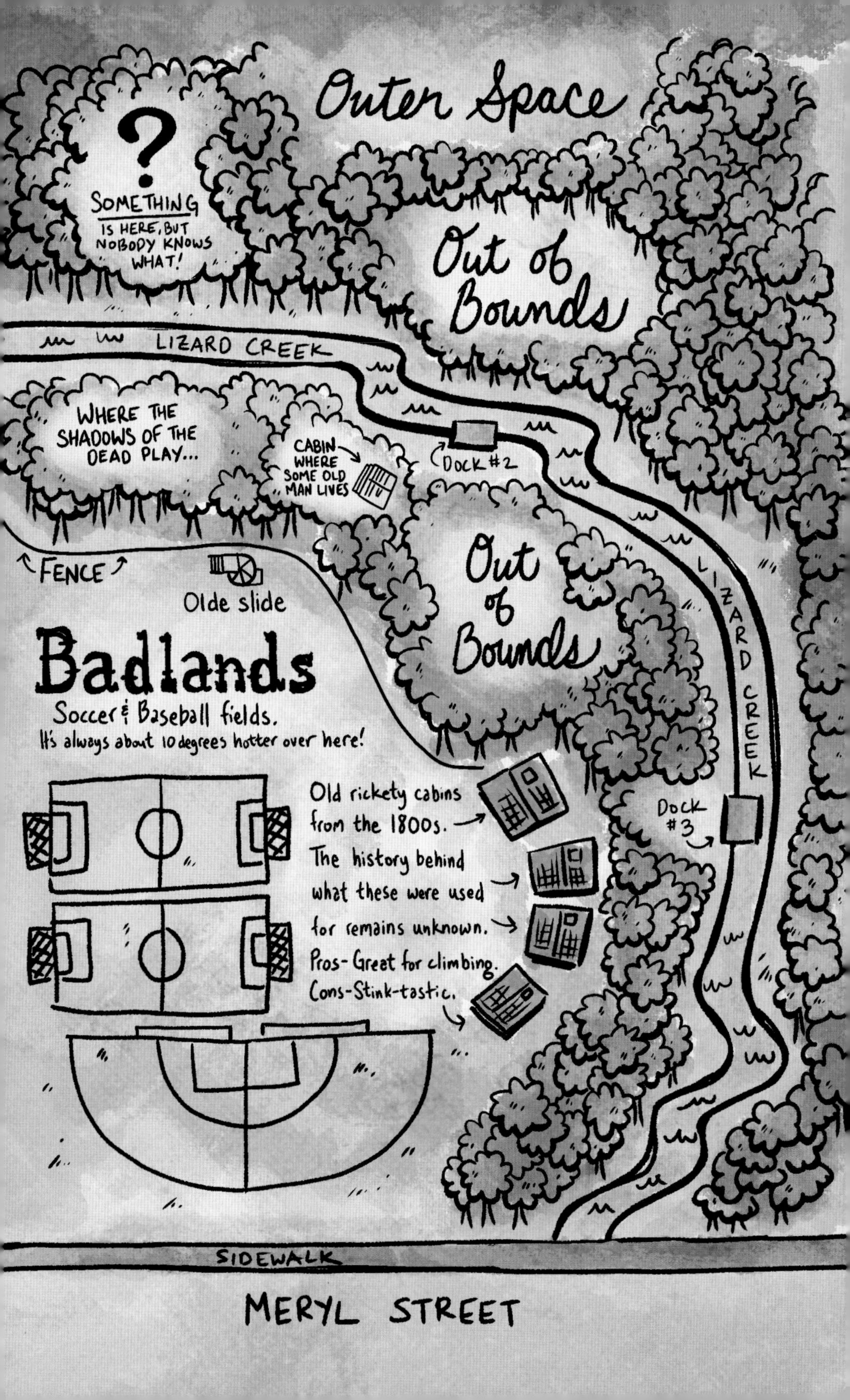
Outer Space
?
SOMETHING
IS HERE, BUT NOBODY KNOWS WHAT!
Out of Bounds
LIZARD CREEK
WHERE THE SHADOWS OF THE DEAD PLAY...
CABIN WHERE SOME OLD MAN LIVES
DOCK #2
Out of Bounds
FENCE
Olde slide
LIZARD CREEK
Badlands
Soccer & Baseball fields.
It's always about 10 degrees hotter over here!
Old rickety cabins from the 1800s. The history behind what these were used for remains unknown. Pros- Great for climbing. Cons-Stink-tastic.
Dock #3
SIDEWALK
MERYL STREET

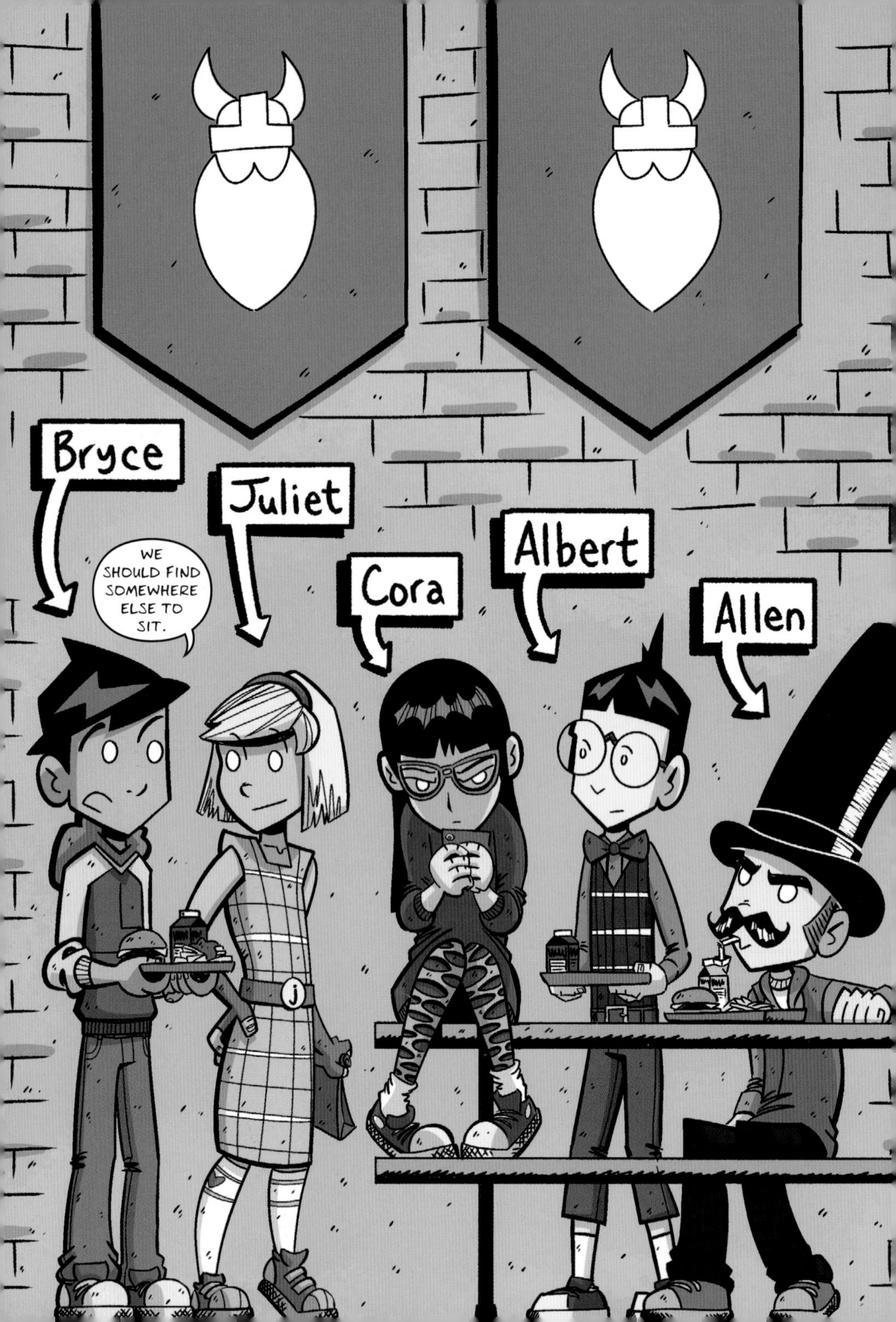
Bryce
Juliet
Cora
Albert
Allen
WE SHOULD FIND SOMEWHERE ELSE TO SIT.

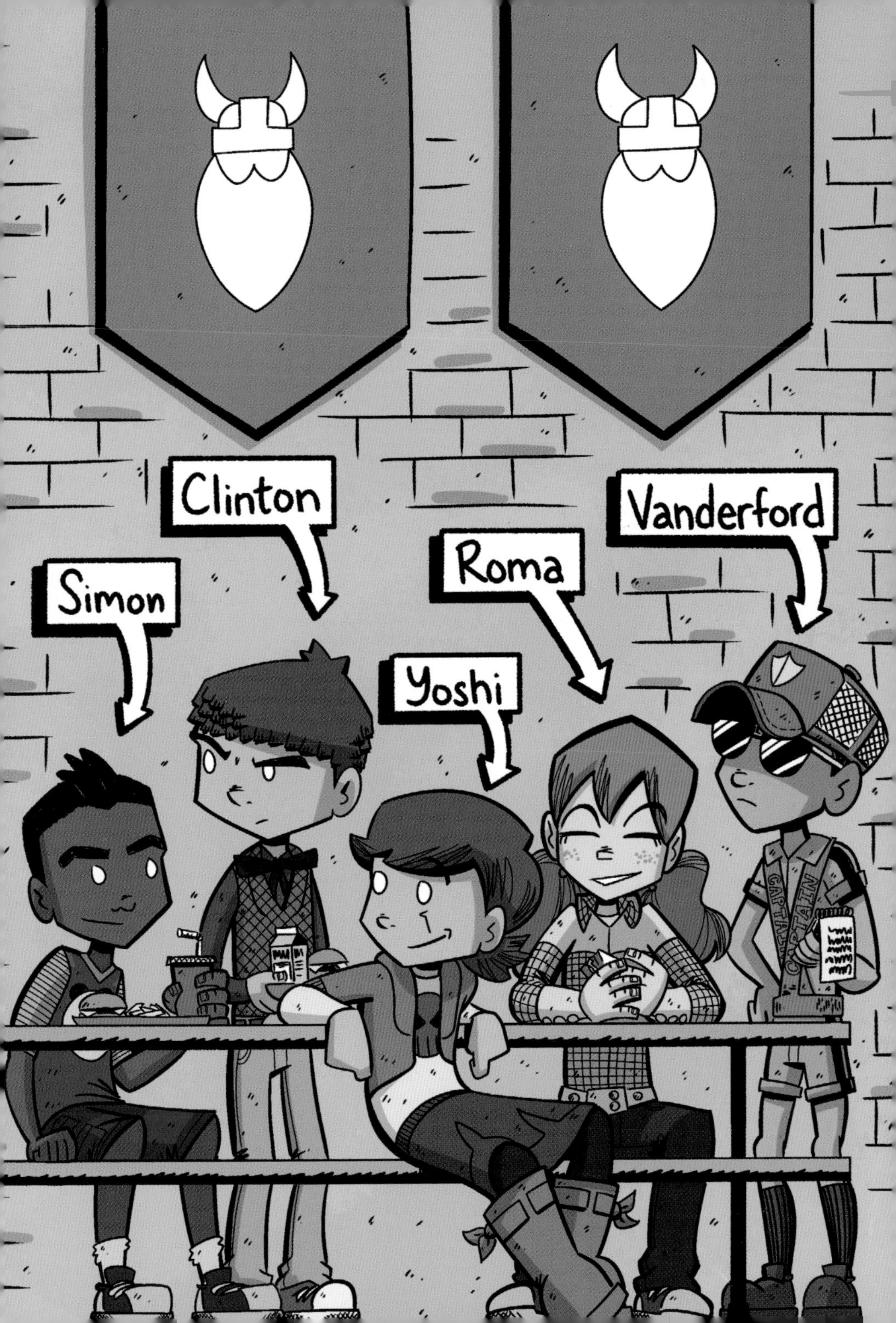
Clinton
Vanderford
Simon
Roma
Yoshi

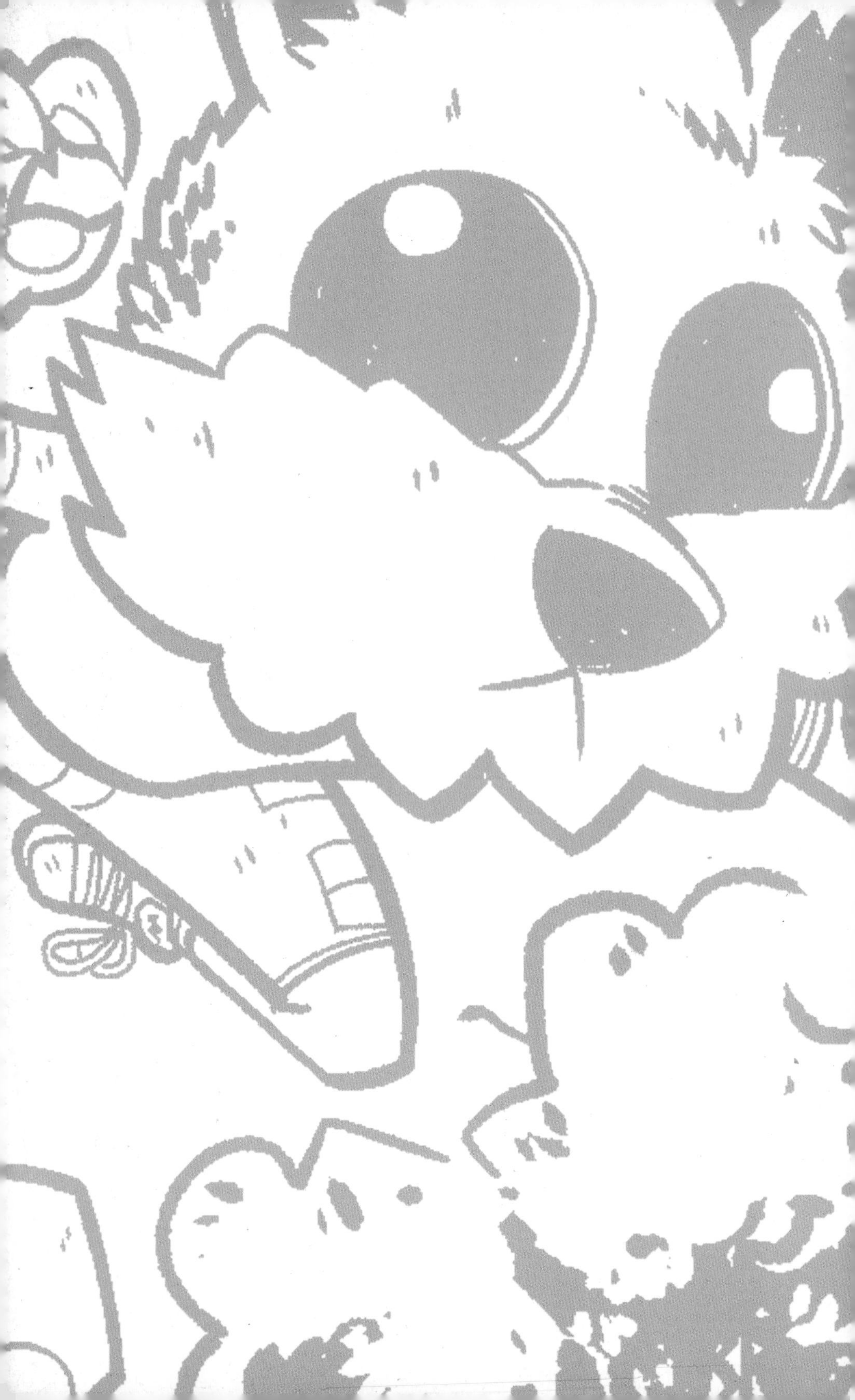

PREVIOUSLY IN

RECESS WARRIORS

IT STARTED WITH A KISS...

LOVESICK 5TH GRADER JULIET FOX USED A SPECIAL LIP GLOSS TO RELEASE THE DEADLY COOTIES VIRUS INTO THE SCHOOLYARD.

HER ENDGAME WAS TO INFECT ONE BOY IN PARTICULAR...

BRYCE. A.K.A.: SCRAP.

BRYCE TRIED TO STOP HER BUT COULDN'T DO IT ALONE. HE SOUGHT HELP FROM HIS EX-BFF, SHERIFF CLINTON. BUT THE COWBOY REFUSED, STILL BURNED BY WHAT HAD HAPPENED IN THEIR PAST...

SO THE MIGHTY SCRAP FACED JULIET FOX ALONE.

ALAS, HE WAS NO MATCH FOR HER RESOLVE AND WAS BESTED BY THE BEST OF THE BESTEST BEST.

AT HIS DARKEST HOUR, SCRAP WAS SAVED BY YOSHI, WHO DEFEATED JULIET WITH NOTHING MORE THAN A TINY LITTLE MOUSE.

BUT YOSHI WAS TOO LATE...

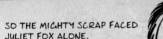

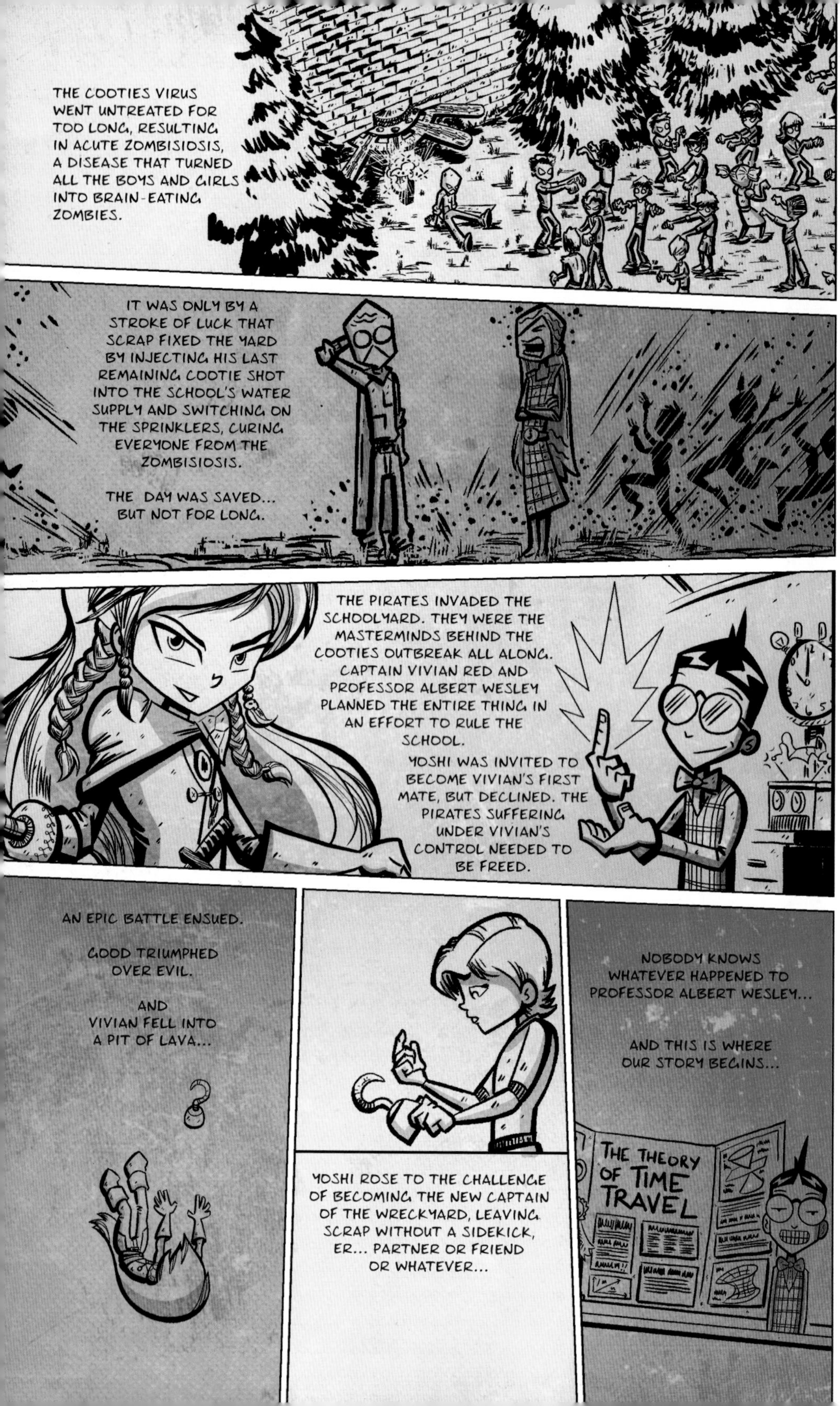
THE COOTIES VIRUS WENT UNTREATED FOR TOO LONG, RESULTING IN ACUTE ZOMBISIOSIS, A DISEASE THAT TURNED ALL THE BOYS AND GIRLS INTO BRAIN-EATING ZOMBIES.
IT WAS ONLY BY A STROKE OF LUCK THAT SCRAP FIXED THE YARD BY INJECTING HIS LAST REMAINING COOTIE SHOT INTO THE SCHOOL'S WATER SUPPLY AND SWITCHING ON THE SPRINKLERS, CURING EVERYONE FROM THE ZOMBISIOSIS.
THE DAY WAS SAVED... BUT NOT FOR LONG.
THE PIRATES INVADED THE SCHOOLYARD. THEY WERE THE MASTERMINDS BEHIND THE COOTIES OUTBREAK ALL ALONG. CAPTAIN VIVIAN RED AND PROFESSOR ALBERT WESLEY PLANNED THE ENTIRE THING IN AN EFFORT TO RULE THE SCHOOL.
YOSHI WAS INVITED TO BECOME VIVIAN'S FIRST MATE, BUT DECLINED. THE PIRATES SUFFERING UNDER VIVIAN'S CONTROL NEEDED TO BE FREED.
AN EPIC BATTLE ENSUED.
GOOD TRIUMPHED OVER EVIL.
AND VIVIAN FELL INTO A PIT OF LAVA...
YOSHI ROSE TO THE CHALLENGE OF BECOMING THE NEW CAPTAIN OF THE WRECKYARD, LEAVING SCRAP WITHOUT A SIDEKICK, ER... PARTNER OR FRIEND OR WHATEVER...
NOBODY KNOWS WHATEVER HAPPENED TO PROFESSOR ALBERT WESLEY...
AND THIS IS WHERE OUR STORY BEGINS...
THE THEORY OF TIME TRAVEL

04 THE BALLAD OF SHERIFF DAVENPORT

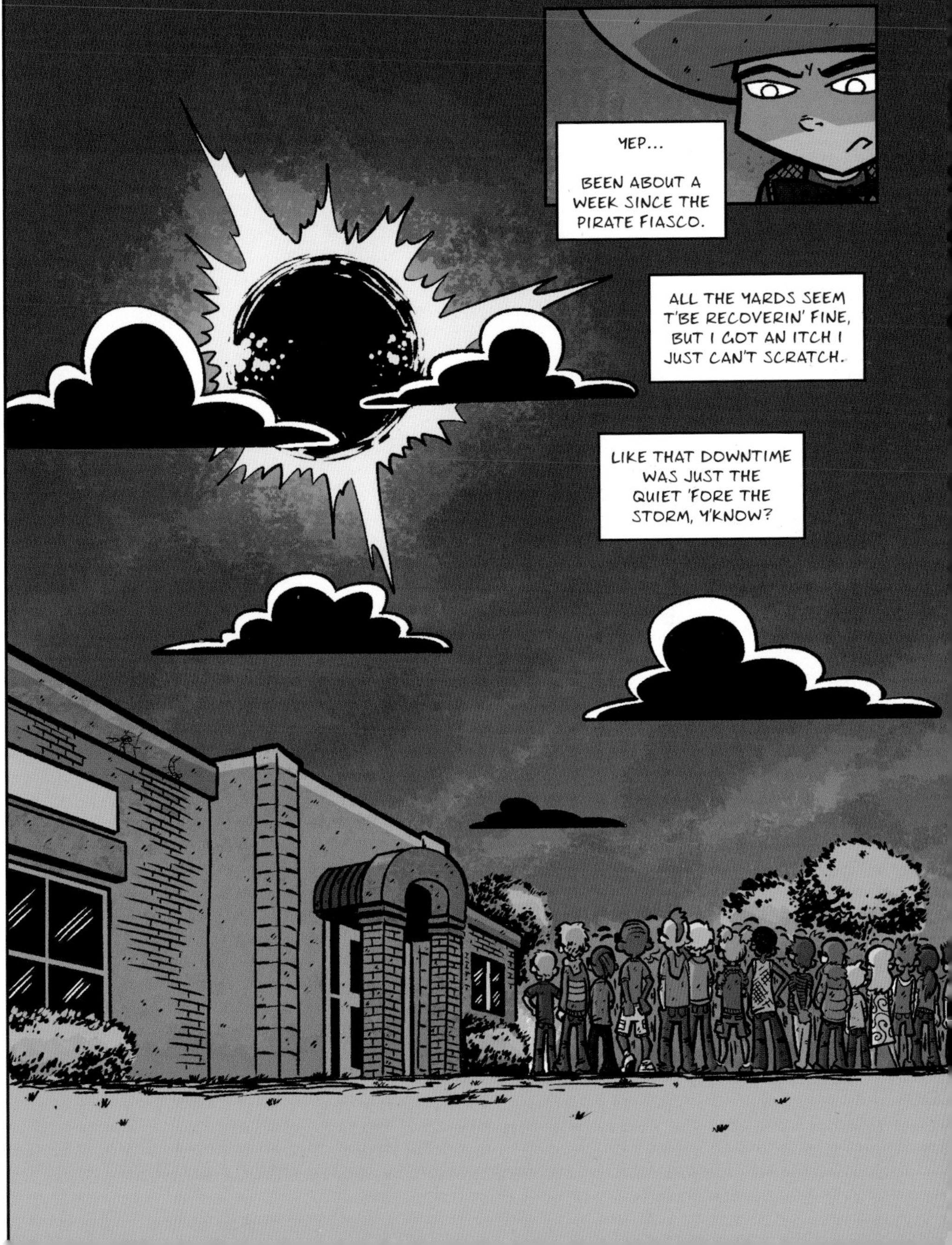
YEP...
BEEN ABOUT A WEEK SINCE THE PIRATE FIASCO.
ALL THE YARDS SEEM T'BE RECOVERIN' FINE, BUT I GOT AN ITCH I JUST CAN'T SCRATCH.
LIKE THAT DOWNTIME WAS JUST THE QUIET 'FORE THE STORM, Y'KNOW?

YOSHI'S BEEN A GOOD LEADER. **REAL GOOD.**

SPENDS SO MUCH TIME IN THE WRECKYARD, WE HARDLY SEE HER 'ROUND THESE PARTS.

THEM GIRLS OWE A LOT TO HER.

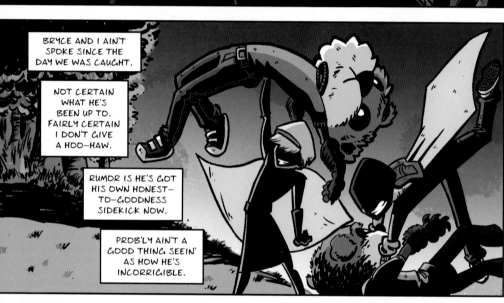

BRYCE AND I AIN'T SPOKE SINCE THE DAY WE WAS CAUGHT.

NOT CERTAIN WHAT HE'S BEEN UP TO. FAIRLY CERTAIN I DON'T GIVE A HOO-HAW.

RUMOR IS HE'S GOT HIS OWN HONEST-TO-GOODNESS SIDEKICK NOW.

PROB'LY AIN'T A GOOD THING SEEIN' AS HOW HE'S INCORRIGIBLE.

BUT THERE'S ANOTHER RUMOR CIRCLIN' THE BADLANDS...

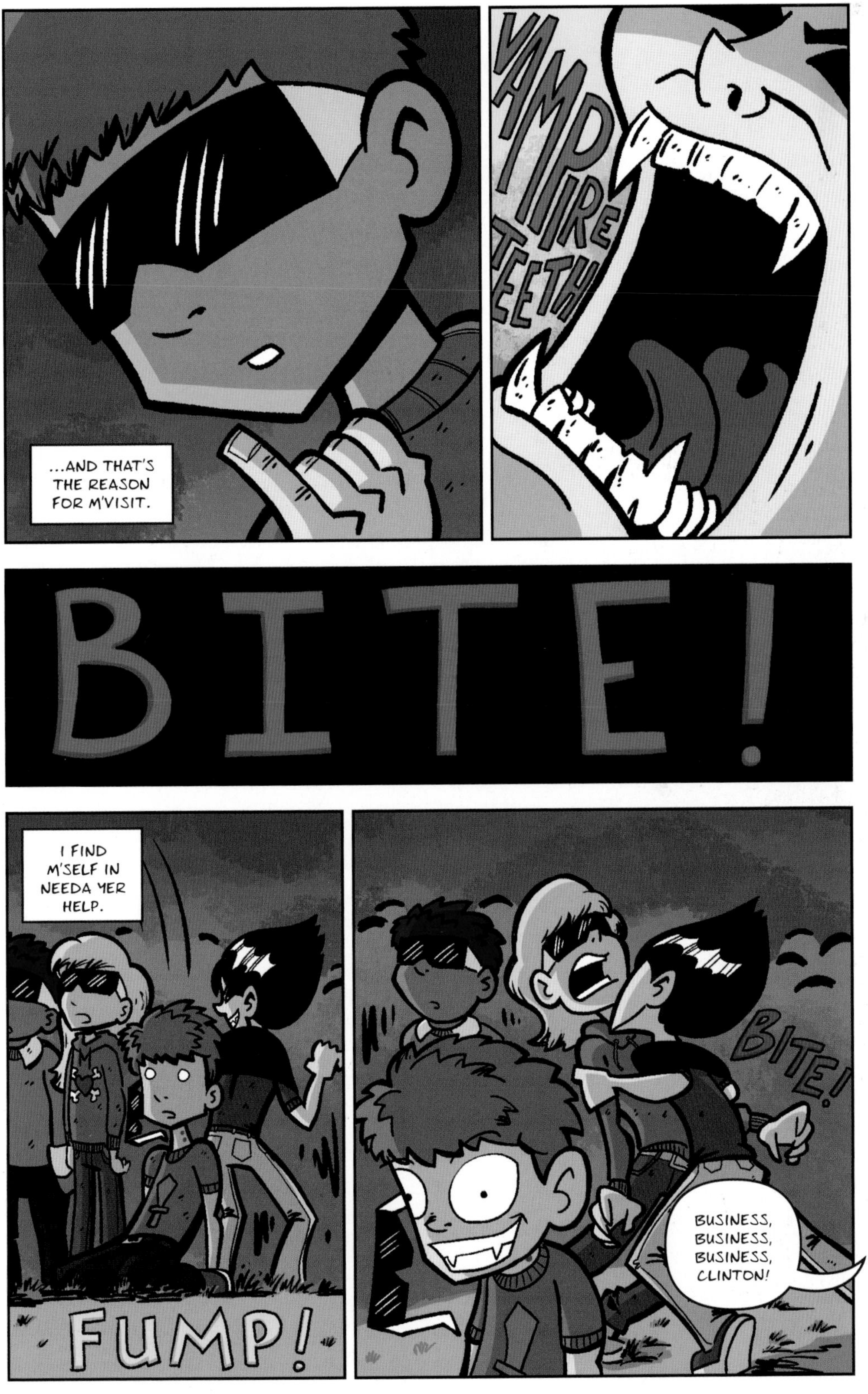
...AND THAT'S THE REASON FOR M'VISIT.
VAMPIRE TEETH
BITE!
I FIND M'SELF IN NEEDA YER HELP.
FUMP!
BITE!
BUSINESS, BUSINESS, BUSINESS, CLINTON!

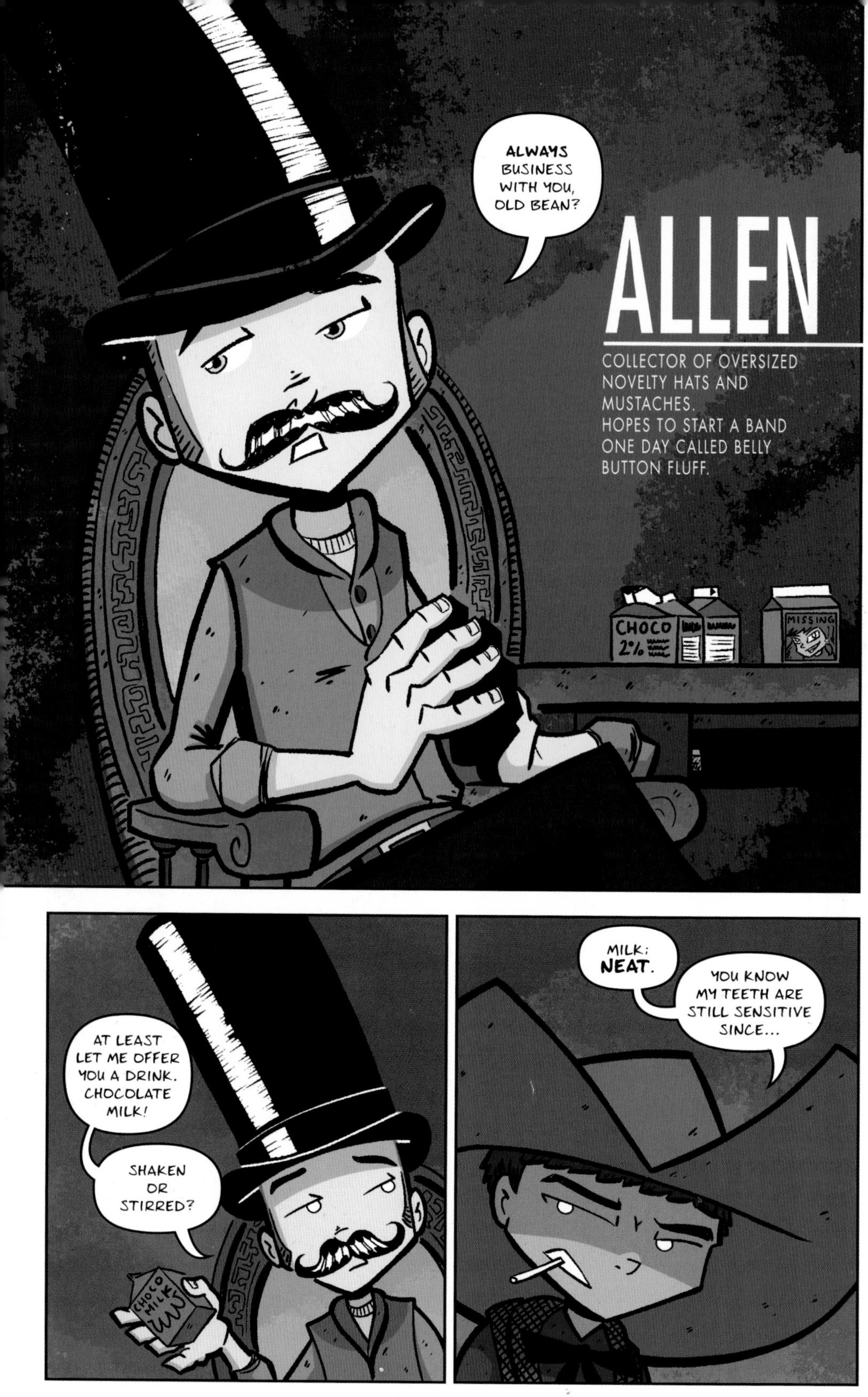
ALWAYS BUSINESS WITH YOU, OLD BEAN?
ALLEN
COLLECTOR OF OVERSIZED NOVELTY HATS AND MUSTACHES.
HOPES TO START A BAND ONE DAY CALLED BELLY BUTTON FLUFF.
CHOCO 2%
MISSING
AT LEAST LET ME OFFER YOU A DRINK. CHOCOLATE MILK!
SHAKEN OR STIRRED?
CHOCO MILK
MILK; **NEAT**.
YOU KNOW MY TEETH ARE STILL SENSITIVE SINCE...

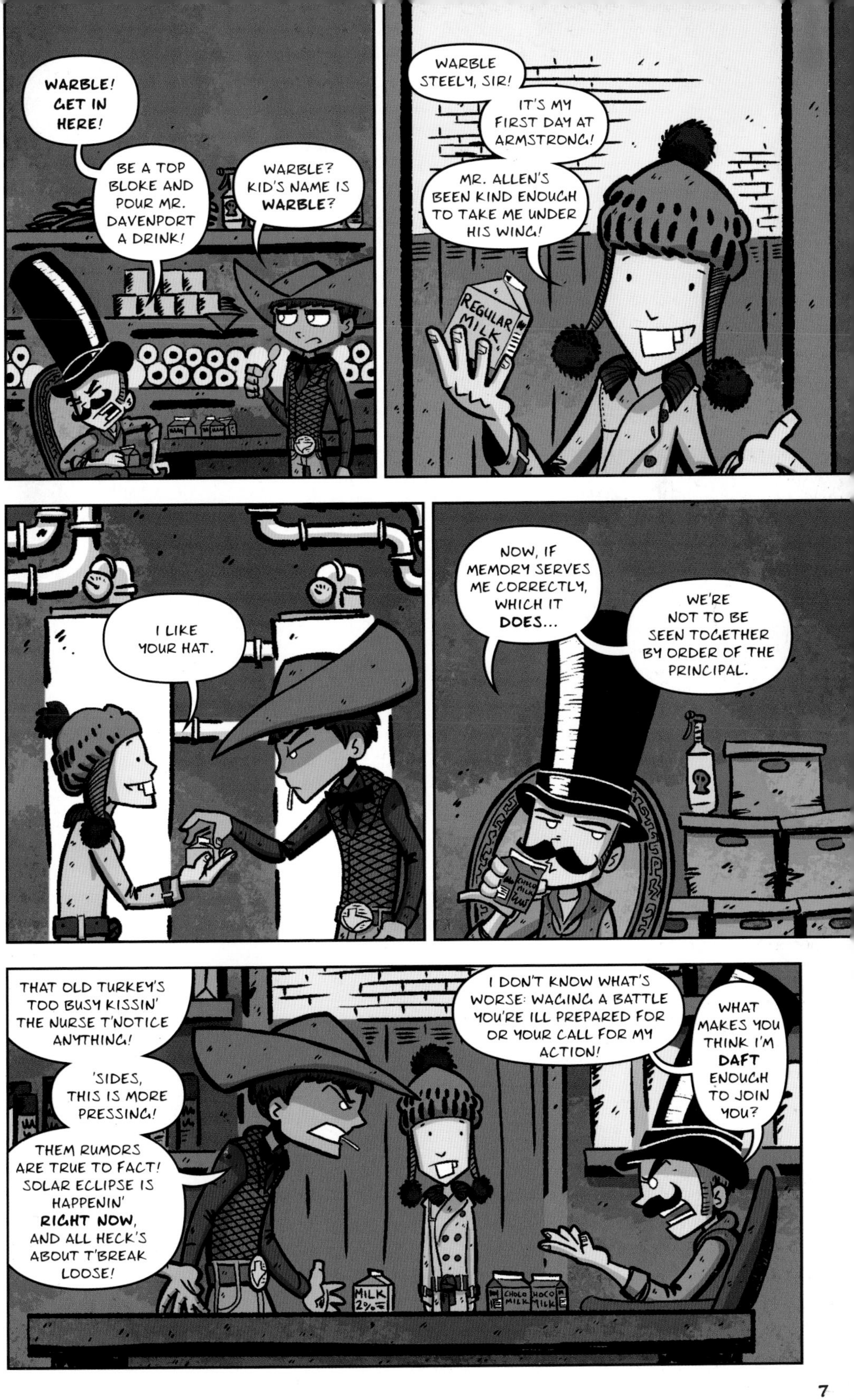
WARBLE! GET IN HERE!
BE A TOP BLOKE AND POUR MR. DAVENPORT A DRINK!
WARBLE? KID'S NAME IS **WARBLE**?
WARBLE STEELY, SIR!
IT'S MY FIRST DAY AT ARMSTRONG!
MR. ALLEN'S BEEN KIND ENOUGH TO TAKE ME UNDER HIS WING!
REGULAR MILK
I LIKE YOUR HAT.
NOW, IF MEMORY SERVES ME CORRECTLY, WHICH IT **DOES**...
WE'RE NOT TO BE SEEN TOGETHER BY ORDER OF THE PRINCIPAL.
THAT OLD TURKEY'S TOO BUSY KISSIN' THE NURSE T'NOTICE ANYTHING!
'SIDES, THIS IS MORE PRESSING!
THEM RUMORS ARE TRUE TO FACT! SOLAR ECLIPSE IS HAPPENIN' **RIGHT NOW**, AND ALL HECK'S ABOUT T'BREAK LOOSE!
I DON'T KNOW WHAT'S WORSE: WAGING A BATTLE YOU'RE ILL PREPARED FOR OR YOUR CALL FOR MY ACTION!
WHAT MAKES YOU THINK I'M **DAFT** ENOUGH TO JOIN YOU?
MILK 2%
CHOCO MILK
CHOCO MILK

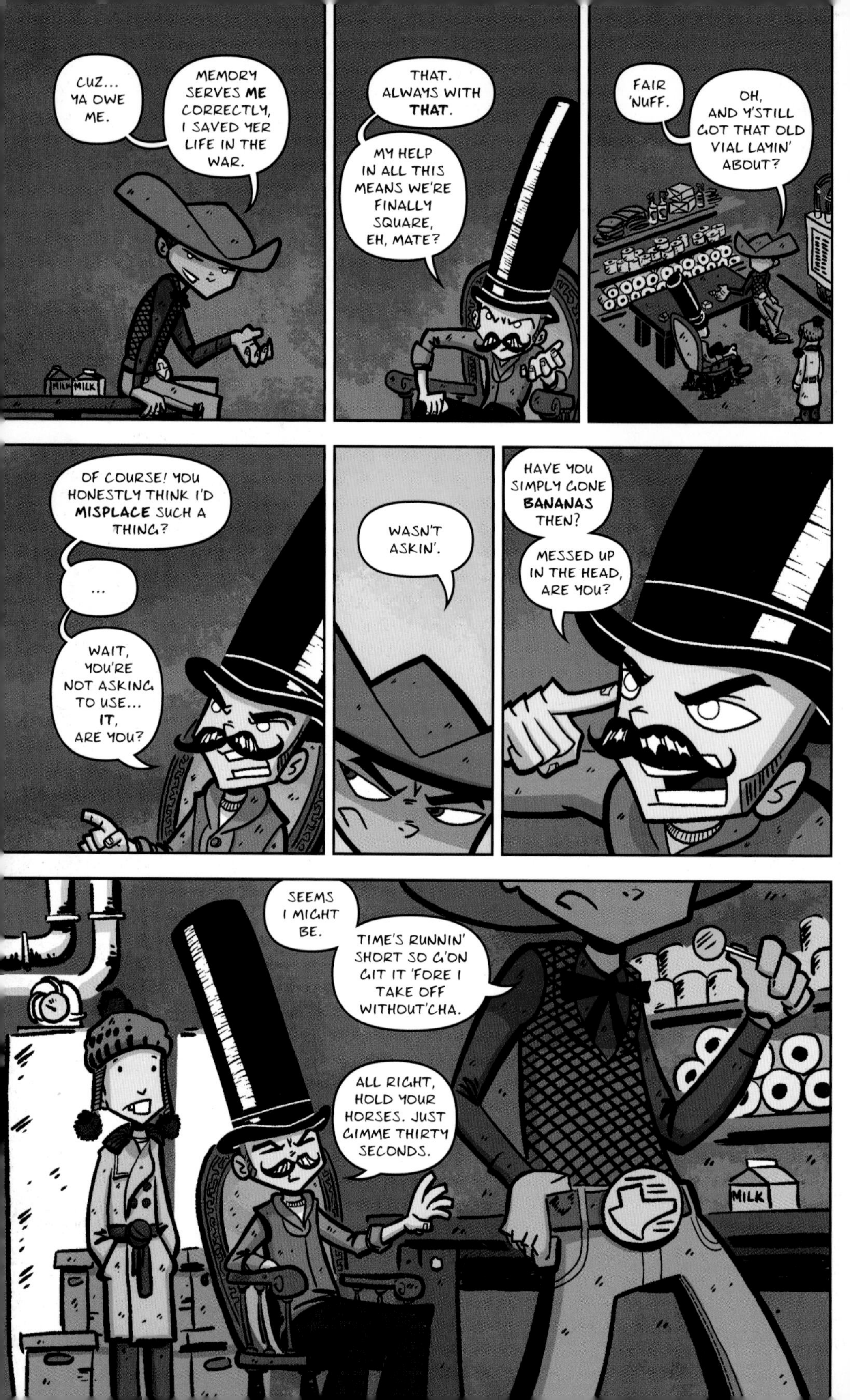
CUZ... YA OWE ME.
MEMORY SERVES **ME** CORRECTLY, I SAVED YER LIFE IN THE WAR.
THAT. ALWAYS WITH **THAT**.
MY HELP IN ALL THIS MEANS WE'RE FINALLY SQUARE, EH, MATE?
FAIR 'NUFF.
OH, AND Y'STILL GOT THAT OLD VIAL LAYIN' ABOUT?
MILK
MILK
OF COURSE! YOU HONESTLY THINK I'D **MISPLACE** SUCH A THING?
...
WAIT, YOU'RE NOT ASKING TO USE... **IT**, ARE YOU?
WASN'T ASKIN'.
HAVE YOU SIMPLY GONE **BANANAS** THEN?
MESSED UP IN THE HEAD, ARE YOU?
SEEMS I MIGHT BE.
TIME'S RUNNIN' SHORT SO G'ON GIT IT 'FORE I TAKE OFF WITHOUT'CHA.
ALL RIGHT, HOLD YOUR HORSES. JUST GIMME THIRTY SECONDS.
MILK

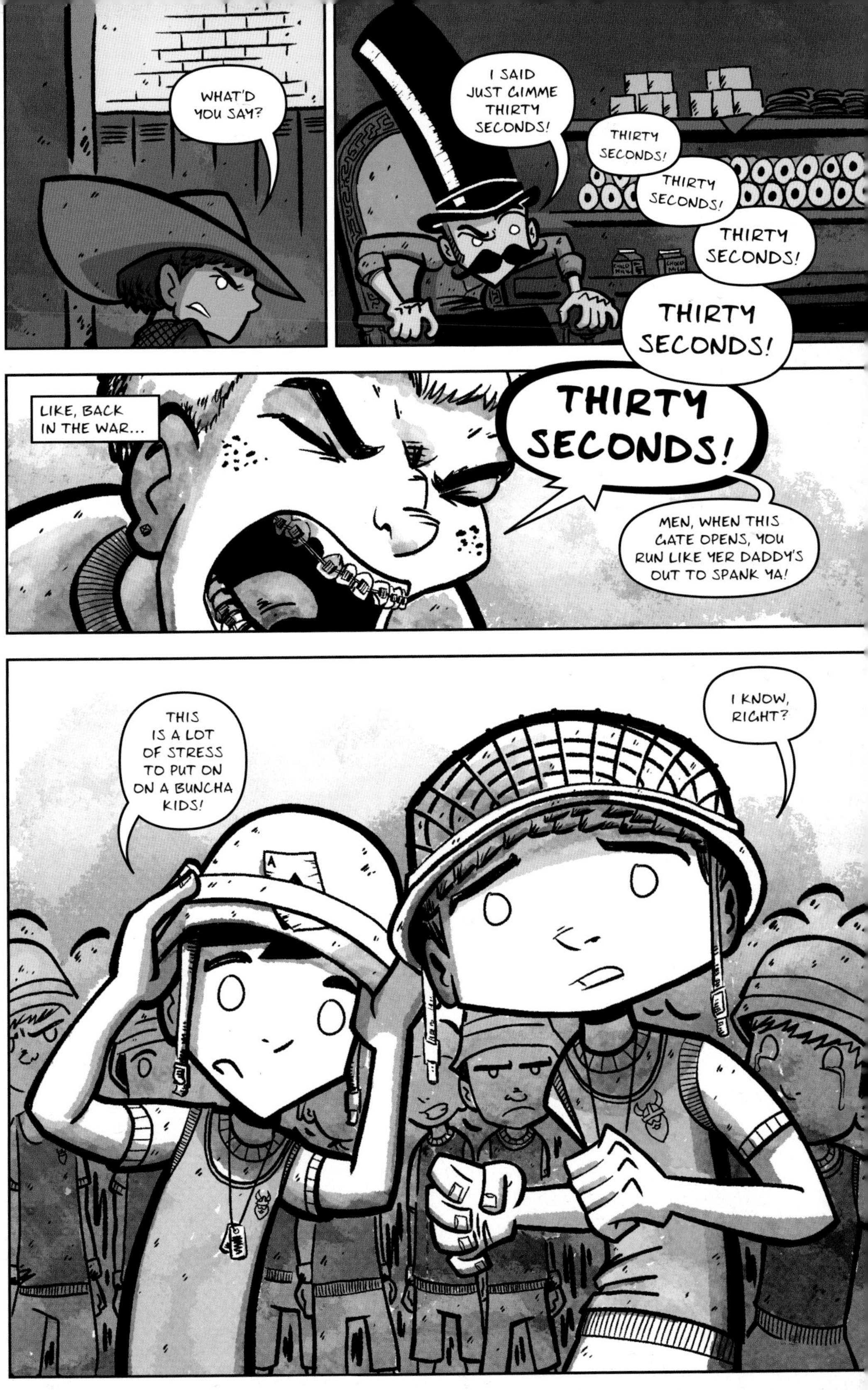
WHAT'D YOU SAY?
I SAID JUST GIMME THIRTY SECONDS!
THIRTY SECONDS!
THIRTY SECONDS!
THIRTY SECONDS!
THIRTY SECONDS!
LIKE, BACK IN THE WAR...
THIRTY SECONDS!
MEN, WHEN THIS GATE OPENS, YOU RUN LIKE YER DADDY'S OUT TO SPANK YA!
THIS IS A LOT OF STRESS TO PUT ON ON A BUNCHA KIDS!
I KNOW, RIGHT?

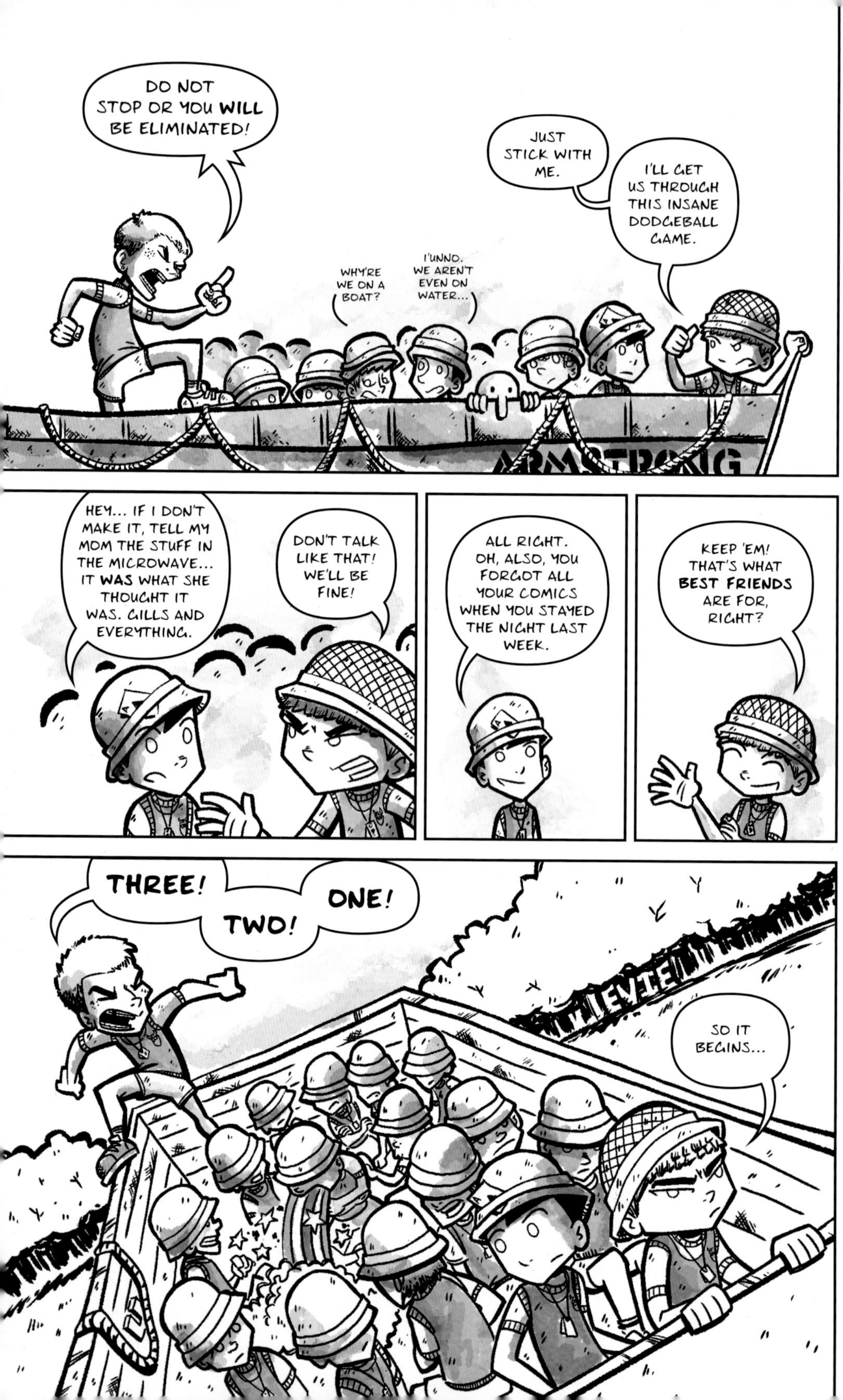
DO NOT STOP OR YOU **WILL** BE ELIMINATED!
WHY'RE WE ON A BOAT?
I'UNNO. WE AREN'T EVEN ON WATER...
JUST STICK WITH ME.
I'LL GET US THROUGH THIS INSANE DODGEBALL GAME.
ARMSTRONG
HEY... IF I DON'T MAKE IT, TELL MY MOM THE STUFF IN THE MICROWAVE... IT **WAS** WHAT SHE THOUGHT IT WAS. GILLS AND EVERYTHING.
DON'T TALK LIKE THAT! WE'LL BE FINE!
ALL RIGHT. OH, ALSO, YOU FORGOT ALL YOUR COMICS WHEN YOU STAYED THE NIGHT LAST WEEK.
KEEP 'EM! THAT'S WHAT **BEST FRIENDS** ARE FOR, RIGHT?
THREE!
TWO!
ONE!
SO IT BEGINS...

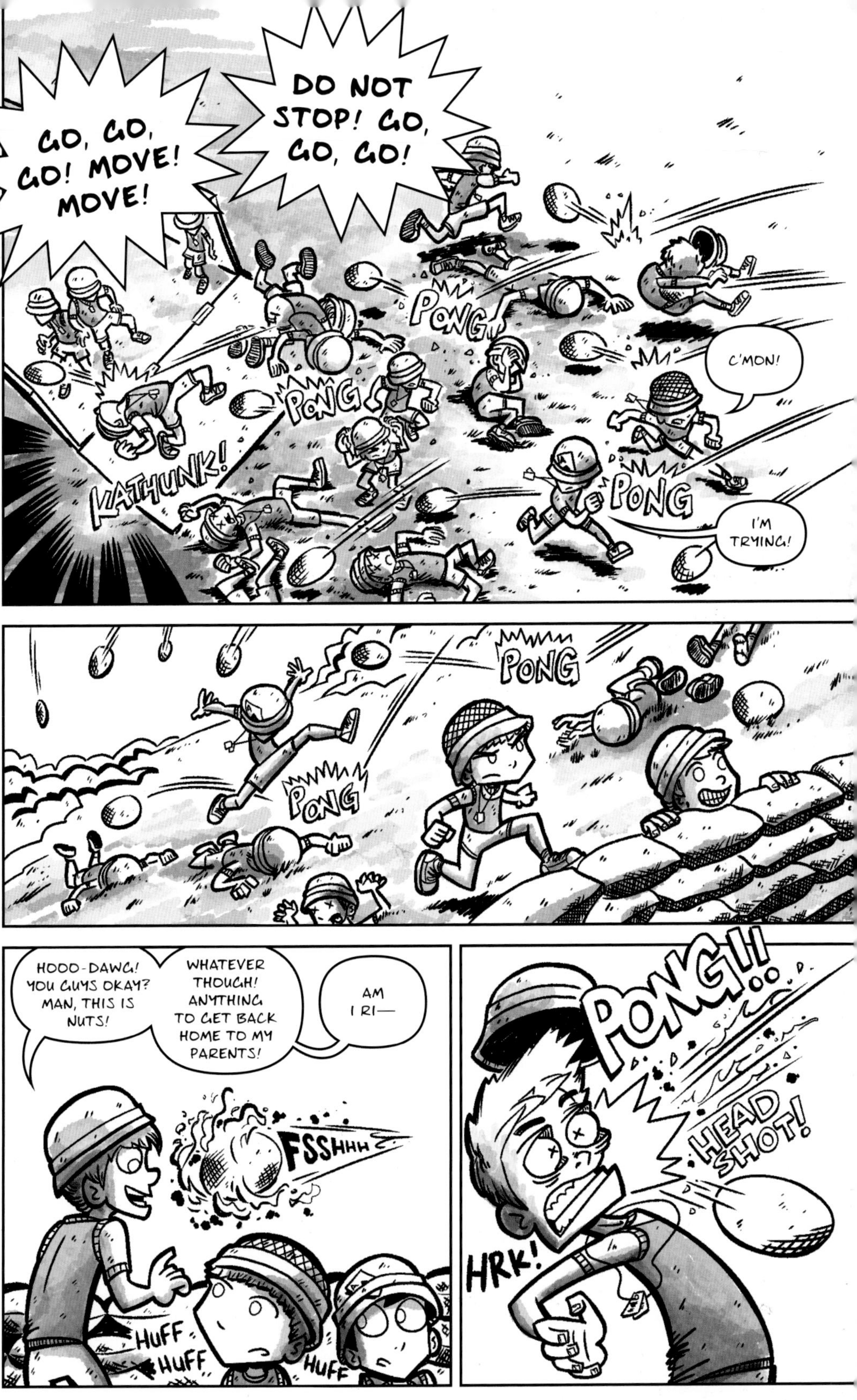
GO, GO, GO! MOVE! MOVE!
DO NOT STOP! GO, GO, GO!
PONG
PONG
KATHUNK!
C'MON!
PONG
I'M TRYING!
PONG
PONG
HOOO-DAWG! YOU GUYS OKAY? MAN, THIS IS NUTS!
WHATEVER THOUGH! ANYTHING TO GET BACK HOME TO MY PARENTS!
AM I RI—
FSSHHH
HUFF HUFF
HUFF
PONG!!
HEAD SHOT!
HRK!

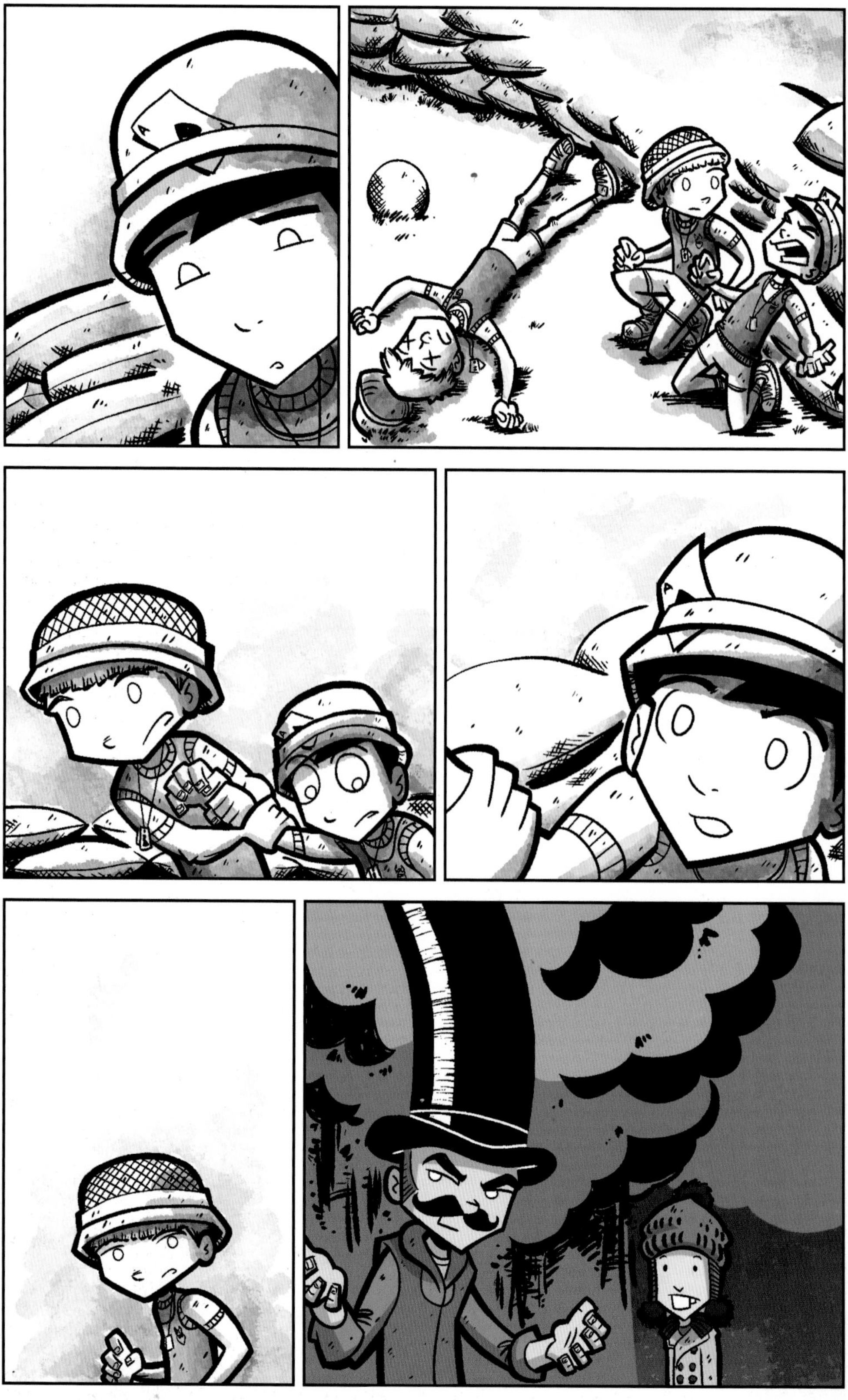

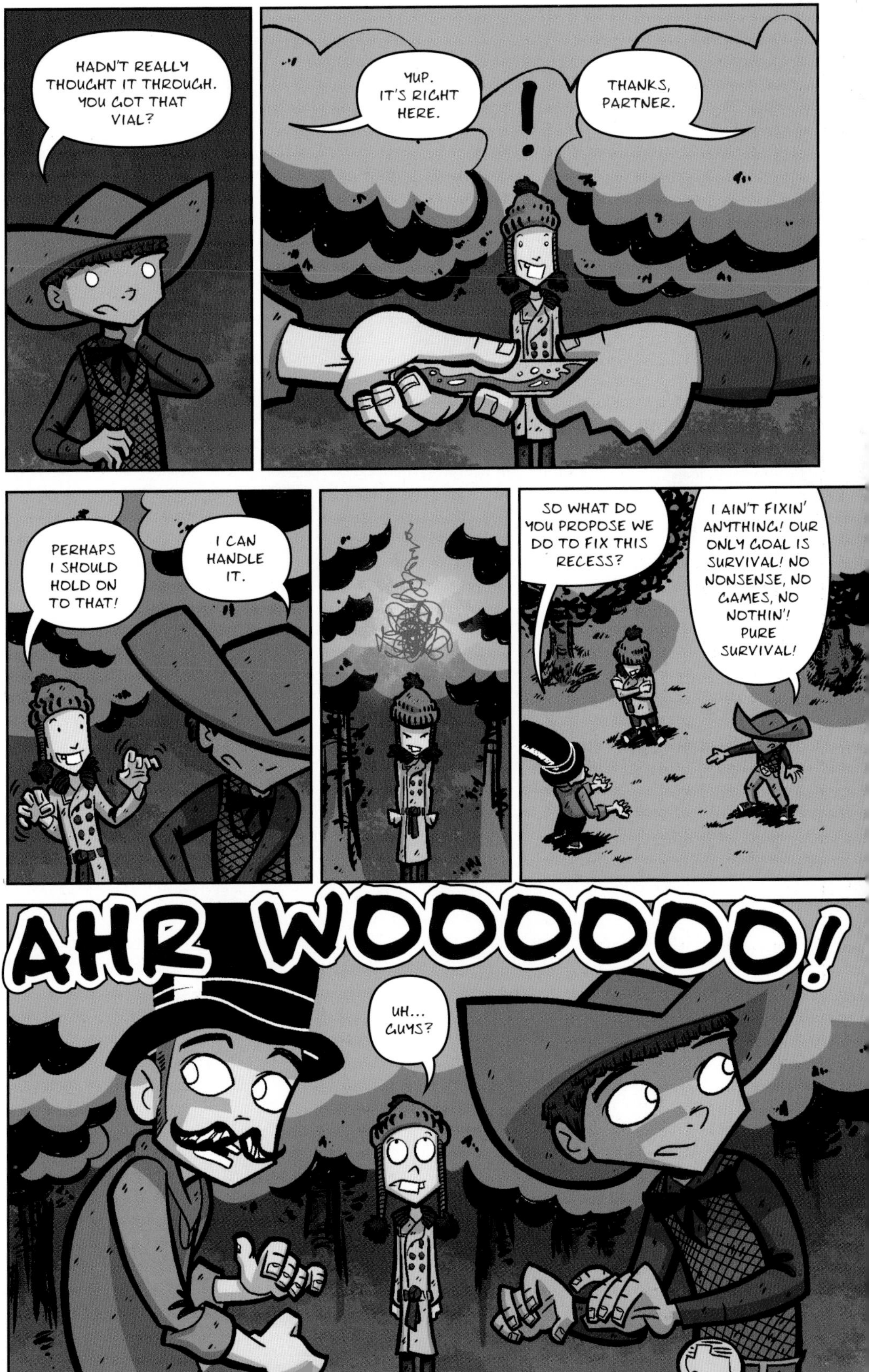
HADN'T REALLY THOUGHT IT THROUGH. YOU GOT THAT VIAL?
YUP. IT'S RIGHT HERE.
!
THANKS, PARTNER.
PERHAPS I SHOULD HOLD ON TO THAT!
I CAN HANDLE IT.
SO WHAT DO YOU PROPOSE WE DO TO FIX THIS RECESS?
I AIN'T FIXIN' ANYTHING! OUR ONLY GOAL IS SURVIVAL! NO NONSENSE, NO GAMES, NO NOTHIN'! PURE SURVIVAL!
AHR WOOOOOO!
UH... GUYS?

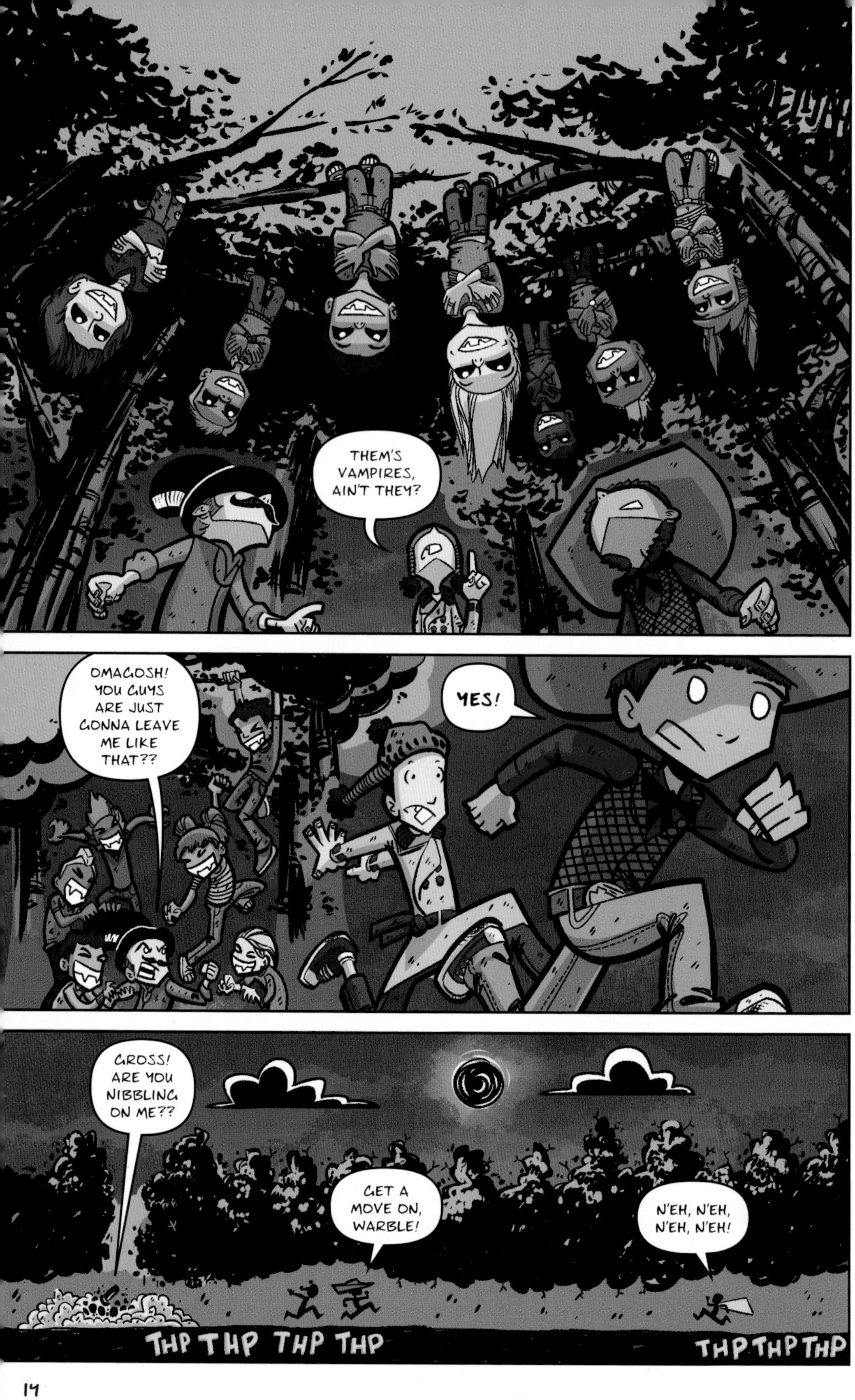
THEM'S VAMPIRES, AIN'T THEY?
OMAGOSH! YOU GUYS ARE JUST GONNA LEAVE ME LIKE THAT??
YES!
GROSS! ARE YOU NIBBLING ON ME??
GET A MOVE ON, WARBLE!
N'EH, N'EH, N'EH, N'EH!
THP THP THP THP
THP THP THP

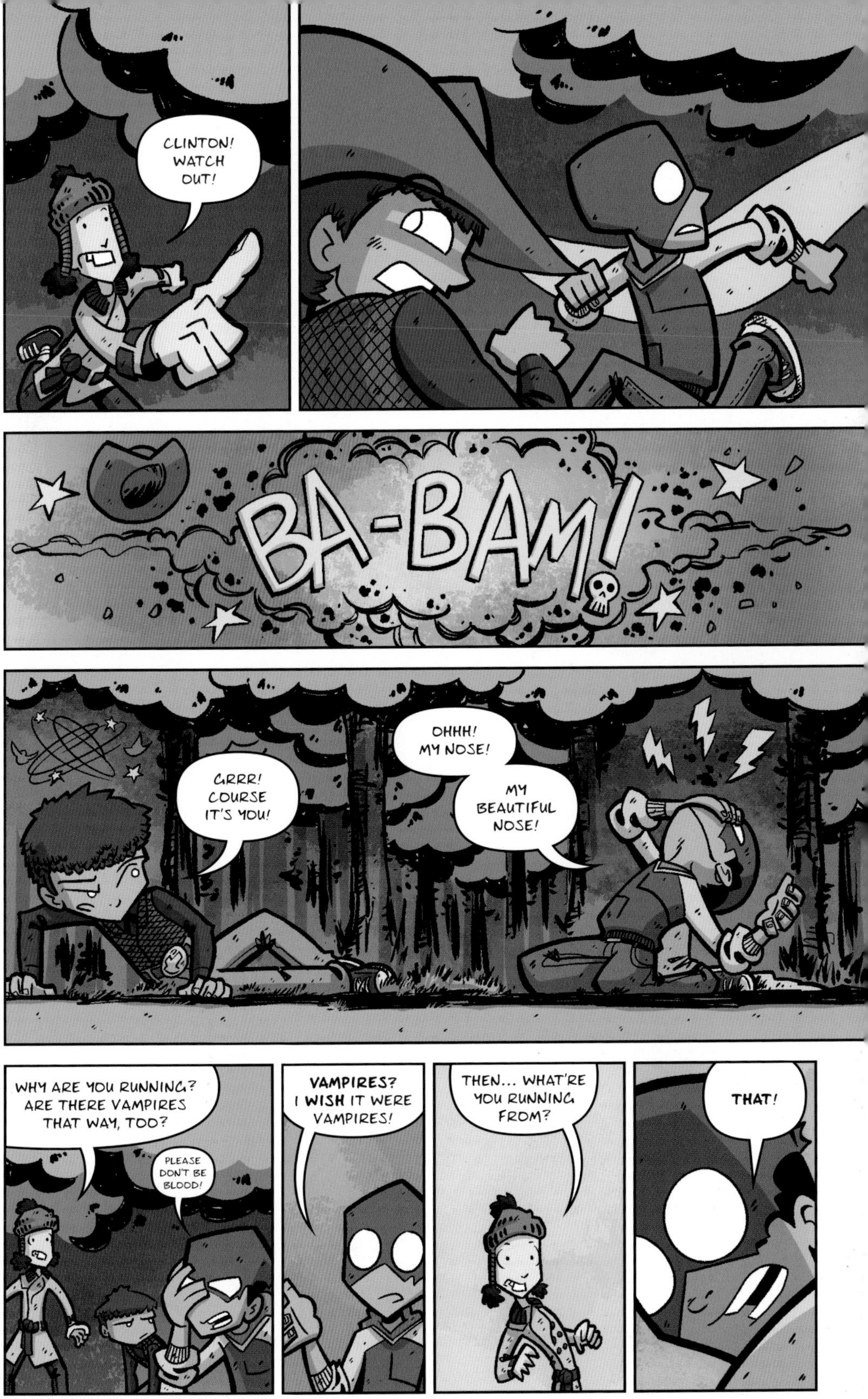
CLINTON! WATCH OUT!
BA-BAM!
GRRR! COURSE IT'S YOU!
OHHH! MY NOSE!
MY BEAUTIFUL NOSE!
WHY ARE YOU RUNNING? ARE THERE VAMPIRES THAT WAY, TOO?
PLEASE DON'T BE BLOOD!
VAMPIRES? I WISH IT WERE VAMPIRES!
THEN... WHAT'RE YOU RUNNING FROM?
THAT!

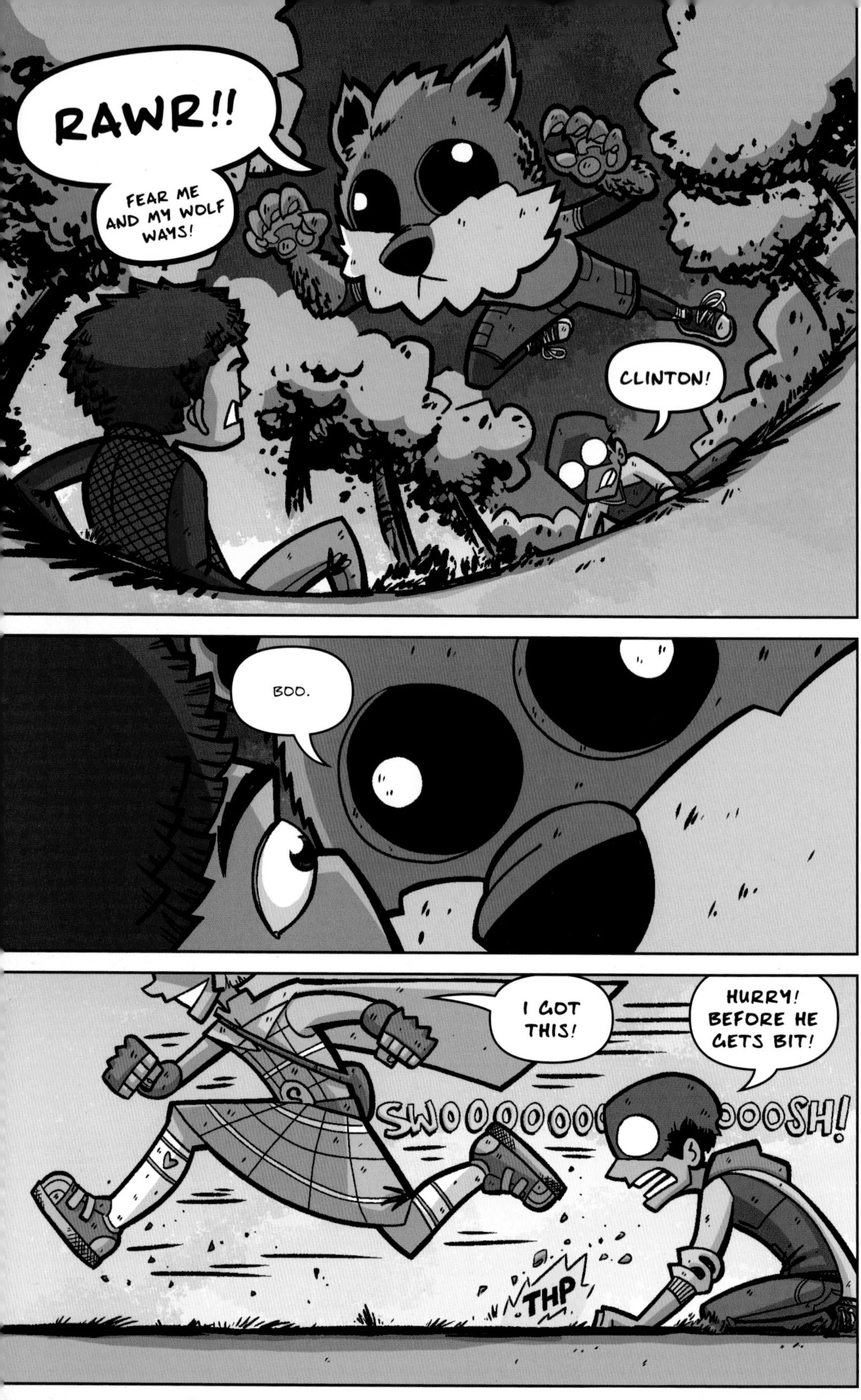
RAWR!!
FEAR ME AND MY WOLF WAYS!
CLINTON!
BOO.
I GOT THIS!
HURRY! BEFORE HE GETS BIT!
SWOOOOOOO OOOSH!
THP

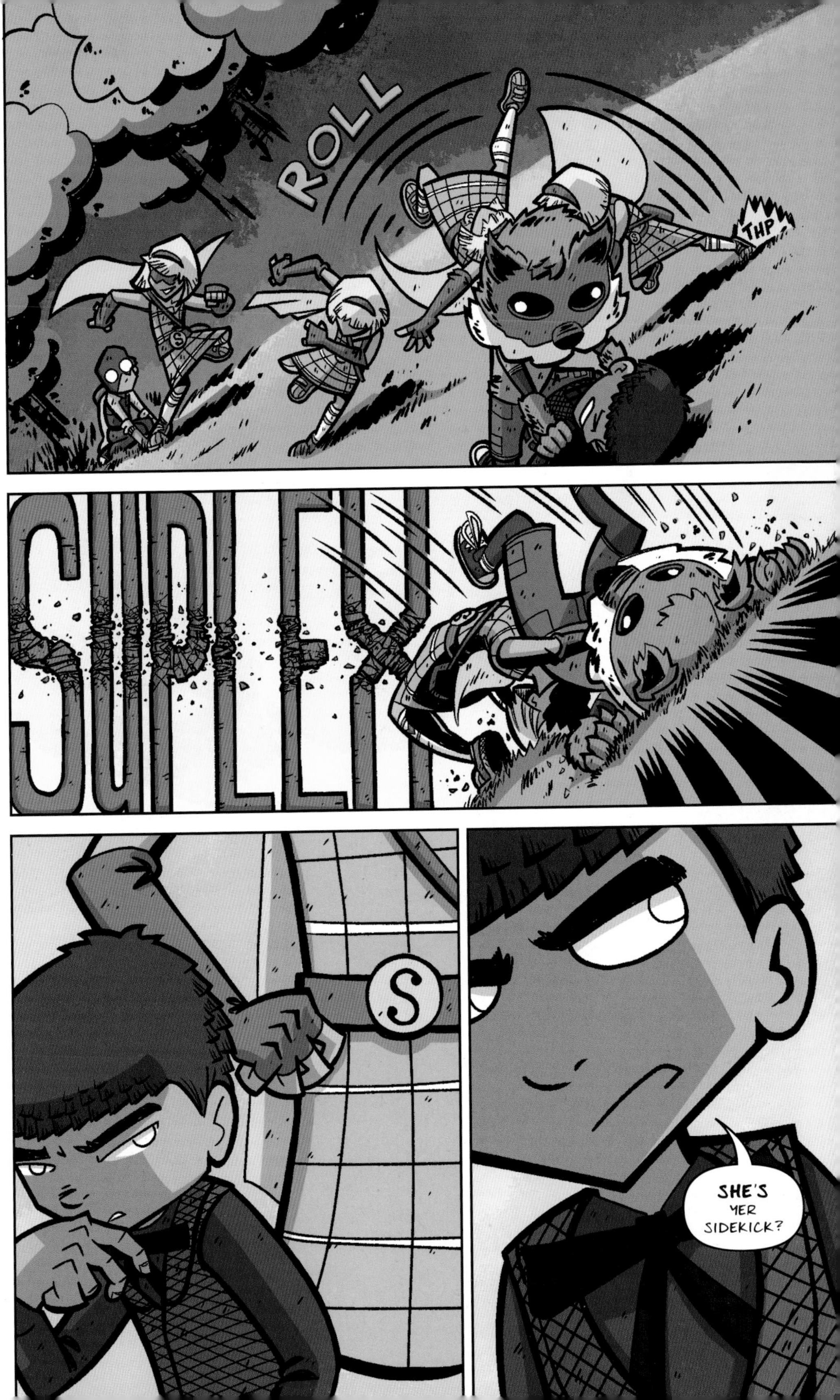
ROLL
THP
SHE'S YER SIDEKICK?

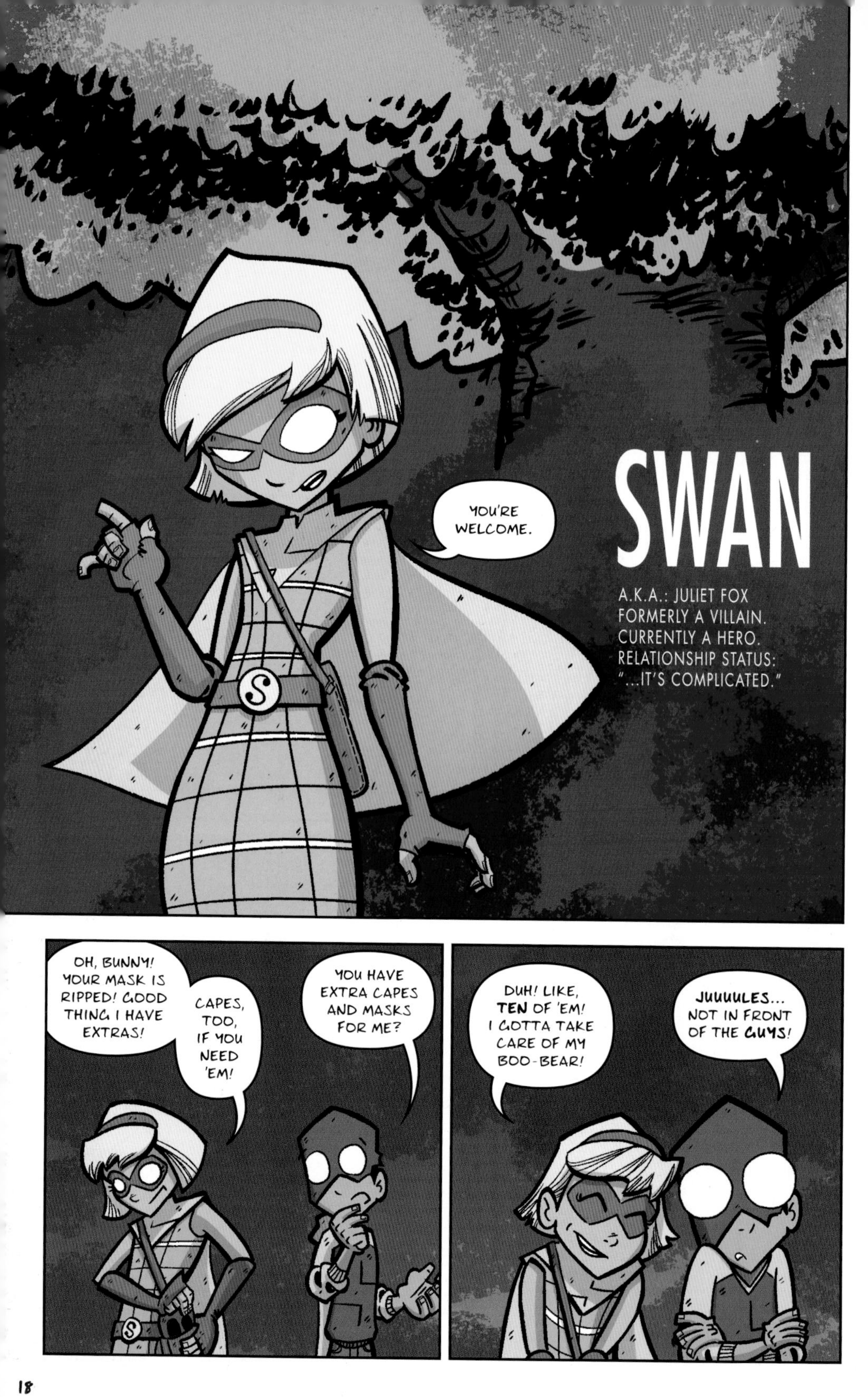
SWAN
A.K.A.: JULIET FOX
FORMERLY A VILLAIN.
CURRENTLY A HERO.
RELATIONSHIP STATUS:
"...IT'S COMPLICATED."
YOU'RE WELCOME.
OH, BUNNY! YOUR MASK IS RIPPED! GOOD THING I HAVE EXTRAS!
CAPES, TOO, IF YOU NEED 'EM!
YOU HAVE EXTRA CAPES AND MASKS FOR ME?
DUH! LIKE, **TEN** OF 'EM! I GOTTA TAKE CARE OF MY BOO-BEAR!
JUUUULES... NOT IN FRONT OF THE **GUYS**!

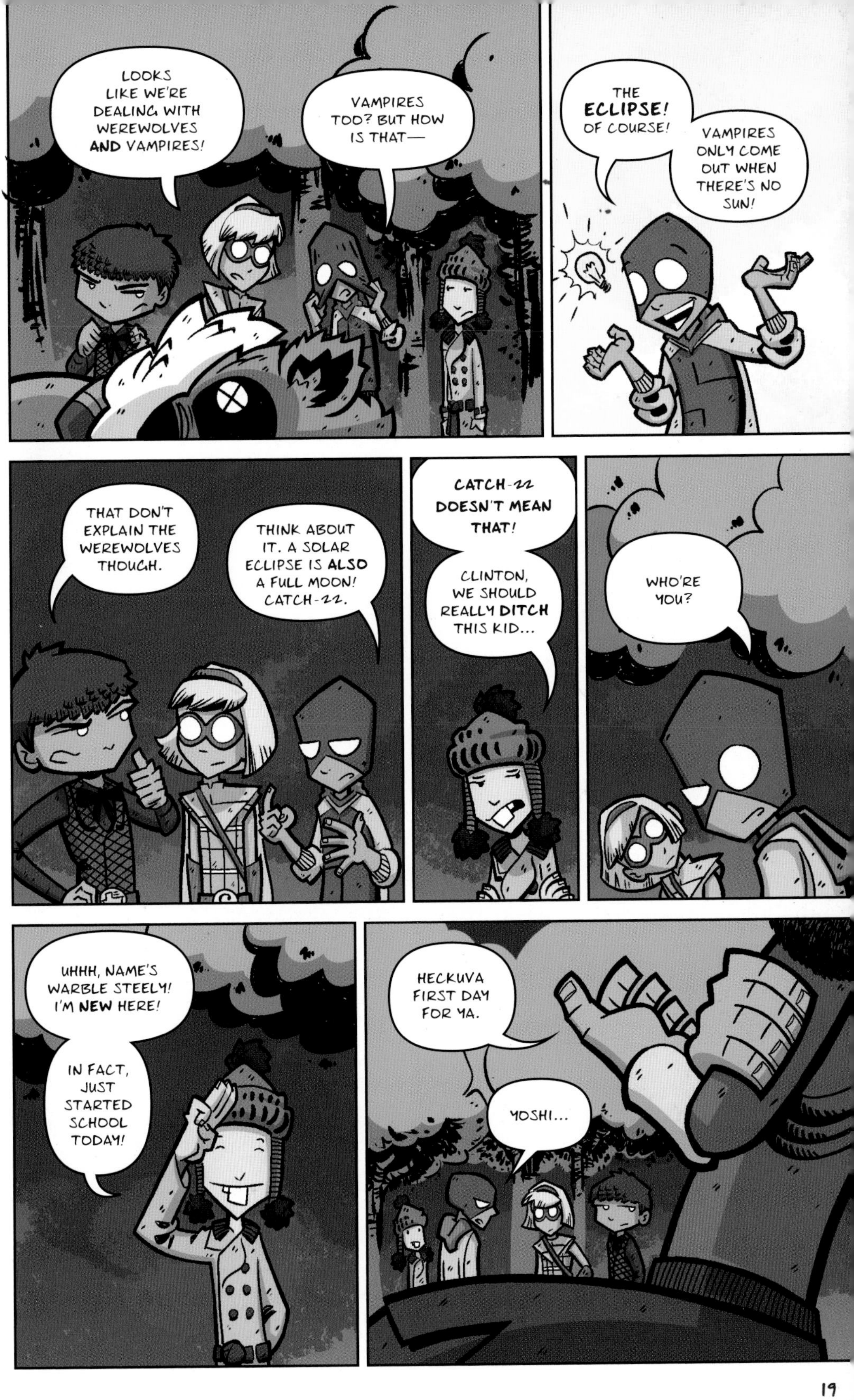
LOOKS LIKE WE'RE DEALING WITH WEREWOLVES **AND** VAMPIRES!
VAMPIRES TOO? BUT HOW IS THAT—
THE **ECLIPSE!** OF COURSE!
VAMPIRES ONLY COME OUT WHEN THERE'S NO SUN!
THAT DON'T EXPLAIN THE WEREWOLVES THOUGH.
THINK ABOUT IT. A SOLAR ECLIPSE IS **ALSO** A FULL MOON! CATCH-22.
CATCH-22 DOESN'T MEAN THAT!
CLINTON, WE SHOULD REALLY **DITCH** THIS KID...
WHO'RE YOU?
UHHH, NAME'S WARBLE STEELY! I'M **NEW** HERE!
IN FACT, JUST STARTED SCHOOL TODAY!
HECKUVA FIRST DAY FOR YA.
YOSHI...

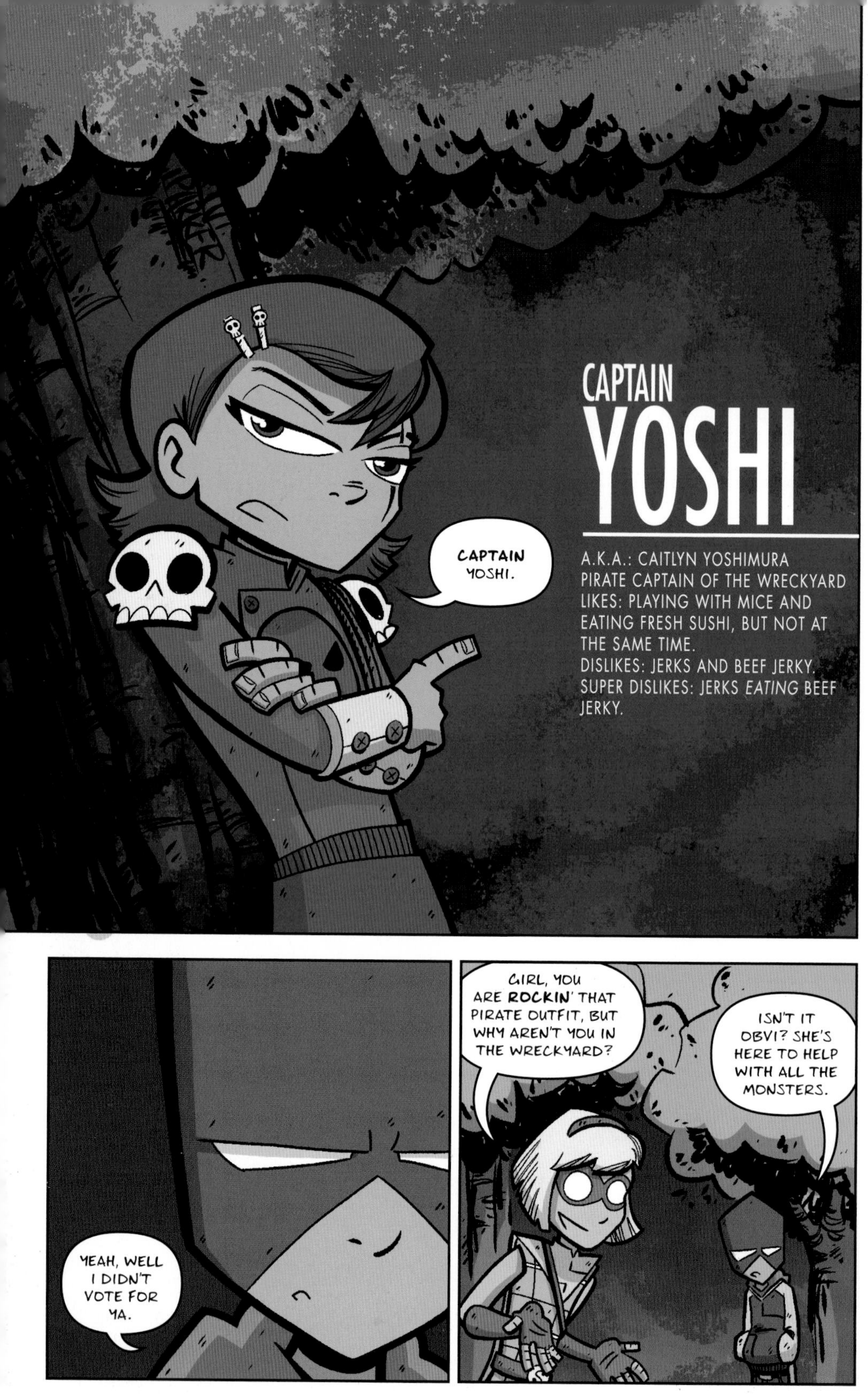
CAPTAIN
YOSHI
A.K.A.: CAITLYN YOSHIMURA
PIRATE CAPTAIN OF THE WRECKYARD
LIKES: PLAYING WITH MICE AND EATING FRESH SUSHI, BUT NOT AT THE SAME TIME.
DISLIKES: JERKS AND BEEF JERKY.
SUPER DISLIKES: JERKS *EATING* BEEF JERKY.
CAPTAIN YOSHI.
YEAH, WELL I DIDN'T VOTE FOR YA.
GIRL, YOU ARE **ROCKIN'** THAT PIRATE OUTFIT, BUT WHY AREN'T YOU IN THE WRECKYARD?
ISN'T IT OBVI? SHE'S HERE TO HELP WITH ALL THE MONSTERS.

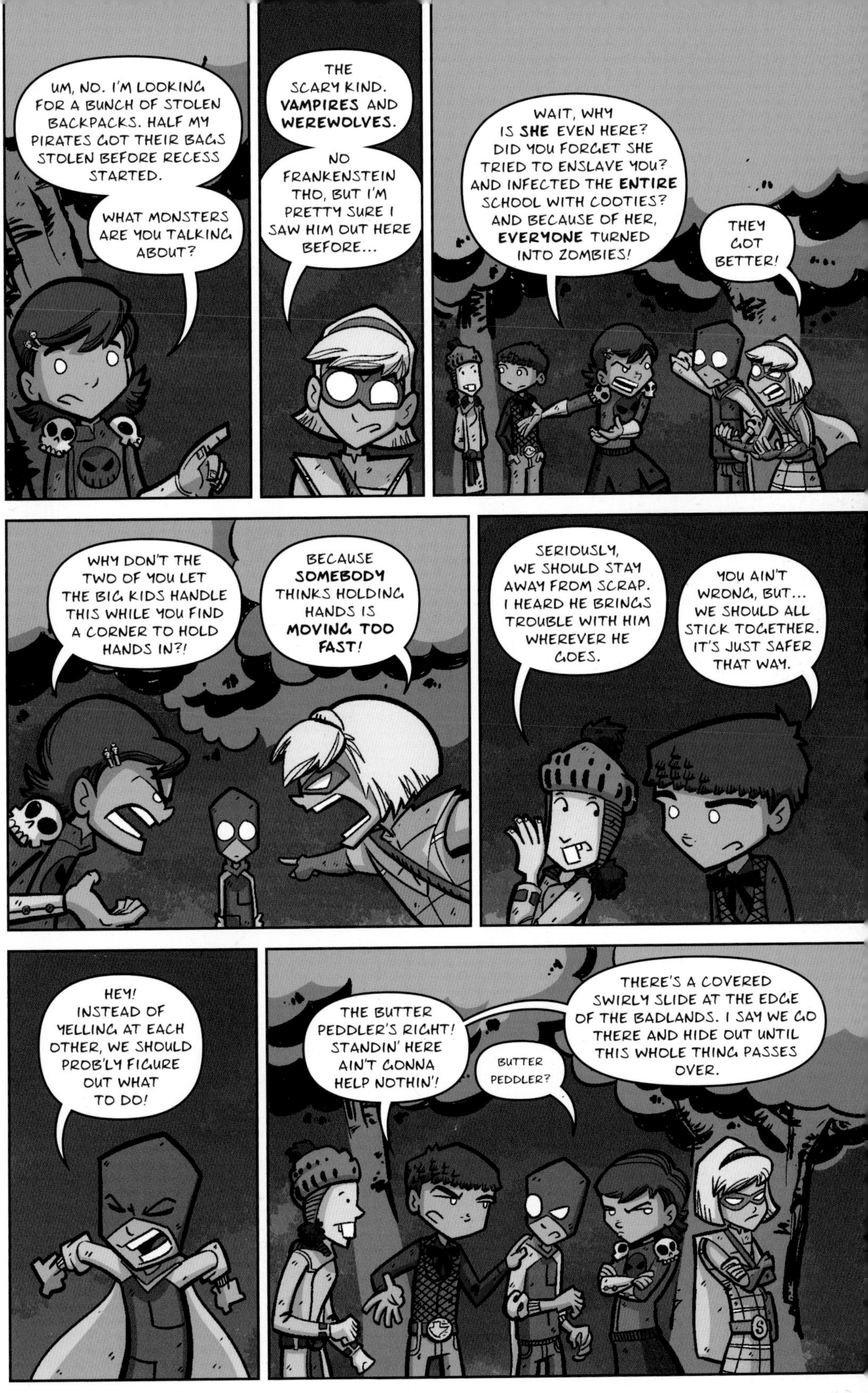

UM, NO. I'M LOOKING FOR A BUNCH OF STOLEN BACKPACKS. HALF MY PIRATES GOT THEIR BAGS STOLEN BEFORE RECESS STARTED.
WHAT MONSTERS ARE YOU TALKING ABOUT?
THE SCARY KIND. VAMPIRES AND WEREWOLVES.
NO FRANKENSTEIN THO, BUT I'M PRETTY SURE I SAW HIM OUT HERE BEFORE...
WAIT, WHY IS SHE EVEN HERE? DID YOU FORGET SHE TRIED TO ENSLAVE YOU? AND INFECTED THE ENTIRE SCHOOL WITH COOTIES? AND BECAUSE OF HER, EVERYONE TURNED INTO ZOMBIES!
THEY GOT BETTER!
WHY DON'T THE TWO OF YOU LET THE BIG KIDS HANDLE THIS WHILE YOU FIND A CORNER TO HOLD HANDS IN?!
BECAUSE SOMEBODY THINKS HOLDING HANDS IS MOVING TOO FAST!
SERIOUSLY, WE SHOULD STAY AWAY FROM SCRAP. I HEARD HE BRINGS TROUBLE WITH HIM WHEREVER HE GOES.
YOU AIN'T WRONG, BUT... WE SHOULD ALL STICK TOGETHER. IT'S JUST SAFER THAT WAY.
HEY! INSTEAD OF YELLING AT EACH OTHER, WE SHOULD PROB'LY FIGURE OUT WHAT TO DO!
THE BUTTER PEDDLER'S RIGHT! STANDIN' HERE AIN'T GONNA HELP NOTHIN'!
BUTTER PEDDLER?
THERE'S A COVERED SWIRLY SLIDE AT THE EDGE OF THE BADLANDS. I SAY WE GO THERE AND HIDE OUT UNTIL THIS WHOLE THING PASSES OVER.

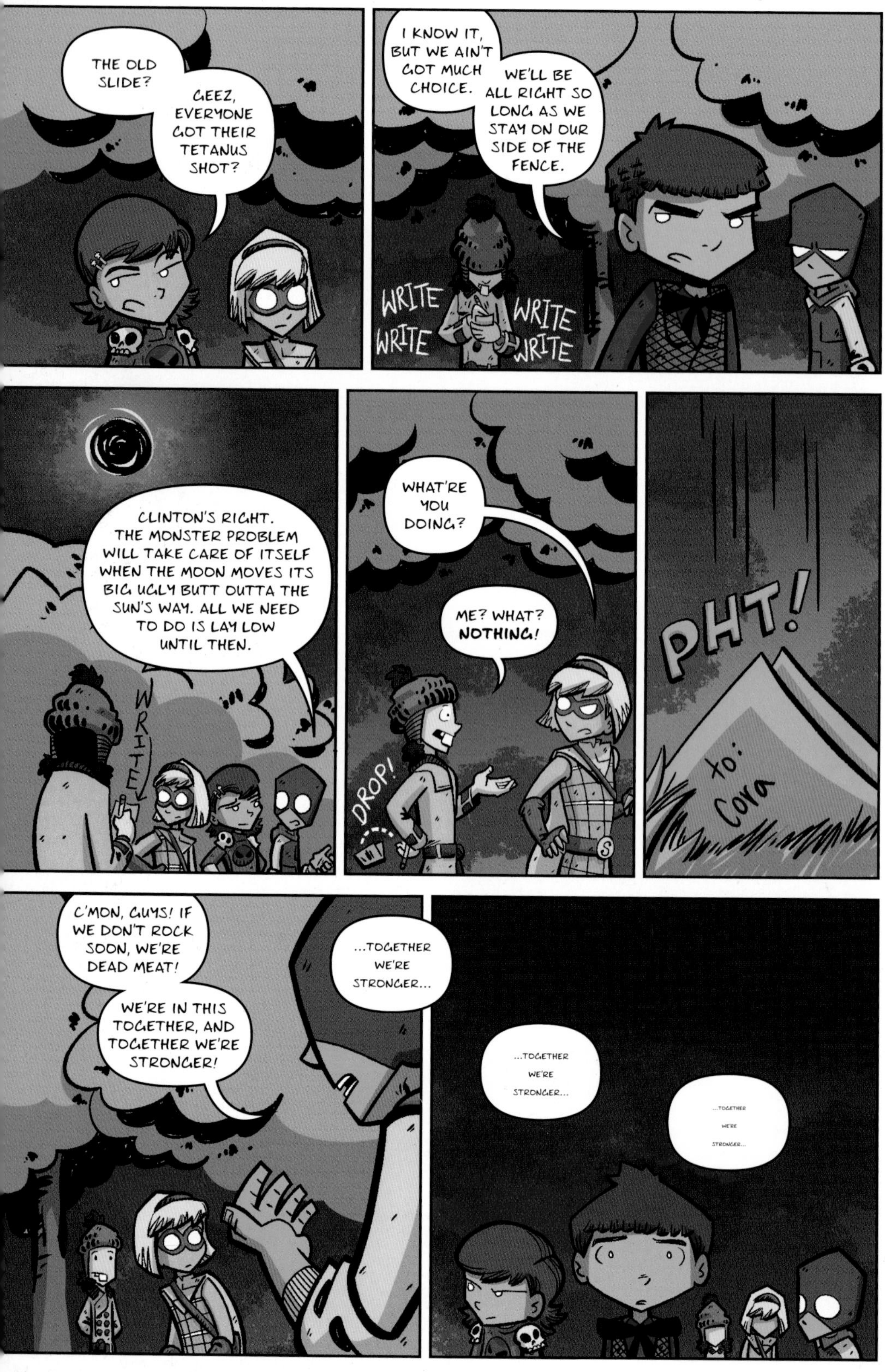
THE OLD SLIDE?
GEEZ, EVERYONE GOT THEIR TETANUS SHOT?
I KNOW IT, BUT WE AIN'T GOT MUCH CHOICE.
WE'LL BE ALL RIGHT SO LONG AS WE STAY ON OUR SIDE OF THE FENCE.
WRITE WRITE
WRITE WRITE
CLINTON'S RIGHT. THE MONSTER PROBLEM WILL TAKE CARE OF ITSELF WHEN THE MOON MOVES ITS BIG UGLY BUTT OUTTA THE SUN'S WAY. ALL WE NEED TO DO IS LAY LOW UNTIL THEN.
WRITE
WHAT'RE YOU DOING?
ME? WHAT? **NOTHING!**
DROP!
PHT!
to: Cora
C'MON, GUYS! IF WE DON'T ROCK SOON, WE'RE DEAD MEAT!
WE'RE IN THIS TOGETHER, AND TOGETHER WE'RE STRONGER!
...TOGETHER WE'RE STRONGER...
...TOGETHER WE'RE STRONGER...
...TOGETHER WE'RE STRONGER...

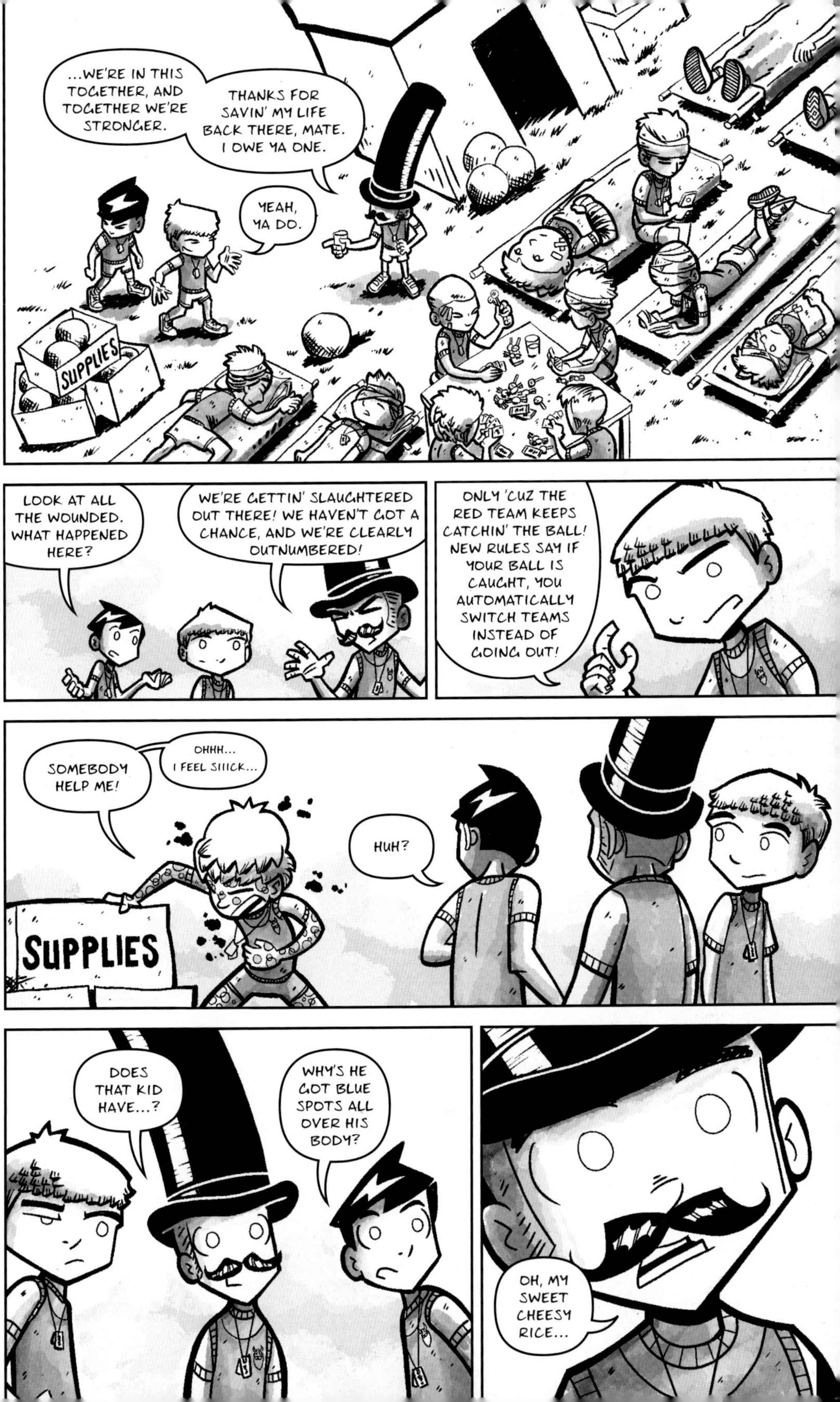
...WE'RE IN THIS TOGETHER, AND TOGETHER WE'RE STRONGER.
THANKS FOR SAVIN' MY LIFE BACK THERE, MATE. I OWE YA ONE.
YEAH, YA DO.
SUPPLIES
LOOK AT ALL THE WOUNDED. WHAT HAPPENED HERE?
WE'RE GETTIN' SLAUGHTERED OUT THERE! WE HAVEN'T GOT A CHANCE, AND WE'RE CLEARLY OUTNUMBERED!
ONLY 'CUZ THE RED TEAM KEEPS CATCHIN' THE BALL! NEW RULES SAY IF YOUR BALL IS CAUGHT, YOU AUTOMATICALLY SWITCH TEAMS INSTEAD OF GOING OUT!
SOMEBODY HELP ME!
OHHH... I FEEL SIIICK...
SUPPLIES
HUH?
DOES THAT KID HAVE...?
WHY'S HE GOT BLUE SPOTS ALL OVER HIS BODY?
OH, MY SWEET CHEESY RICE...

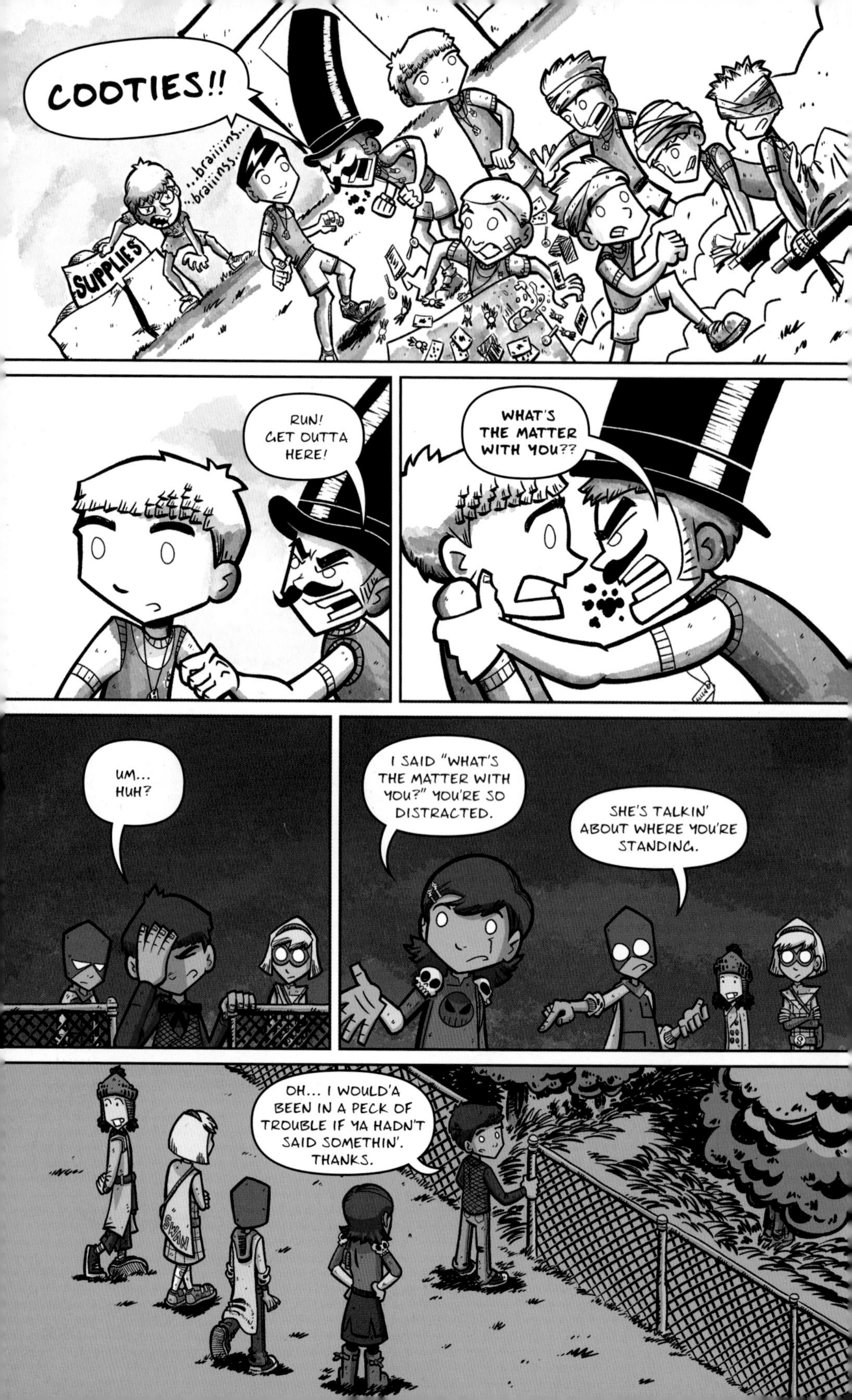
COOTIES!!
...braiiins...
...braiiinss...
SUPPLIES
RUN! GET OUTTA HERE!
WHAT'S THE MATTER WITH YOU??
UM... HUH?
I SAID "WHAT'S THE MATTER WITH YOU?" YOU'RE SO DISTRACTED.
SHE'S TALKIN' ABOUT WHERE YOU'RE STANDING.
OH... I WOULD'A BEEN IN A PECK OF TROUBLE IF YA HADN'T SAID SOMETHIN'. THANKS.
SWAN

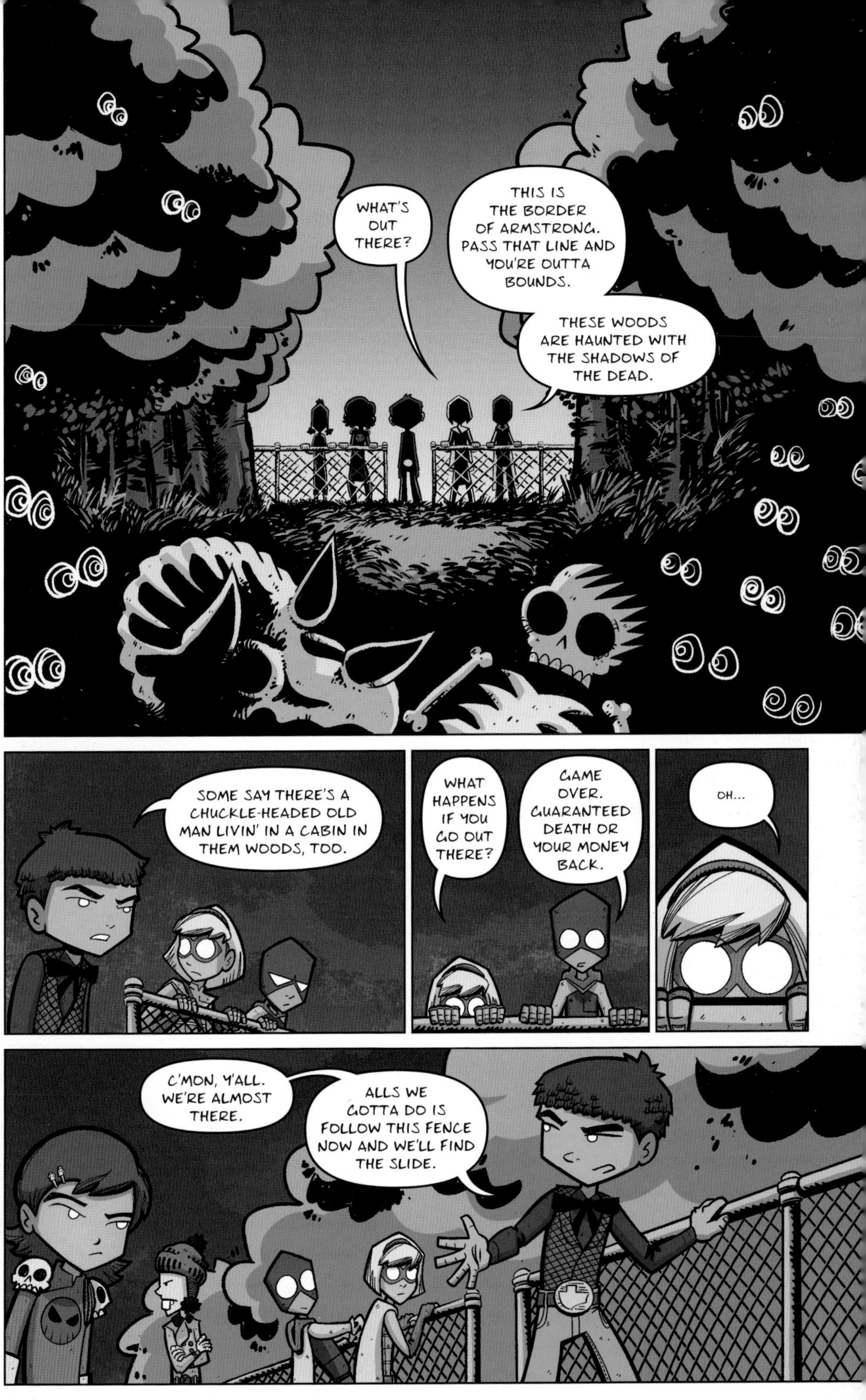
WHAT'S OUT THERE?
THIS IS THE BORDER OF ARMSTRONG. PASS THAT LINE AND YOU'RE OUTTA BOUNDS.
THESE WOODS ARE HAUNTED WITH THE SHADOWS OF THE DEAD.
SOME SAY THERE'S A CHUCKLE-HEADED OLD MAN LIVIN' IN A CABIN IN THEM WOODS, TOO.
WHAT HAPPENS IF YOU GO OUT THERE?
GAME OVER. GUARANTEED DEATH OR YOUR MONEY BACK.
OH...
C'MON, Y'ALL. WE'RE ALMOST THERE.
ALLS WE GOTTA DO IS FOLLOW THIS FENCE NOW AND WE'LL FIND THE SLIDE.

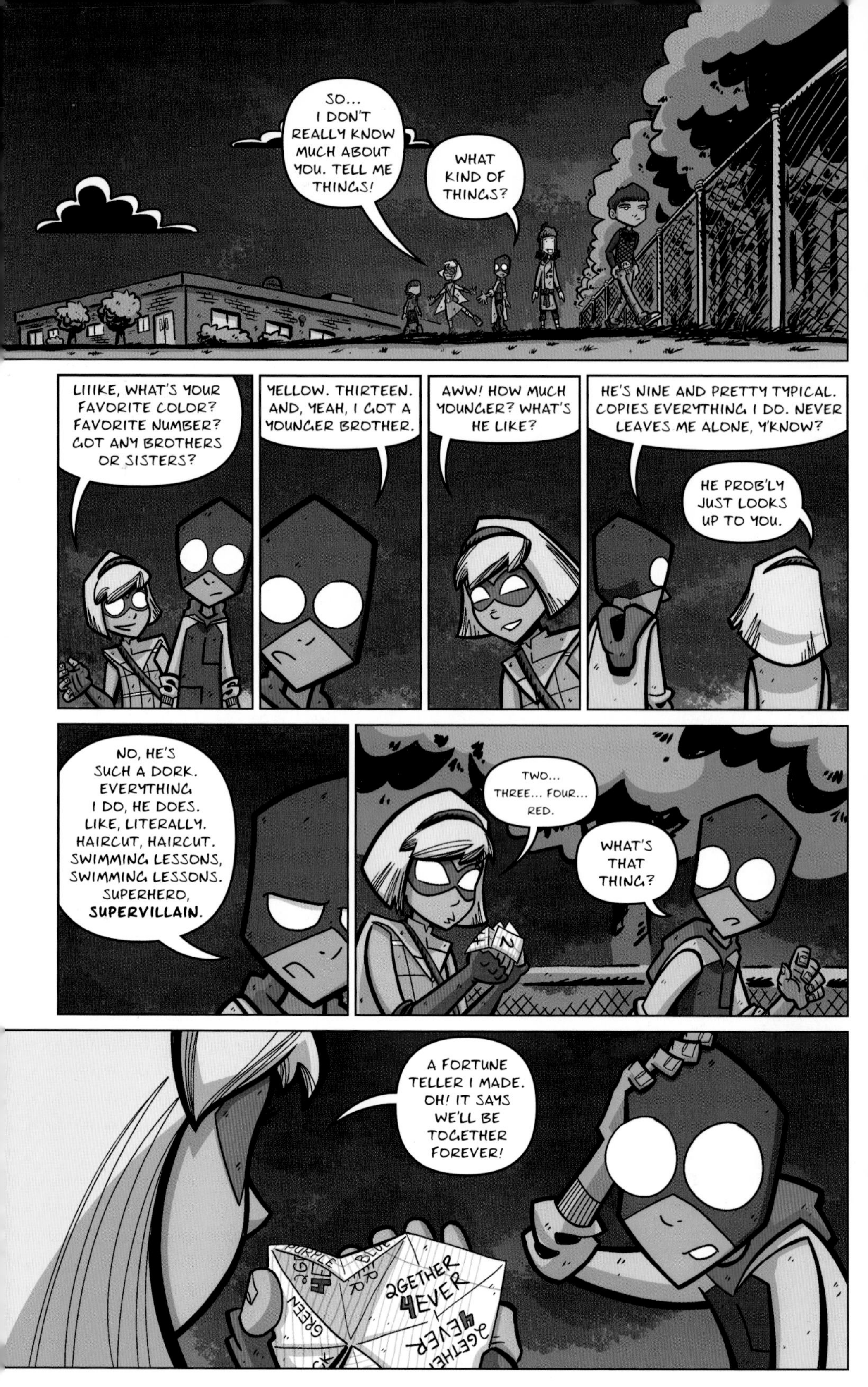
SO... I DON'T REALLY KNOW MUCH ABOUT YOU. TELL ME THINGS!
WHAT KIND OF THINGS?
LIIIKE, WHAT'S YOUR FAVORITE COLOR? FAVORITE NUMBER? GOT ANY BROTHERS OR SISTERS?
YELLOW. THIRTEEN. AND, YEAH, I GOT A YOUNGER BROTHER.
AWW! HOW MUCH YOUNGER? WHAT'S HE LIKE?
HE'S NINE AND PRETTY TYPICAL. COPIES EVERYTHING I DO. NEVER LEAVES ME ALONE, Y'KNOW?
HE PROB'LY JUST LOOKS UP TO YOU.
NO, HE'S SUCH A DORK. EVERYTHING I DO, HE DOES. LIKE, LITERALLY. HAIRCUT, HAIRCUT. SWIMMING LESSONS, SWIMMING LESSONS. SUPERHERO, **SUPERVILLAIN**.
TWO... THREE... FOUR... RED.
WHAT'S THAT THING?
A FORTUNE TELLER I MADE. OH! IT SAYS WE'LL BE TOGETHER FOREVER!
PURPLE
BLUE
GREEN
2GETHER 4EVER
2GETHER 4EVER

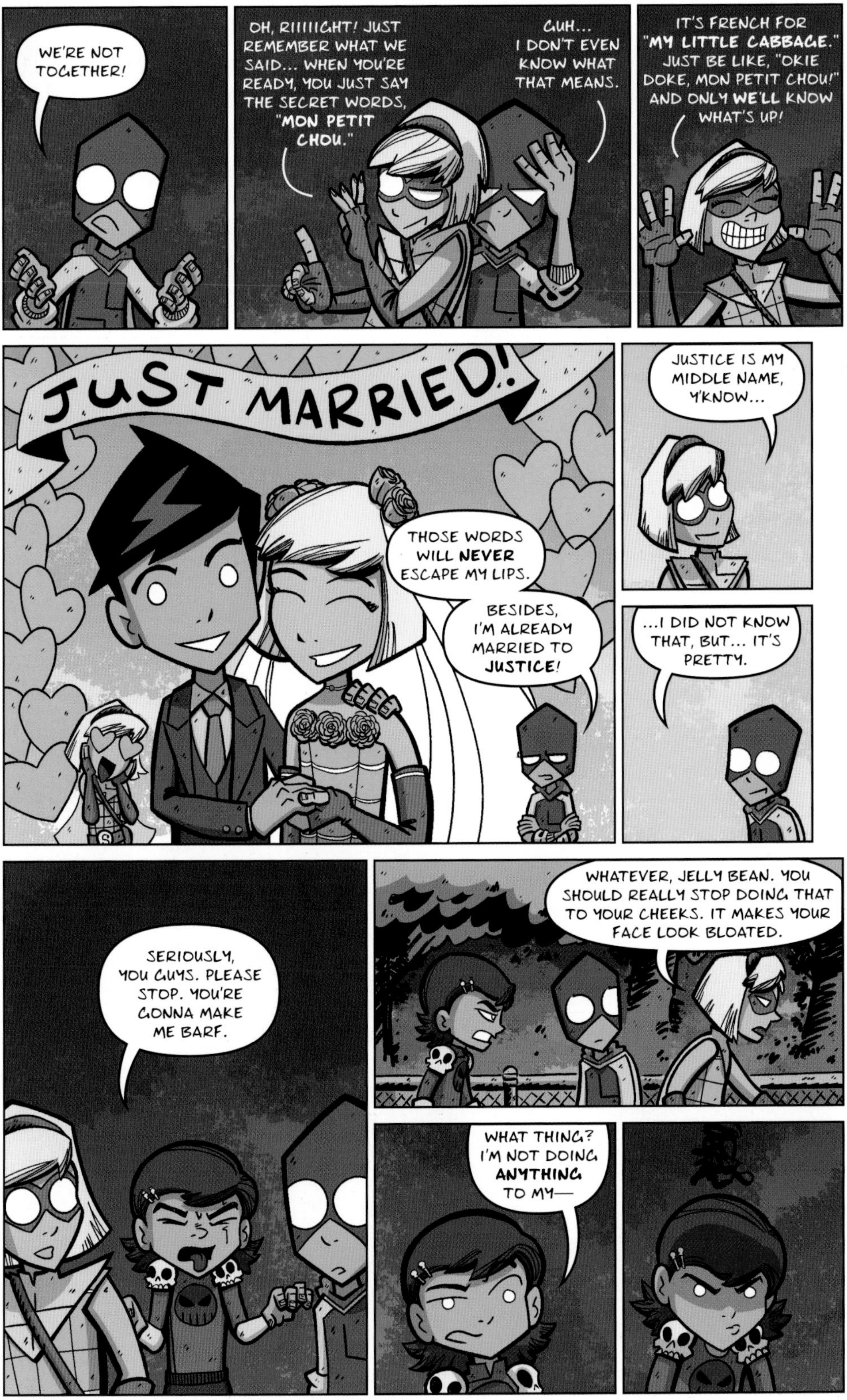
WE'RE NOT TOGETHER!
OH, RIIIIIGHT! JUST REMEMBER WHAT WE SAID... WHEN YOU'RE READY, YOU JUST SAY THE SECRET WORDS, "MON PETIT CHOU."
GUH... I DON'T EVEN KNOW WHAT THAT MEANS.
IT'S FRENCH FOR "MY LITTLE CABBAGE." JUST BE LIKE, "OKIE DOKE, MON PETIT CHOU!" AND ONLY WE'LL KNOW WHAT'S UP!
JUST MARRIED!
THOSE WORDS WILL NEVER ESCAPE MY LIPS.
BESIDES, I'M ALREADY MARRIED TO JUSTICE!
JUSTICE IS MY MIDDLE NAME, Y'KNOW...
...I DID NOT KNOW THAT, BUT... IT'S PRETTY.
SERIOUSLY, YOU GUYS. PLEASE STOP. YOU'RE GONNA MAKE ME BARF.
WHATEVER, JELLY BEAN. YOU SHOULD REALLY STOP DOING THAT TO YOUR CHEEKS. IT MAKES YOUR FACE LOOK BLOATED.
WHAT THING? I'M NOT DOING ANYTHING TO MY—

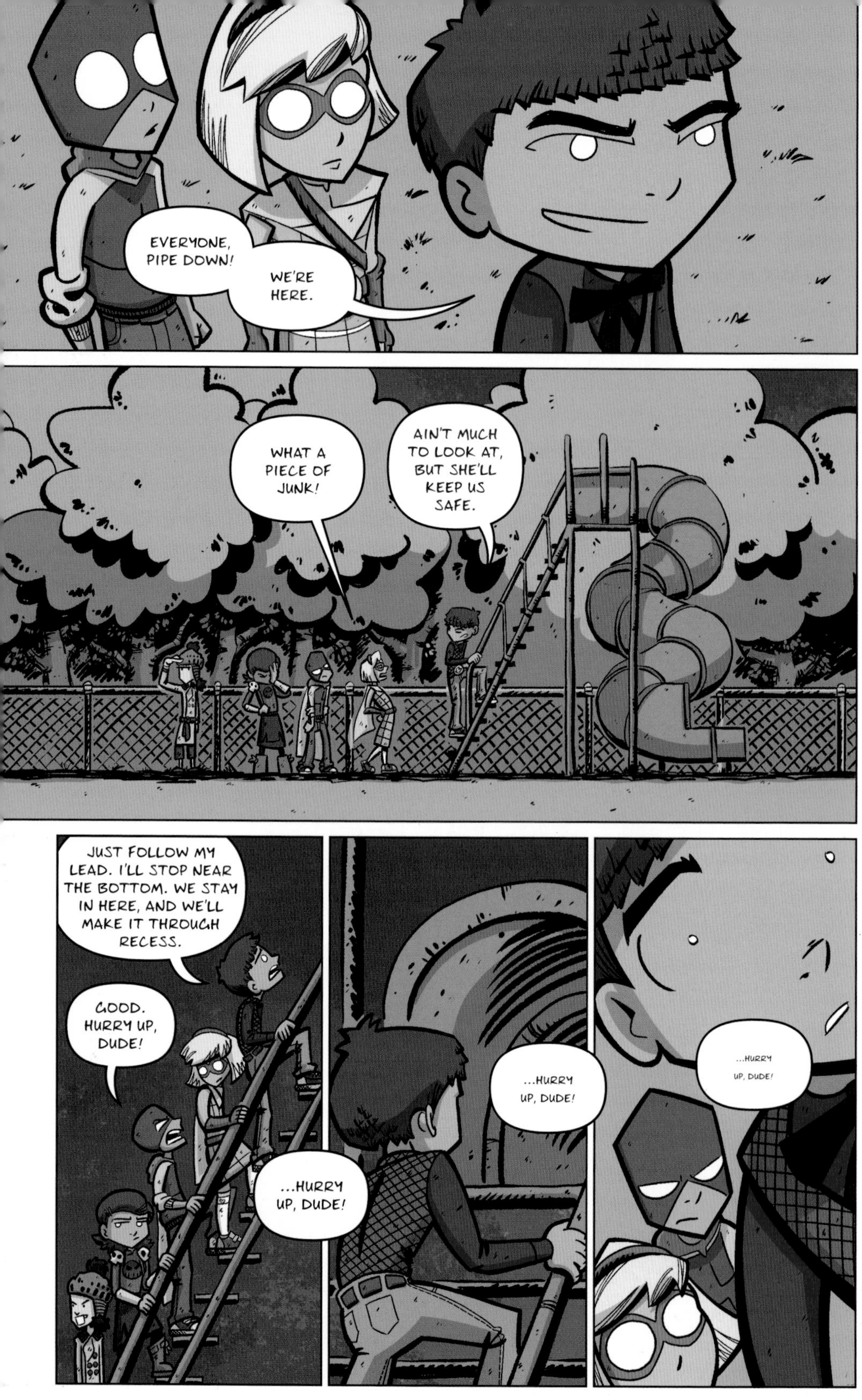
EVERYONE, PIPE DOWN!
WE'RE HERE.
WHAT A PIECE OF JUNK!
AIN'T MUCH TO LOOK AT, BUT SHE'LL KEEP US SAFE.
JUST FOLLOW MY LEAD. I'LL STOP NEAR THE BOTTOM. WE STAY IN HERE, AND WE'LL MAKE IT THROUGH RECESS.
GOOD. HURRY UP, DUDE!
...HURRY UP, DUDE!
...HURRY UP, DUDE!
...HURRY UP, DUDE!

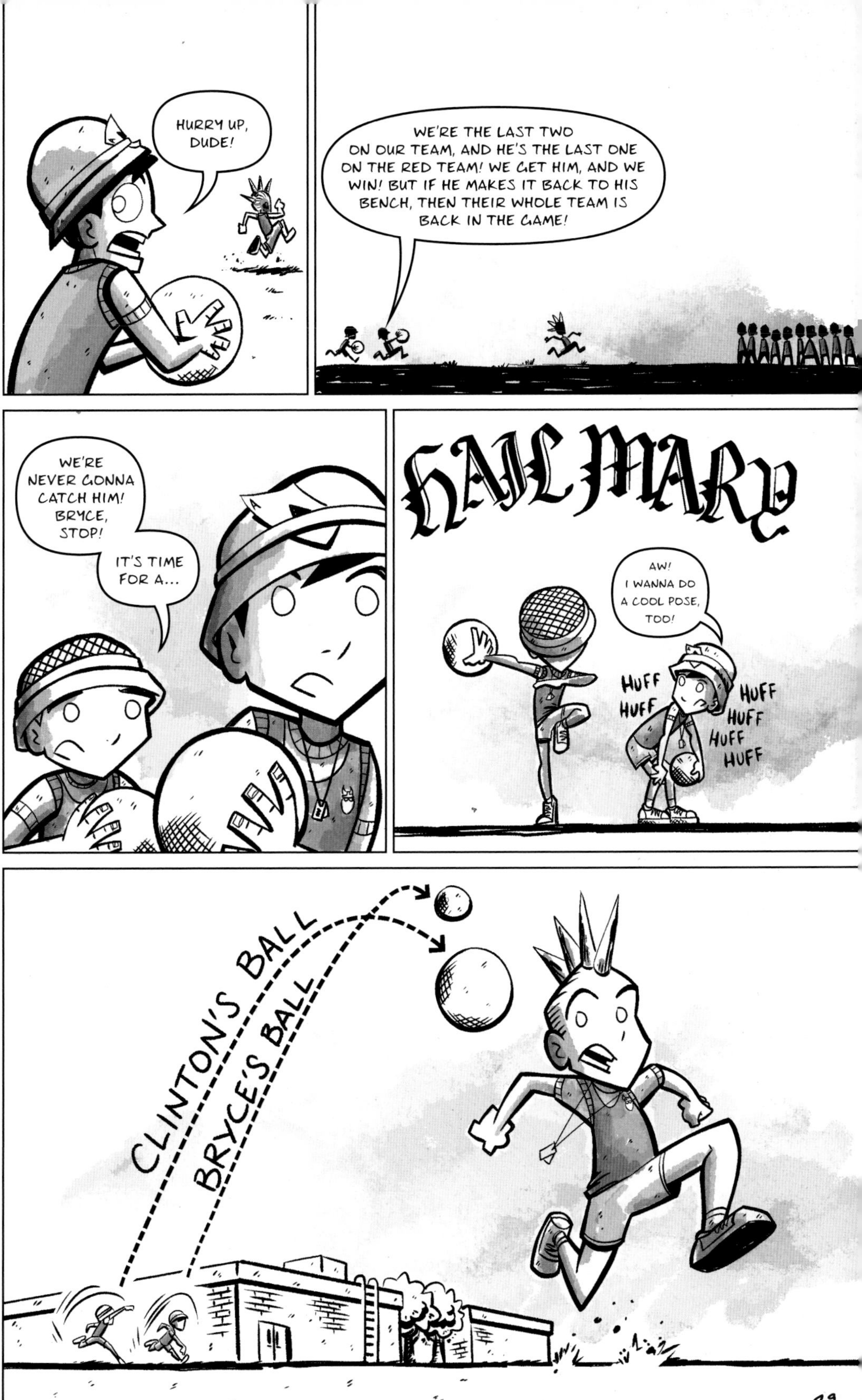
HURRY UP, DUDE!
WE'RE THE LAST TWO ON OUR TEAM, AND HE'S THE LAST ONE ON THE RED TEAM! WE GET HIM, AND WE WIN! BUT IF HE MAKES IT BACK TO HIS BENCH, THEN THEIR WHOLE TEAM IS BACK IN THE GAME!
WE'RE NEVER GONNA CATCH HIM! BRYCE, STOP!
IT'S TIME FOR A...
HAIL MARY
AW! I WANNA DO A COOL POSE, TOO!
HUFF HUFF
HUFF HUFF HUFF HUFF
CLINTON'S BALL
BRYCE'S BALL

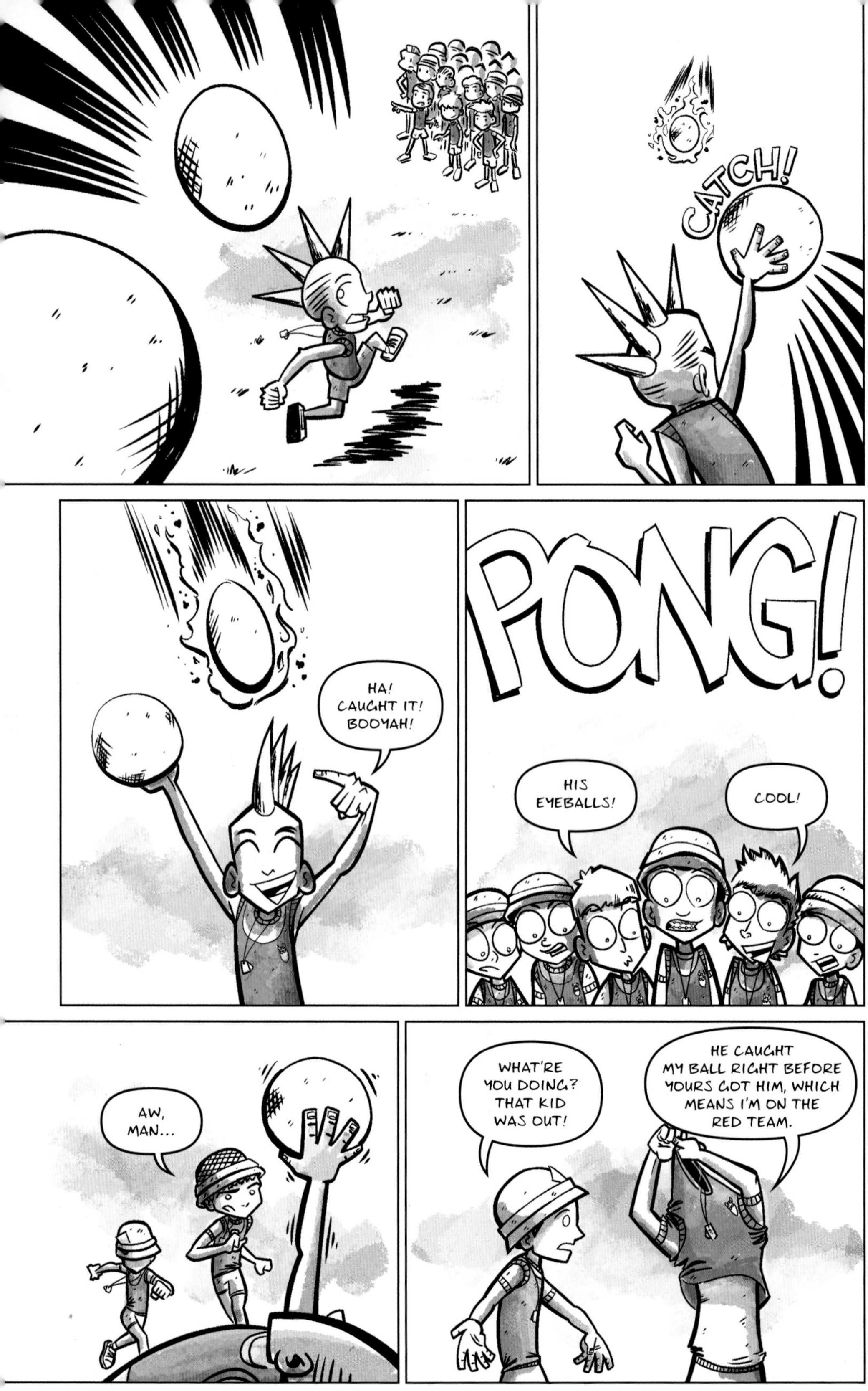
CATCH!
HA! CAUGHT IT! BOOYAH!
PONG!
HIS EYEBALLS!
COOL!
AW, MAN...
WHAT'RE YOU DOING? THAT KID WAS OUT!
HE CAUGHT MY BALL RIGHT BEFORE YOURS GOT HIM, WHICH MEANS I'M ON THE RED TEAM.

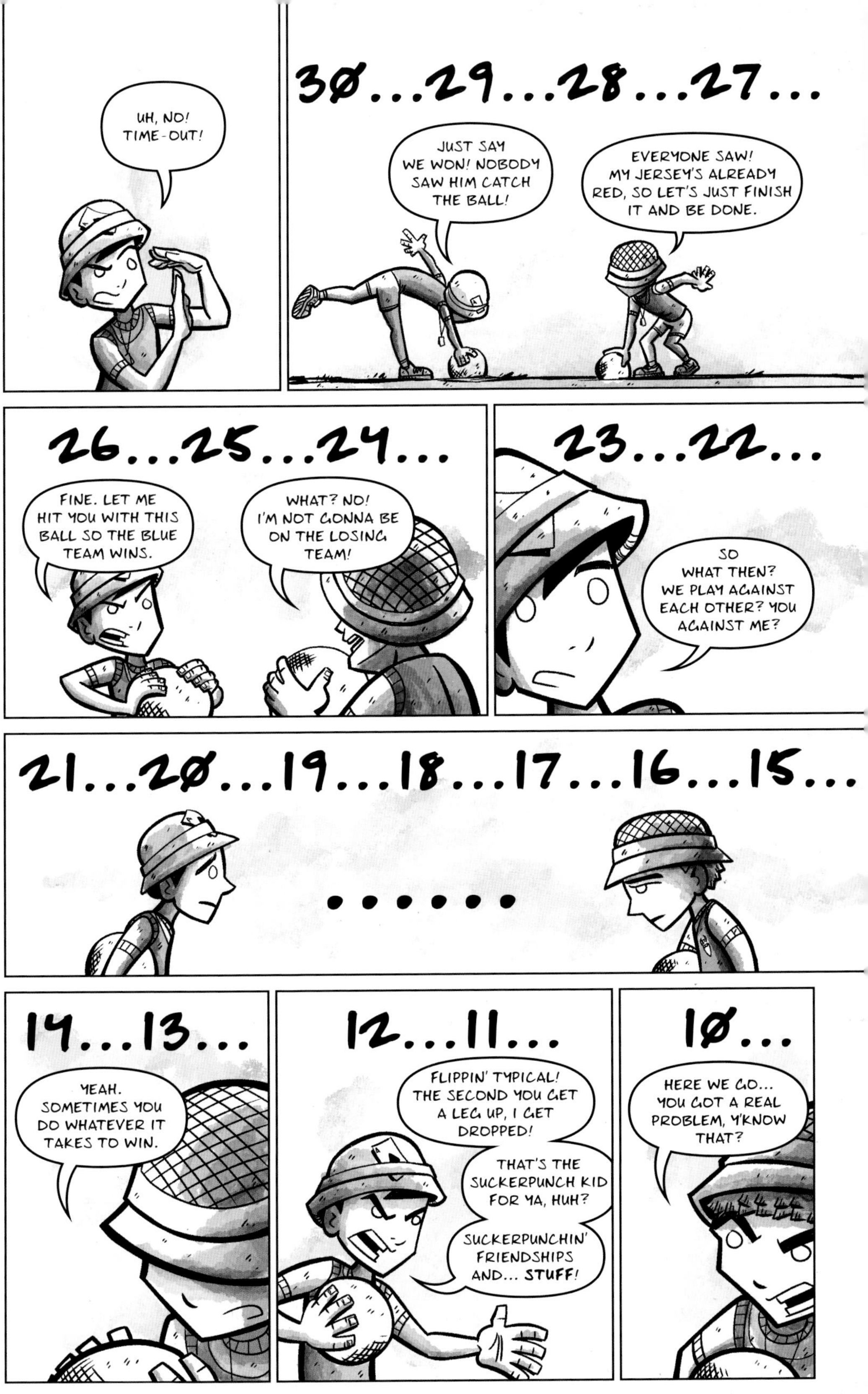
UH, NO! TIME-OUT!
30...29...28...27...
JUST SAY WE WON! NOBODY SAW HIM CATCH THE BALL!
EVERYONE SAW! MY JERSEY'S ALREADY RED, SO LET'S JUST FINISH IT AND BE DONE.
26...25...24...
FINE. LET ME HIT YOU WITH THIS BALL SO THE BLUE TEAM WINS.
WHAT? NO! I'M NOT GONNA BE ON THE LOSING TEAM!
23...22...
SO WHAT THEN? WE PLAY AGAINST EACH OTHER? YOU AGAINST ME?
21...20...19...18...17...16...15...
......
14...13...
YEAH. SOMETIMES YOU DO WHATEVER IT TAKES TO WIN.
12...11...
FLIPPIN' TYPICAL! THE SECOND YOU GET A LEG UP, I GET DROPPED!
THAT'S THE SUCKERPUNCH KID FOR YA, HUH?
SUCKERPUNCHIN' FRIENDSHIPS AND... STUFF!
10...
HERE WE GO... YOU GOT A REAL PROBLEM, Y'KNOW THAT?

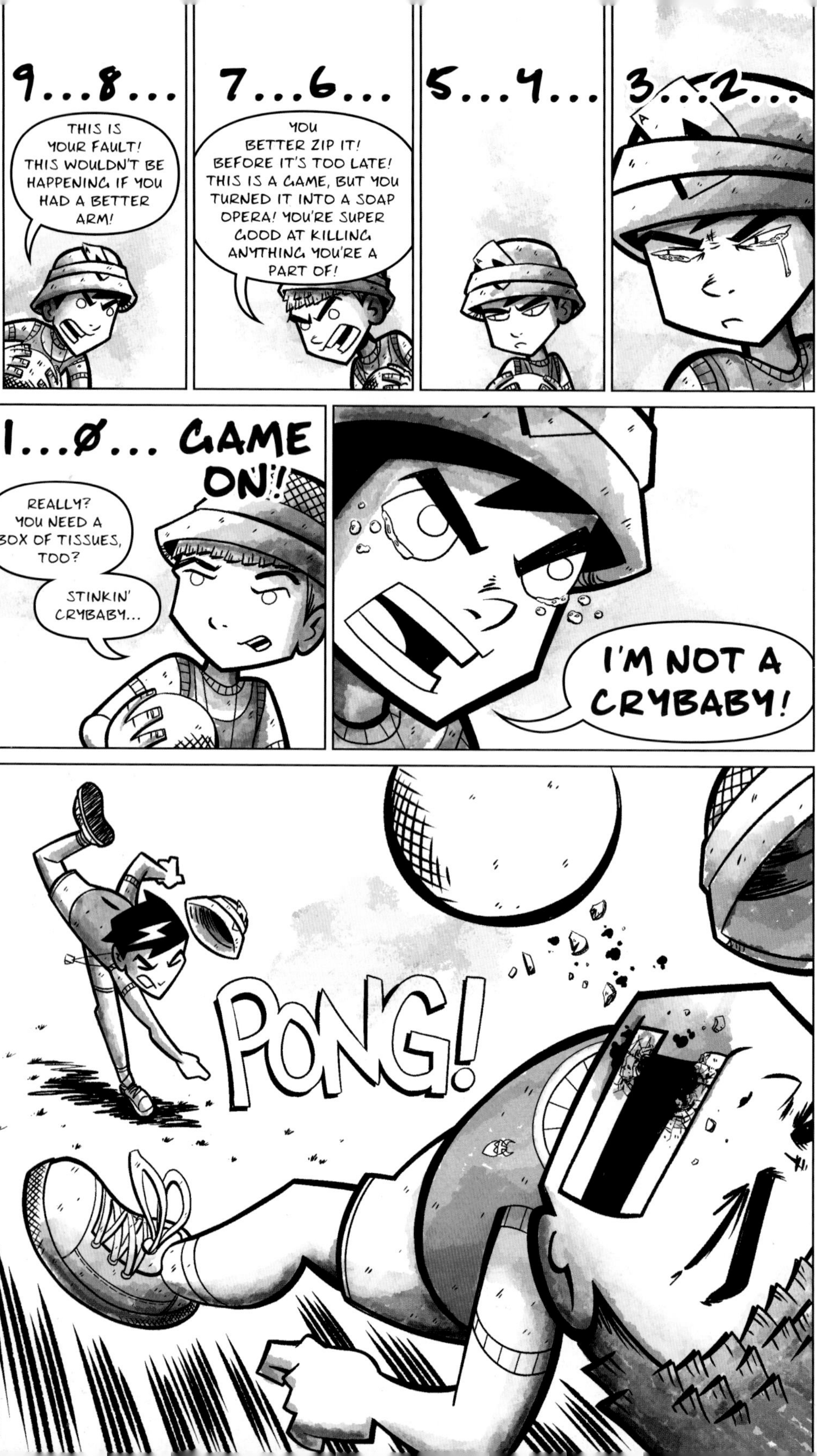
9...8...
THIS IS YOUR FAULT! THIS WOULDN'T BE HAPPENING IF YOU HAD A BETTER ARM!
7...6...
YOU BETTER ZIP IT! BEFORE IT'S TOO LATE! THIS IS A GAME, BUT YOU TURNED IT INTO A SOAP OPERA! YOU'RE SUPER GOOD AT KILLING ANYTHING YOU'RE A PART OF!
5...4...
3...2...
1...Ø... GAME ON!
REALLY? YOU NEED A BOX OF TISSUES, TOO?
STINKIN' CRYBABY...
I'M NOT A CRYBABY!
PONG!

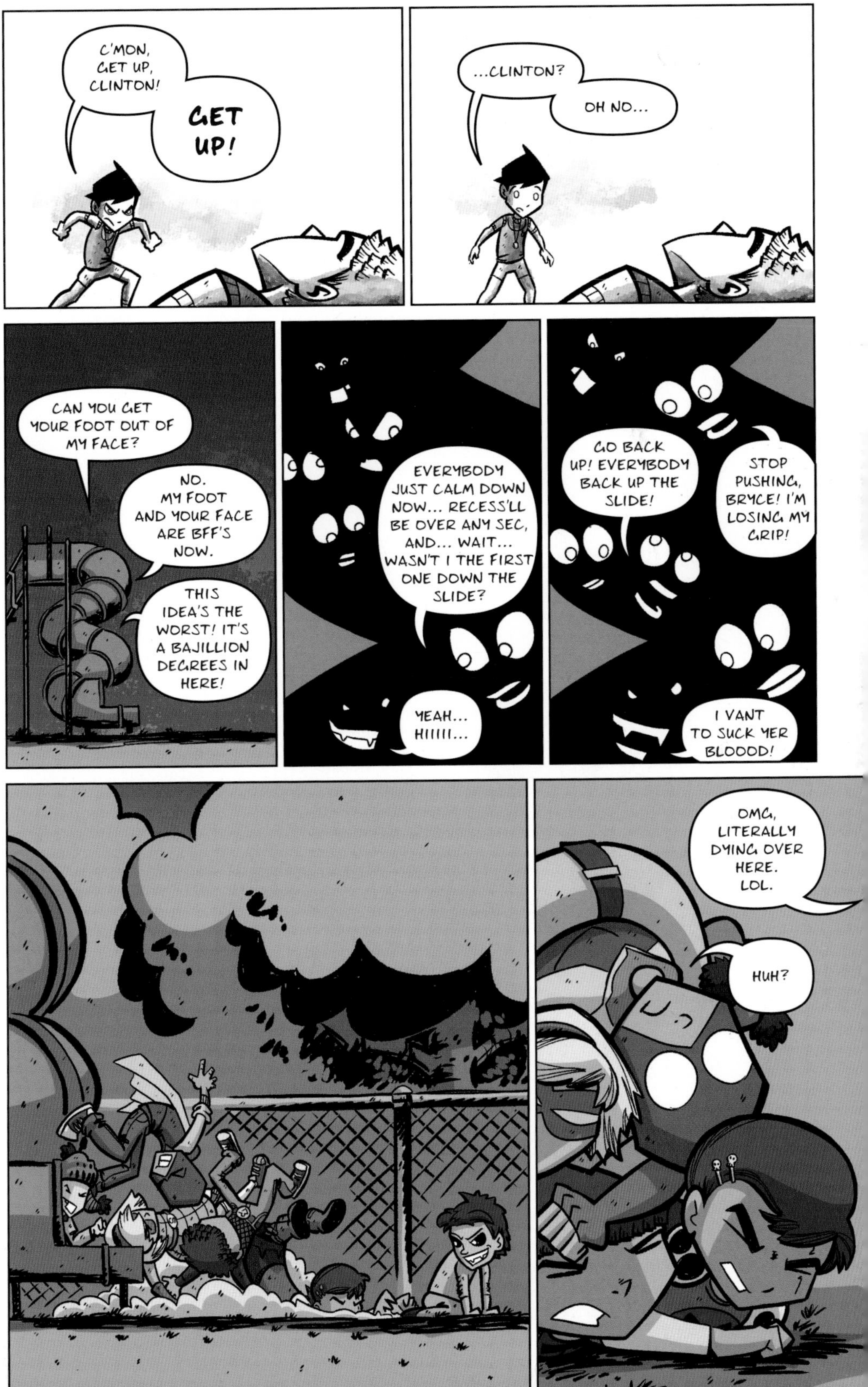
C'MON, GET UP, CLINTON!
GET UP!
...CLINTON?
OH NO...
CAN YOU GET YOUR FOOT OUT OF MY FACE?
NO. MY FOOT AND YOUR FACE ARE BFF'S NOW.
THIS IDEA'S THE WORST! IT'S A BAJILLION DEGREES IN HERE!
EVERYBODY JUST CALM DOWN NOW... RECESS'LL BE OVER ANY SEC, AND... WAIT... WASN'T I THE FIRST ONE DOWN THE SLIDE?
YEAH... HIIIII...
GO BACK UP! EVERYBODY BACK UP THE SLIDE!
STOP PUSHING, BRYCE! I'M LOSING MY GRIP!
I VANT TO SUCK YER BLOOOD!
OMG, LITERALLY DYING OVER HERE. LOL.
HUH?

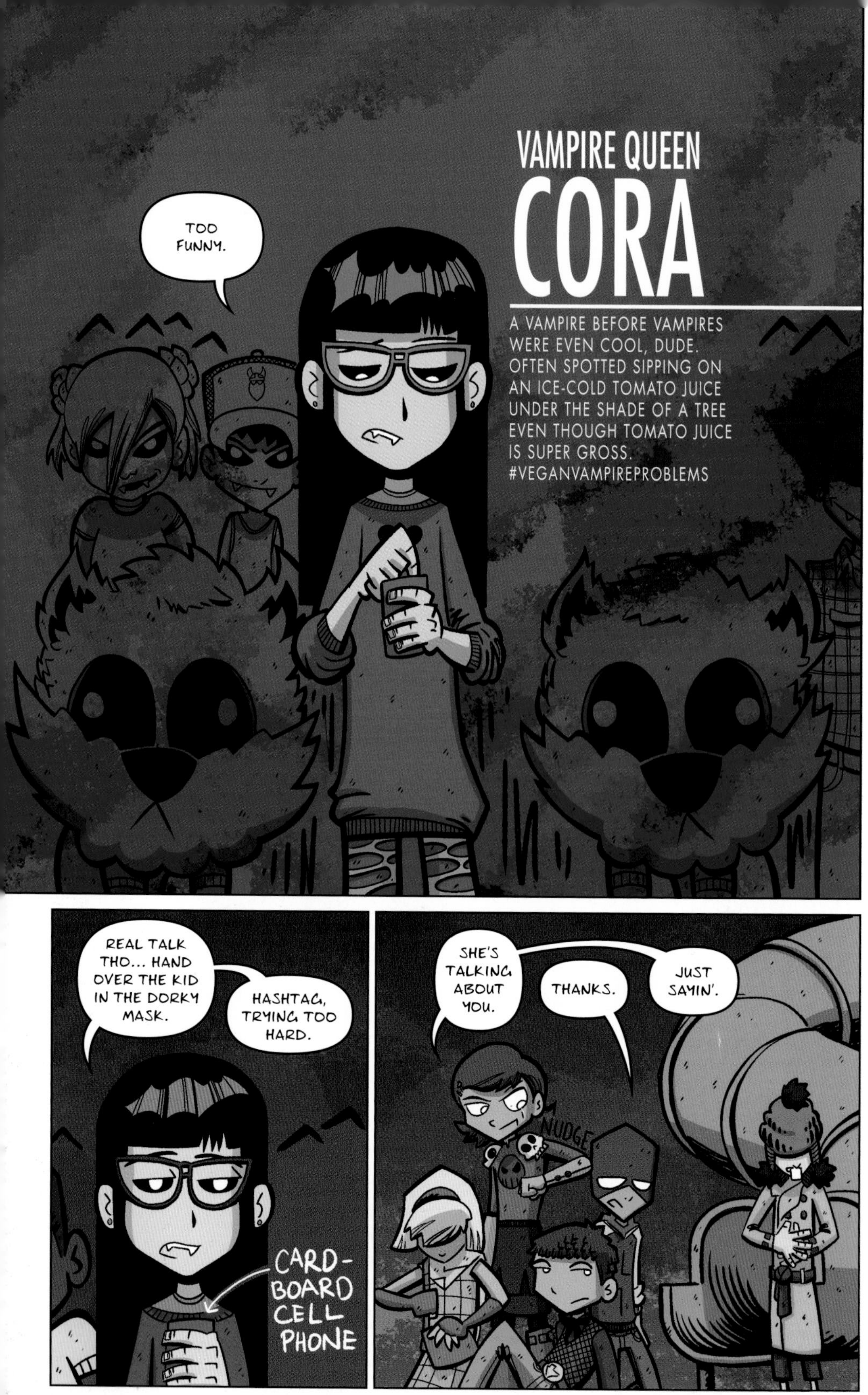
VAMPIRE QUEEN
CORA
A VAMPIRE BEFORE VAMPIRES WERE EVEN COOL, DUDE. OFTEN SPOTTED SIPPING ON AN ICE-COLD TOMATO JUICE UNDER THE SHADE OF A TREE EVEN THOUGH TOMATO JUICE IS SUPER GROSS. #VEGANVAMPIREPROBLEMS
TOO FUNNY.
REAL TALK THO... HAND OVER THE KID IN THE DORKY MASK.
HASHTAG, TRYING TOO HARD.
CARD-BOARD CELL PHONE
SHE'S TALKING ABOUT YOU.
THANKS.
JUST SAYIN'.
NUDGE

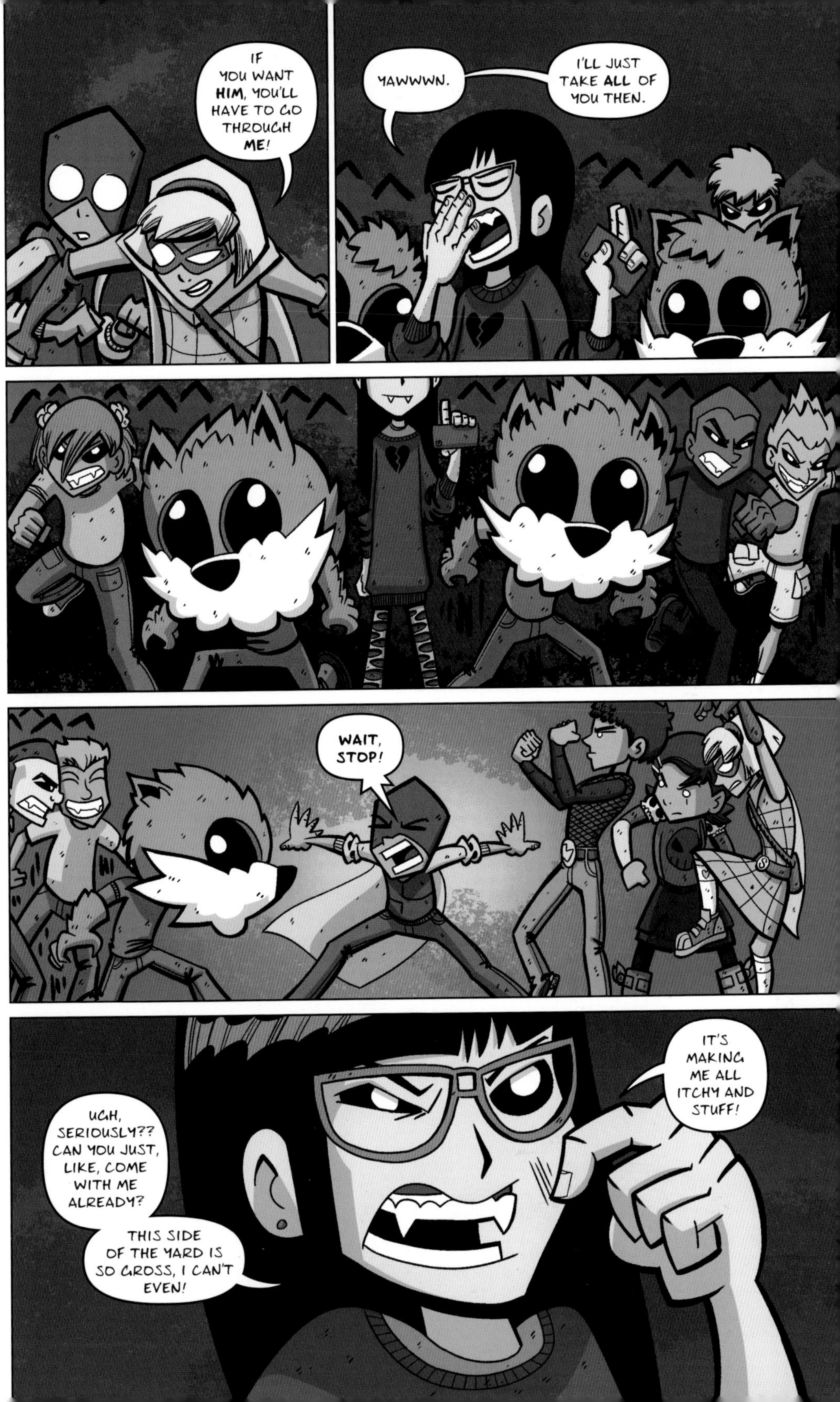
IF YOU WANT HIM, YOU'LL HAVE TO GO THROUGH ME!
YAWWWN.
I'LL JUST TAKE ALL OF YOU THEN.
WAIT, STOP!
UGH, SERIOUSLY?? CAN YOU JUST, LIKE, COME WITH ME ALREADY?
THIS SIDE OF THE YARD IS SO GROSS, I CAN'T EVEN!
IT'S MAKING ME ALL ITCHY AND STUFF!

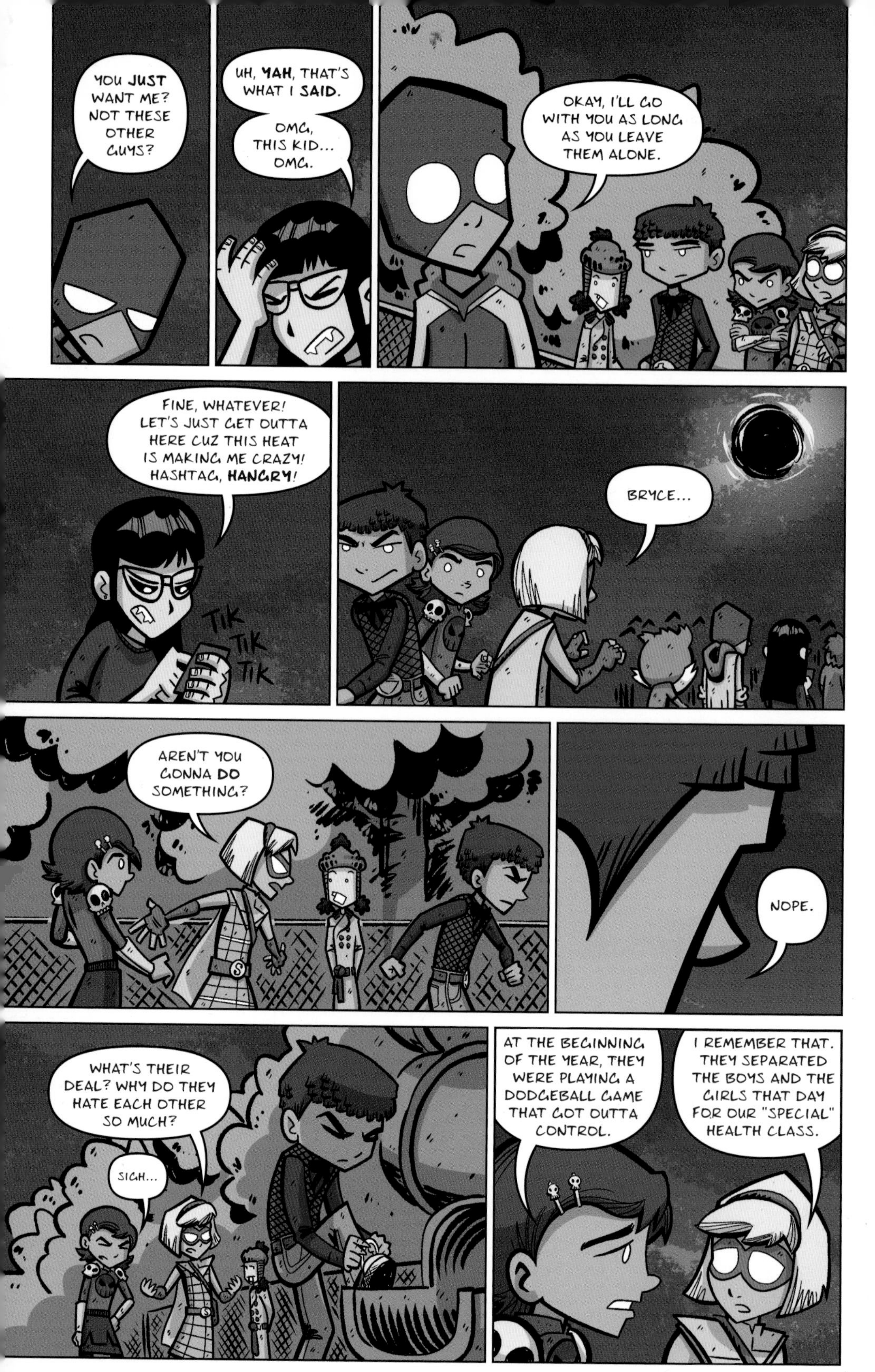
YOU JUST WANT ME? NOT THESE OTHER GUYS?
UH, YAH, THAT'S WHAT I SAID.
OMG, THIS KID... OMG.
OKAY, I'LL GO WITH YOU AS LONG AS YOU LEAVE THEM ALONE.
FINE, WHATEVER! LET'S JUST GET OUTTA HERE CUZ THIS HEAT IS MAKING ME CRAZY! HASHTAG, HANGRY!
TIK TIK TIK
BRYCE...
AREN'T YOU GONNA DO SOMETHING?
NOPE.
WHAT'S THEIR DEAL? WHY DO THEY HATE EACH OTHER SO MUCH?
SIGH...
AT THE BEGINNING OF THE YEAR, THEY WERE PLAYING A DODGEBALL GAME THAT GOT OUTTA CONTROL.
I REMEMBER THAT. THEY SEPARATED THE BOYS AND THE GIRLS THAT DAY FOR OUR "SPECIAL" HEALTH CLASS.

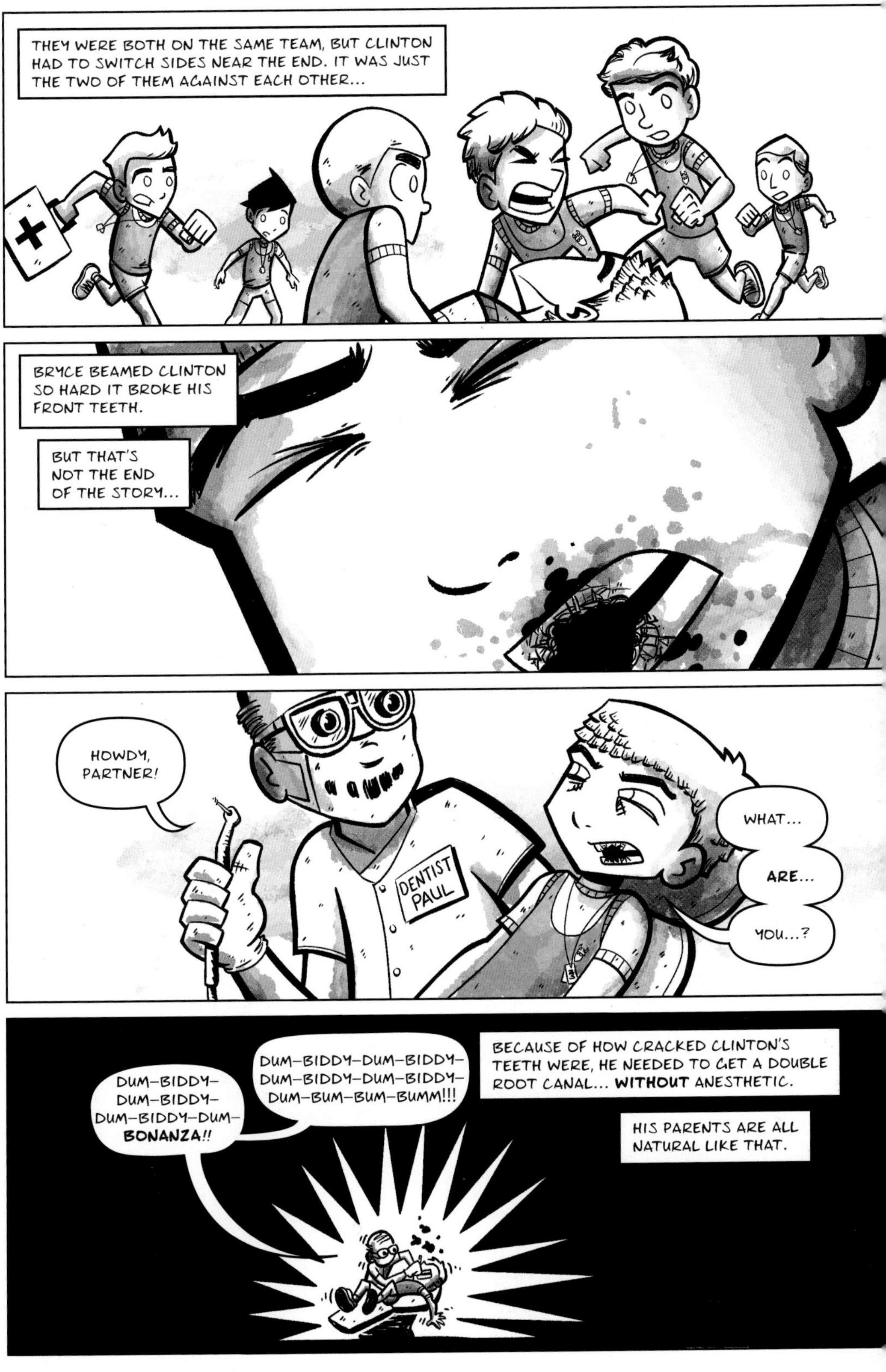
THEY WERE BOTH ON THE SAME TEAM, BUT CLINTON HAD TO SWITCH SIDES NEAR THE END. IT WAS JUST THE TWO OF THEM AGAINST EACH OTHER...
BRYCE BEAMED CLINTON SO HARD IT BROKE HIS FRONT TEETH.
BUT THAT'S NOT THE END OF THE STORY...
HOWDY, PARTNER!
DENTIST PAUL
WHAT...
ARE...
YOU...?
BECAUSE OF HOW CRACKED CLINTON'S TEETH WERE, HE NEEDED TO GET A DOUBLE ROOT CANAL... **WITHOUT** ANESTHETIC.
HIS PARENTS ARE ALL NATURAL LIKE THAT.
DUM-BIDDY-DUM-BIDDY-DUM-BIDDY-DUM-**BONANZA**!!
DUM-BIDDY-DUM-BIDDY-DUM-BIDDY-DUM-BIDDY-DUM-BUM-BUM-BUMM!!!

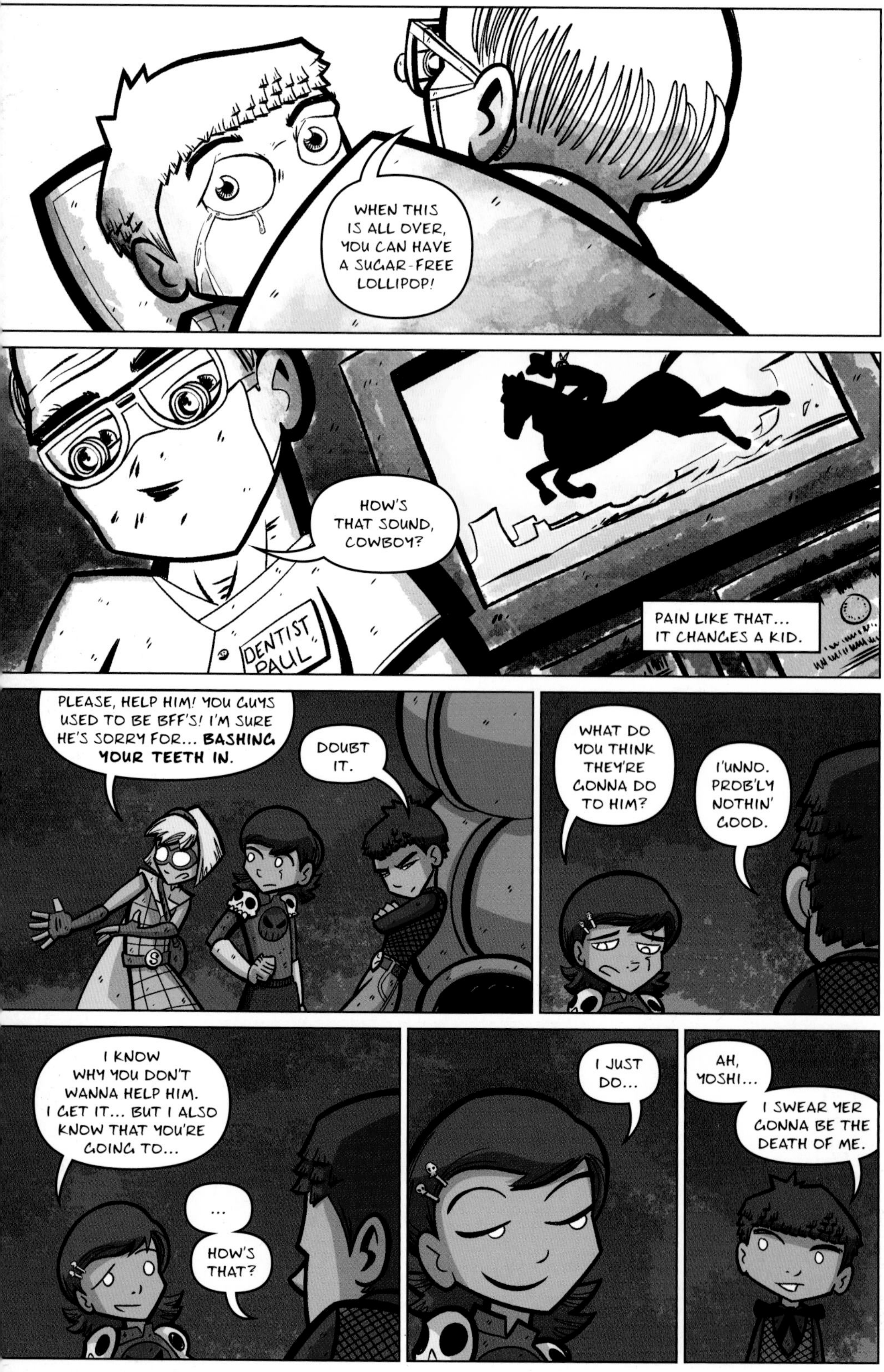
WHEN THIS IS ALL OVER, YOU CAN HAVE A SUGAR-FREE LOLLIPOP!
HOW'S THAT SOUND, COWBOY?
DENTIST PAUL
PAIN LIKE THAT... IT CHANGES A KID.
PLEASE, HELP HIM! YOU GUYS USED TO BE BFF'S! I'M SURE HE'S SORRY FOR... BASHING YOUR TEETH IN.
DOUBT IT.
WHAT DO YOU THINK THEY'RE GONNA DO TO HIM?
I'UNNO. PROB'LY NOTHIN' GOOD.
I KNOW WHY YOU DON'T WANNA HELP HIM. I GET IT... BUT I ALSO KNOW THAT YOU'RE GOING TO...
...
HOW'S THAT?
I JUST DO...
AH, YOSHI...
I SWEAR YER GONNA BE THE DEATH OF ME.

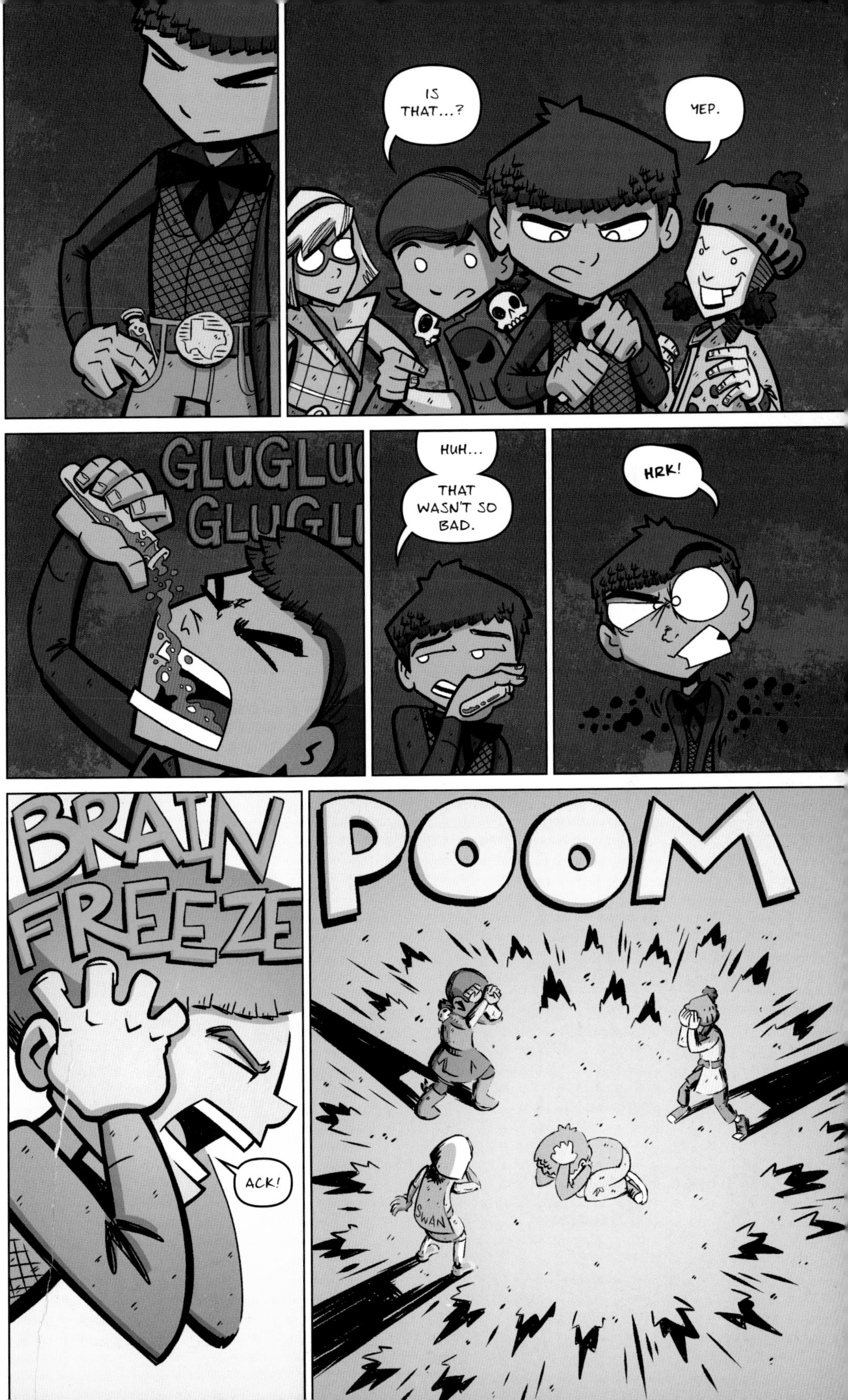
IS THAT...?
YEP.
GLUGLUG GLUGLU
HUH...
THAT WASN'T SO BAD.
HRK!
BRAIN FREEZE
ACK!
POOM
SWAN

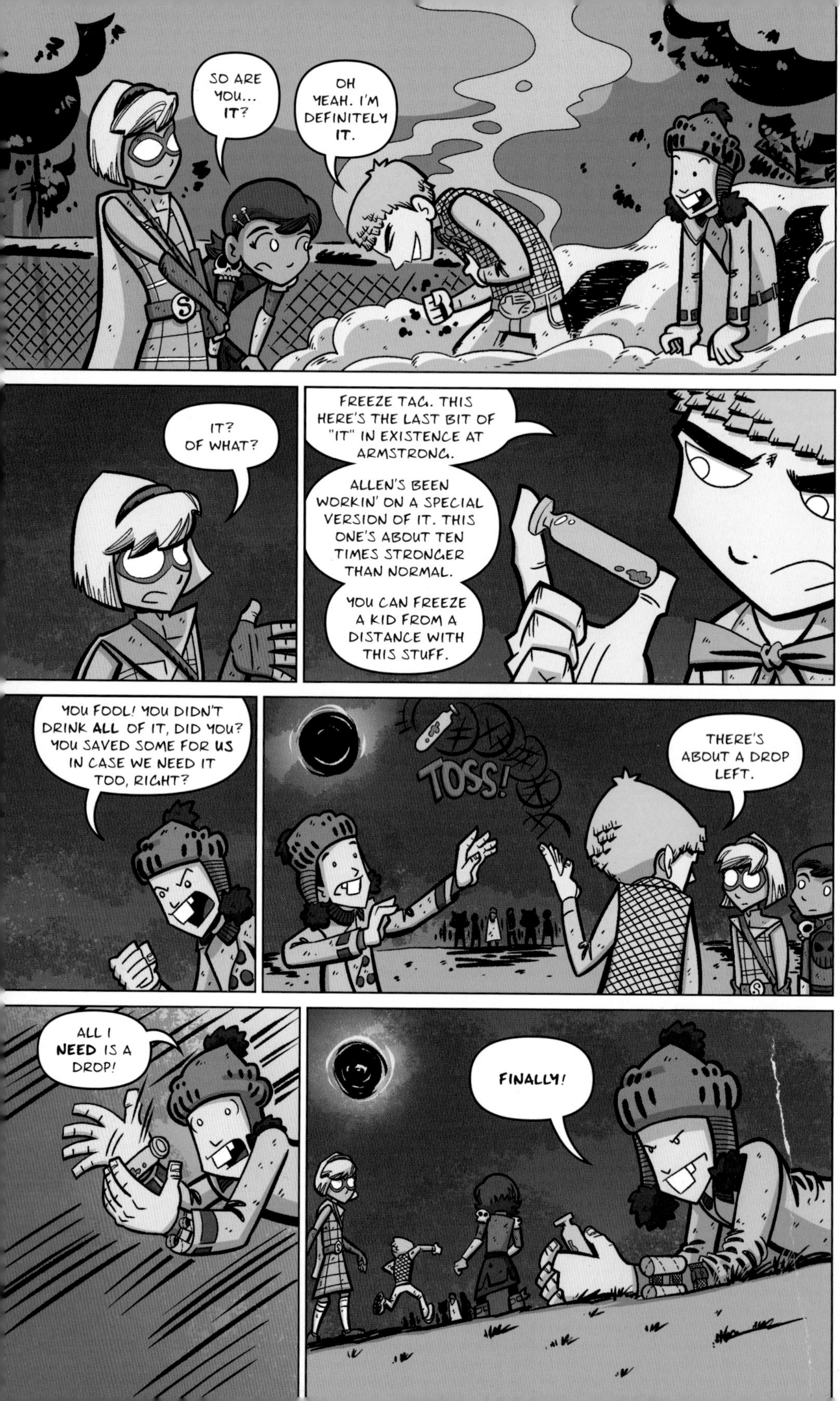
SO ARE YOU... IT?
OH YEAH. I'M DEFINITELY IT.
IT? OF WHAT?
FREEZE TAG. THIS HERE'S THE LAST BIT OF "IT" IN EXISTENCE AT ARMSTRONG.
ALLEN'S BEEN WORKIN' ON A SPECIAL VERSION OF IT. THIS ONE'S ABOUT TEN TIMES STRONGER THAN NORMAL.
YOU CAN FREEZE A KID FROM A DISTANCE WITH THIS STUFF.
YOU FOOL! YOU DIDN'T DRINK ALL OF IT, DID YOU? YOU SAVED SOME FOR US IN CASE WE NEED IT TOO, RIGHT?
TOSS!
THERE'S ABOUT A DROP LEFT.
ALL I NEED IS A DROP!
FINALLY!

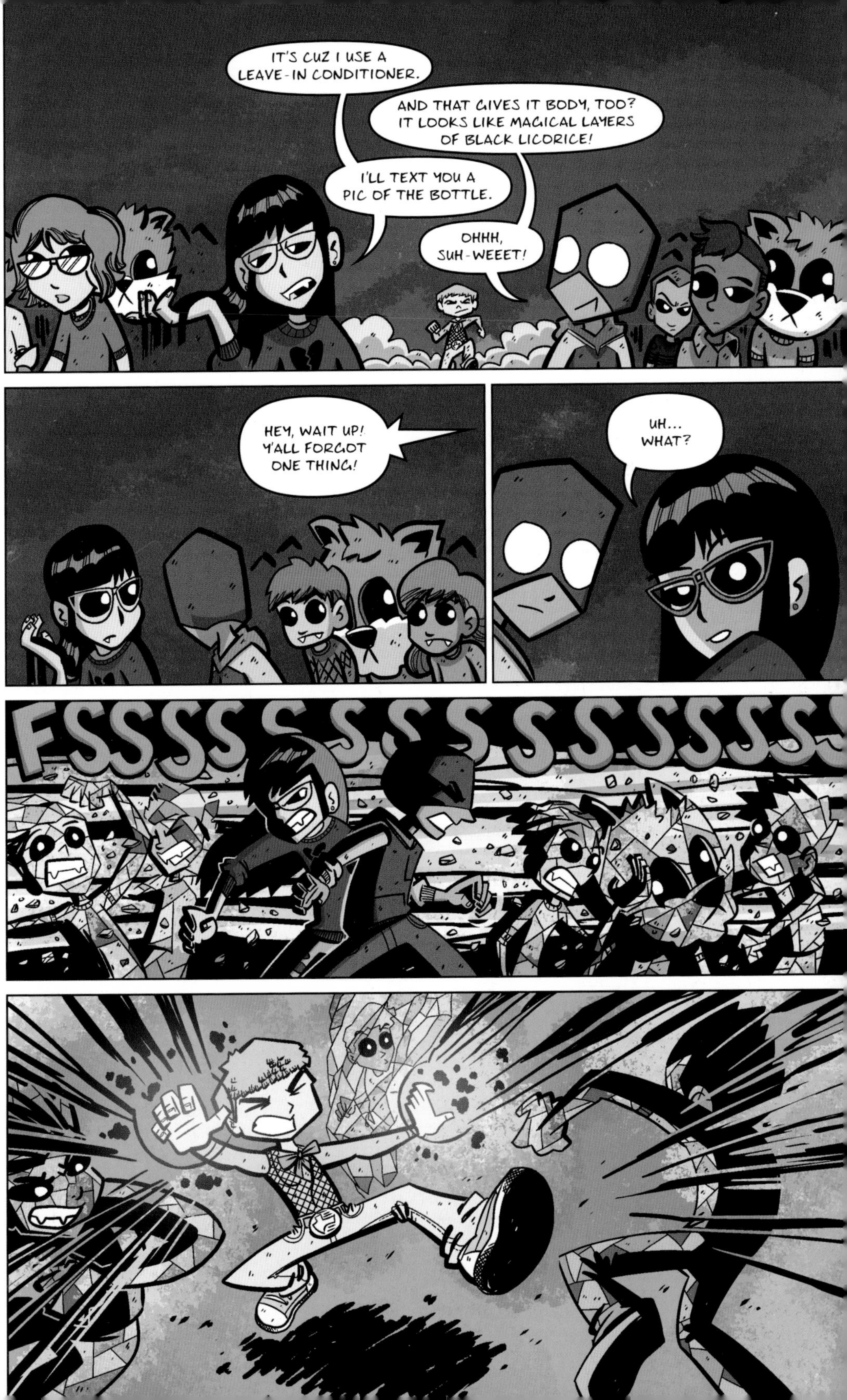
IT'S CUZ I USE A LEAVE-IN CONDITIONER.
AND THAT GIVES IT BODY, TOO? IT LOOKS LIKE MAGICAL LAYERS OF BLACK LICORICE!
I'LL TEXT YOU A PIC OF THE BOTTLE.
OHHH, SUH-WEEET!
HEY, WAIT UP! Y'ALL FORGOT ONE THING!
UH... WHAT?
FSSSSSSSSSSSSSS

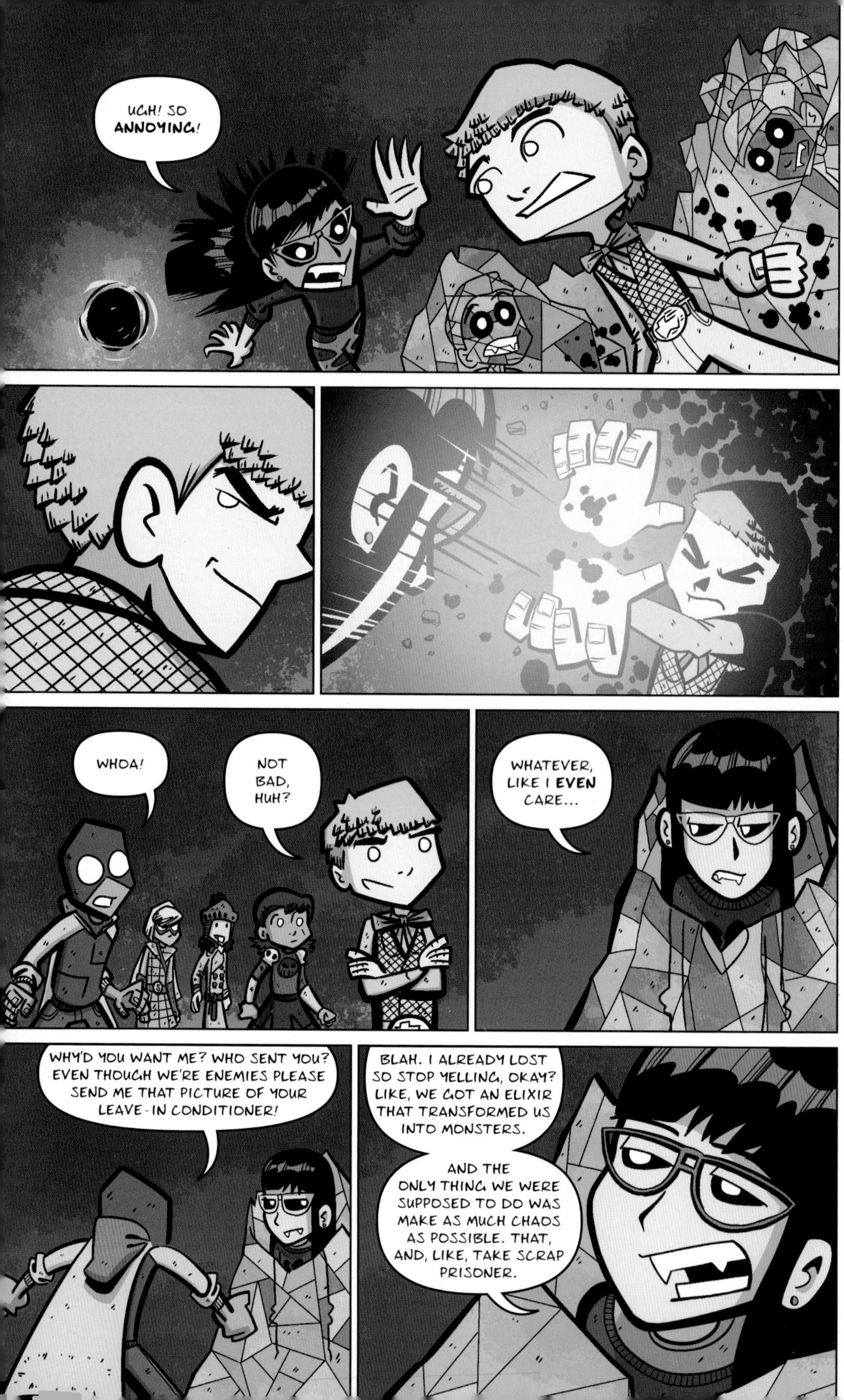
UGH! SO **ANNOYING**!
WHOA!
NOT BAD, HUH?
WHATEVER, LIKE I **EVEN** CARE...
WHY'D YOU WANT ME? WHO SENT YOU? EVEN THOUGH WE'RE ENEMIES PLEASE SEND ME THAT PICTURE OF YOUR LEAVE-IN CONDITIONER!
BLAH. I ALREADY LOST SO STOP YELLING, OKAY? LIKE, WE GOT AN ELIXIR THAT TRANSFORMED US INTO MONSTERS.
AND THE ONLY THING WE WERE SUPPOSED TO DO WAS MAKE AS MUCH CHAOS AS POSSIBLE. THAT, AND, LIKE, TAKE SCRAP PRISONER.

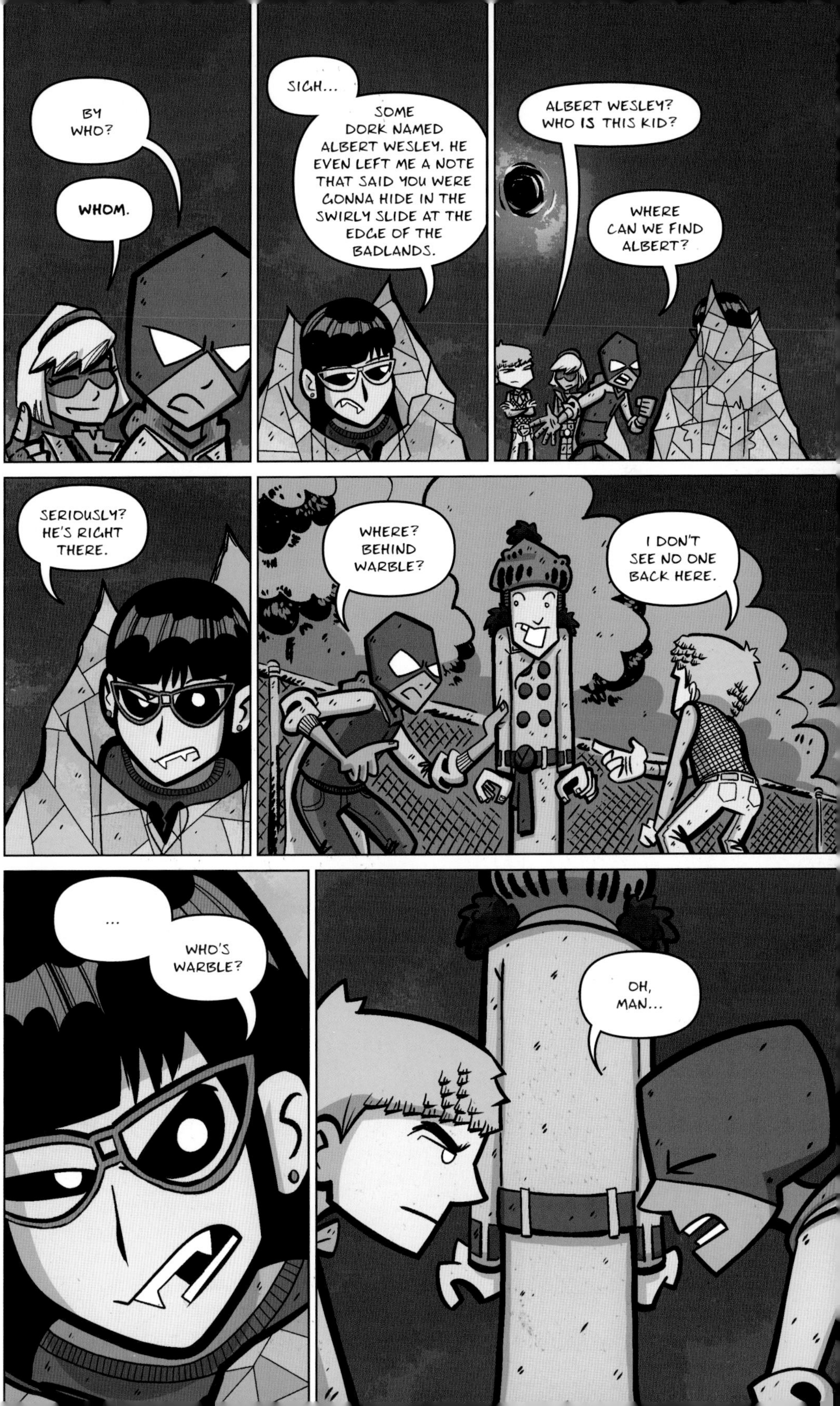
BY WHO?
WHOM.
SIGH...
SOME DORK NAMED ALBERT WESLEY. HE EVEN LEFT ME A NOTE THAT SAID YOU WERE GONNA HIDE IN THE SWIRLY SLIDE AT THE EDGE OF THE BADLANDS.
ALBERT WESLEY? WHO IS THIS KID?
WHERE CAN WE FIND ALBERT?
SERIOUSLY? HE'S RIGHT THERE.
WHERE? BEHIND WARBLE?
I DON'T SEE NO ONE BACK HERE.
...
WHO'S WARBLE?
OH, MAN...

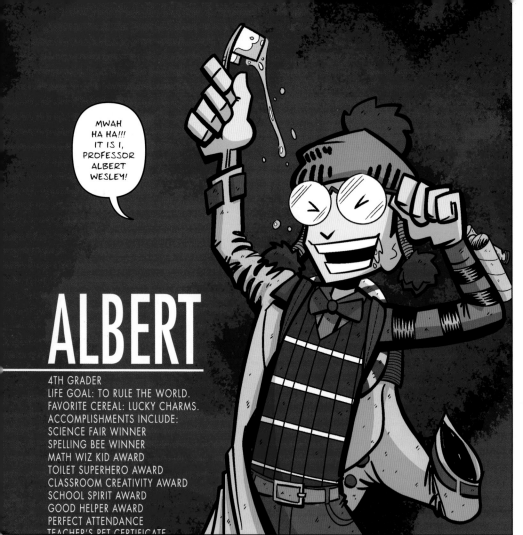

MWAH HA HA!!! IT IS I, PROFESSOR ALBERT WESLEY!

ALBERT

4TH GRADER
LIFE GOAL: TO RULE THE WORLD.
FAVORITE CEREAL: LUCKY CHARMS.
ACCOMPLISHMENTS INCLUDE:
SCIENCE FAIR WINNER
SPELLING BEE WINNER
MATH WIZ KID AWARD
TOILET SUPERHERO AWARD
CLASSROOM CREATIVITY AWARD
SCHOOL SPIRIT AWARD
GOOD HELPER AWARD
PERFECT ATTENDANCE
TEACHER'S PET CERTIFICATE

WARBLE STEELY? ALBERT WESLEY? HIS NAME IS A **MAMMOGRAM**!

ANAGRAM.

ANAGRAM!

I'M ABOUT TO PUT A STOP TO ALL THIS RIGHT NOW...

VMMMM

DOOT! DOOT! DOOT! DOOT! DOOT!

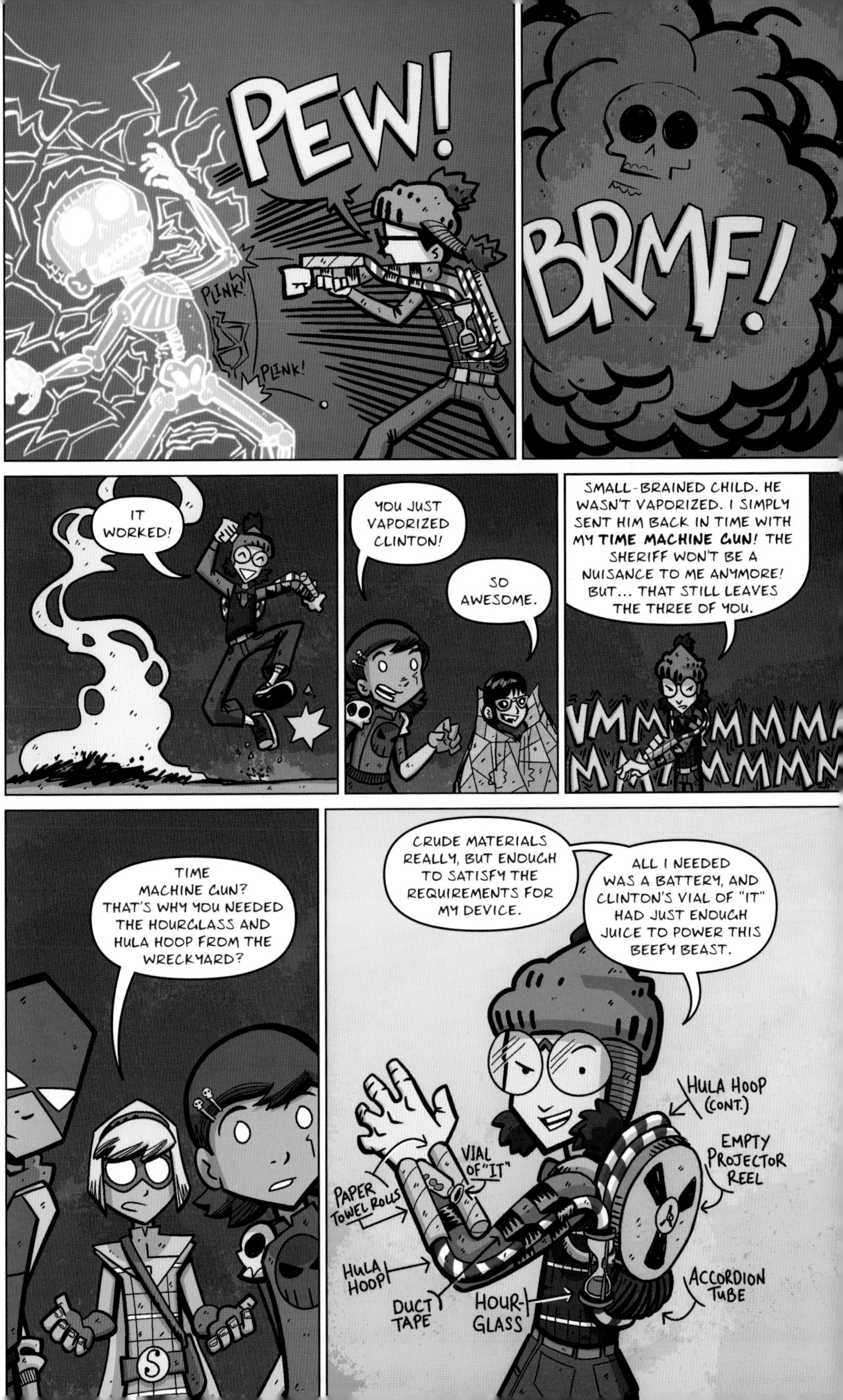
PEW!
PLINK!
PLINK!
BRMF!
IT WORKED!
YOU JUST VAPORIZED CLINTON!
SO AWESOME.
SMALL-BRAINED CHILD. HE WASN'T VAPORIZED. I SIMPLY SENT HIM BACK IN TIME WITH MY TIME MACHINE GUN! THE SHERIFF WON'T BE A NUISANCE TO ME ANYMORE! BUT... THAT STILL LEAVES THE THREE OF YOU.
VMMMMMMMMMMMMMMMMMMM
TIME MACHINE GUN? THAT'S WHY YOU NEEDED THE HOURGLASS AND HULA HOOP FROM THE WRECKYARD?
CRUDE MATERIALS REALLY, BUT ENOUGH TO SATISFY THE REQUIREMENTS FOR MY DEVICE.
ALL I NEEDED WAS A BATTERY, AND CLINTON'S VIAL OF "IT" HAD JUST ENOUGH JUICE TO POWER THIS BEEFY BEAST.
HULA HOOP (CONT.)
EMPTY PROJECTOR REEL
VIAL OF "IT"
PAPER TOWEL ROLLS
HULA HOOP
DUCT TAPE
HOUR-GLASS
ACCORDION TUBE

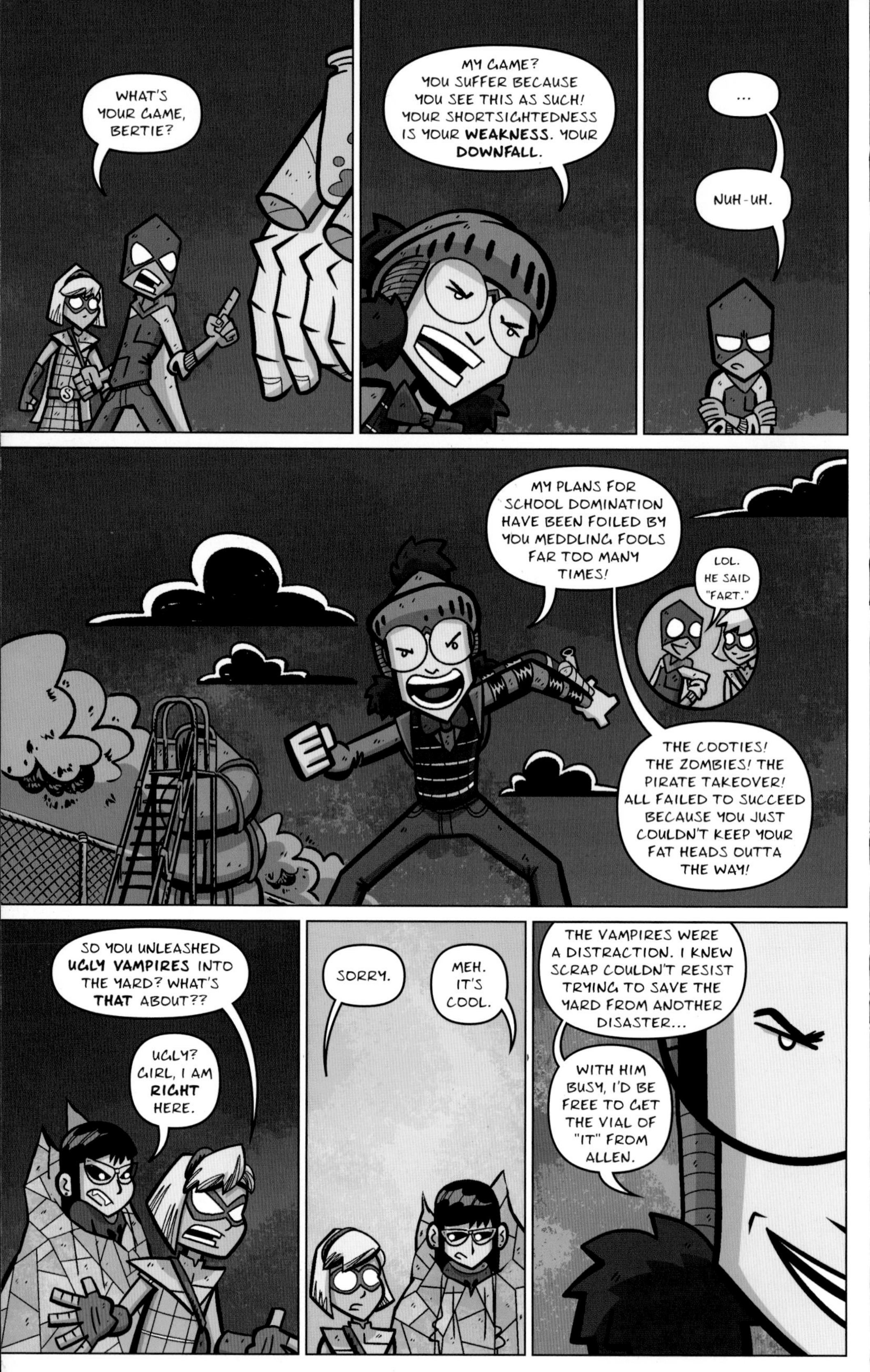
WHAT'S YOUR GAME, BERTIE?
MY GAME? YOU SUFFER BECAUSE YOU SEE THIS AS SUCH! YOUR SHORTSIGHTEDNESS IS YOUR WEAKNESS. YOUR DOWNFALL.
...
NUH-UH.
MY PLANS FOR SCHOOL DOMINATION HAVE BEEN FOILED BY YOU MEDDLING FOOLS FAR TOO MANY TIMES!
LOL. HE SAID "FART."
THE COOTIES! THE ZOMBIES! THE PIRATE TAKEOVER! ALL FAILED TO SUCCEED BECAUSE YOU JUST COULDN'T KEEP YOUR FAT HEADS OUTTA THE WAY!
SO YOU UNLEASHED UGLY VAMPIRES INTO THE YARD? WHAT'S THAT ABOUT??
UGLY? GIRL, I AM RIGHT HERE.
SORRY.
MEH. IT'S COOL.
THE VAMPIRES WERE A DISTRACTION. I KNEW SCRAP COULDN'T RESIST TRYING TO SAVE THE YARD FROM ANOTHER DISASTER...
WITH HIM BUSY, I'D BE FREE TO GET THE VIAL OF "IT" FROM ALLEN.

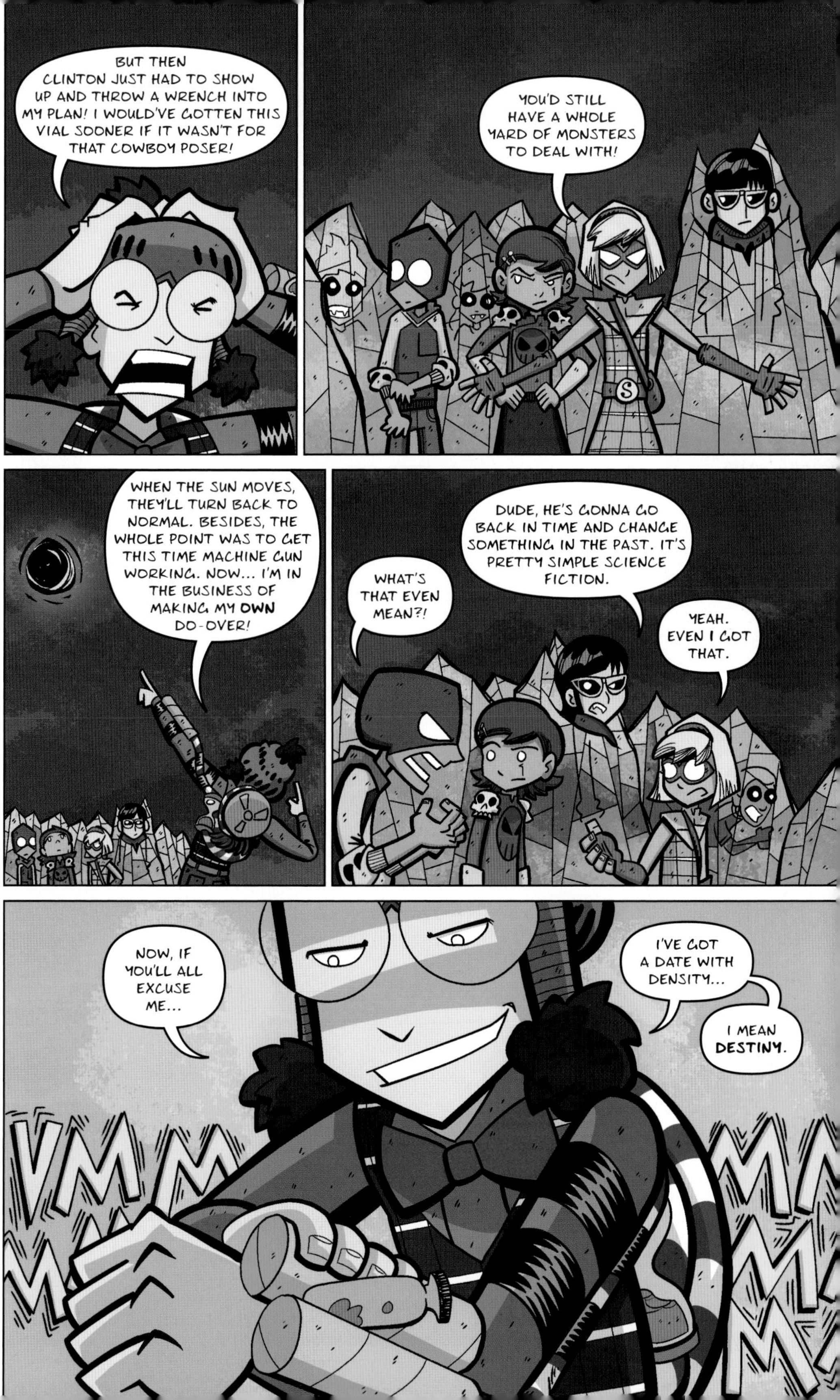
BUT THEN CLINTON JUST HAD TO SHOW UP AND THROW A WRENCH INTO MY PLAN! I WOULD'VE GOTTEN THIS VIAL SOONER IF IT WASN'T FOR THAT COWBOY POSER!
YOU'D STILL HAVE A WHOLE YARD OF MONSTERS TO DEAL WITH!
WHEN THE SUN MOVES, THEY'LL TURN BACK TO NORMAL. BESIDES, THE WHOLE POINT WAS TO GET THIS TIME MACHINE GUN WORKING. NOW... I'M IN THE BUSINESS OF MAKING MY **OWN** DO-OVER!
WHAT'S THAT EVEN MEAN?!
DUDE, HE'S GONNA GO BACK IN TIME AND CHANGE SOMETHING IN THE PAST. IT'S PRETTY SIMPLE SCIENCE FICTION.
YEAH. EVEN I GOT THAT.
NOW, IF YOU'LL ALL EXCUSE ME...
I'VE GOT A DATE WITH DENSITY...
I MEAN **DESTINY**.
VMMM
MMMM

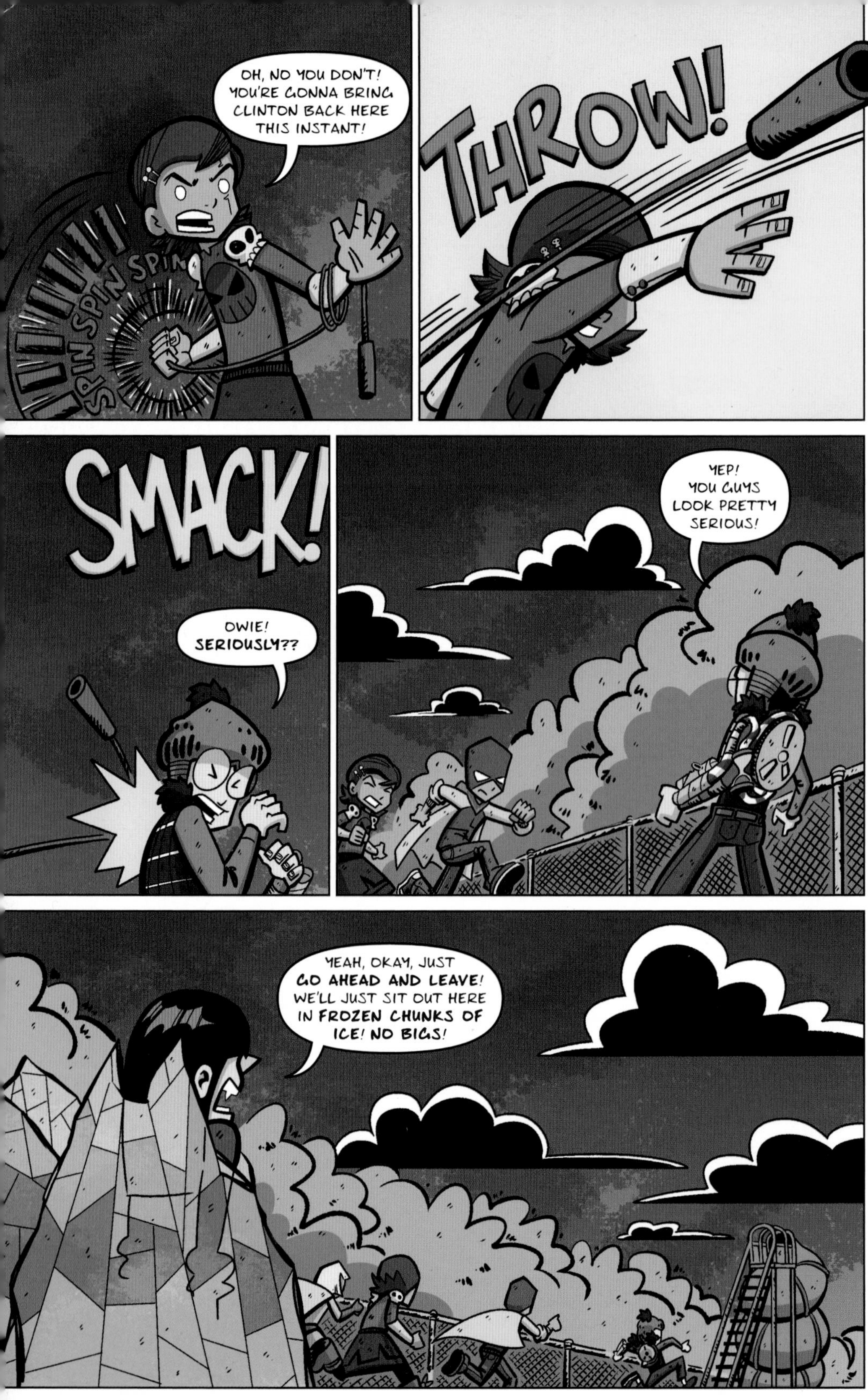
OH, NO YOU DON'T! YOU'RE GONNA BRING CLINTON BACK HERE THIS INSTANT!
SPIN SPIN SPIN SPIN
THROW!
SMACK!
OWIE! SERIOUSLY??
YEP! YOU GUYS LOOK PRETTY SERIOUS!
YEAH, OKAY, JUST GO AHEAD AND LEAVE! WE'LL JUST SIT OUT HERE IN FROZEN CHUNKS OF ICE! NO BIGS!

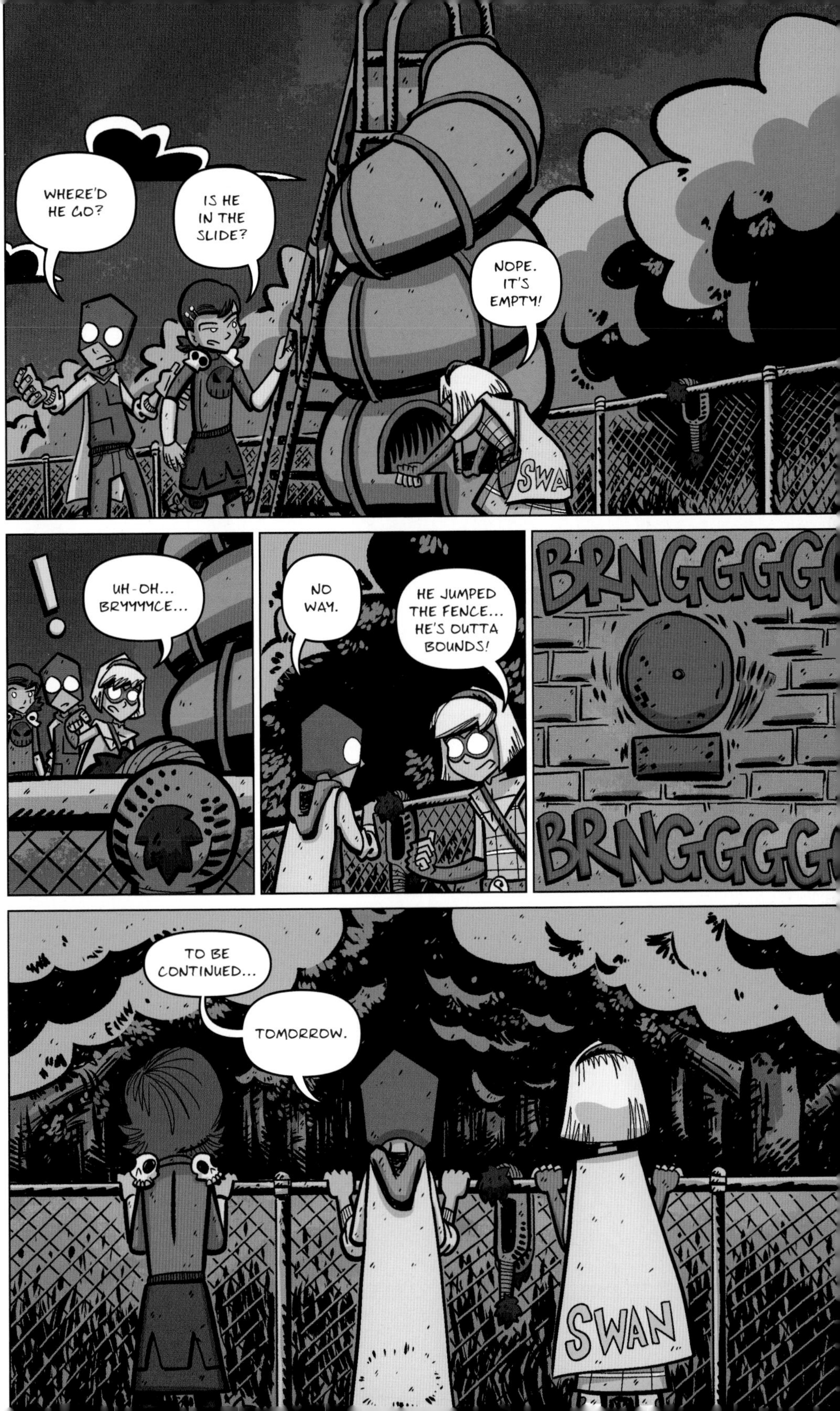
WHERE'D HE GO?
IS HE IN THE SLIDE?
NOPE. IT'S EMPTY!
SWAN
!
UH-OH... BRYYYYCE...
NO WAY.
HE JUMPED THE FENCE... HE'S OUTTA BOUNDS!
BRNGGGGG
BRNGGGGG
TO BE CONTINUED...
TOMORROW.
FINN
SWAN

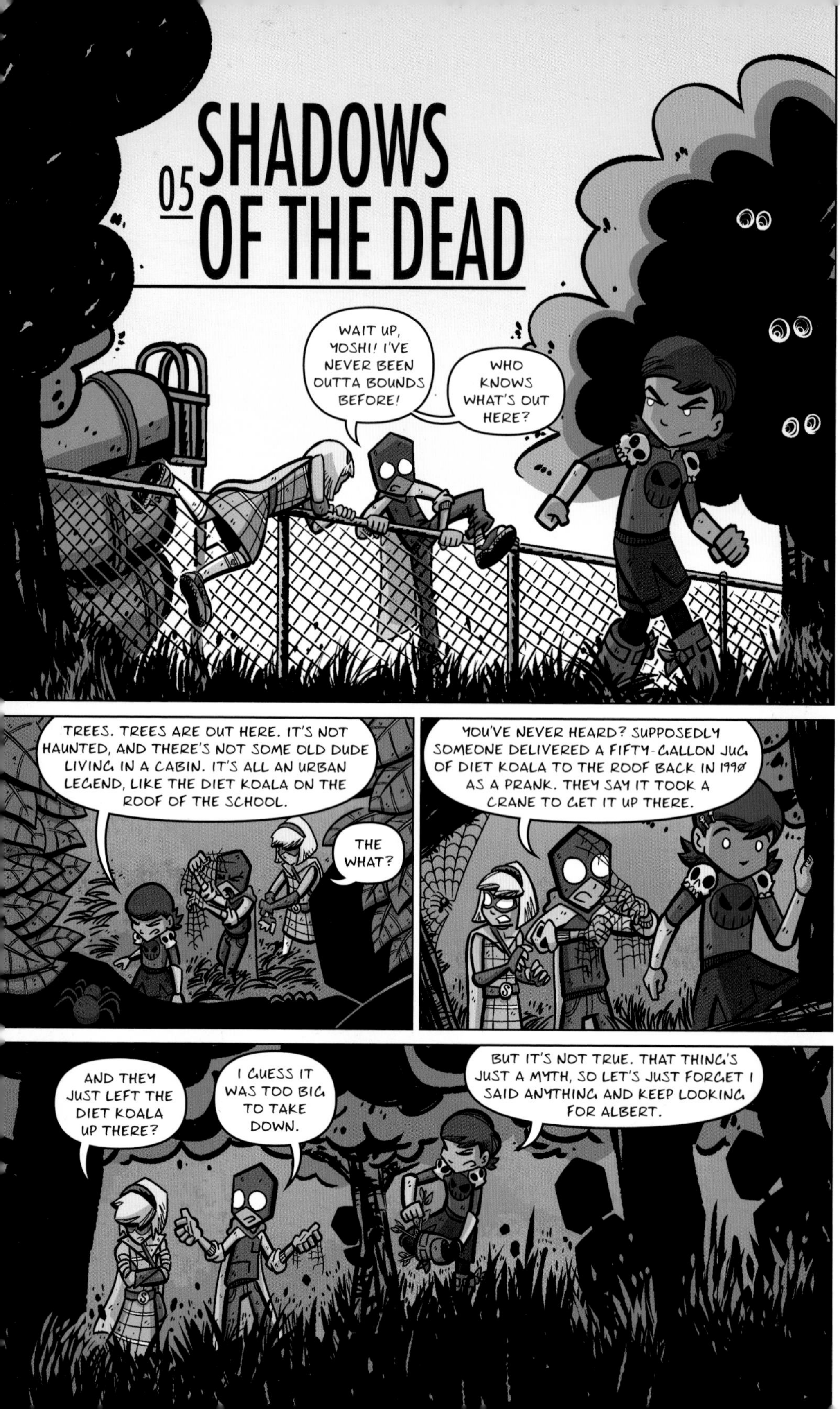
05 SHADOWS OF THE DEAD
WAIT UP, YOSHI! I'VE NEVER BEEN OUTTA BOUNDS BEFORE!
WHO KNOWS WHAT'S OUT HERE?
TREES. TREES ARE OUT HERE. IT'S NOT HAUNTED, AND THERE'S NOT SOME OLD DUDE LIVING IN A CABIN. IT'S ALL AN URBAN LEGEND, LIKE THE DIET KOALA ON THE ROOF OF THE SCHOOL.
THE WHAT?
YOU'VE NEVER HEARD? SUPPOSEDLY SOMEONE DELIVERED A FIFTY-GALLON JUG OF DIET KOALA TO THE ROOF BACK IN 1990 AS A PRANK. THEY SAY IT TOOK A CRANE TO GET IT UP THERE.
AND THEY JUST LEFT THE DIET KOALA UP THERE?
I GUESS IT WAS TOO BIG TO TAKE DOWN.
BUT IT'S NOT TRUE. THAT THING'S JUST A MYTH, SO LET'S JUST FORGET I SAID ANYTHING AND KEEP LOOKING FOR ALBERT.

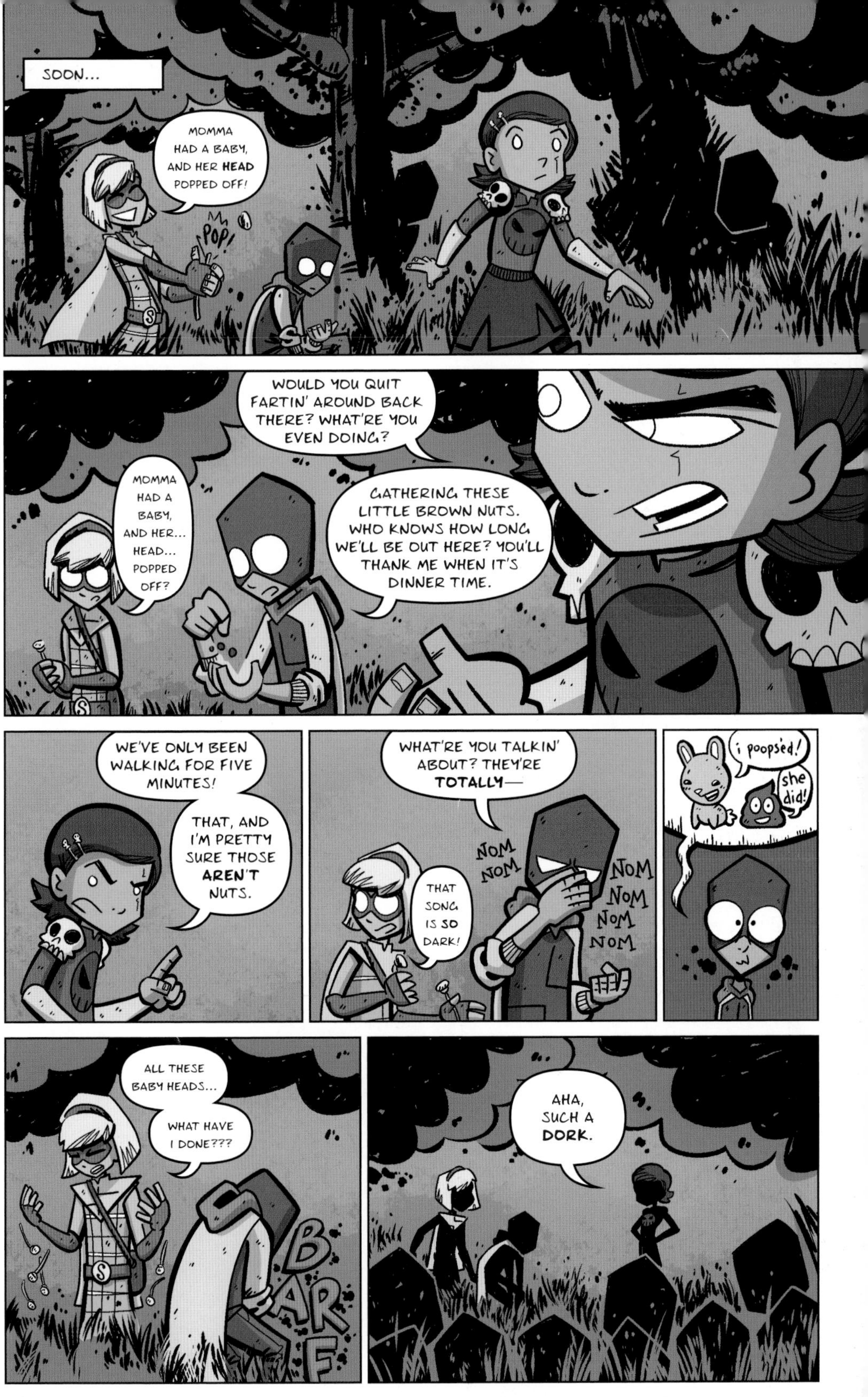
SOON...
MOMMA HAD A BABY, AND HER HEAD POPPED OFF!
POP!
WOULD YOU QUIT FARTIN' AROUND BACK THERE? WHAT'RE YOU EVEN DOING?
MOMMA HAD A BABY, AND HER... HEAD... POPPED OFF?
GATHERING THESE LITTLE BROWN NUTS. WHO KNOWS HOW LONG WE'LL BE OUT HERE? YOU'LL THANK ME WHEN IT'S DINNER TIME.
WE'VE ONLY BEEN WALKING FOR FIVE MINUTES!
THAT, AND I'M PRETTY SURE THOSE AREN'T NUTS.
WHAT'RE YOU TALKIN' ABOUT? THEY'RE TOTALLY—
NOM NOM
NOM NOM NOM NOM
THAT SONG IS SO DARK!
i poopsed!
she did!
ALL THESE BABY HEADS...
WHAT HAVE I DONE???
BARF
AHA, SUCH A DORK.

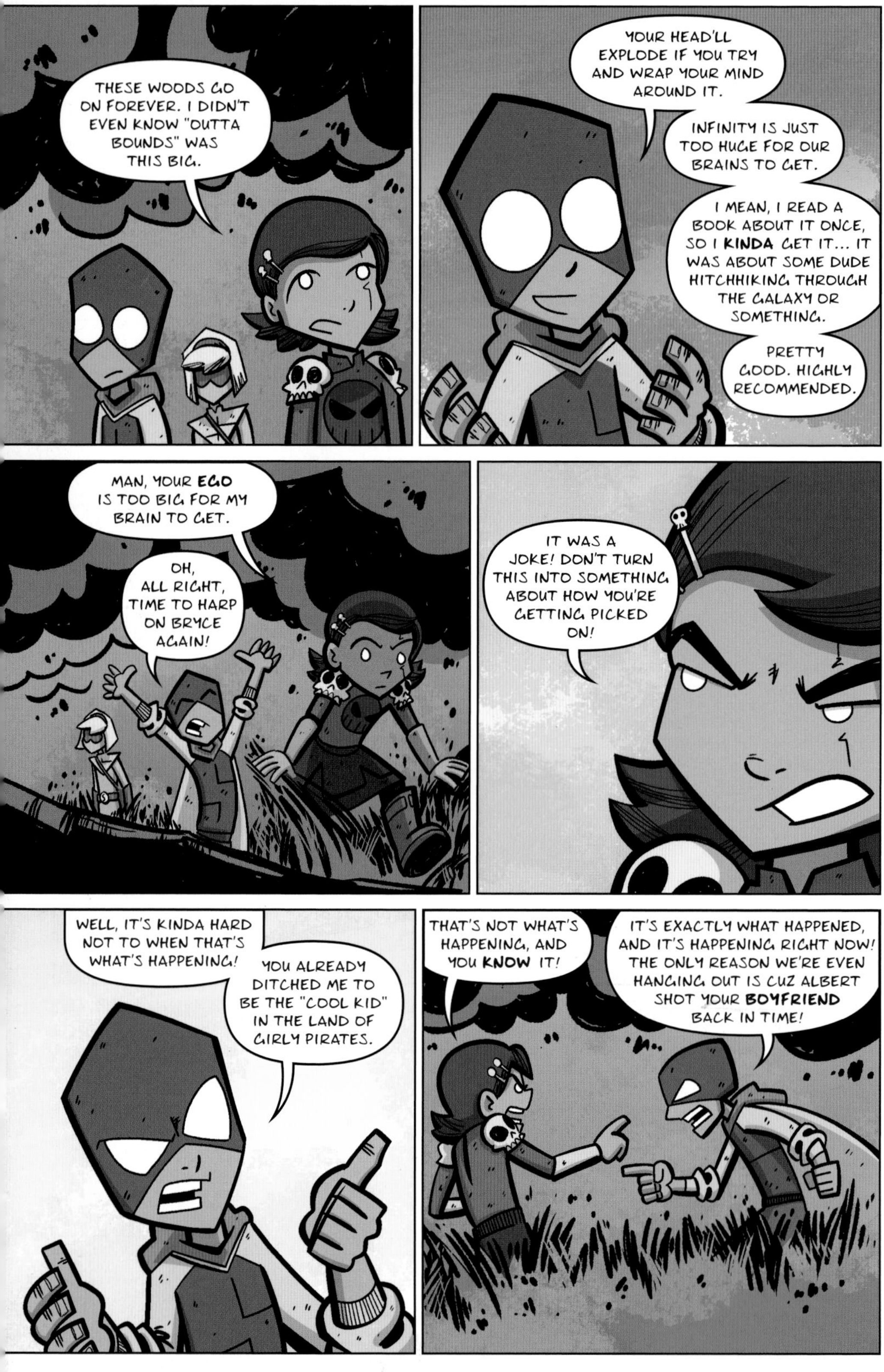
THESE WOODS GO ON FOREVER. I DIDN'T EVEN KNOW "OUTTA BOUNDS" WAS THIS BIG.
YOUR HEAD'LL EXPLODE IF YOU TRY AND WRAP YOUR MIND AROUND IT.
INFINITY IS JUST TOO HUGE FOR OUR BRAINS TO GET.
I MEAN, I READ A BOOK ABOUT IT ONCE, SO I **KINDA** GET IT... IT WAS ABOUT SOME DUDE HITCHHIKING THROUGH THE GALAXY OR SOMETHING.
PRETTY GOOD. HIGHLY RECOMMENDED.
MAN, YOUR **EGO** IS TOO BIG FOR MY BRAIN TO GET.
OH, ALL RIGHT, TIME TO HARP ON BRYCE AGAIN!
IT WAS A JOKE! DON'T TURN THIS INTO SOMETHING ABOUT HOW YOU'RE GETTING PICKED ON!
WELL, IT'S KINDA HARD NOT TO WHEN THAT'S WHAT'S HAPPENING!
YOU ALREADY DITCHED ME TO BE THE "COOL KID" IN THE LAND OF GIRLY PIRATES.
THAT'S NOT WHAT'S HAPPENING, AND YOU **KNOW** IT!
IT'S EXACTLY WHAT HAPPENED, AND IT'S HAPPENING RIGHT NOW! THE ONLY REASON WE'RE EVEN HANGING OUT IS CUZ ALBERT SHOT YOUR **BOYFRIEND** BACK IN TIME!

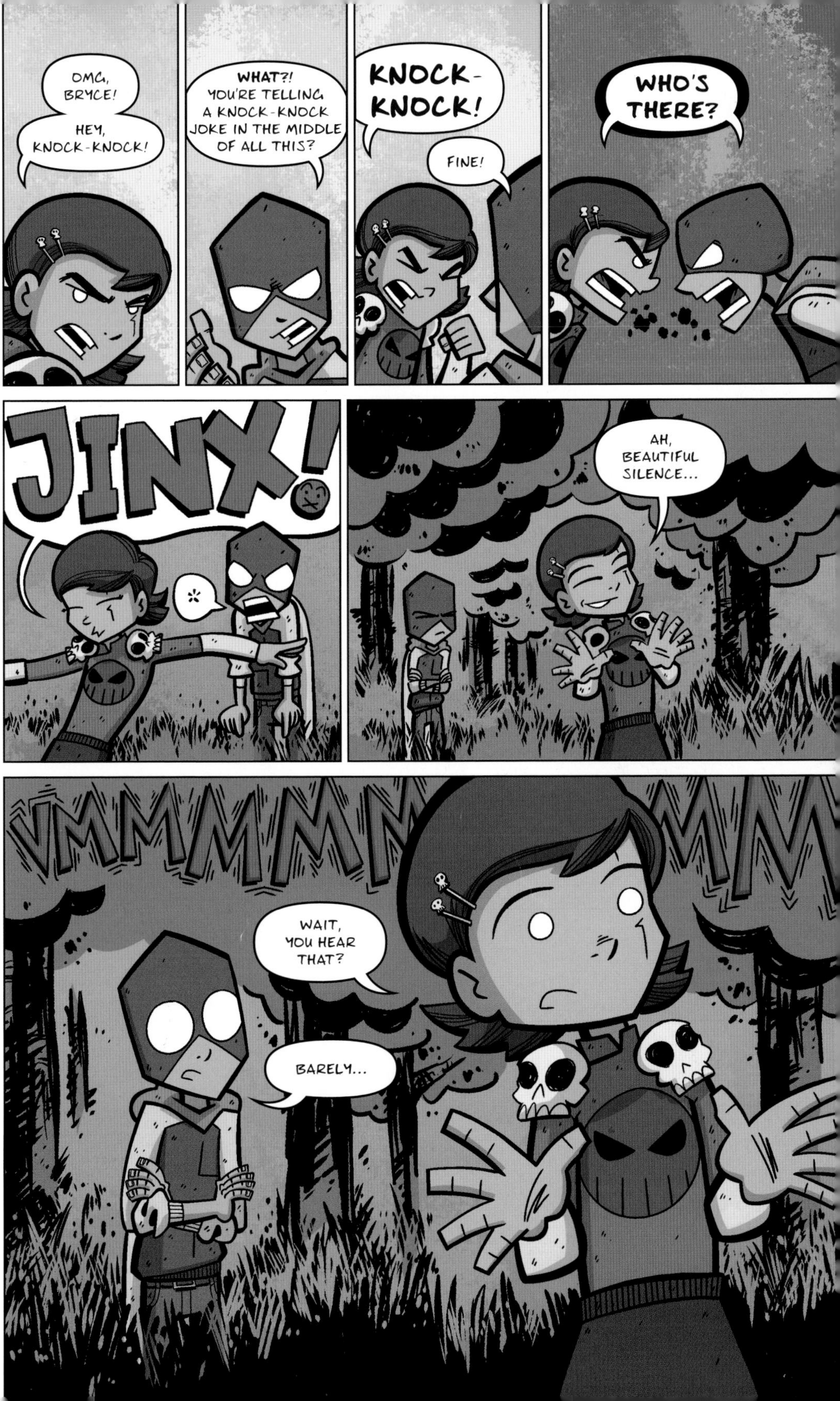
OMG, BRYCE!
HEY, KNOCK-KNOCK!
WHAT?! YOU'RE TELLING A KNOCK-KNOCK JOKE IN THE MIDDLE OF ALL THIS?
KNOCK-KNOCK!
FINE!
WHO'S THERE?
JINX!
AH, BEAUTIFUL SILENCE...
VMMMMMMMMM
WAIT, YOU HEAR THAT?
BARELY...

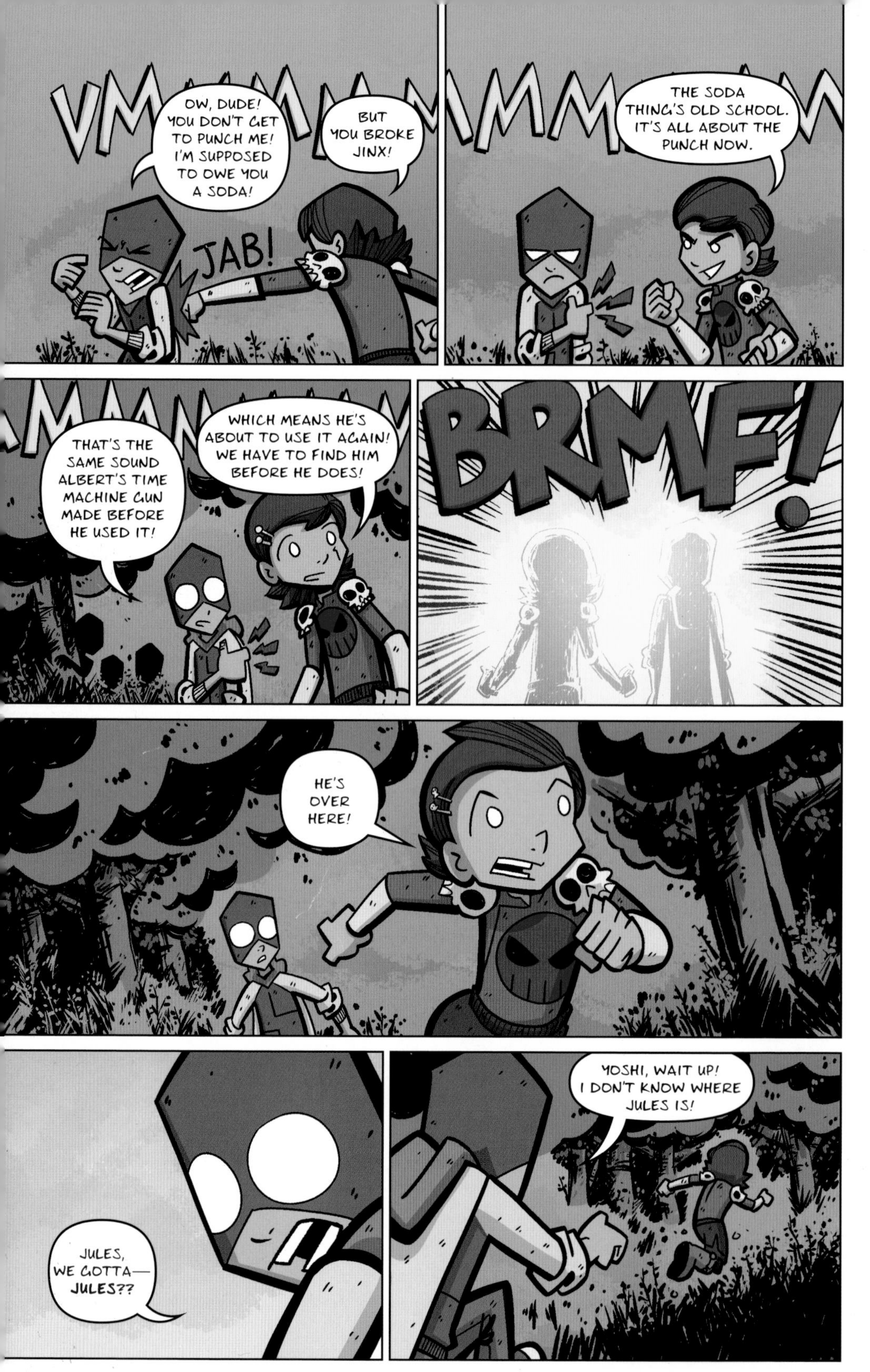
VMMMMMMMMMMMMMMMMMMMMMMMM
OW, DUDE! YOU DON'T GET TO PUNCH ME! I'M SUPPOSED TO OWE YOU A SODA!
BUT YOU BROKE JINX!
JAB!
THE SODA THING'S OLD SCHOOL. IT'S ALL ABOUT THE PUNCH NOW.
THAT'S THE SAME SOUND ALBERT'S TIME MACHINE GUN MADE BEFORE HE USED IT!
WHICH MEANS HE'S ABOUT TO USE IT AGAIN! WE HAVE TO FIND HIM BEFORE HE DOES!
BRMF!
HE'S OVER HERE!
JULES, WE GOTTA— JULES??
YOSHI, WAIT UP! I DON'T KNOW WHERE JULES IS!

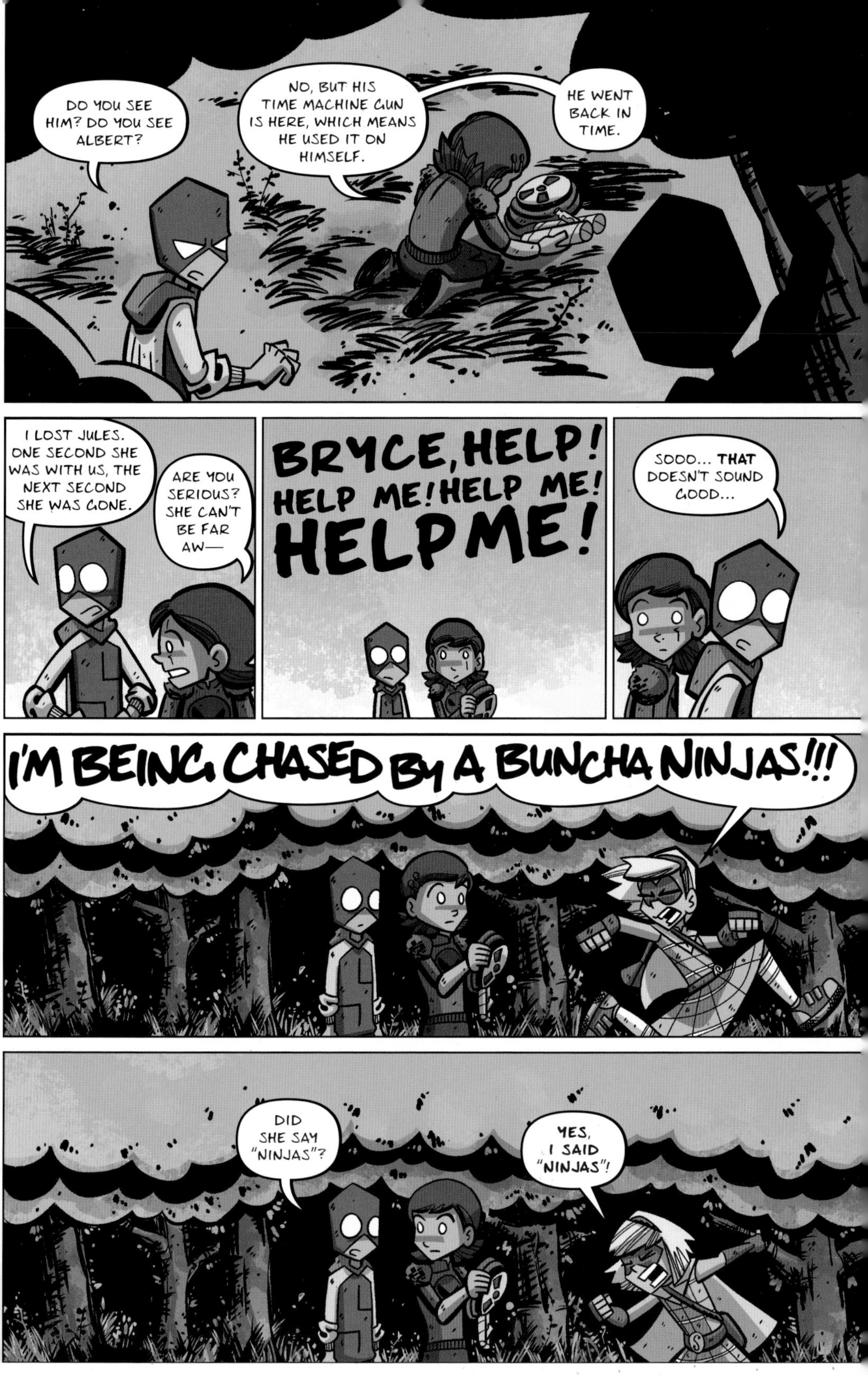
DO YOU SEE HIM? DO YOU SEE ALBERT?
NO, BUT HIS TIME MACHINE GUN IS HERE, WHICH MEANS HE USED IT ON HIMSELF.
HE WENT BACK IN TIME.
I LOST JULES. ONE SECOND SHE WAS WITH US, THE NEXT SECOND SHE WAS GONE.
ARE YOU SERIOUS? SHE CAN'T BE FAR AW—
BRYCE, HELP! HELP ME! HELP ME! HELP ME!
SOOO... **THAT** DOESN'T SOUND GOOD...
I'M BEING CHASED BY A BUNCHA NINJAS!!!
DID SHE SAY "NINJAS"?
YES, I SAID "**NINJAS**"!

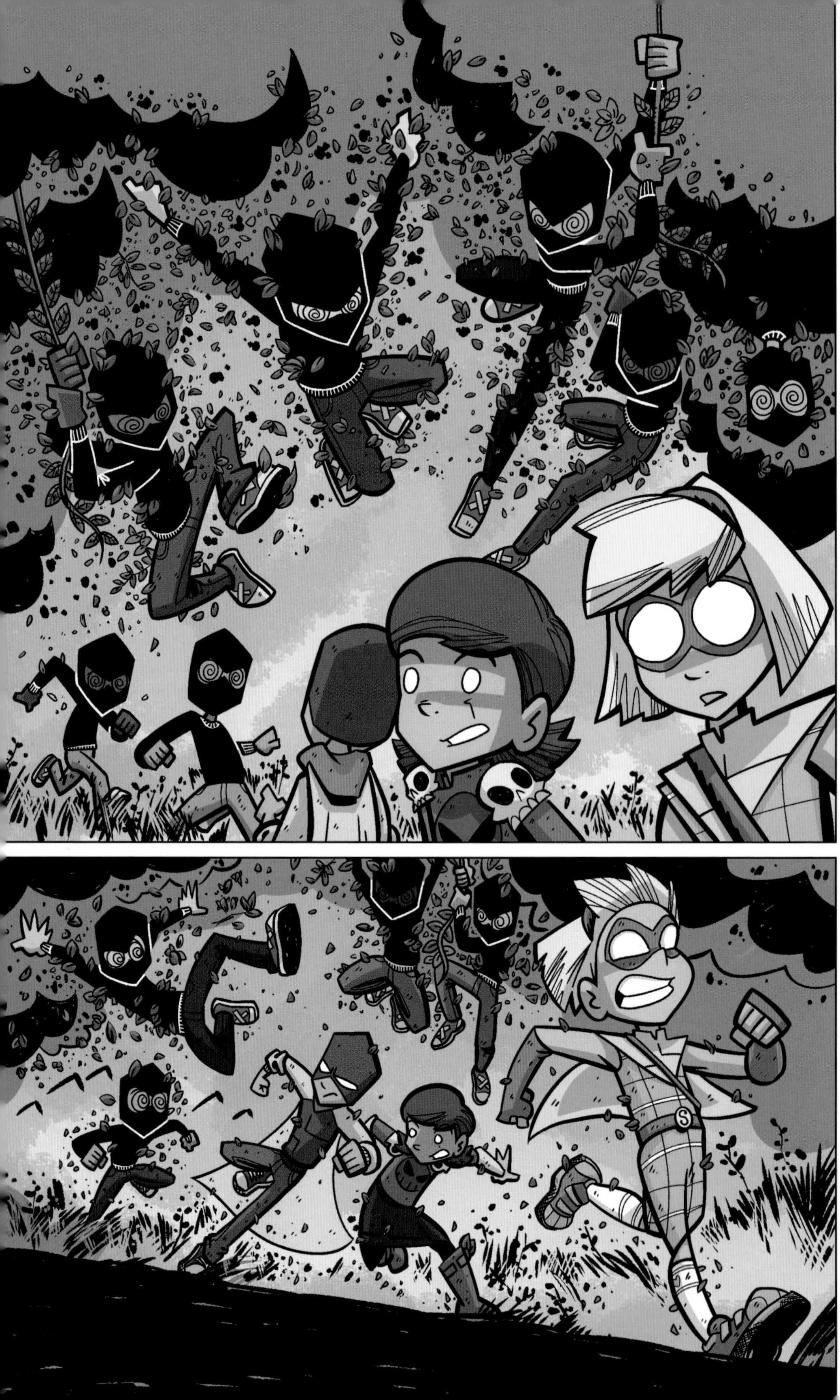

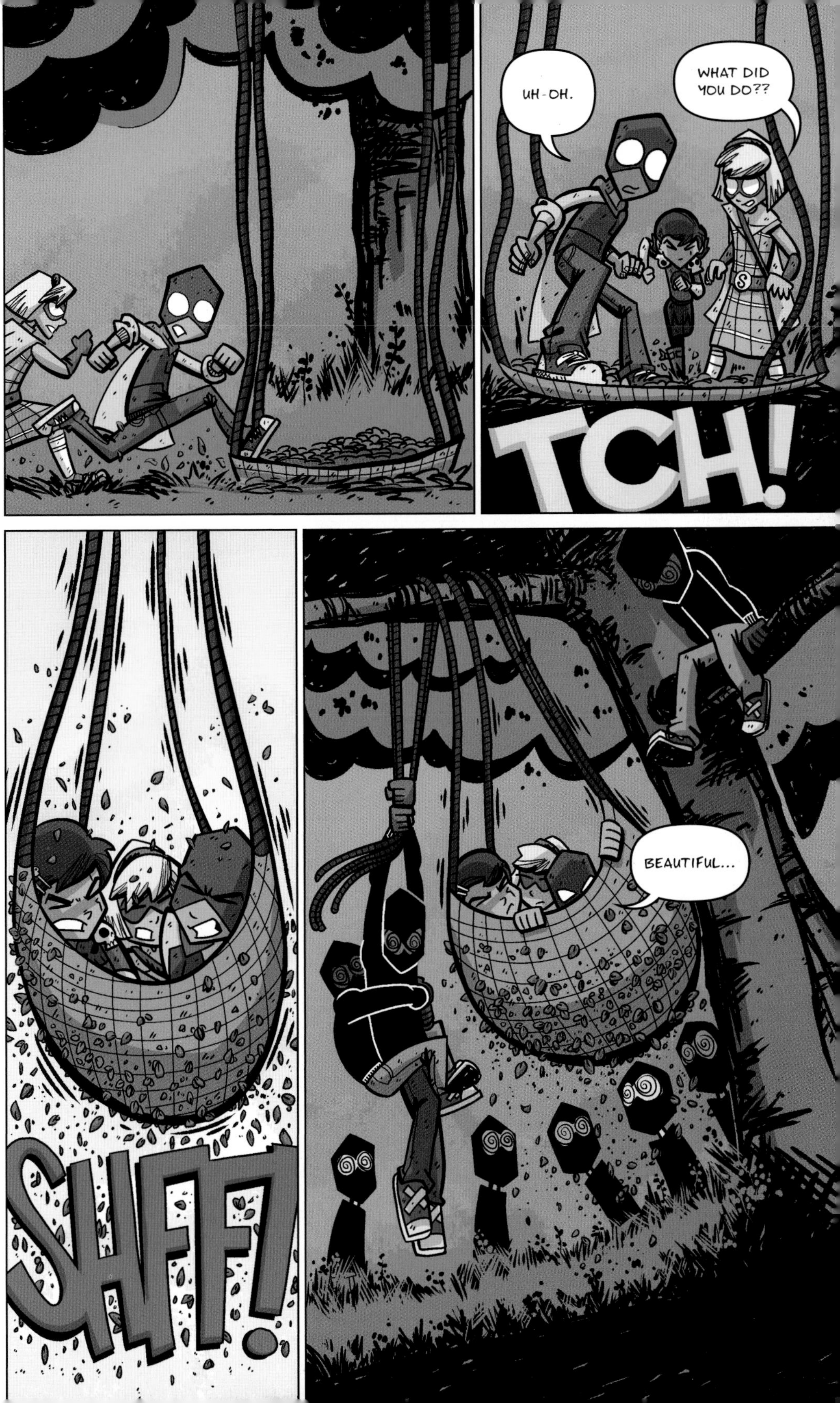
UH-OH.
WHAT DID YOU DO??
TCH!
SHFF!
BEAUTIFUL...

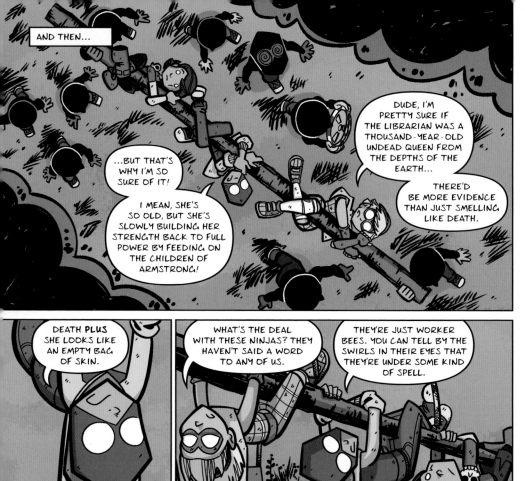

AND THEN...

...BUT THAT'S WHY I'M SO SURE OF IT!

I MEAN, SHE'S SO OLD, BUT SHE'S SLOWLY BUILDING HER STRENGTH BACK TO FULL POWER BY FEEDING ON THE CHILDREN OF ARMSTRONG!

DUDE, I'M PRETTY SURE IF THE LIBRARIAN WAS A THOUSAND-YEAR-OLD UNDEAD QUEEN FROM THE DEPTHS OF THE EARTH...

THERE'D BE MORE EVIDENCE THAN JUST SMELLING LIKE DEATH.

DEATH **PLUS** SHE LOOKS LIKE AN EMPTY BAG OF SKIN.

WHAT'S THE DEAL WITH THESE NINJAS? THEY HAVEN'T SAID A WORD TO ANY OF US.

THEY'RE JUST WORKER BEES. YOU CAN TELL BY THE SWIRLS IN THEIR EYES THAT THEY'RE UNDER SOME KIND OF SPELL.

I'M REALLY STARTING TO HATE THIS SCHOOL.

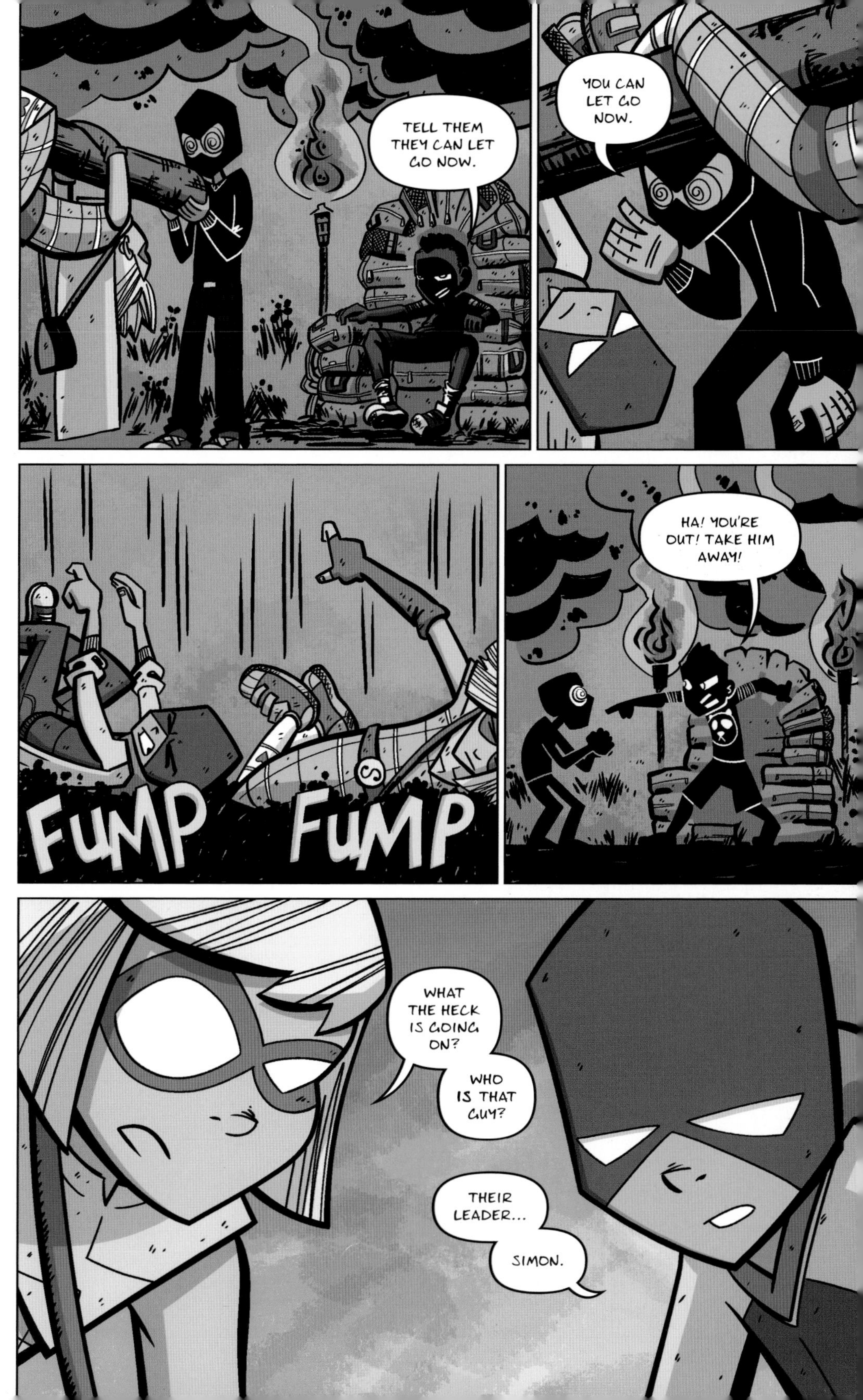
TELL THEM THEY CAN LET GO NOW.
YOU CAN LET GO NOW.
FUMP FUMP
HA! YOU'RE OUT! TAKE HIM AWAY!
WHAT THE HECK IS GOING ON?
WHO IS THAT GUY?
THEIR LEADER...
SIMON.

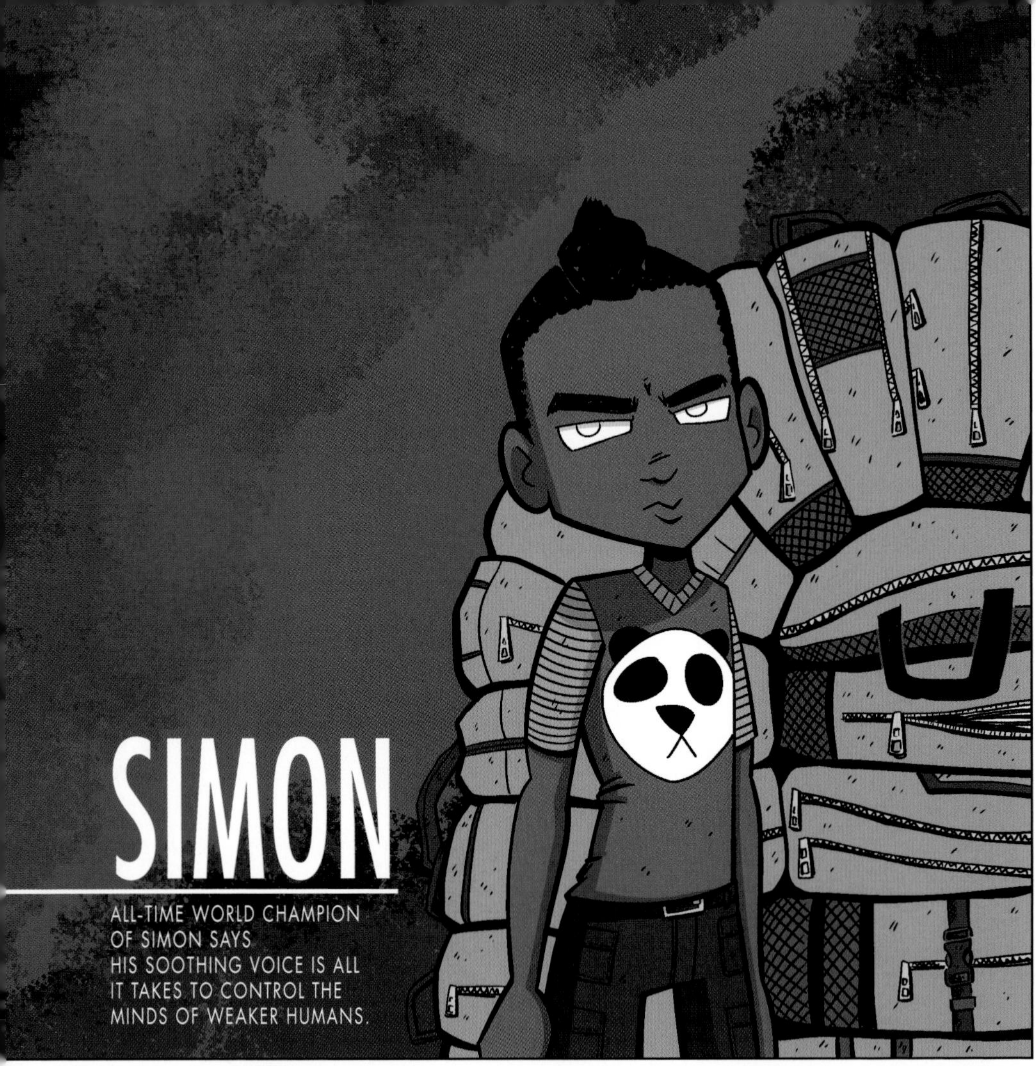
SIMON
ALL-TIME WORLD CHAMPION OF SIMON SAYS
HIS SOOTHING VOICE IS ALL IT TAKES TO CONTROL THE MINDS OF WEAKER HUMANS.

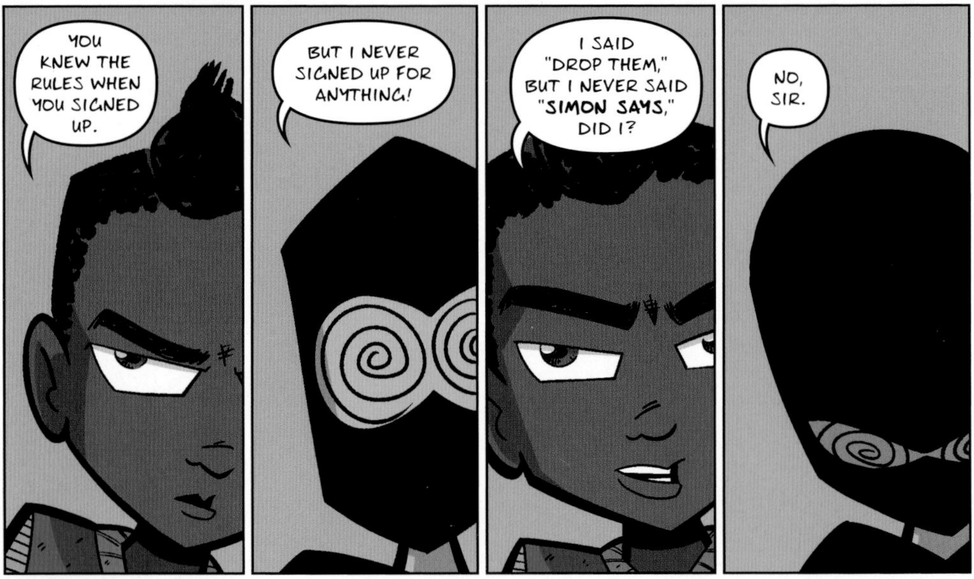
YOU KNEW THE RULES WHEN YOU SIGNED UP.
BUT I NEVER SIGNED UP FOR ANYTHING!
I SAID "DROP THEM," BUT I NEVER SAID "SIMON SAYS," DID I?
NO, SIR.

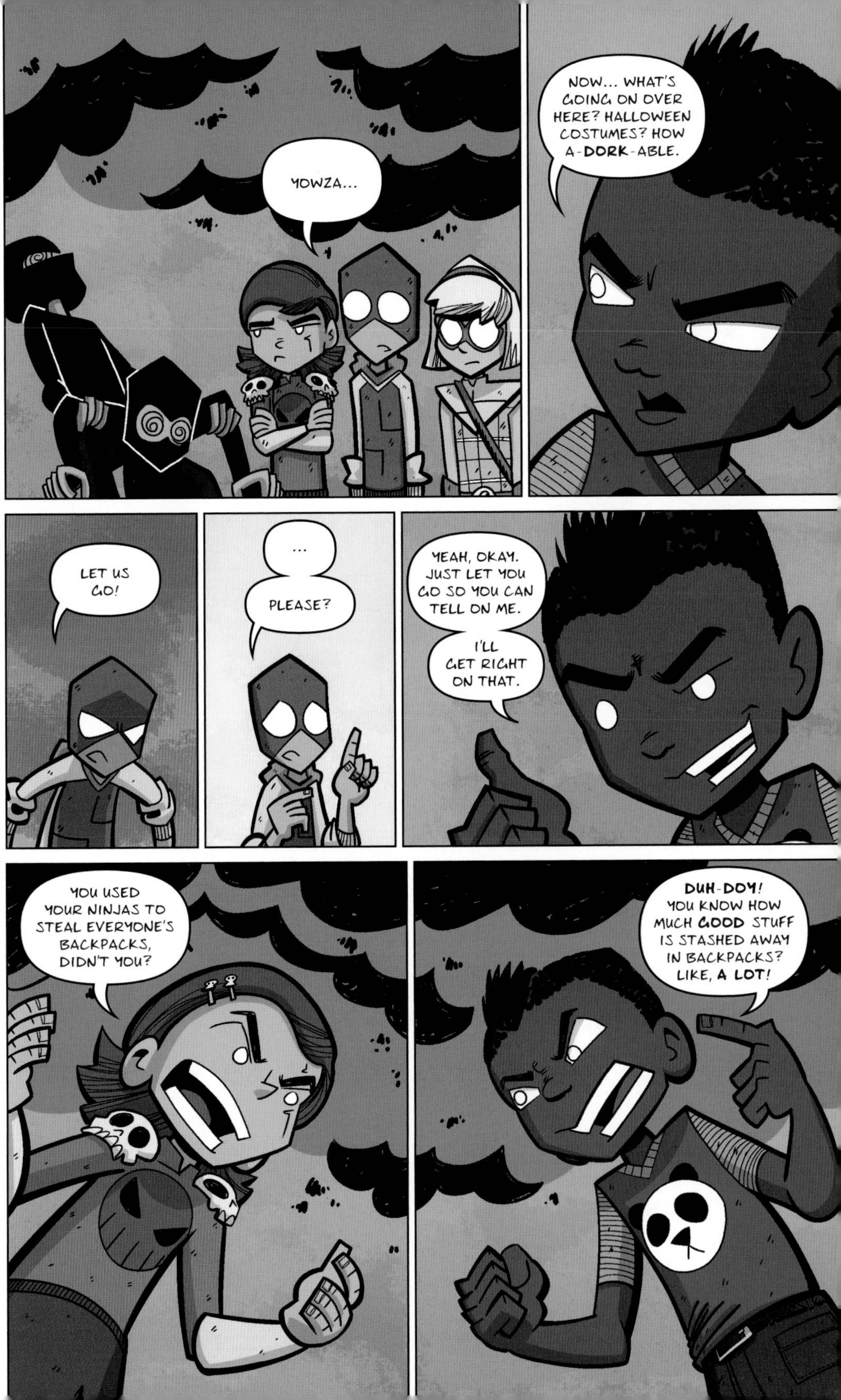
YOWZA...
NOW... WHAT'S GOING ON OVER HERE? HALLOWEEN COSTUMES? HOW A-**DORK**-ABLE.
LET US GO!
...
PLEASE?
YEAH, OKAY. JUST LET YOU GO SO YOU CAN TELL ON ME.
I'LL GET RIGHT ON THAT.
YOU USED YOUR NINJAS TO STEAL EVERYONE'S BACKPACKS, DIDN'T YOU?
DUH-DOY! YOU KNOW HOW MUCH **GOOD** STUFF IS STASHED AWAY IN BACKPACKS? LIKE, **A LOT**!

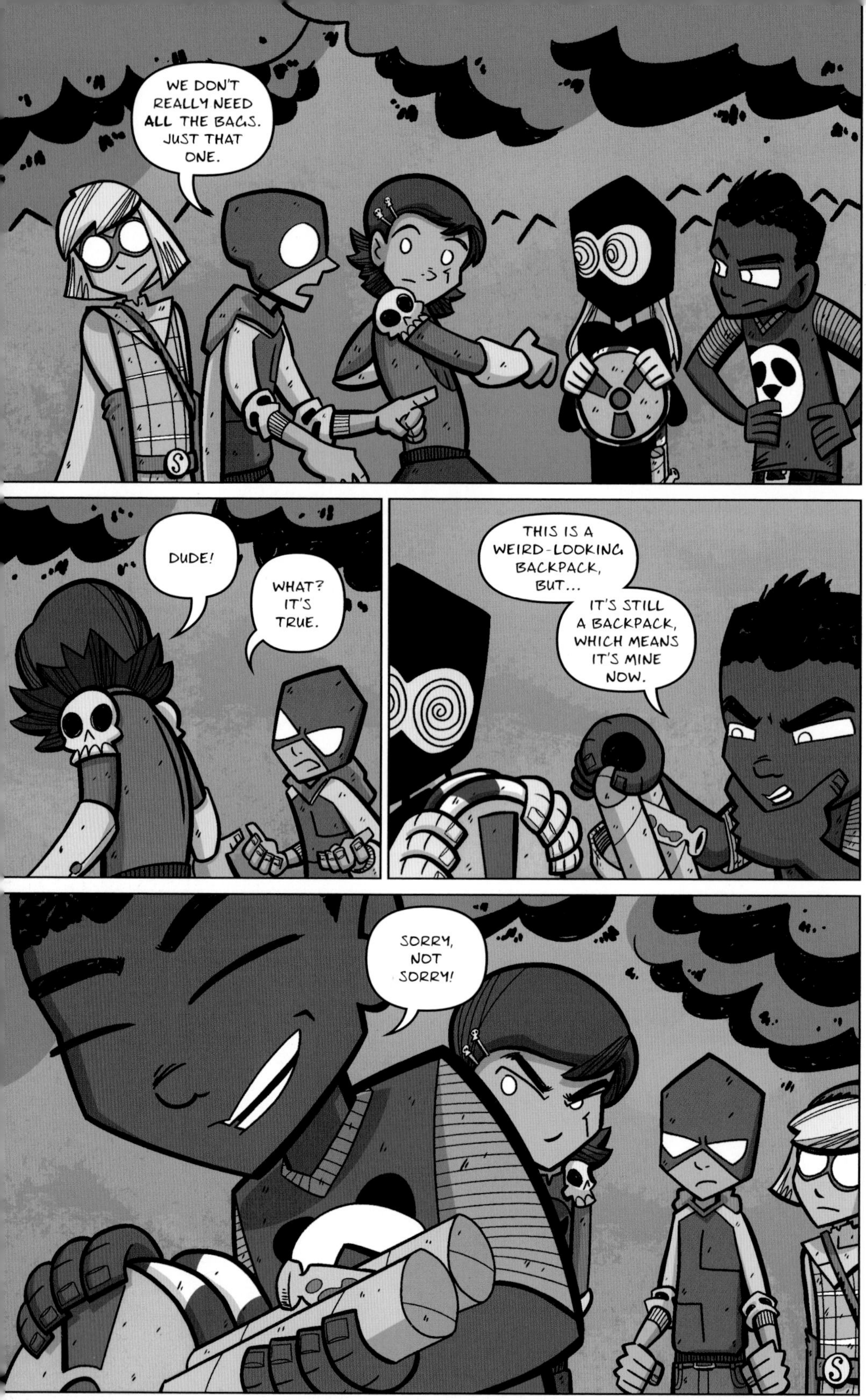

WE DON'T REALLY NEED **ALL** THE BAGS. JUST THAT ONE.
DUDE!
WHAT? IT'S TRUE.
THIS IS A WEIRD-LOOKING BACKPACK, BUT...
IT'S STILL A BACKPACK, WHICH MEANS IT'S MINE NOW.
SORRY, NOT SORRY!

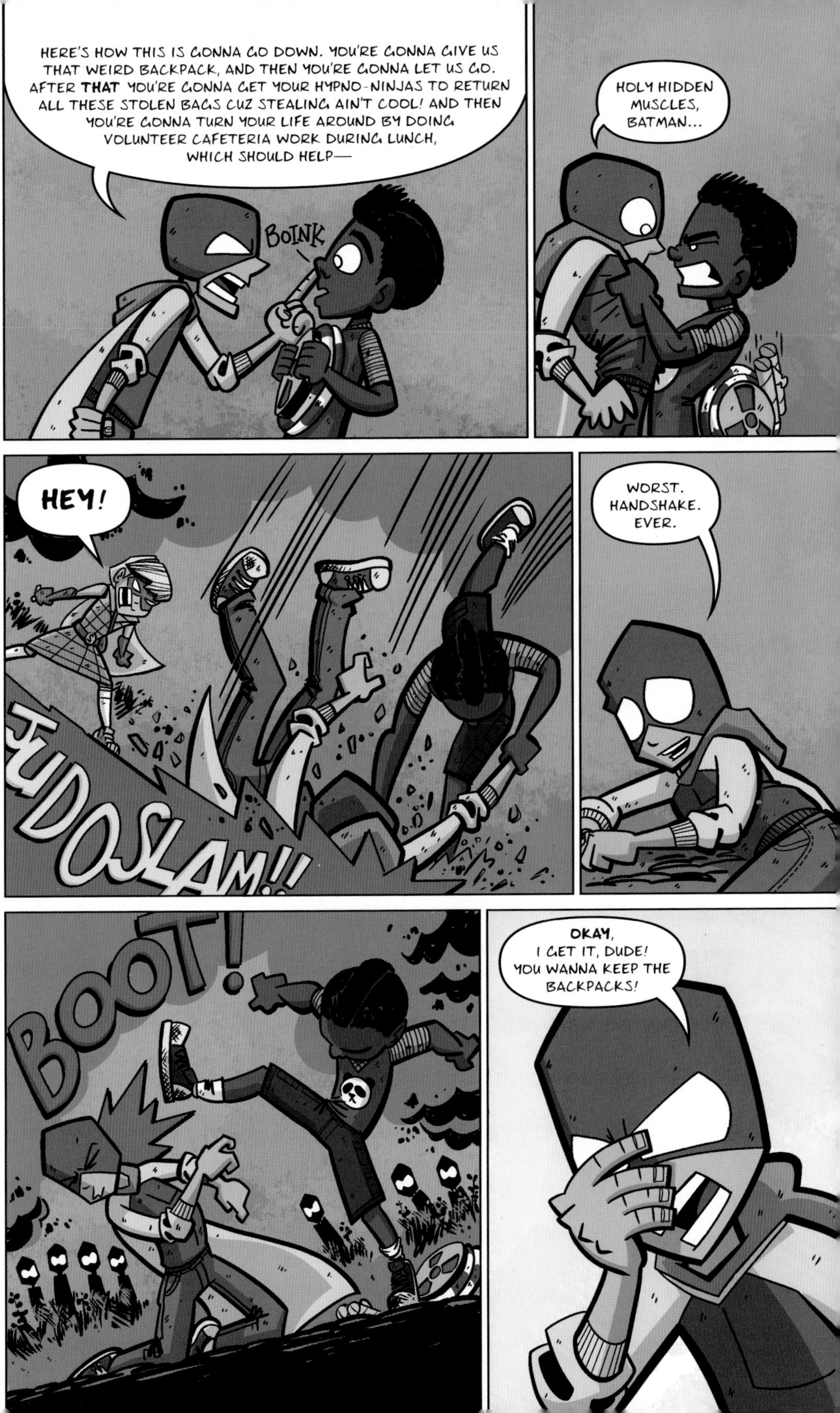
HERE'S HOW THIS IS GONNA GO DOWN. YOU'RE GONNA GIVE US THAT WEIRD BACKPACK, AND THEN YOU'RE GONNA LET US GO. AFTER **THAT** YOU'RE GONNA GET YOUR HYPNO-NINJAS TO RETURN ALL THESE STOLEN BAGS CUZ STEALING AIN'T COOL! AND THEN YOU'RE GONNA TURN YOUR LIFE AROUND BY DOING VOLUNTEER CAFETERIA WORK DURING LUNCH, WHICH SHOULD HELP—
BOINK
HOLY HIDDEN MUSCLES, BATMAN...
HEY!
JUDOSLAM!!
WORST. HANDSHAKE. EVER.
BOOT!
OKAY, I GET IT, DUDE! YOU WANNA KEEP THE BACKPACKS!

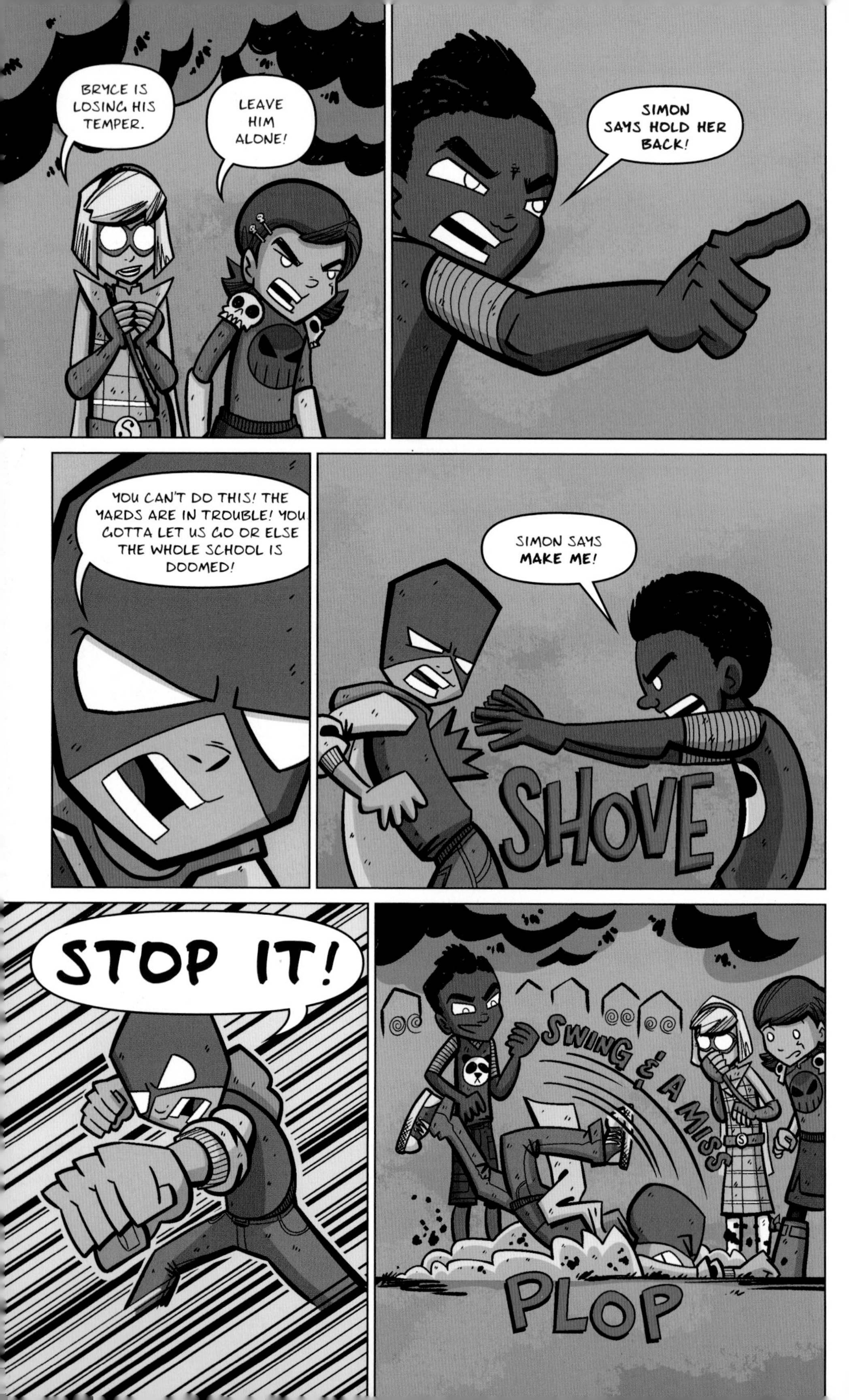
BRYCE IS LOSING HIS TEMPER.
LEAVE HIM ALONE!
SIMON SAYS HOLD HER BACK!
YOU CAN'T DO THIS! THE YARDS ARE IN TROUBLE! YOU GOTTA LET US GO OR ELSE THE WHOLE SCHOOL IS DOOMED!
SIMON SAYS MAKE ME!
SHOVE
STOP IT!
SWING & A MISS
PLOP

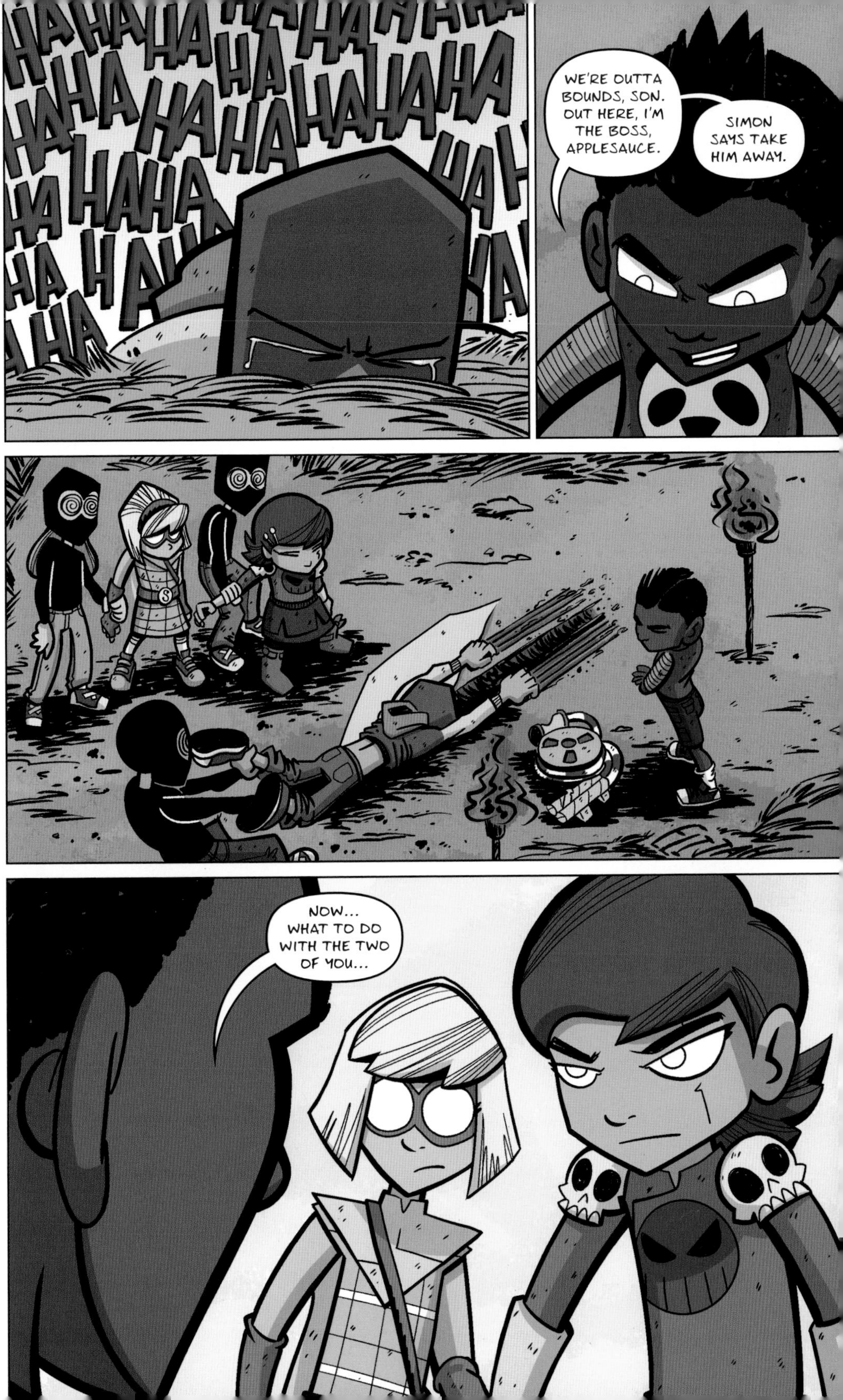
HAHAHAHAHA HAHAHAHAHA HAHAHAHAHA
WE'RE OUTTA BOUNDS, SON. OUT HERE, I'M THE BOSS, APPLESAUCE.
SIMON SAYS TAKE HIM AWAY.
NOW... WHAT TO DO WITH THE TWO OF YOU...

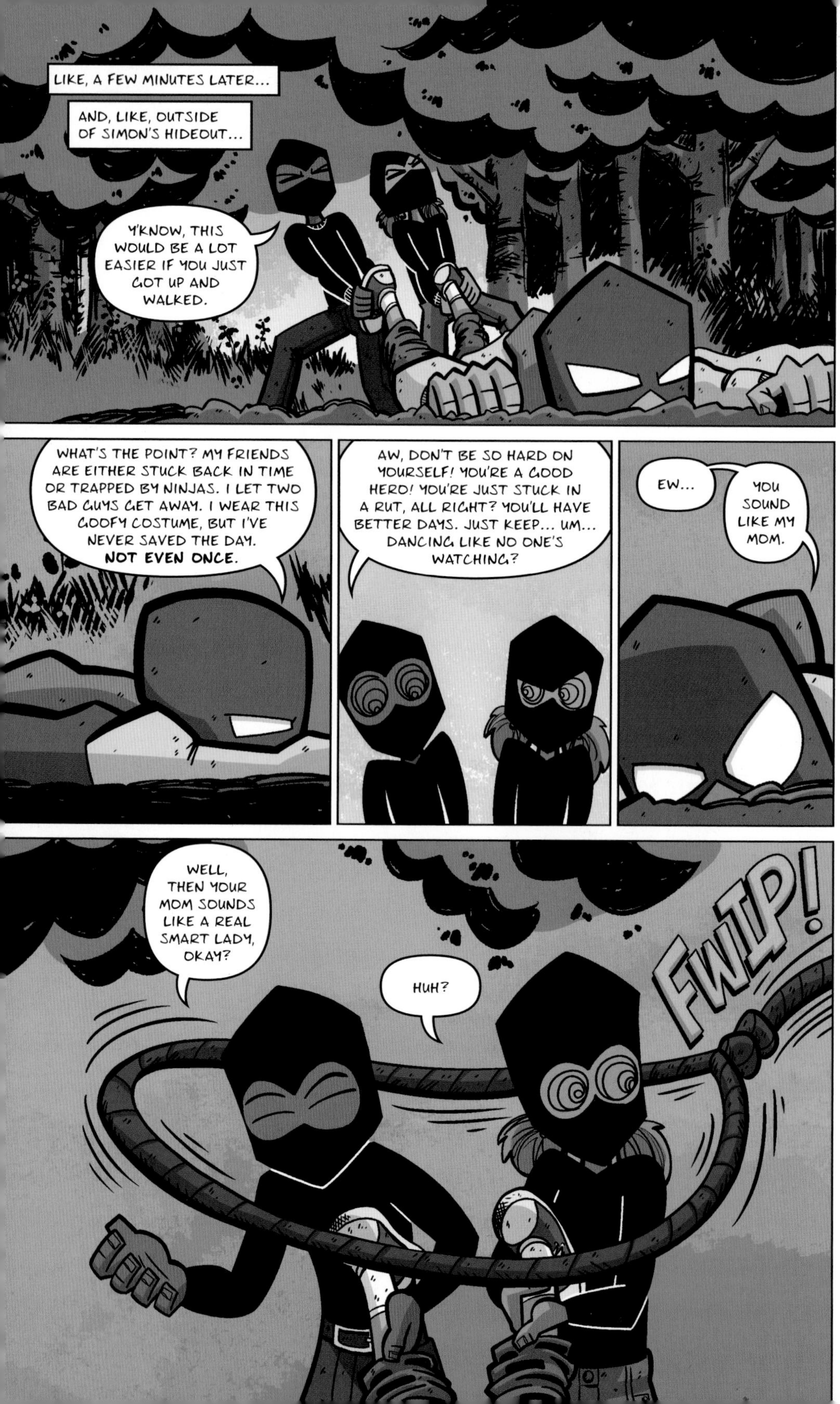
LIKE, A FEW MINUTES LATER...
AND, LIKE, OUTSIDE OF SIMON'S HIDEOUT...
Y'KNOW, THIS WOULD BE A LOT EASIER IF YOU JUST GOT UP AND WALKED.
WHAT'S THE POINT? MY FRIENDS ARE EITHER STUCK BACK IN TIME OR TRAPPED BY NINJAS. I LET TWO BAD GUYS GET AWAY. I WEAR THIS GOOFY COSTUME, BUT I'VE NEVER SAVED THE DAY. **NOT EVEN ONCE.**
AW, DON'T BE SO HARD ON YOURSELF! YOU'RE A GOOD HERO! YOU'RE JUST STUCK IN A RUT, ALL RIGHT? YOU'LL HAVE BETTER DAYS. JUST KEEP... UM... DANCING LIKE NO ONE'S WATCHING?
EW...
YOU SOUND LIKE MY MOM.
WELL, THEN YOUR MOM SOUNDS LIKE A REAL SMART LADY, OKAY?
HUH?
FWIP!

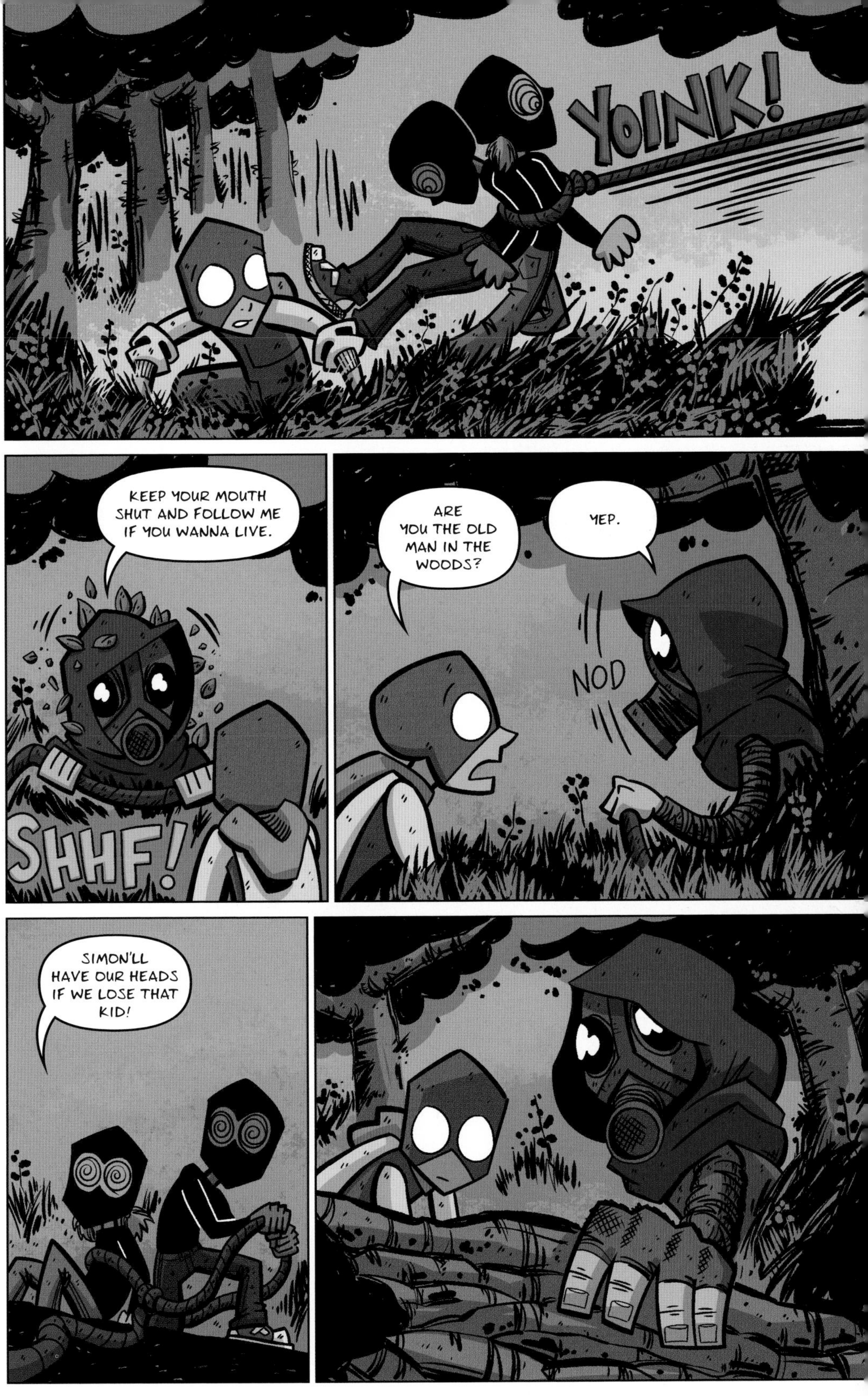
YOINK!
KEEP YOUR MOUTH SHUT AND FOLLOW ME IF YOU WANNA LIVE.
SHHF!
ARE YOU THE OLD MAN IN THE WOODS?
YEP.
NOD
SIMON'LL HAVE OUR HEADS IF WE LOSE THAT KID!

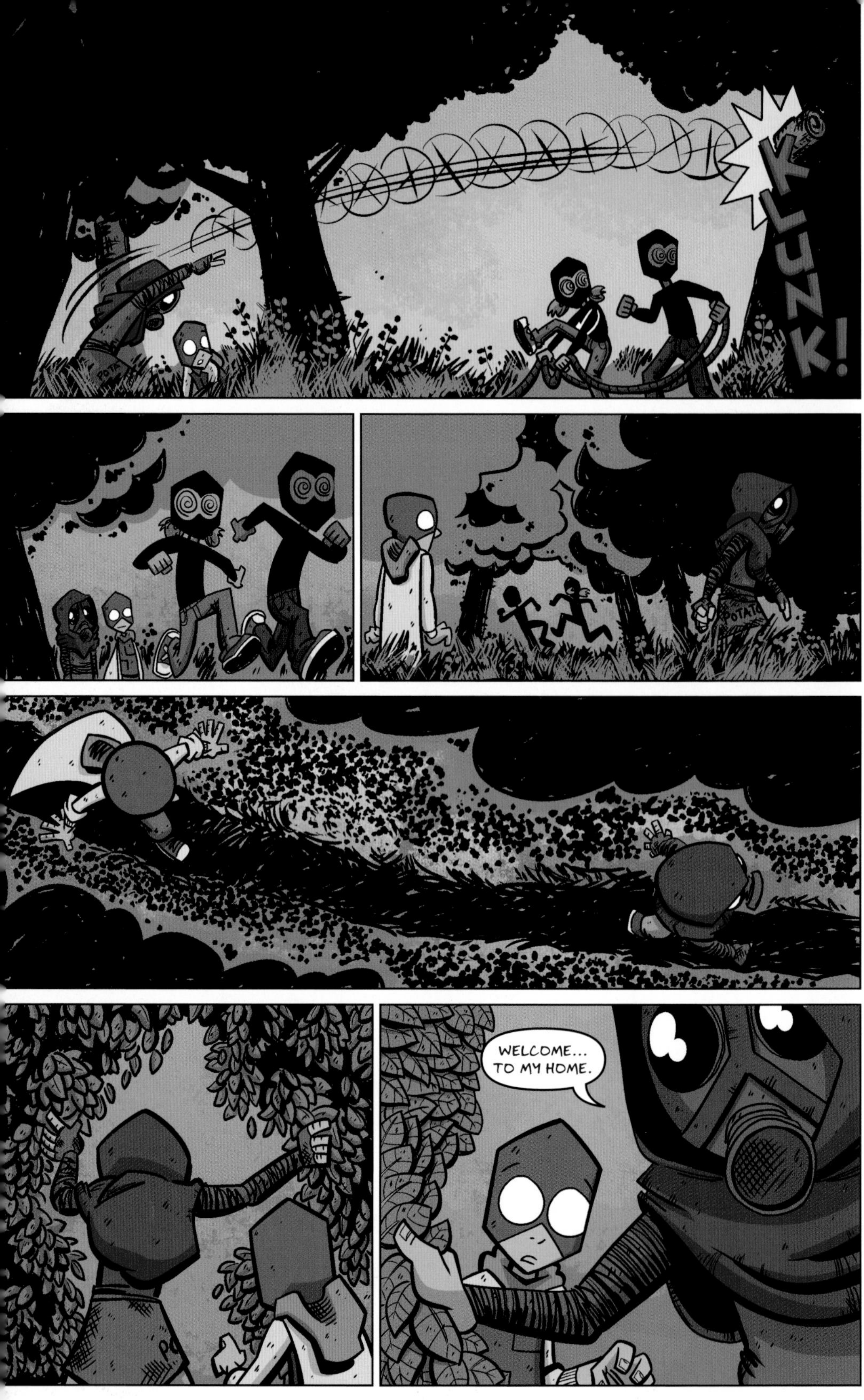
KLUNK!
WELCOME...
TO MY HOME.

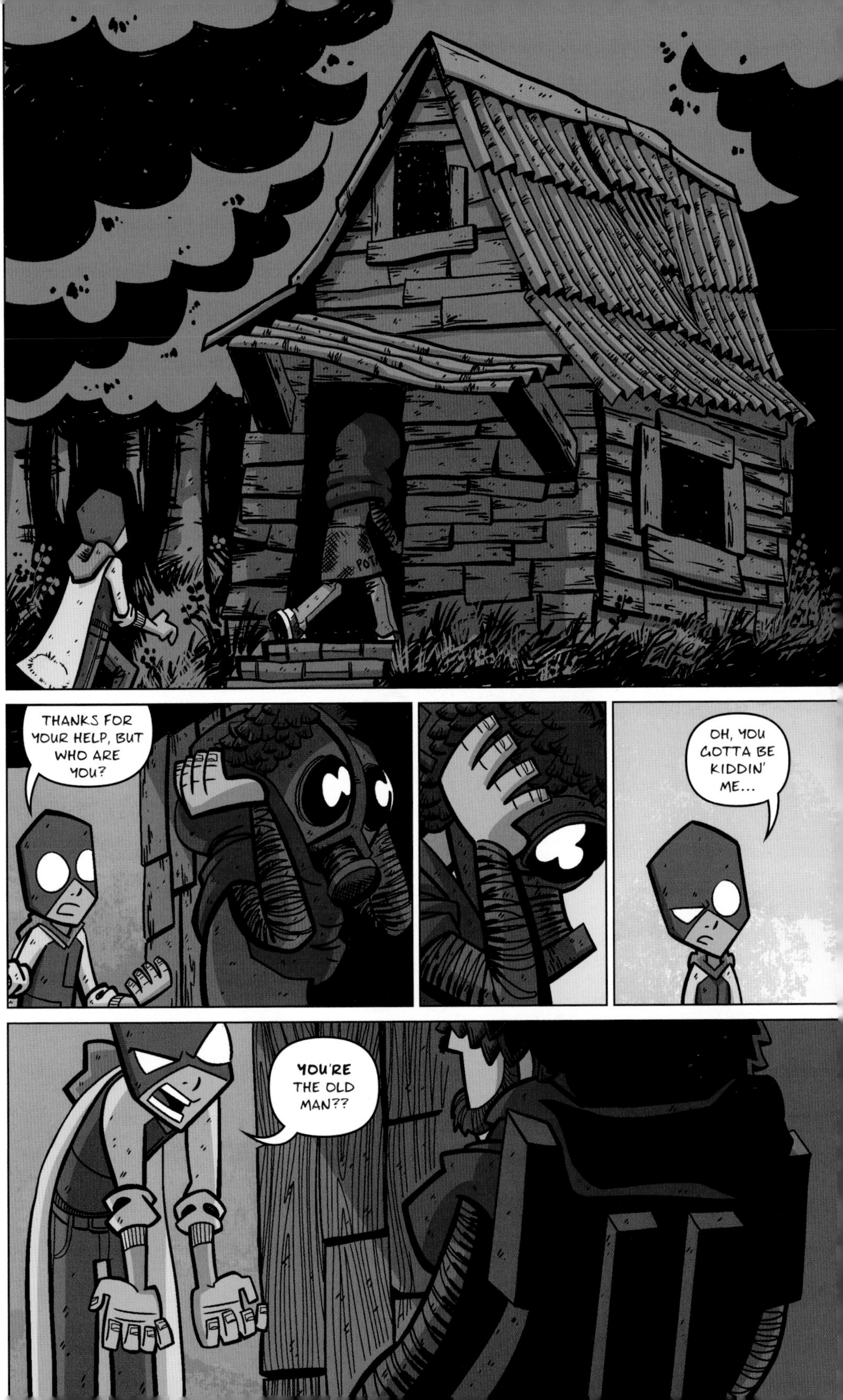

THANKS FOR YOUR HELP, BUT WHO ARE YOU?
OH, YOU GOTTA BE KIDDIN' ME...
YOU'RE THE OLD MAN??

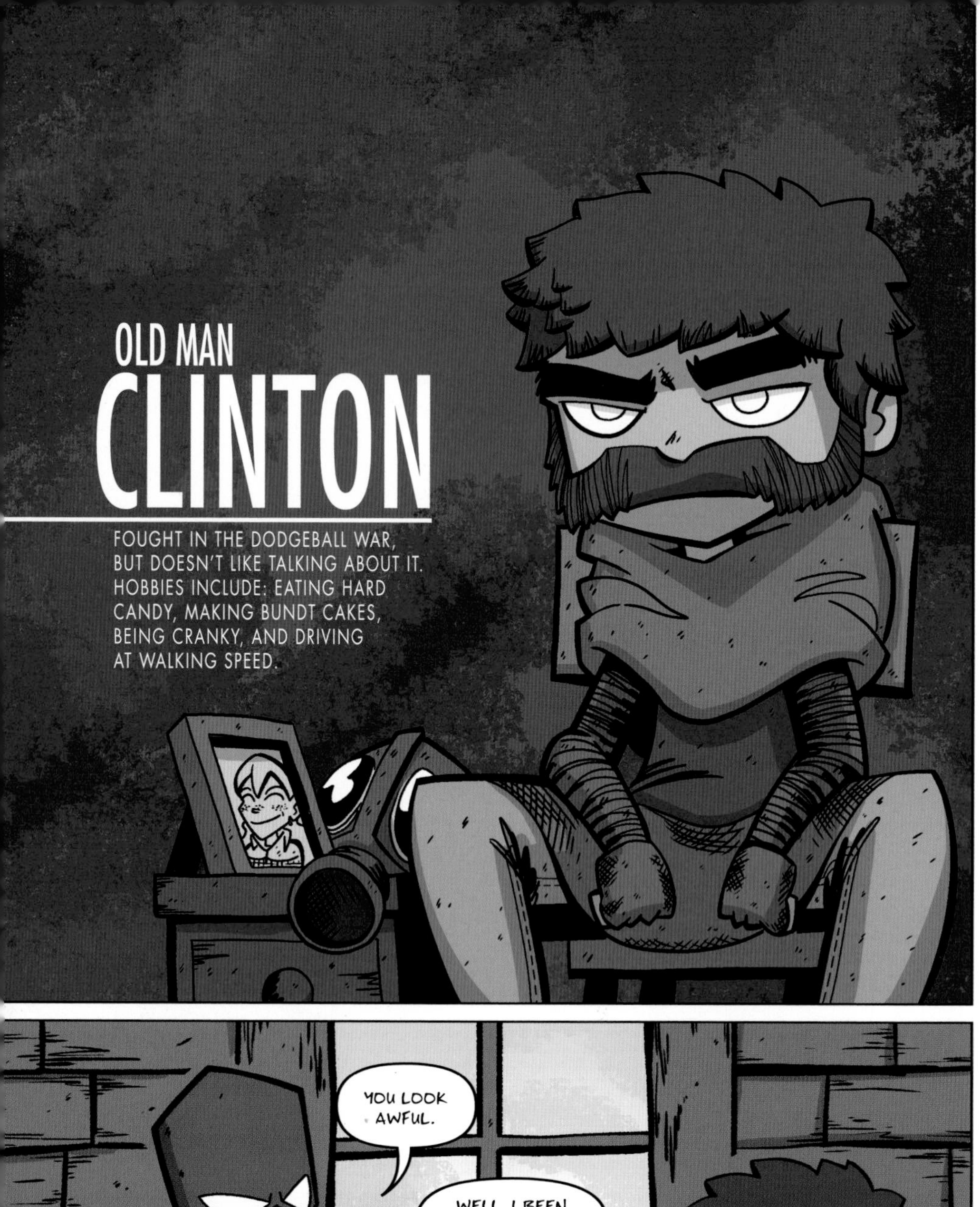
OLD MAN
CLINTON
FOUGHT IN THE DODGEBALL WAR, BUT DOESN'T LIKE TALKING ABOUT IT. HOBBIES INCLUDE: EATING HARD CANDY, MAKING BUNDT CAKES, BEING CRANKY, AND DRIVING AT WALKING SPEED.

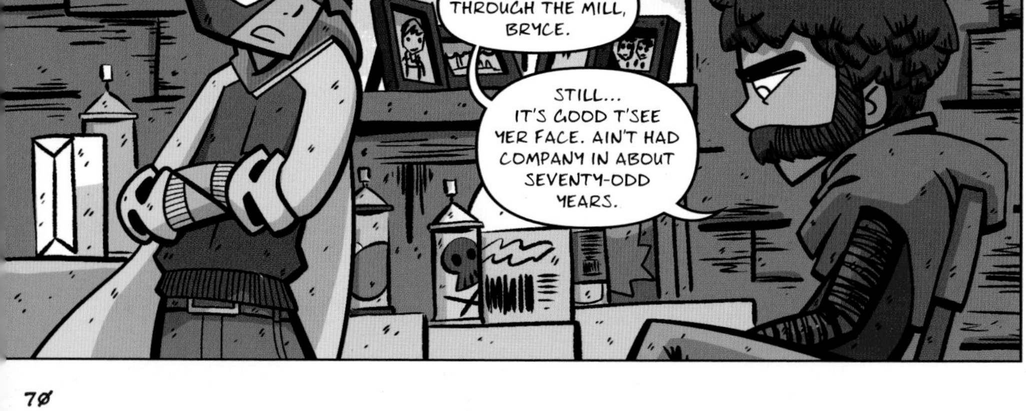
YOU LOOK AWFUL.
WELL, I BEEN THROUGH THE MILL, BRYCE.
STILL... IT'S GOOD T'SEE YER FACE. AIN'T HAD COMPANY IN ABOUT SEVENTY-ODD YEARS.

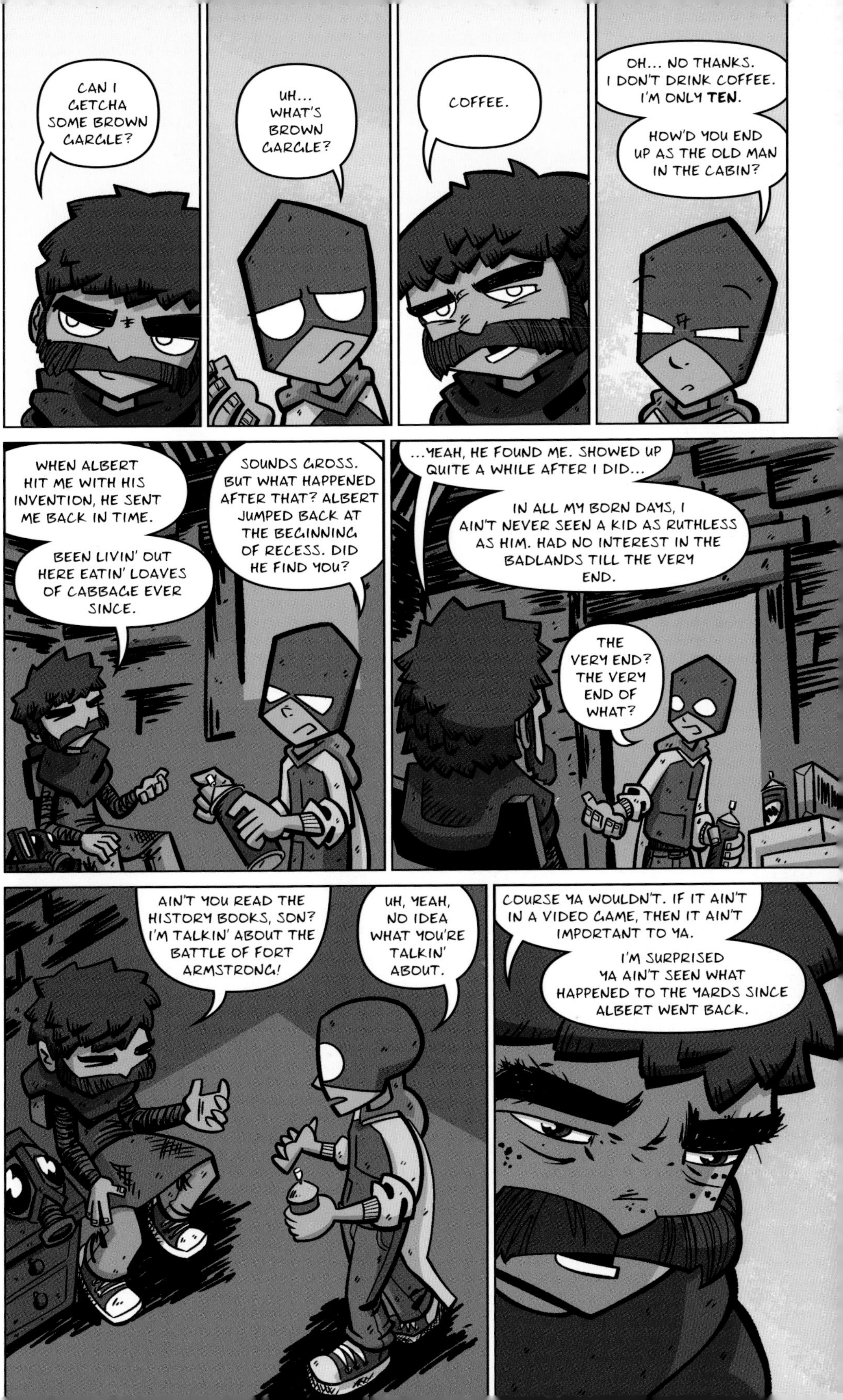
CAN I GETCHA SOME BROWN GARGLE?
UH... WHAT'S BROWN GARGLE?
COFFEE.
OH... NO THANKS. I DON'T DRINK COFFEE. I'M ONLY **TEN**.
HOW'D YOU END UP AS THE OLD MAN IN THE CABIN?
WHEN ALBERT HIT ME WITH HIS INVENTION, HE SENT ME BACK IN TIME.
BEEN LIVIN' OUT HERE EATIN' LOAVES OF CABBAGE EVER SINCE.
SOUNDS GROSS. BUT WHAT HAPPENED AFTER THAT? ALBERT JUMPED BACK AT THE BEGINNING OF RECESS. DID HE FIND YOU?
...YEAH, HE FOUND ME. SHOWED UP QUITE A WHILE AFTER I DID...
IN ALL MY BORN DAYS, I AIN'T NEVER SEEN A KID AS RUTHLESS AS HIM. HAD NO INTEREST IN THE BADLANDS TILL THE VERY END.
THE VERY END? THE VERY END OF WHAT?
AIN'T YOU READ THE HISTORY BOOKS, SON? I'M TALKIN' ABOUT THE BATTLE OF FORT ARMSTRONG!
UH, YEAH, NO IDEA WHAT YOU'RE TALKIN' ABOUT.
COURSE YA WOULDN'T. IF IT AIN'T IN A VIDEO GAME, THEN IT AIN'T IMPORTANT TO YA.
I'M SURPRISED YA AIN'T SEEN WHAT HAPPENED TO THE YARDS SINCE ALBERT WENT BACK.

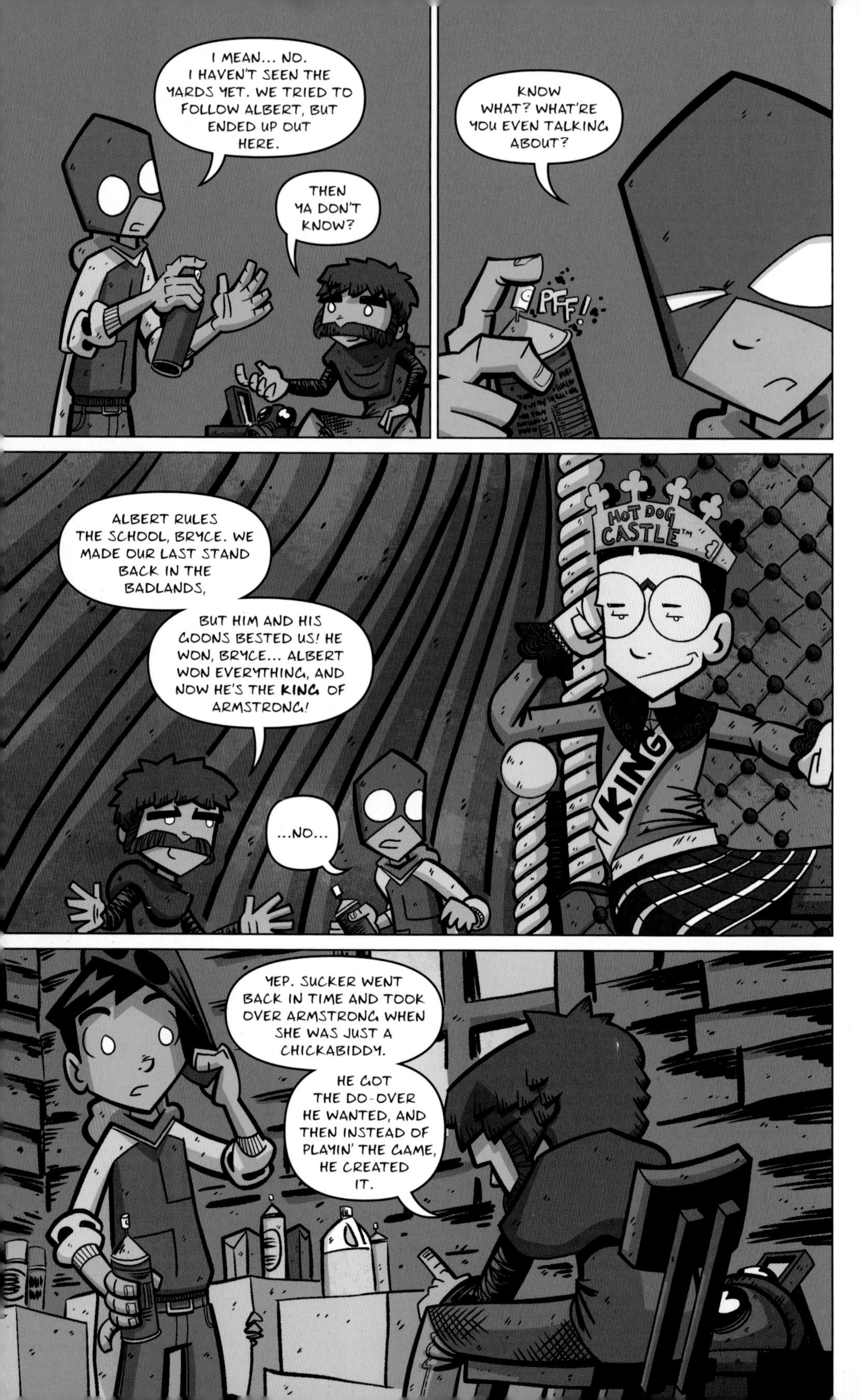
I MEAN... NO. I HAVEN'T SEEN THE YARDS YET. WE TRIED TO FOLLOW ALBERT, BUT ENDED UP OUT HERE.
THEN YA DON'T KNOW?
KNOW WHAT? WHAT'RE YOU EVEN TALKING ABOUT?
PFF!
ALBERT RULES THE SCHOOL, BRYCE. WE MADE OUR LAST STAND BACK IN THE BADLANDS,
BUT HIM AND HIS GOONS BESTED US! HE WON, BRYCE... ALBERT WON EVERYTHING, AND NOW HE'S THE **KING** OF ARMSTRONG!
HOT DOG CASTLE™
KING
...NO...
YEP. SUCKER WENT BACK IN TIME AND TOOK OVER ARMSTRONG WHEN SHE WAS JUST A CHICKABIDDY.
HE GOT THE DO-OVER HE WANTED, AND THEN INSTEAD OF PLAYIN' THE GAME, HE CREATED IT.

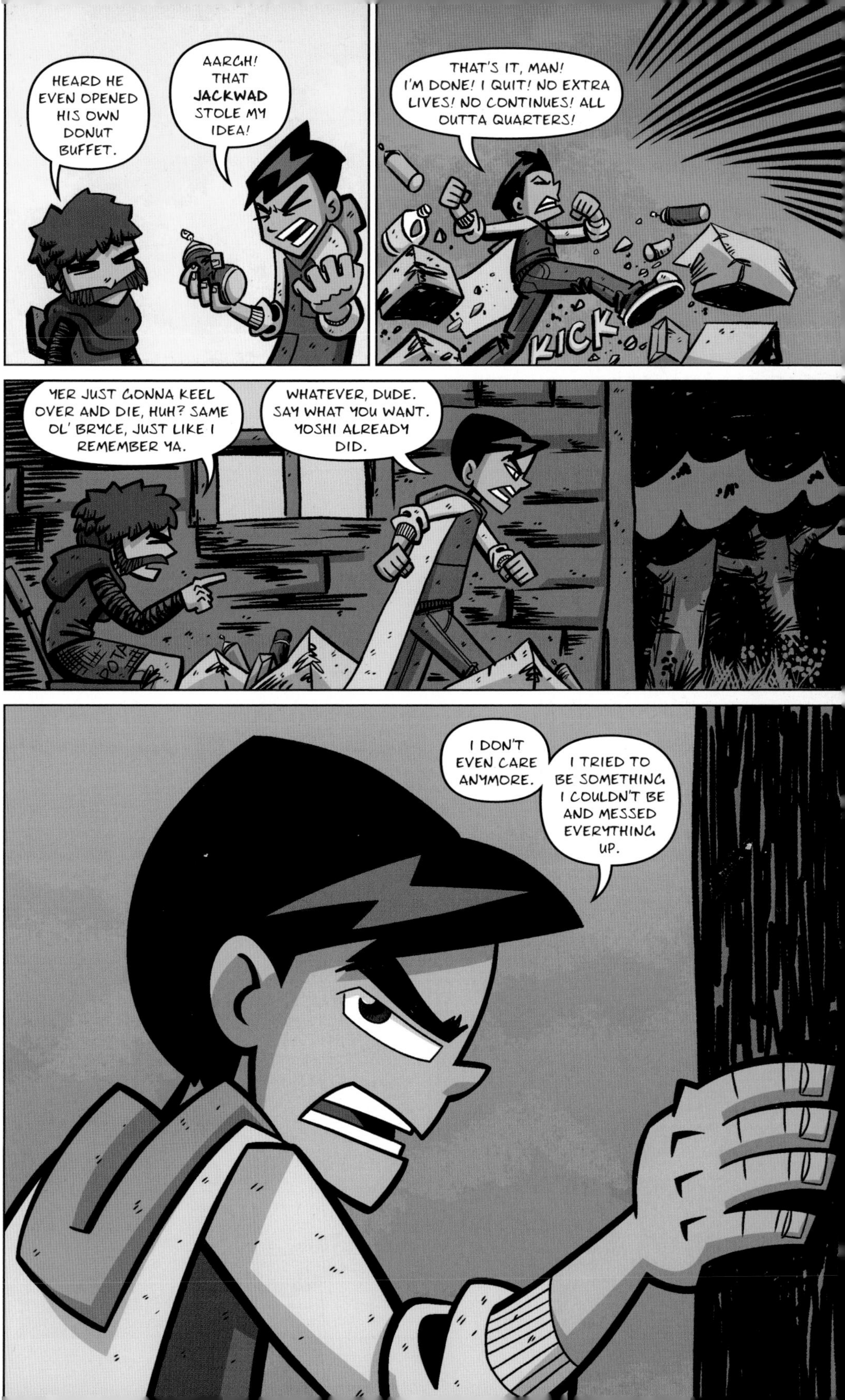
HEARD HE EVEN OPENED HIS OWN DONUT BUFFET.
AARGH! THAT JACKWAD STOLE MY IDEA!
THAT'S IT, MAN! I'M DONE! I QUIT! NO EXTRA LIVES! NO CONTINUES! ALL OUTTA QUARTERS!
KICK
YER JUST GONNA KEEL OVER AND DIE, HUH? SAME OL' BRYCE, JUST LIKE I REMEMBER YA.
WHATEVER, DUDE. SAY WHAT YOU WANT. YOSHI ALREADY DID.
I DON'T EVEN CARE ANYMORE.
I TRIED TO BE SOMETHING I COULDN'T BE AND MESSED EVERYTHING UP.

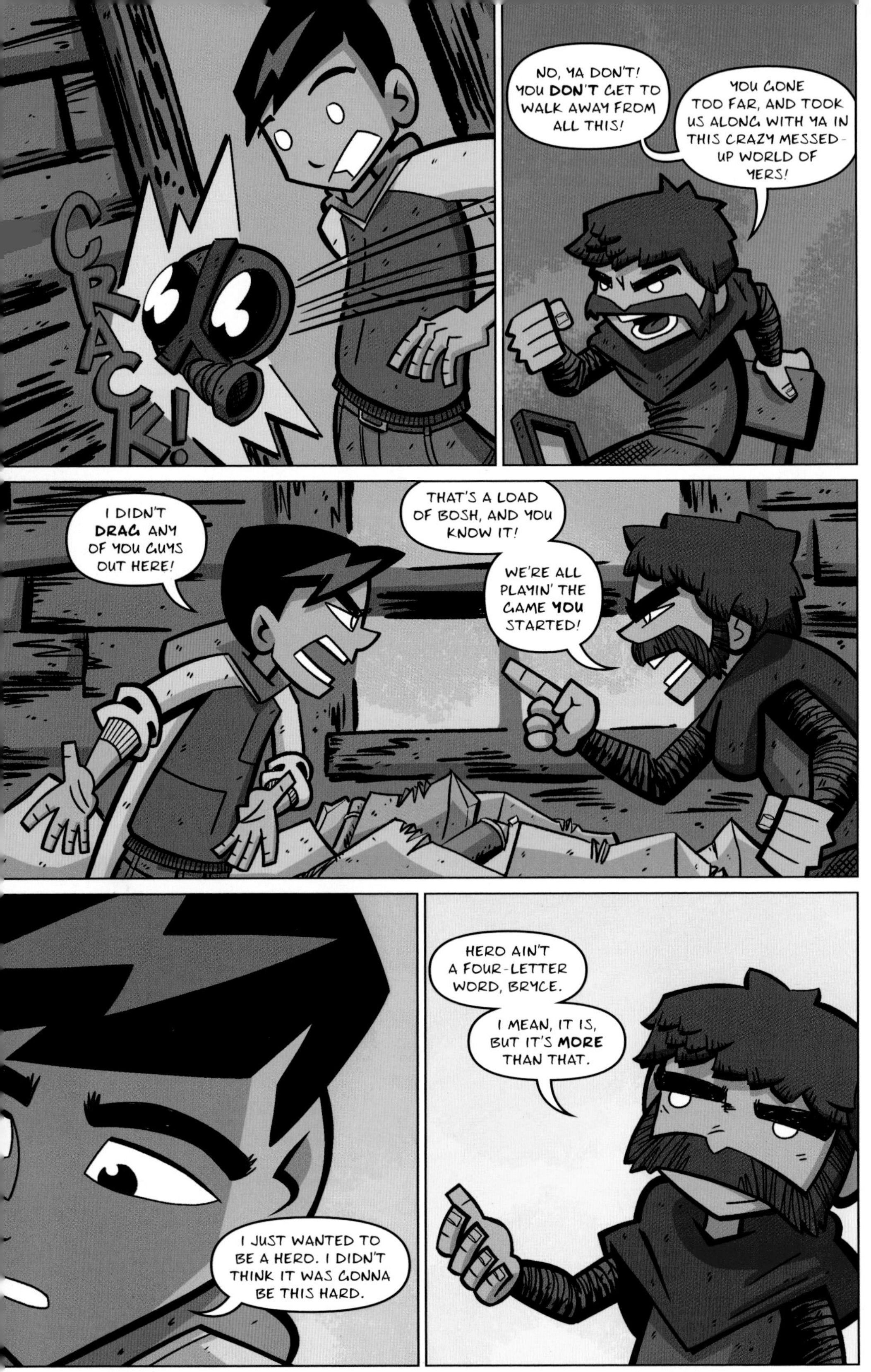
CRACK!
NO, YA DON'T! YOU DON'T GET TO WALK AWAY FROM ALL THIS!
YOU GONE TOO FAR, AND TOOK US ALONG WITH YA IN THIS CRAZY MESSED-UP WORLD OF YERS!
I DIDN'T DRAG ANY OF YOU GUYS OUT HERE!
THAT'S A LOAD OF BOSH, AND YOU KNOW IT!
WE'RE ALL PLAYIN' THE GAME YOU STARTED!
I JUST WANTED TO BE A HERO. I DIDN'T THINK IT WAS GONNA BE THIS HARD.
HERO AIN'T A FOUR-LETTER WORD, BRYCE.
I MEAN, IT IS, BUT IT'S MORE THAN THAT.

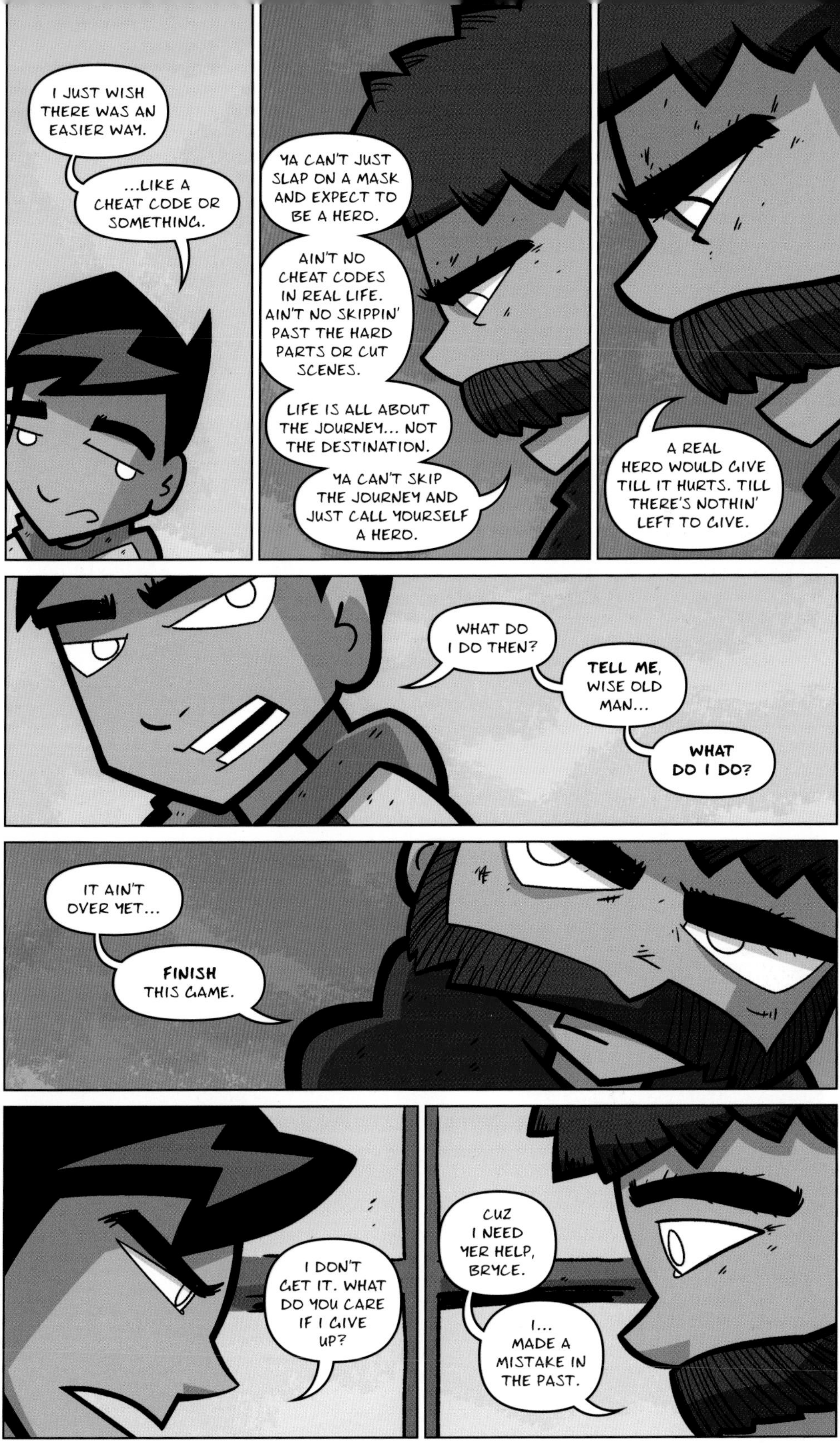
I JUST WISH THERE WAS AN EASIER WAY.
...LIKE A CHEAT CODE OR SOMETHING.
YA CAN'T JUST SLAP ON A MASK AND EXPECT TO BE A HERO.
AIN'T NO CHEAT CODES IN REAL LIFE. AIN'T NO SKIPPIN' PAST THE HARD PARTS OR CUT SCENES.
LIFE IS ALL ABOUT THE JOURNEY... NOT THE DESTINATION.
YA CAN'T SKIP THE JOURNEY AND JUST CALL YOURSELF A HERO.
A REAL HERO WOULD GIVE TILL IT HURTS. TILL THERE'S NOTHIN' LEFT TO GIVE.
WHAT DO I DO THEN?
TELL ME, WISE OLD MAN...
WHAT DO I DO?
IT AIN'T OVER YET...
FINISH THIS GAME.
I DON'T GET IT. WHAT DO YOU CARE IF I GIVE UP?
CUZ I NEED YER HELP, BRYCE.
I... MADE A MISTAKE IN THE PAST.

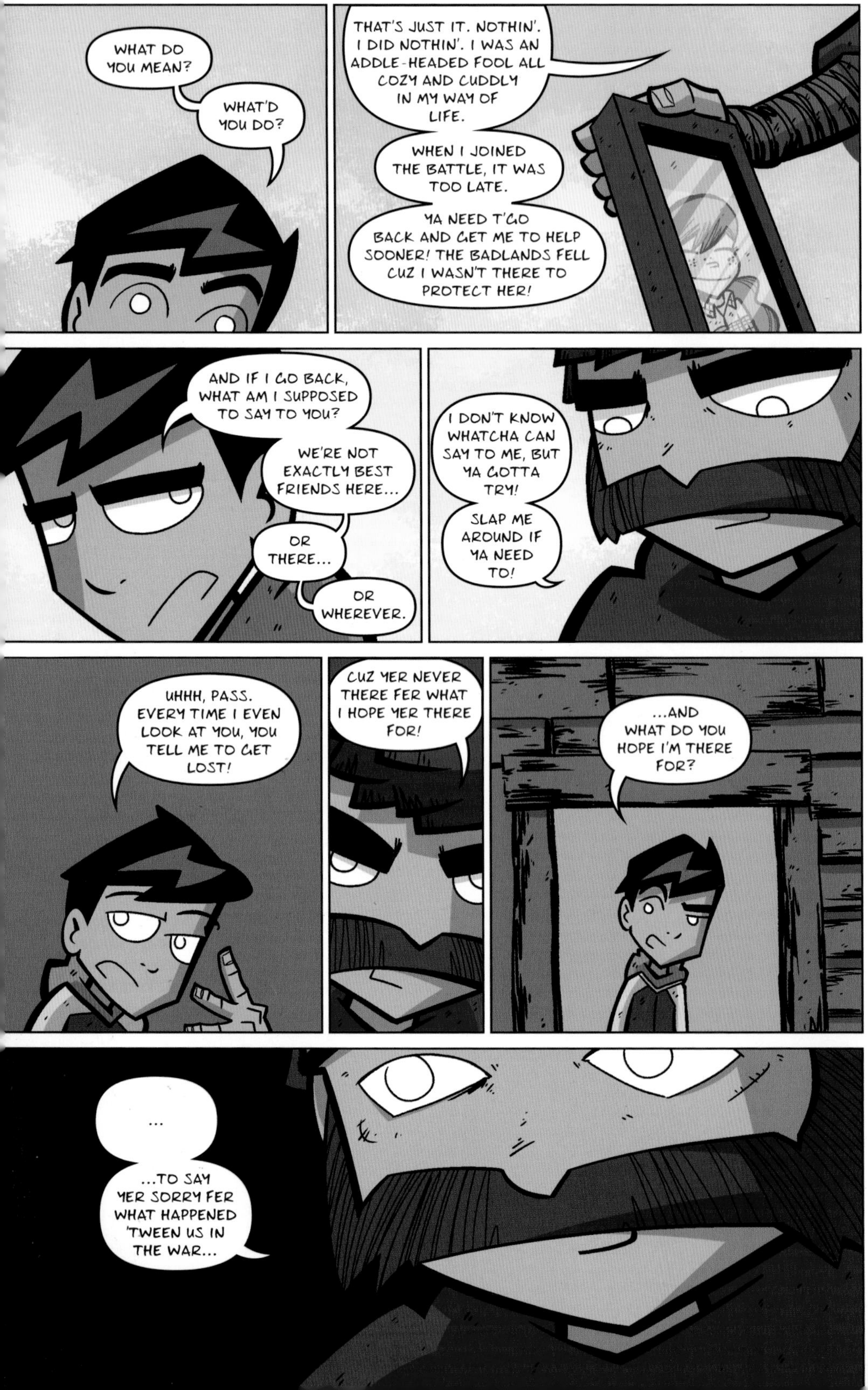
WHAT DO YOU MEAN?
WHAT'D YOU DO?
THAT'S JUST IT. NOTHIN'. I DID NOTHIN'. I WAS AN ADDLE-HEADED FOOL ALL COZY AND CUDDLY IN MY WAY OF LIFE.
WHEN I JOINED THE BATTLE, IT WAS TOO LATE.
YA NEED T'GO BACK AND GET ME TO HELP SOONER! THE BADLANDS FELL CUZ I WASN'T THERE TO PROTECT HER!
AND IF I GO BACK, WHAT AM I SUPPOSED TO SAY TO YOU?
WE'RE NOT EXACTLY BEST FRIENDS HERE...
OR THERE...
OR WHEREVER.
I DON'T KNOW WHATCHA CAN SAY TO ME, BUT YA GOTTA TRY!
SLAP ME AROUND IF YA NEED TO!
UHHH, PASS. EVERY TIME I EVEN LOOK AT YOU, YOU TELL ME TO GET LOST!
CUZ YER NEVER THERE FER WHAT I HOPE YER THERE FOR!
...AND WHAT DO YOU HOPE I'M THERE FOR?
...
...TO SAY YER SORRY FER WHAT HAPPENED 'TWEEN US IN THE WAR...

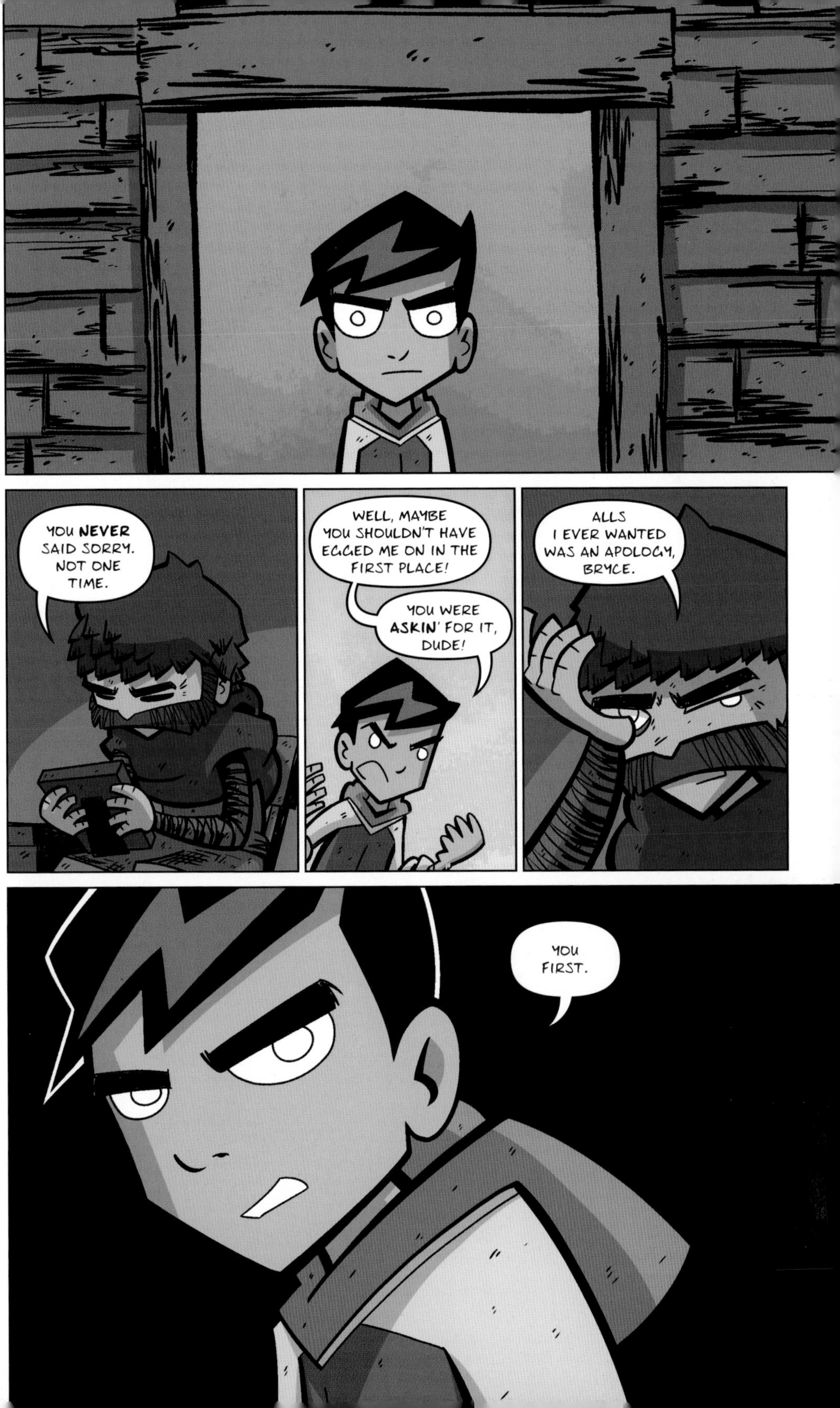
YOU NEVER SAID SORRY. NOT ONE TIME.
WELL, MAYBE YOU SHOULDN'T HAVE EGGED ME ON IN THE FIRST PLACE!
YOU WERE ASKIN' FOR IT, DUDE!
ALLS I EVER WANTED WAS AN APOLOGY, BRYCE.
YOU FIRST.

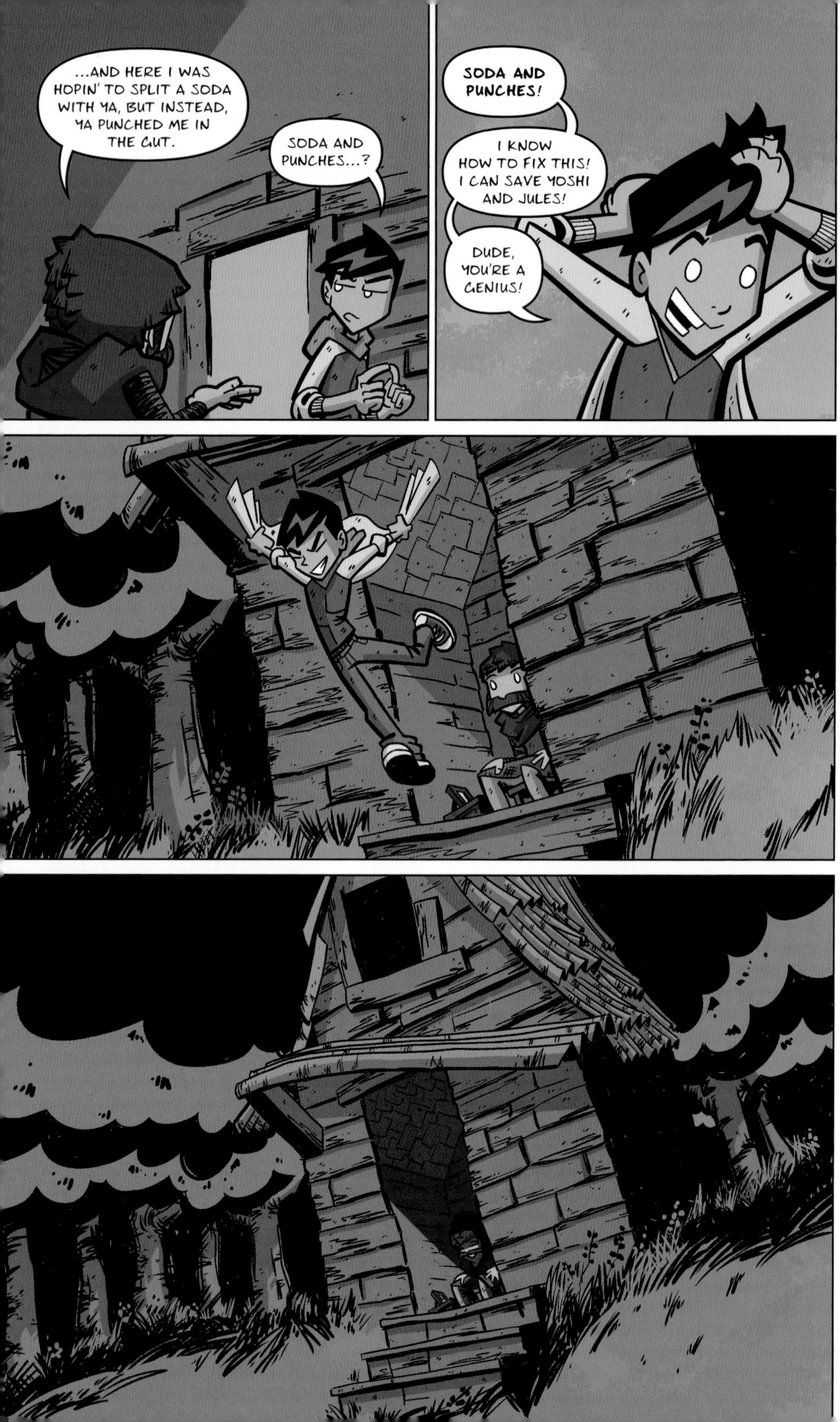
...AND HERE I WAS HOPIN' TO SPLIT A SODA WITH YA, BUT INSTEAD, YA PUNCHED ME IN THE GUT.
SODA AND PUNCHES...?
SODA AND PUNCHES!
I KNOW HOW TO FIX THIS! I CAN SAVE YOSHI AND JULES!
DUDE, YOU'RE A GENIUS!

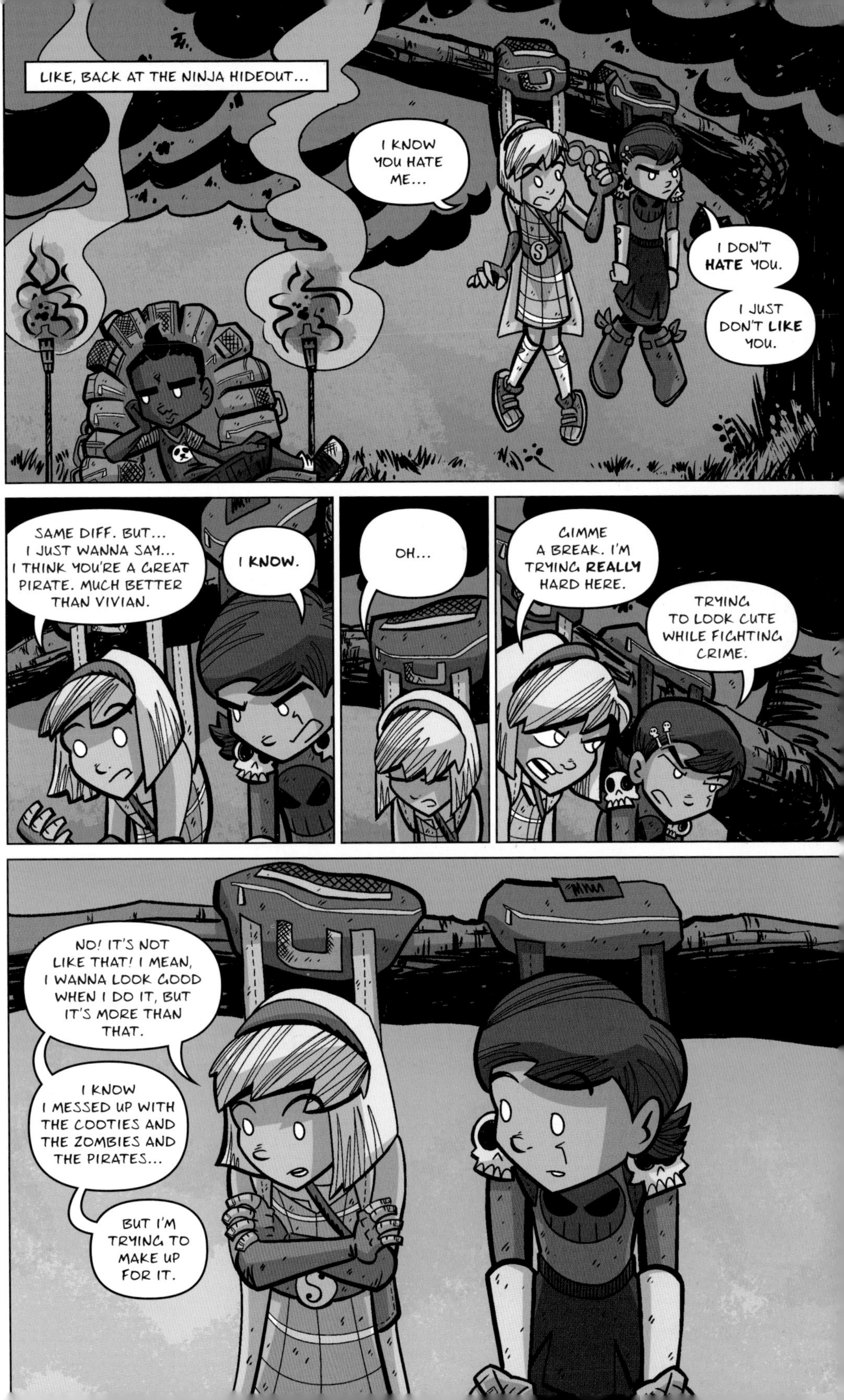
LIKE, BACK AT THE NINJA HIDEOUT...
I KNOW YOU HATE ME...
I DON'T **HATE** YOU.
I JUST DON'T **LIKE** YOU.
SAME DIFF. BUT... I JUST WANNA SAY... I THINK YOU'RE A GREAT PIRATE. MUCH BETTER THAN VIVIAN.
I **KNOW**.
OH...
GIMME A BREAK. I'M TRYING **REALLY** HARD HERE.
TRYING TO LOOK CUTE WHILE FIGHTING CRIME.
NO! IT'S NOT LIKE THAT! I MEAN, I WANNA LOOK GOOD WHEN I DO IT, BUT IT'S MORE THAN THAT.
I KNOW I MESSED UP WITH THE COOTIES AND THE ZOMBIES AND THE PIRATES...
BUT I'M TRYING TO MAKE UP FOR IT.

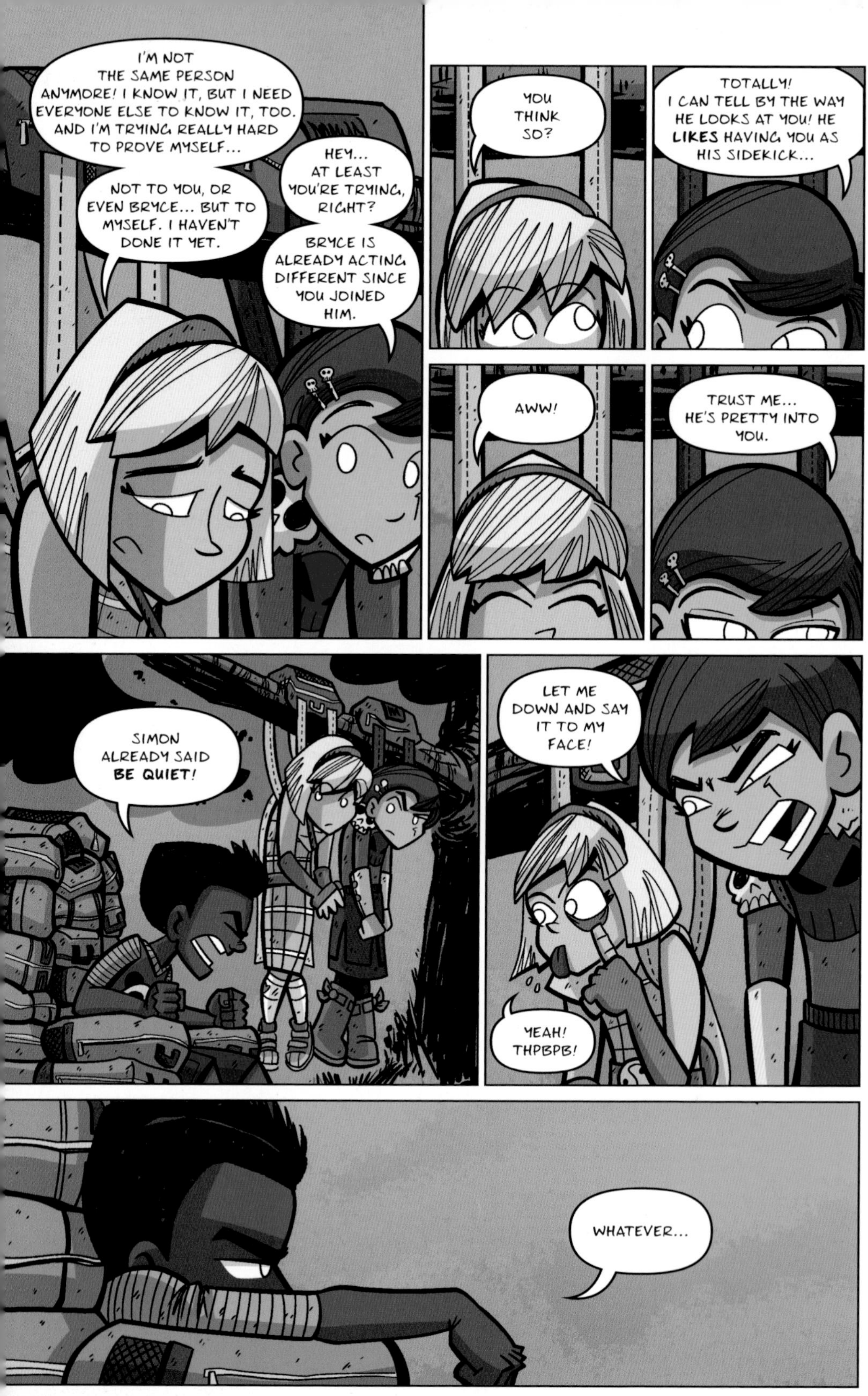
I'M NOT THE SAME PERSON ANYMORE! I KNOW IT, BUT I NEED EVERYONE ELSE TO KNOW IT, TOO. AND I'M TRYING REALLY HARD TO PROVE MYSELF...
NOT TO YOU, OR EVEN BRYCE... BUT TO MYSELF. I HAVEN'T DONE IT YET.
HEY... AT LEAST YOU'RE TRYING, RIGHT?
BRYCE IS ALREADY ACTING DIFFERENT SINCE YOU JOINED HIM.
YOU THINK SO?
TOTALLY! I CAN TELL BY THE WAY HE LOOKS AT YOU! HE **LIKES** HAVING YOU AS HIS SIDEKICK...
AWW!
TRUST ME... HE'S PRETTY INTO YOU.
SIMON ALREADY SAID **BE QUIET**!
LET ME DOWN AND SAY IT TO MY FACE!
YEAH! THPBPB!
WHATEVER...

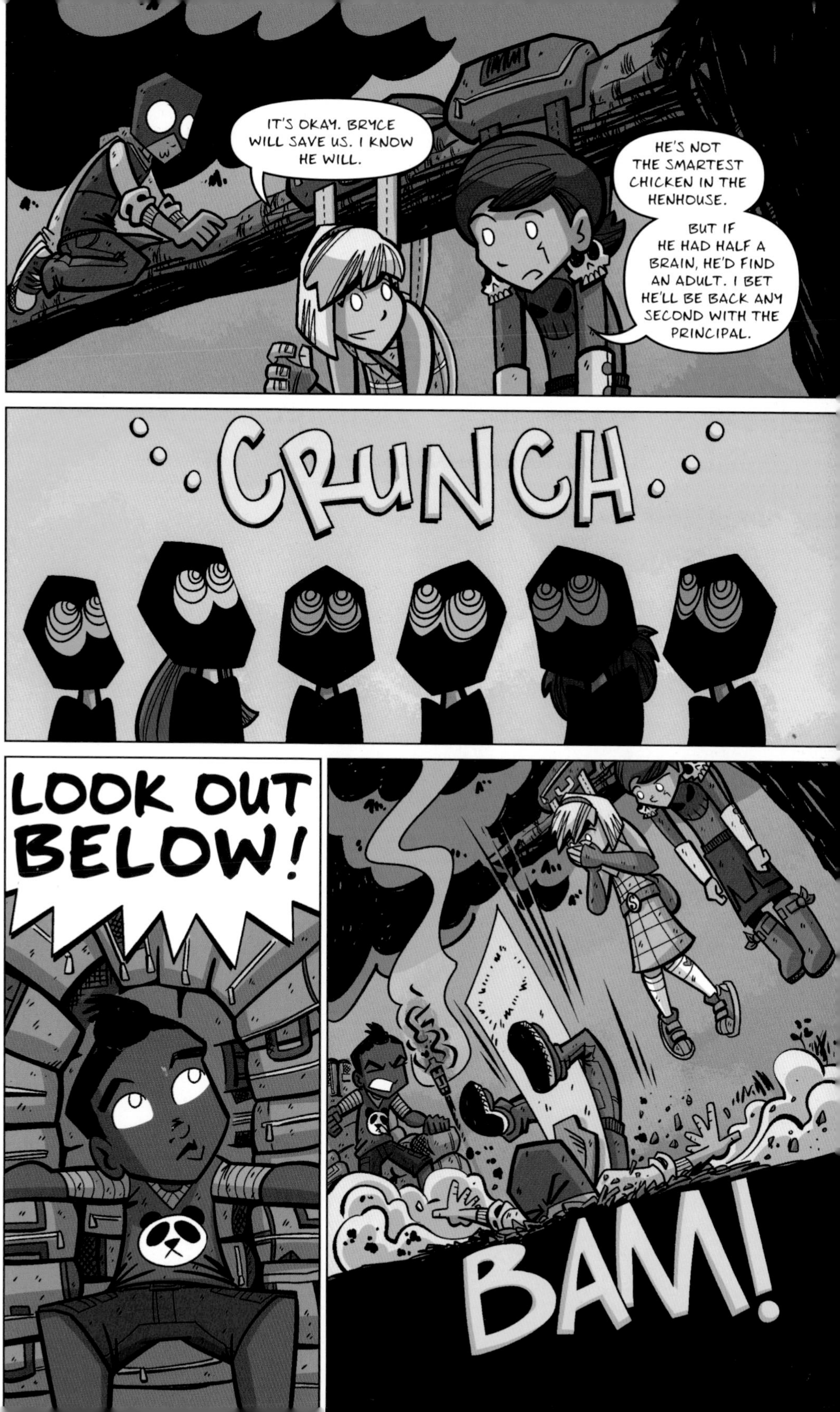
IT'S OKAY. BRYCE WILL SAVE US. I KNOW HE WILL.
HE'S NOT THE SMARTEST CHICKEN IN THE HENHOUSE.
BUT IF HE HAD HALF A BRAIN, HE'D FIND AN ADULT. I BET HE'LL BE BACK ANY SECOND WITH THE PRINCIPAL.
CRUNCH
LOOK OUT BELOW!
BAM!

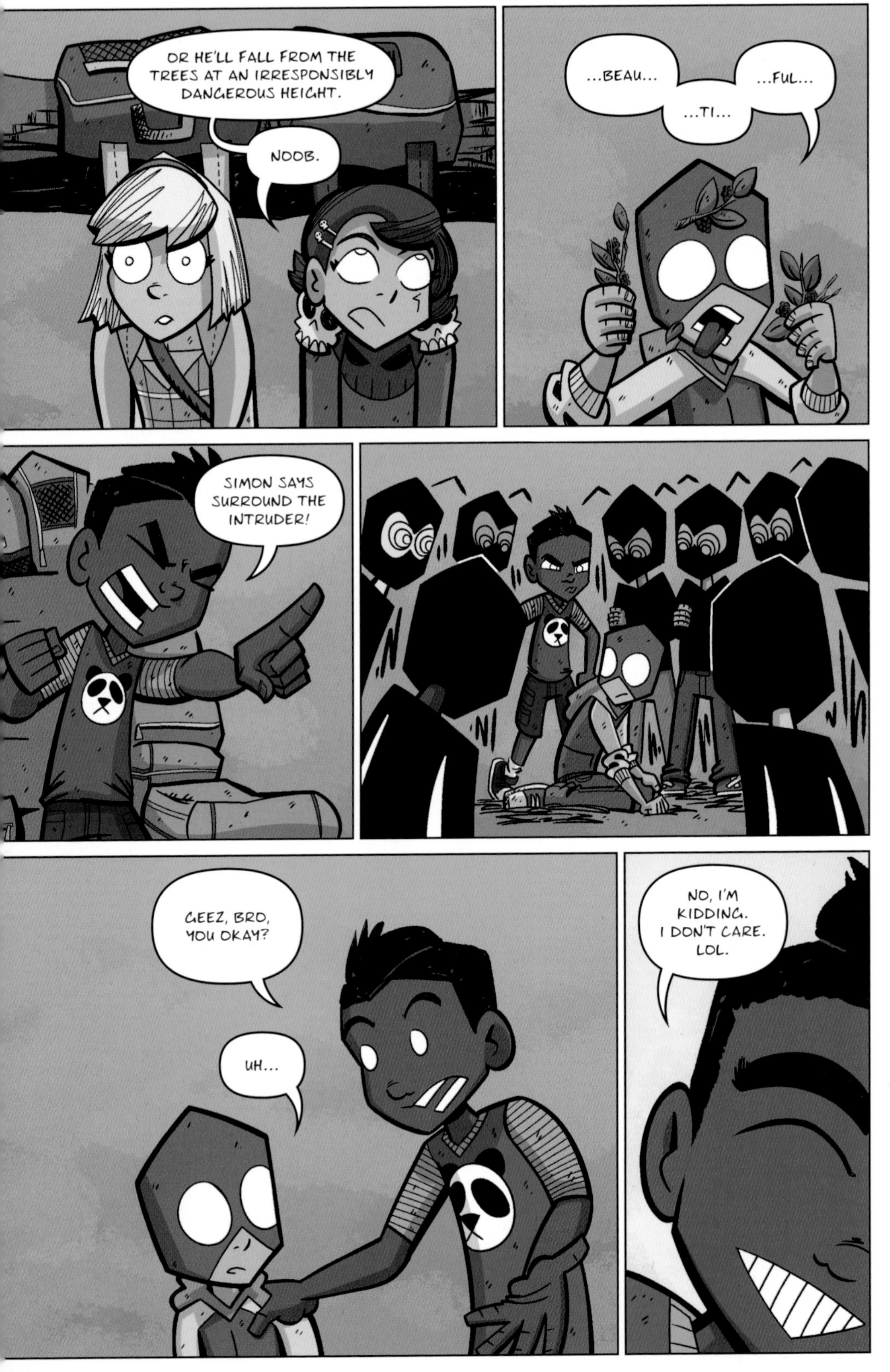
OR HE'LL FALL FROM THE TREES AT AN IRRESPONSIBLY DANGEROUS HEIGHT.
NOOB.
...BEAU...
...TI...
...FUL...
SIMON SAYS SURROUND THE INTRUDER!
GEEZ, BRO, YOU OKAY?
UH...
NO, I'M KIDDING. I DON'T CARE. LOL.

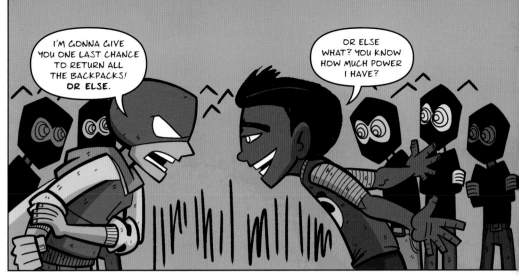

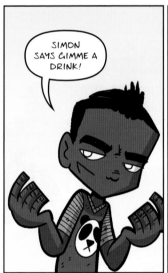

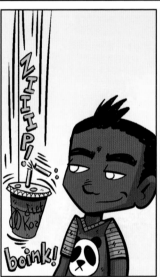

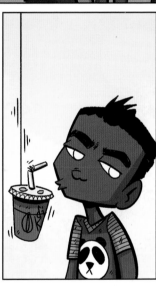

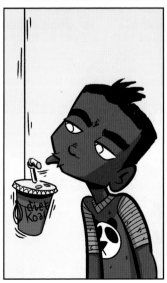

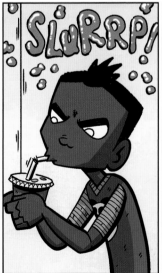

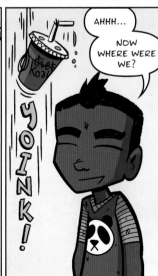

83

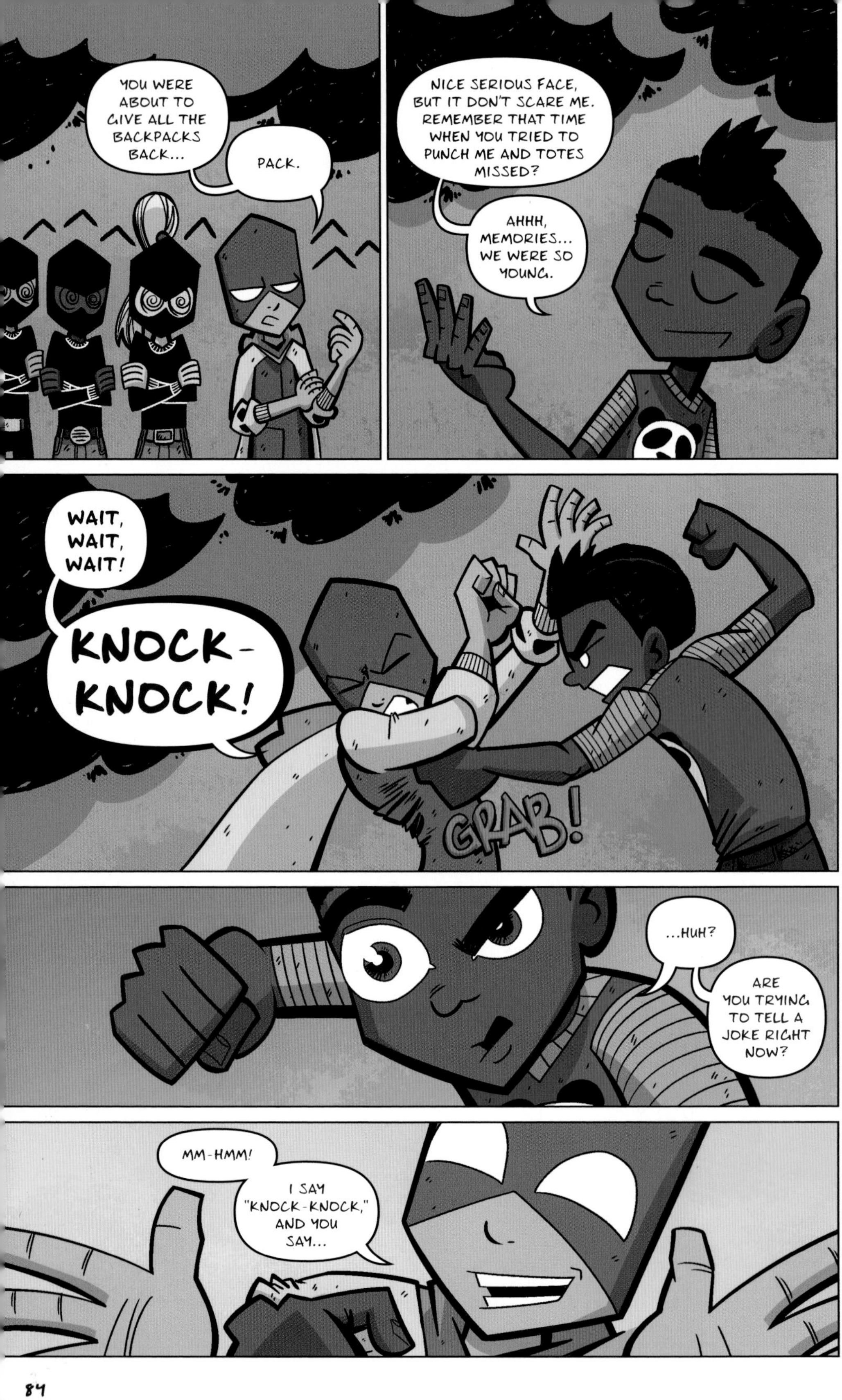
YOU WERE ABOUT TO GIVE ALL THE BACKPACKS BACK...
PACK.
NICE SERIOUS FACE, BUT IT DON'T SCARE ME. REMEMBER THAT TIME WHEN YOU TRIED TO PUNCH ME AND TOTES MISSED?
AHHH, MEMORIES... WE WERE SO YOUNG.
WAIT, WAIT, WAIT!
KNOCK-KNOCK!
GRAB!
...HUH?
ARE YOU TRYING TO TELL A JOKE RIGHT NOW?
MM-HMM!
I SAY "KNOCK-KNOCK," AND YOU SAY...

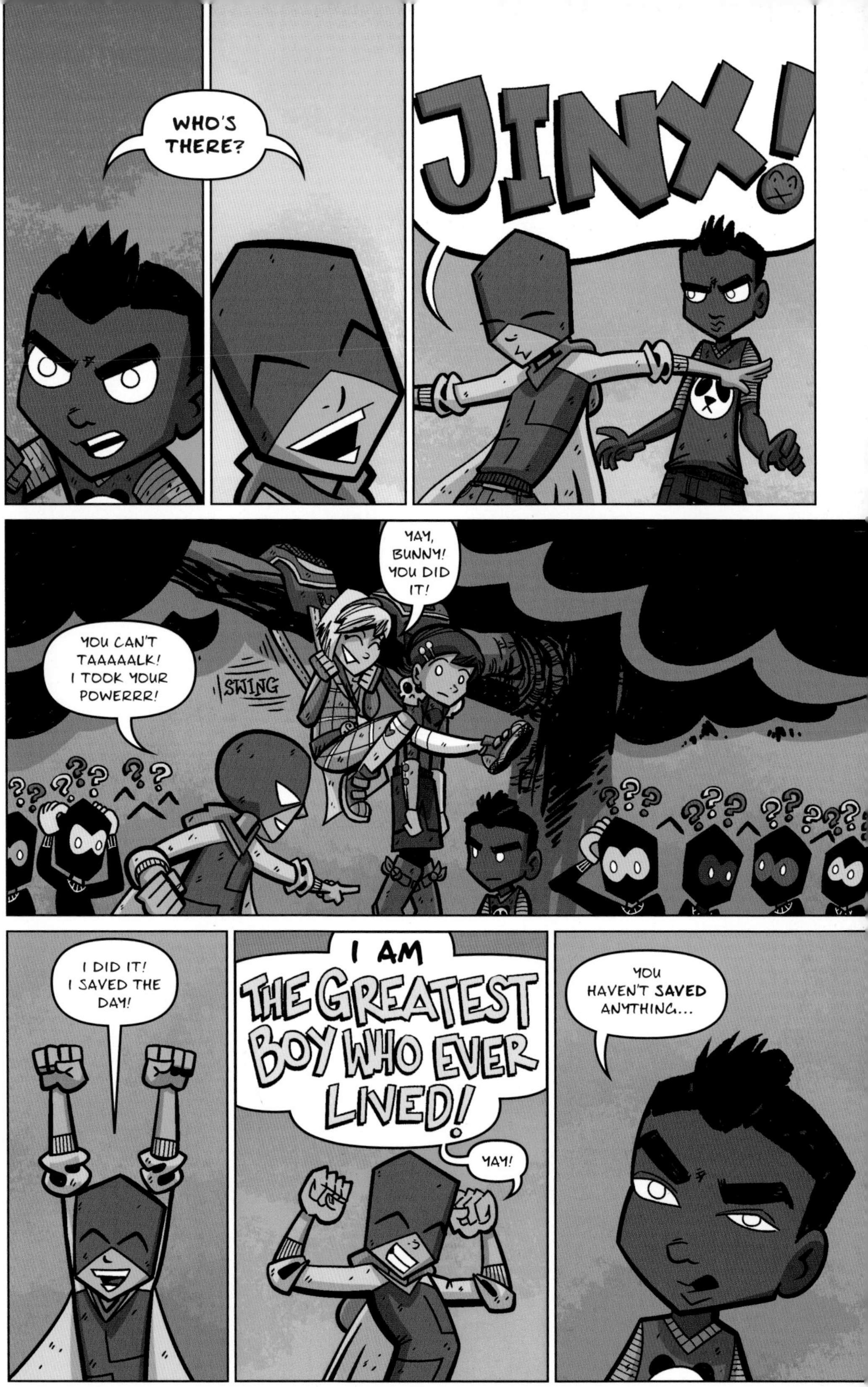
WHO'S THERE?
JINX!
YAY, BUNNY! YOU DID IT!
YOU CAN'T TAAAAALK! I TOOK YOUR POWERRR!
SWING
I DID IT! I SAVED THE DAY!
I AM THE GREATEST BOY WHO EVER LIVED!
YAY!
YOU HAVEN'T **SAVED** ANYTHING...

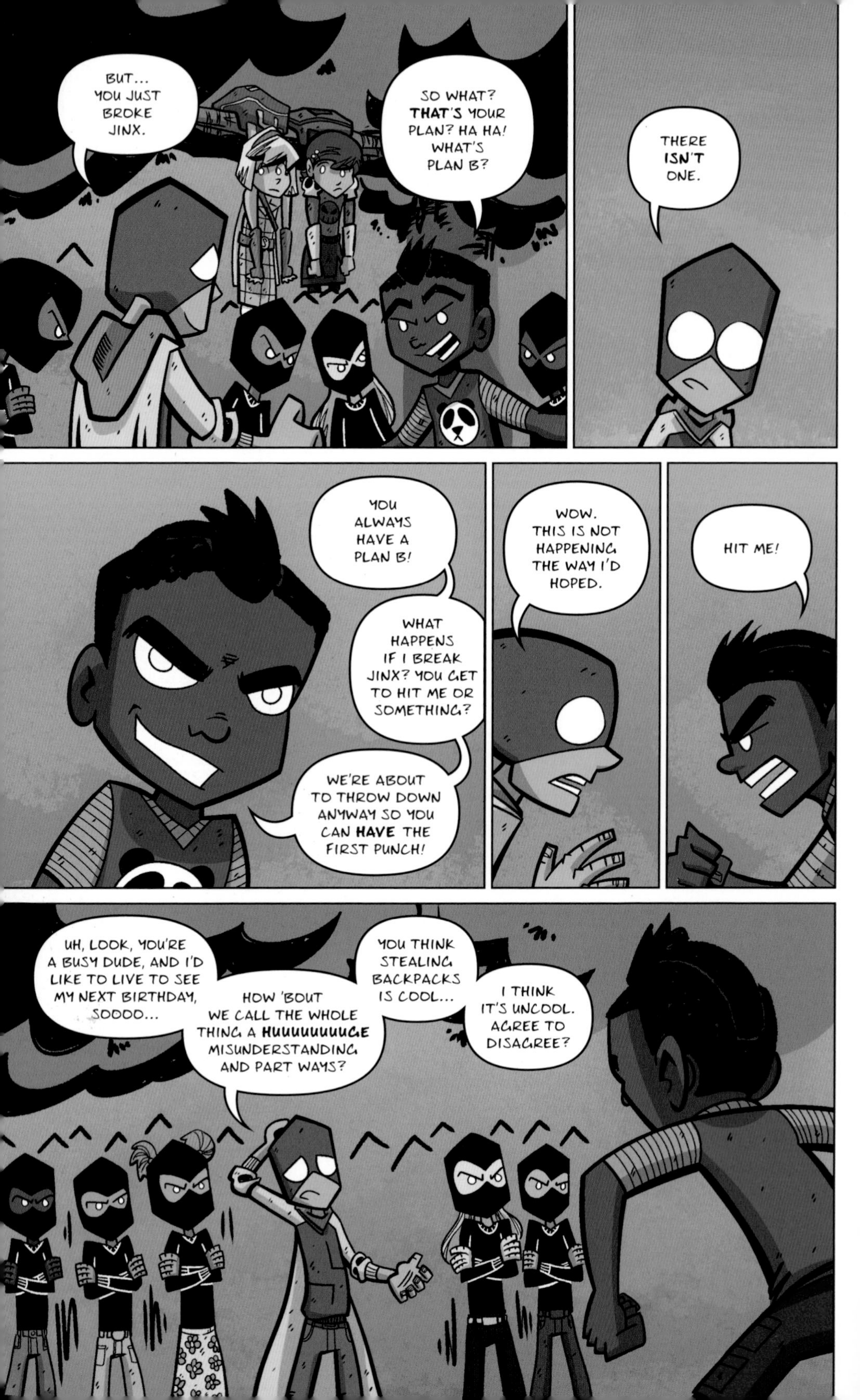
BUT... YOU JUST BROKE JINX.
SO WHAT? THAT'S YOUR PLAN? HA HA! WHAT'S PLAN B?
THERE ISN'T ONE.
YOU ALWAYS HAVE A PLAN B!
WHAT HAPPENS IF I BREAK JINX? YOU GET TO HIT ME OR SOMETHING?
WE'RE ABOUT TO THROW DOWN ANYWAY SO YOU CAN HAVE THE FIRST PUNCH!
WOW. THIS IS NOT HAPPENING THE WAY I'D HOPED.
HIT ME!
UH, LOOK, YOU'RE A BUSY DUDE, AND I'D LIKE TO LIVE TO SEE MY NEXT BIRTHDAY, SOOOO...
HOW 'BOUT WE CALL THE WHOLE THING A HUUUUUUUUGE MISUNDERSTANDING AND PART WAYS?
YOU THINK STEALING BACKPACKS IS COOL...
I THINK IT'S UNCOOL. AGREE TO DISAGREE?

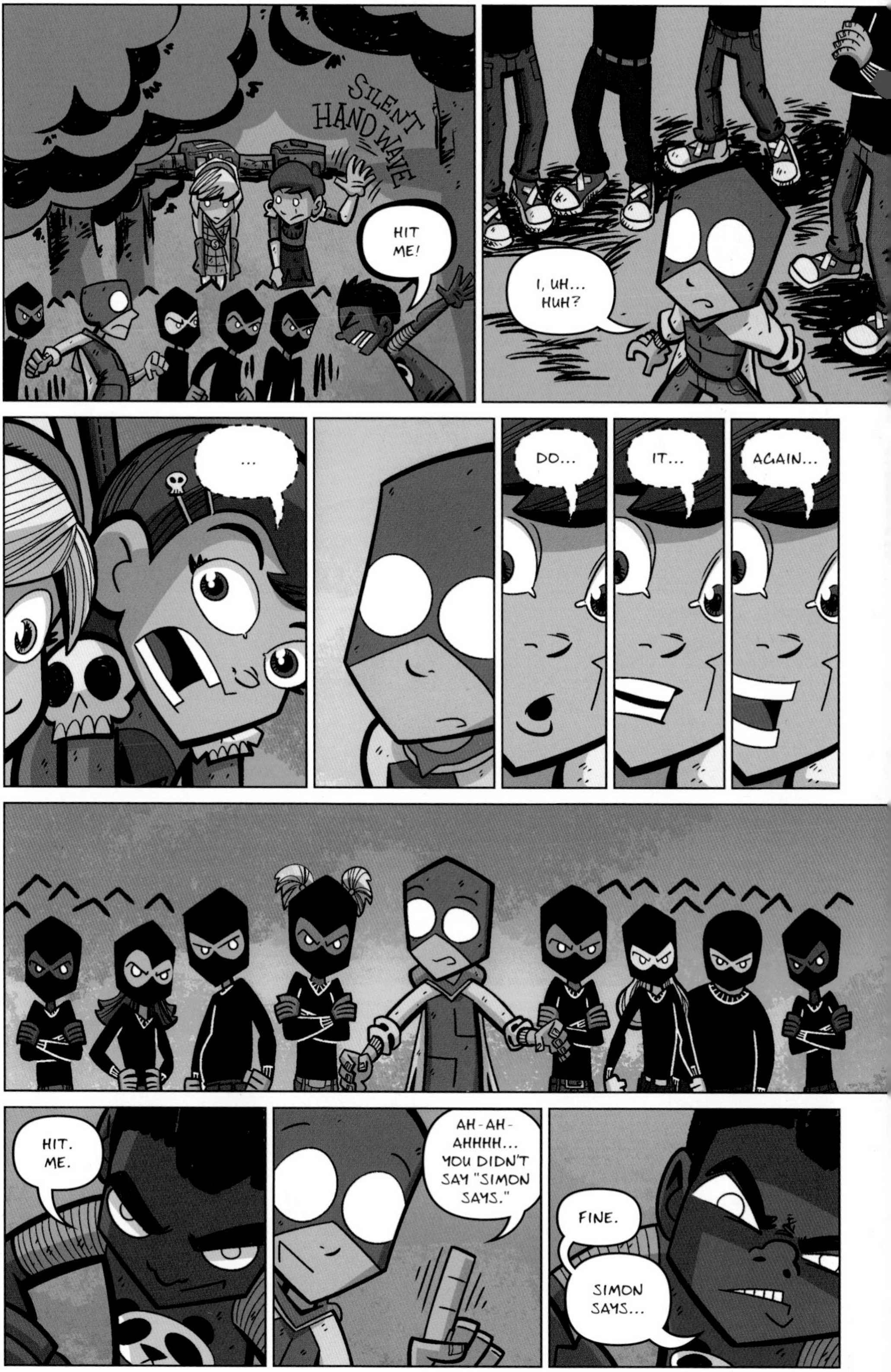
SILENT HANDWAVE
HIT ME!
I, UH... HUH?
...
DO...
IT...
AGAIN...
HIT. ME.
AH-AH-AHHHH... YOU DIDN'T SAY "SIMON SAYS."
FINE.
SIMON SAYS...

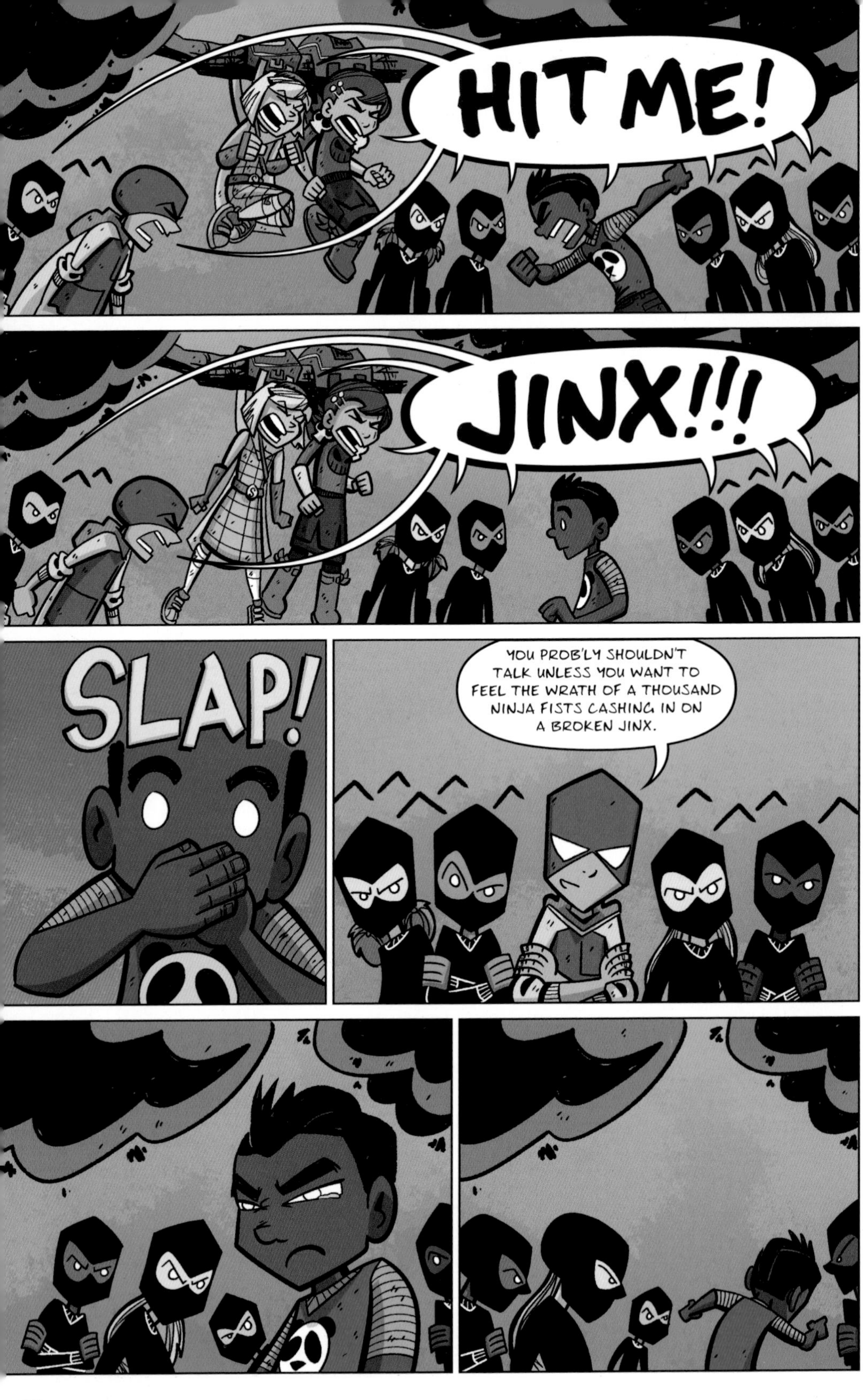
HIT ME!
JINX!!!
SLAP!
YOU PROB'LY SHOULDN'T TALK UNLESS YOU WANT TO FEEL THE WRATH OF A THOUSAND NINJA FISTS CASHING IN ON A BROKEN JINX.

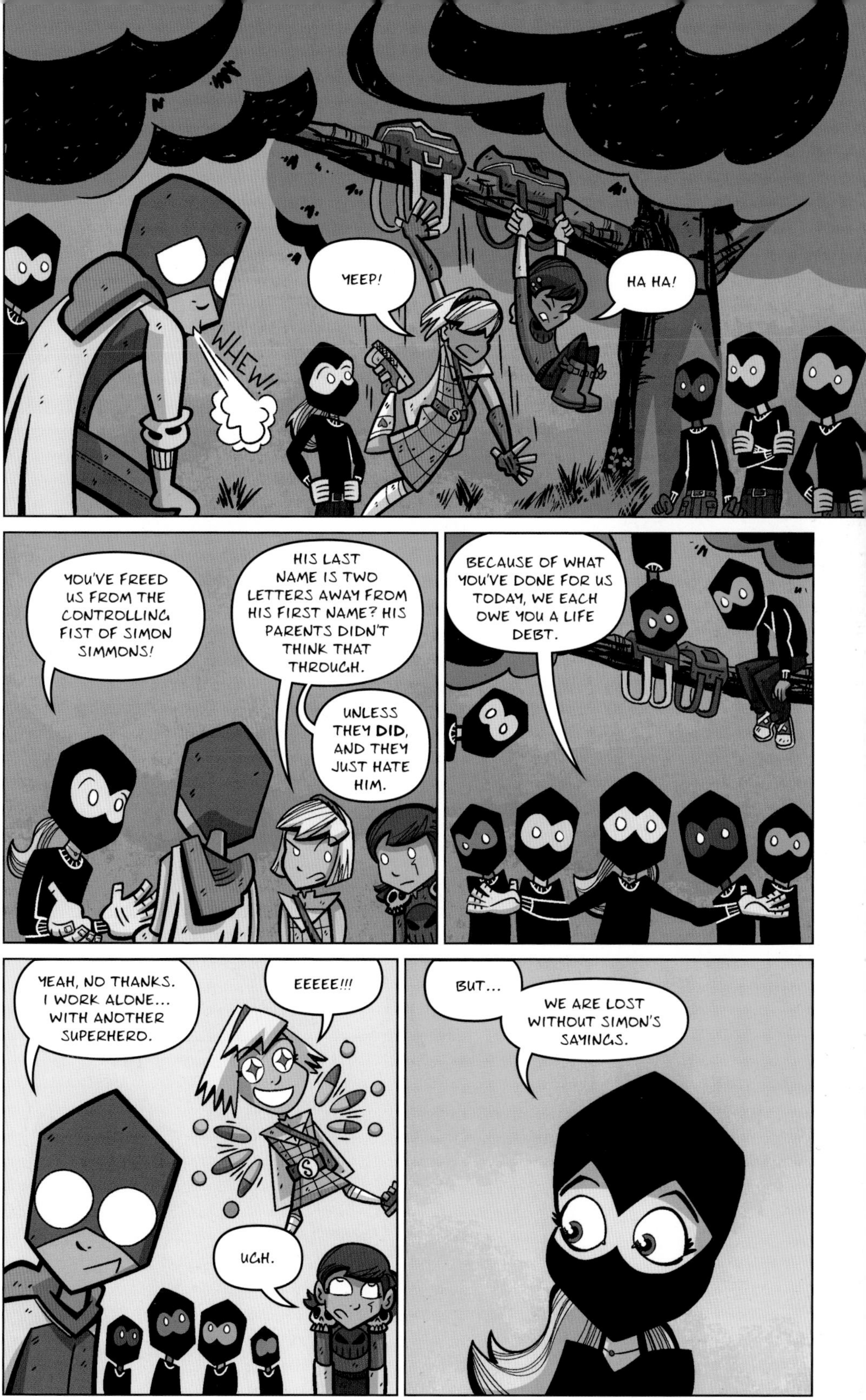
WHEW!
YEEP!
HA HA!
YOU'VE FREED US FROM THE CONTROLLING FIST OF SIMON SIMMONS!
HIS LAST NAME IS TWO LETTERS AWAY FROM HIS FIRST NAME? HIS PARENTS DIDN'T THINK THAT THROUGH.
UNLESS THEY DID, AND THEY JUST HATE HIM.
BECAUSE OF WHAT YOU'VE DONE FOR US TODAY, WE EACH OWE YOU A LIFE DEBT.
YEAH, NO THANKS. I WORK ALONE... WITH ANOTHER SUPERHERO.
EEEEE!!!
UGH.
BUT...
WE ARE LOST WITHOUT SIMON'S SAYINGS.

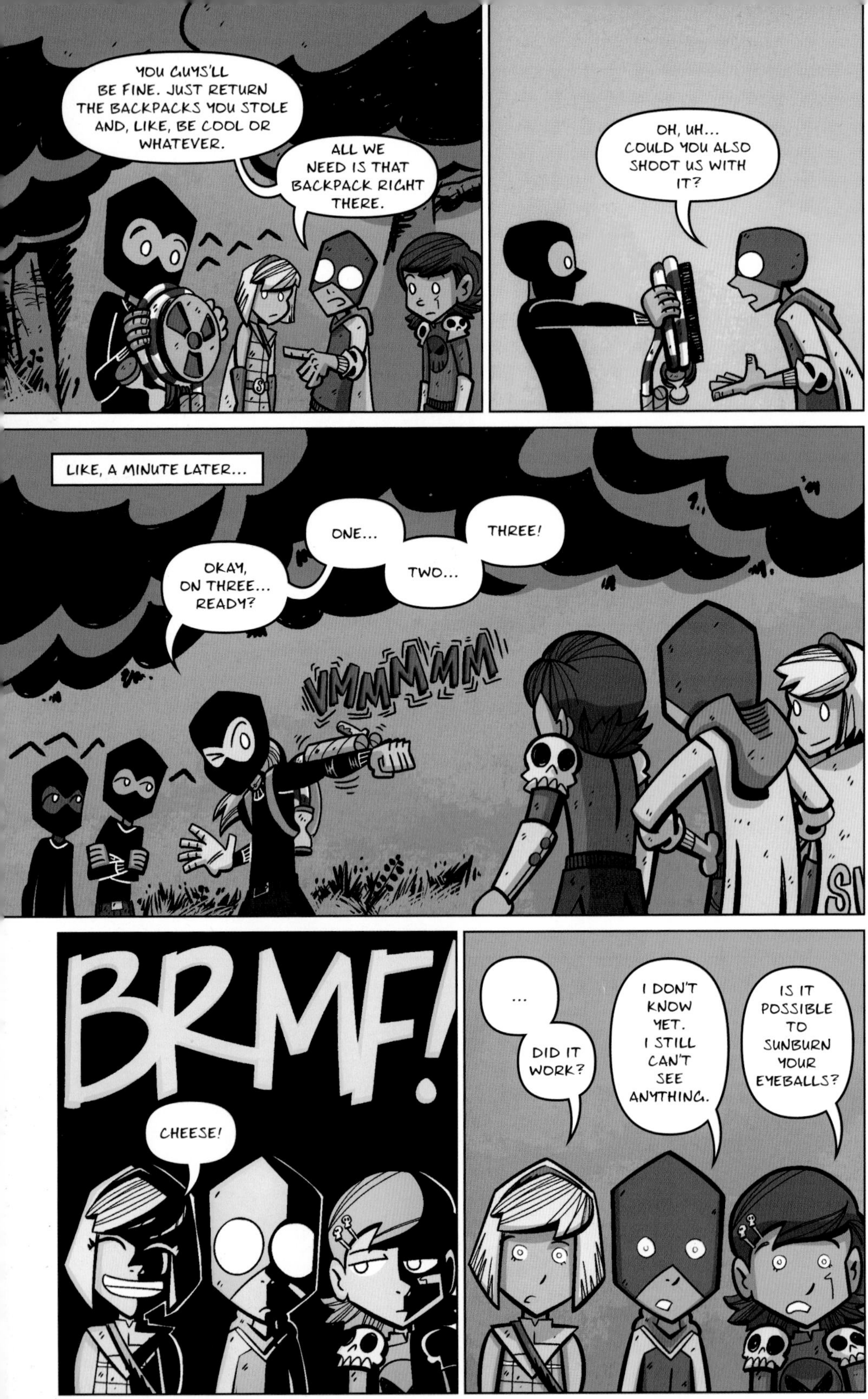
YOU GUYS'LL BE FINE. JUST RETURN THE BACKPACKS YOU STOLE AND, LIKE, BE COOL OR WHATEVER.
ALL WE NEED IS THAT BACKPACK RIGHT THERE.
OH, UH... COULD YOU ALSO SHOOT US WITH IT?
LIKE, A MINUTE LATER...
OKAY, ON THREE... READY?
ONE...
TWO...
THREE!
VMMMMMM
BRMF!
CHEESE!
...
DID IT WORK?
I DON'T KNOW YET. I STILL CAN'T SEE ANYTHING.
IS IT POSSIBLE TO SUNBURN YOUR EYEBALLS?

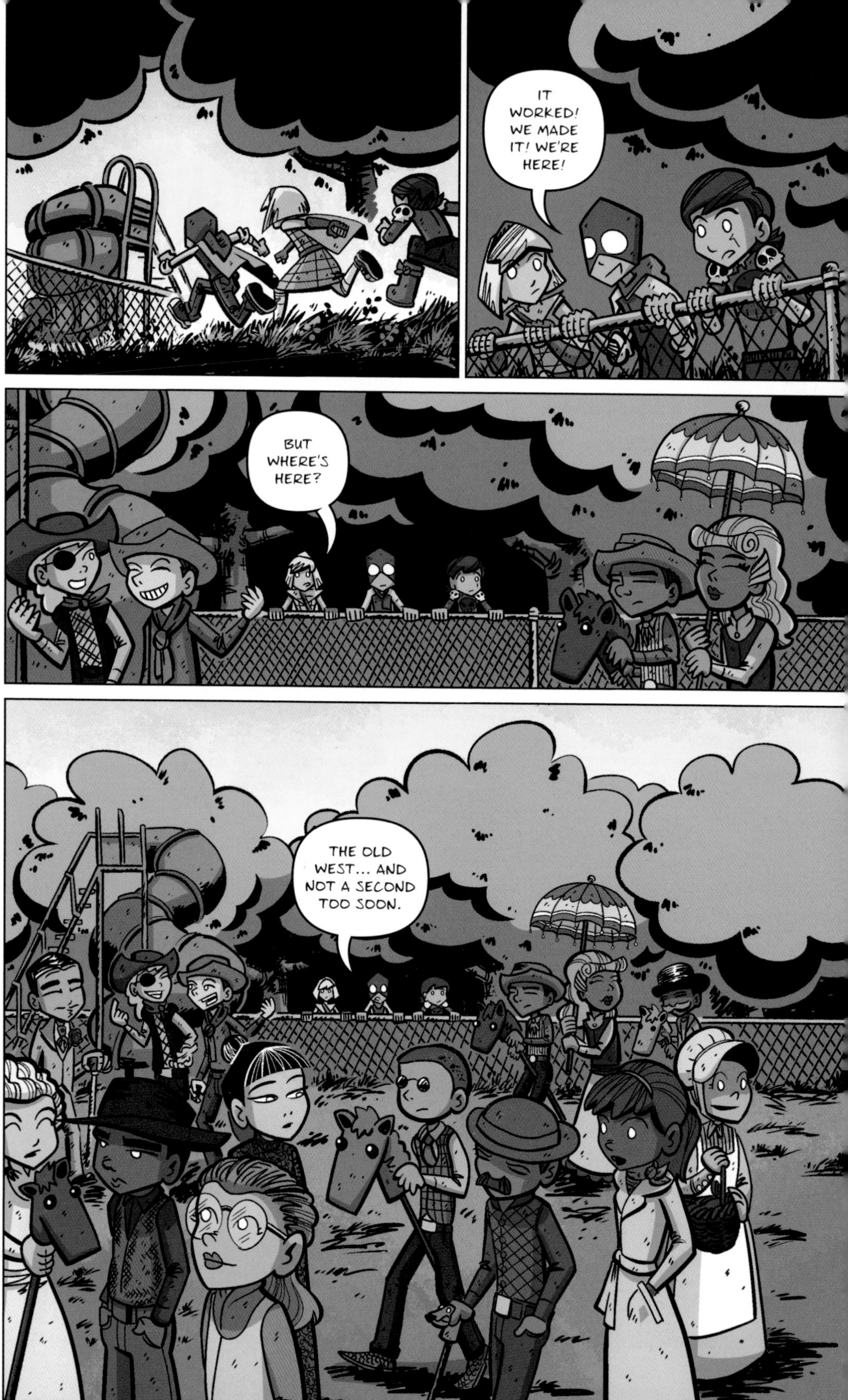
IT WORKED! WE MADE IT! WE'RE HERE!
BUT WHERE'S HERE?
THE OLD WEST... AND NOT A SECOND TOO SOON.

06 THE BATTLE OF FORT ARMSTRONG

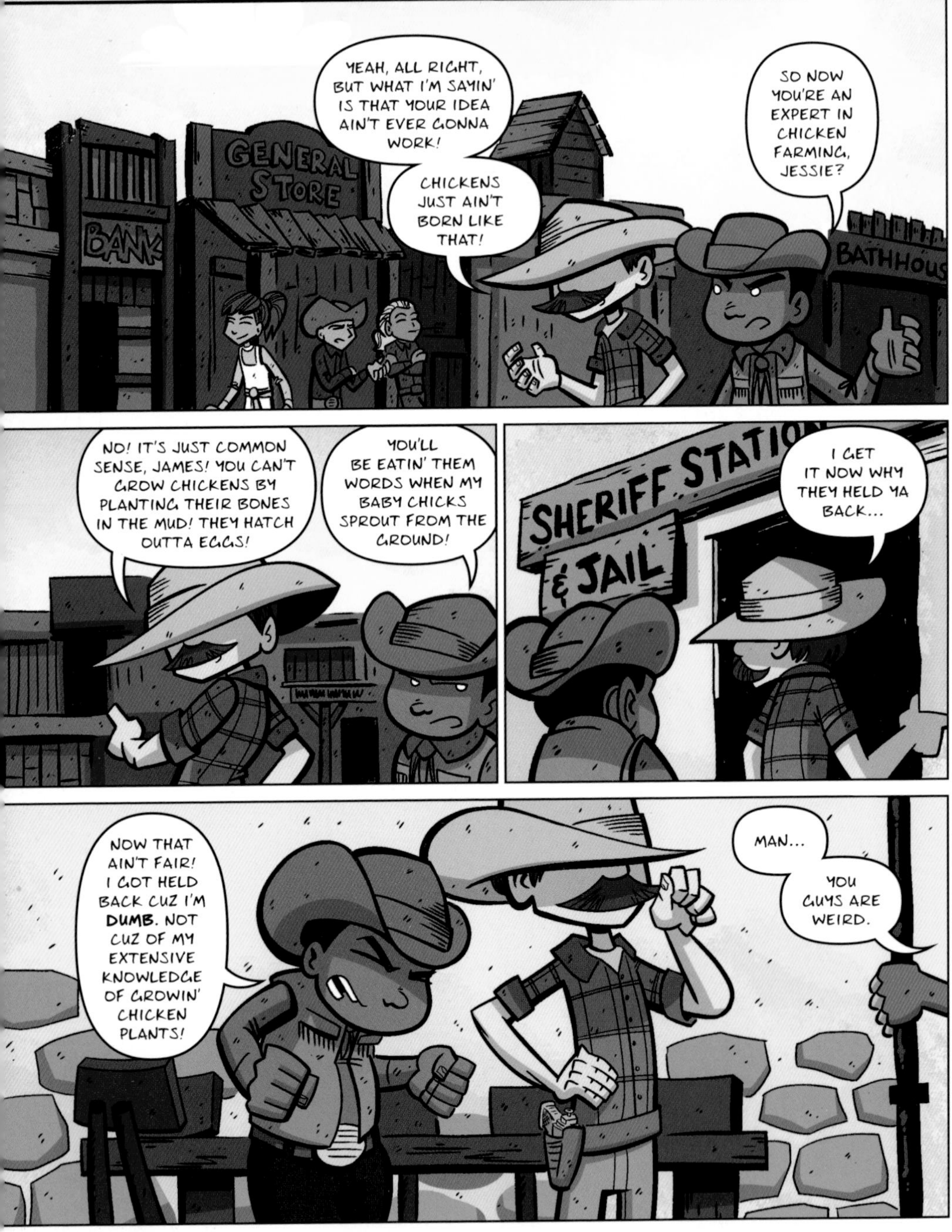

YEAH, ALL RIGHT, BUT WHAT I'M SAYIN' IS THAT YOUR IDEA AIN'T EVER GONNA WORK!
CHICKENS JUST AIN'T BORN LIKE THAT!
SO NOW YOU'RE AN EXPERT IN CHICKEN FARMING, JESSIE?
GENERAL STORE
BANK
BATHHOUS
NO! IT'S JUST COMMON SENSE, JAMES! YOU CAN'T GROW CHICKENS BY PLANTING THEIR BONES IN THE MUD! THEY HATCH OUTTA EGGS!
YOU'LL BE EATIN' THEM WORDS WHEN MY BABY CHICKS SPROUT FROM THE GROUND!
SHERIFF STATIO
& JAIL
I GET IT NOW WHY THEY HELD YA BACK...
NOW THAT AIN'T FAIR! I GOT HELD BACK CUZ I'M **DUMB**. NOT CUZ OF MY EXTENSIVE KNOWLEDGE OF GROWIN' CHICKEN PLANTS!
MAN...
YOU GUYS ARE WEIRD.

WE'RE WEIRD? Y'ALL ARE THE ONES WEARIN' YELLA CAPES AND PIRATE GARMENTS, SO DON'T BE CALLIN' NO ONE WEIRD BUT YERSELF, YA YOUNG BIDDY.

LET US OUT ALREADY! WE DIDN'T EVEN DO ANYTHING!

UGH! I **REALLY** HATE GETTING TAKEN PRISONER!

SEEMS TO BE HAPPENING TO YOU A LOT LATELY.

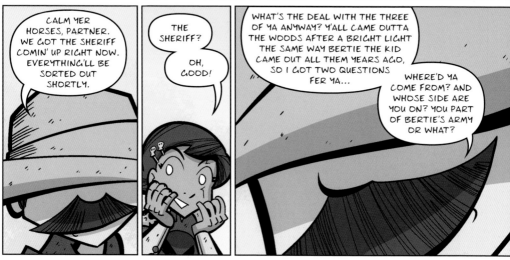

CALM YER HORSES, PARTNER. WE GOT THE SHERIFF COMIN' UP RIGHT NOW. EVERYTHING'LL BE SORTED OUT SHORTLY.

THE SHERIFF?

OH, GOOD!

WHAT'S THE DEAL WITH THE THREE OF YA ANYWAY? Y'ALL CAME OUTTA THE WOODS AFTER A BRIGHT LIGHT THE SAME WAY BERTIE THE KID CAME OUT ALL THEM YEARS AGO, SO I GOT TWO QUESTIONS FER YA...

WHERE'D YA COME FROM? AND WHOSE SIDE ARE YOU ON? YOU PART OF BERTIE'S ARMY OR WHAT?

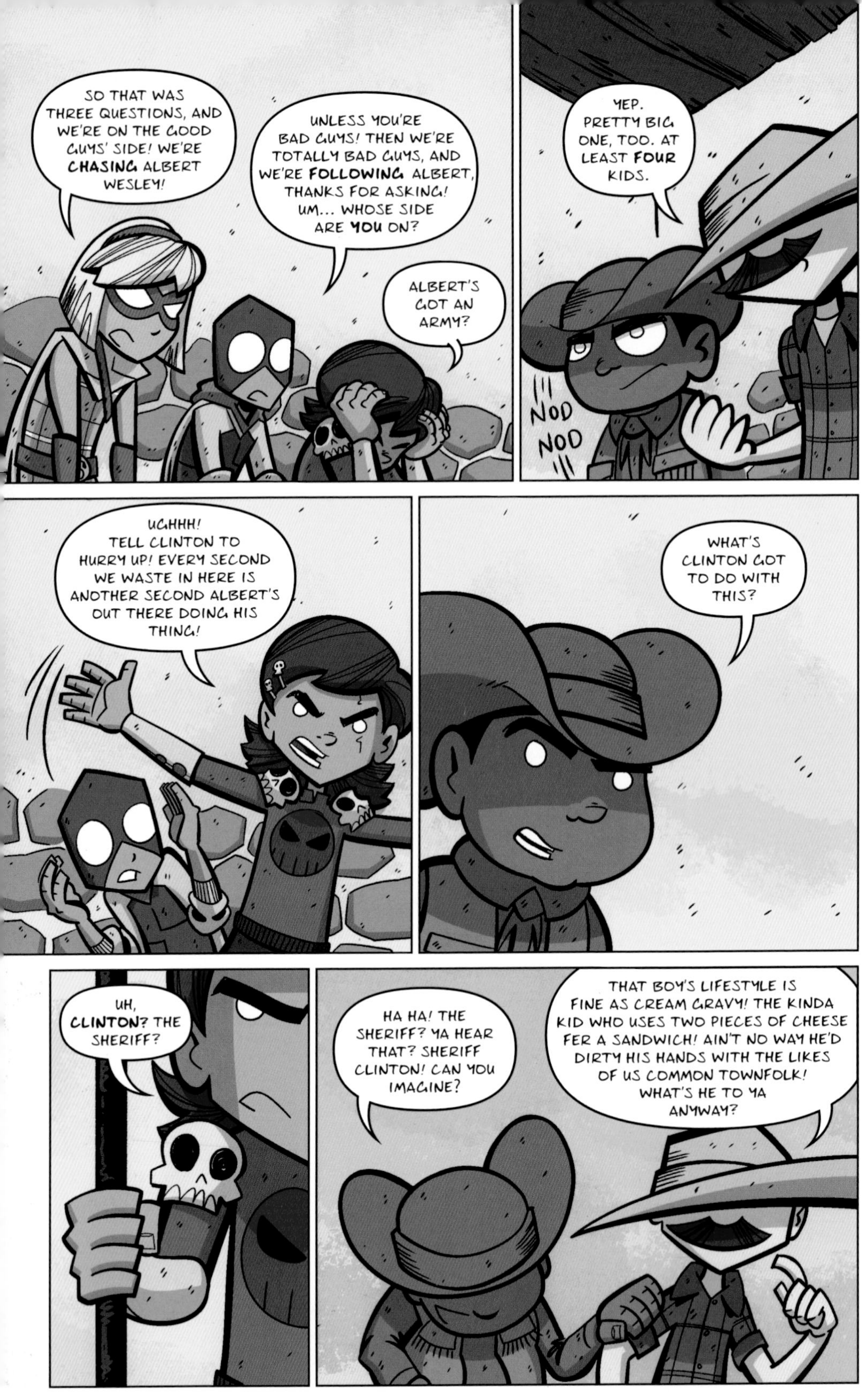
SO THAT WAS THREE QUESTIONS, AND WE'RE ON THE GOOD GUYS' SIDE! WE'RE **CHASING** ALBERT WESLEY!
UNLESS YOU'RE BAD GUYS! THEN WE'RE TOTALLY BAD GUYS, AND WE'RE **FOLLOWING** ALBERT, THANKS FOR ASKING! UM... WHOSE SIDE ARE **YOU** ON?
ALBERT'S GOT AN ARMY?
YEP. PRETTY BIG ONE, TOO. AT LEAST **FOUR** KIDS.
NOD NOD
UGHHH! TELL CLINTON TO HURRY UP! EVERY SECOND WE WASTE IN HERE IS ANOTHER SECOND ALBERT'S OUT THERE DOING HIS THING!
WHAT'S CLINTON GOT TO DO WITH THIS?
UH, **CLINTON**? THE SHERIFF?
HA HA! THE SHERIFF? YA HEAR THAT? SHERIFF CLINTON! CAN YOU IMAGINE?
THAT BOY'S LIFESTYLE IS FINE AS CREAM GRAVY! THE KINDA KID WHO USES TWO PIECES OF CHEESE FER A SANDWICH! AIN'T NO WAY HE'D DIRTY HIS HANDS WITH THE LIKES OF US COMMON TOWNFOLK! WHAT'S HE TO YA ANYWAY?

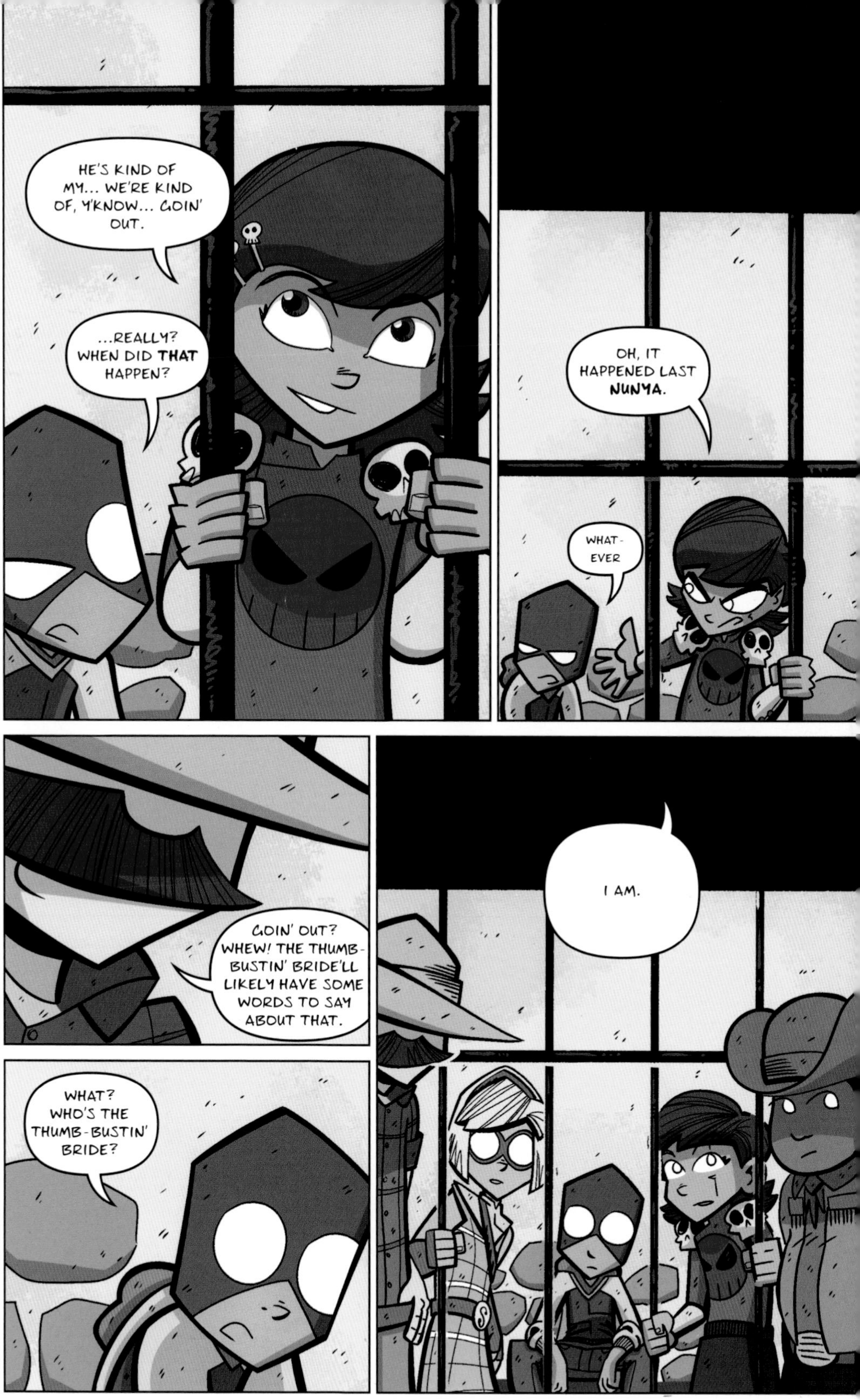
HE'S KIND OF MY... WE'RE KIND OF, Y'KNOW... GOIN' OUT.
...REALLY? WHEN DID THAT HAPPEN?
OH, IT HAPPENED LAST NUNYA.
WHAT-EVER
GOIN' OUT? WHEW! THE THUMB-BUSTIN' BRIDE'LL LIKELY HAVE SOME WORDS TO SAY ABOUT THAT.
WHAT? WHO'S THE THUMB-BUSTIN' BRIDE?
I AM.

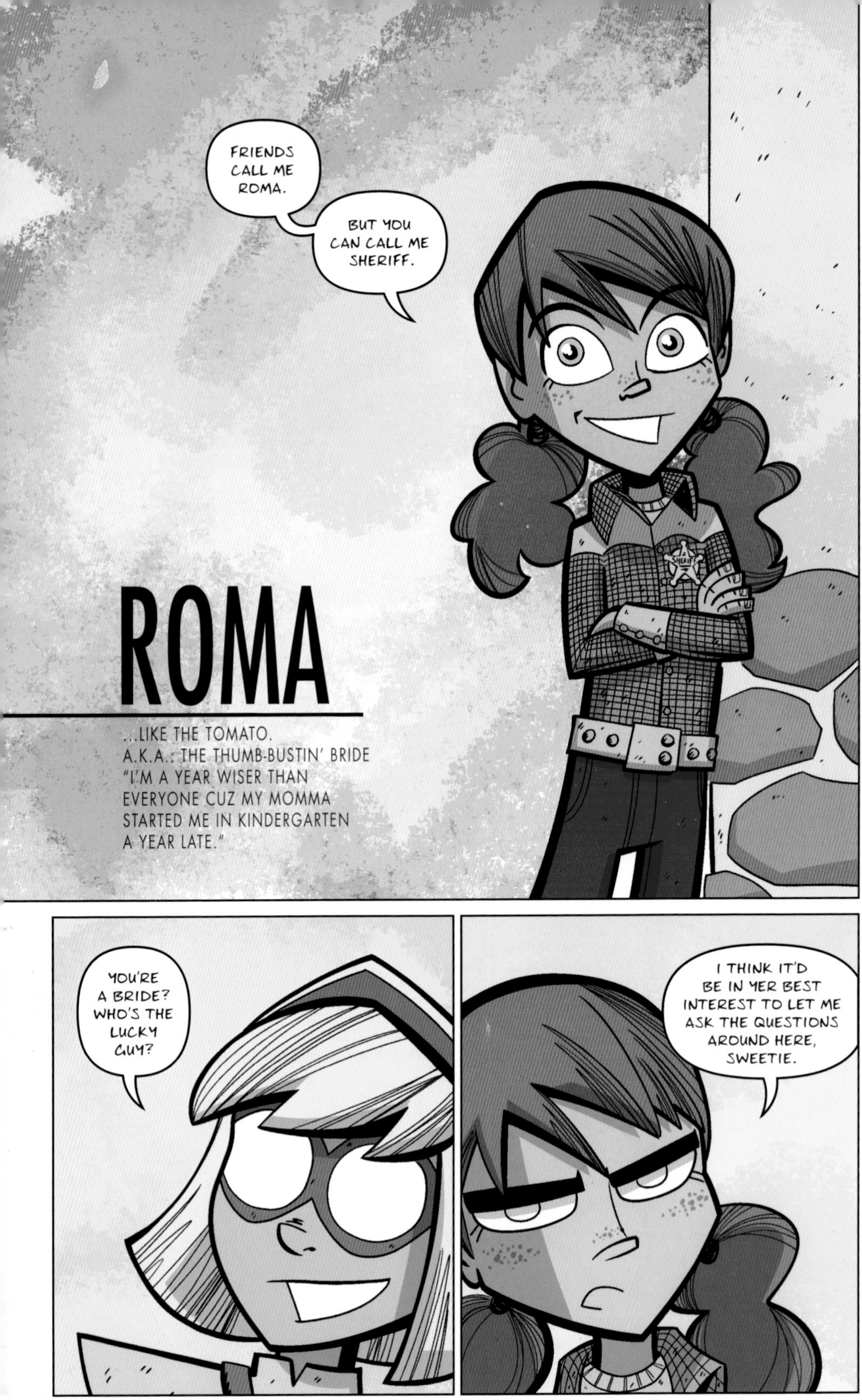
FRIENDS CALL ME ROMA.
BUT YOU CAN CALL ME SHERIFF.
SHERIFF
ROMA
...LIKE THE TOMATO.
A.K.A.: THE THUMB-BUSTIN' BRIDE
"I'M A YEAR WISER THAN EVERYONE CUZ MY MOMMA STARTED ME IN KINDERGARTEN A YEAR LATE."
YOU'RE A BRIDE? WHO'S THE LUCKY GUY?
I THINK IT'D BE IN YER BEST INTEREST TO LET ME ASK THE QUESTIONS AROUND HERE, SWEETIE.

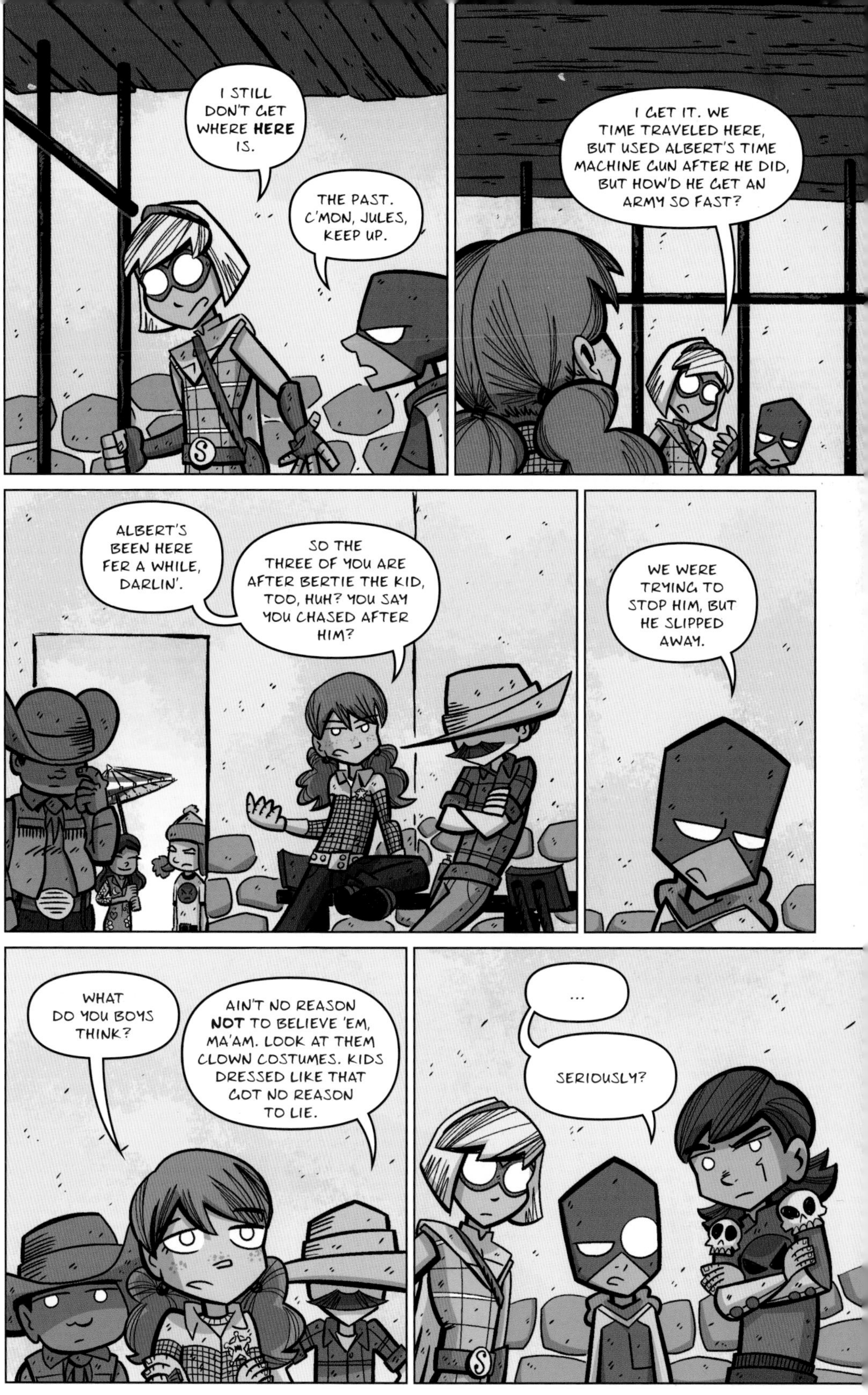
I STILL DON'T GET WHERE **HERE** IS.
THE PAST. C'MON, JULES, KEEP UP.
I GET IT. WE TIME TRAVELED HERE, BUT USED ALBERT'S TIME MACHINE GUN AFTER HE DID, BUT HOW'D HE GET AN ARMY SO FAST?
ALBERT'S BEEN HERE FER A WHILE, DARLIN'.
SO THE THREE OF YOU ARE AFTER BERTIE THE KID, TOO, HUH? YOU SAY YOU CHASED AFTER HIM?
WE WERE TRYING TO STOP HIM, BUT HE SLIPPED AWAY.
WHAT DO YOU BOYS THINK?
AIN'T NO REASON **NOT** TO BELIEVE 'EM, MA'AM. LOOK AT THEM CLOWN COSTUMES. KIDS DRESSED LIKE THAT GOT NO REASON TO LIE.
...
SERIOUSLY?

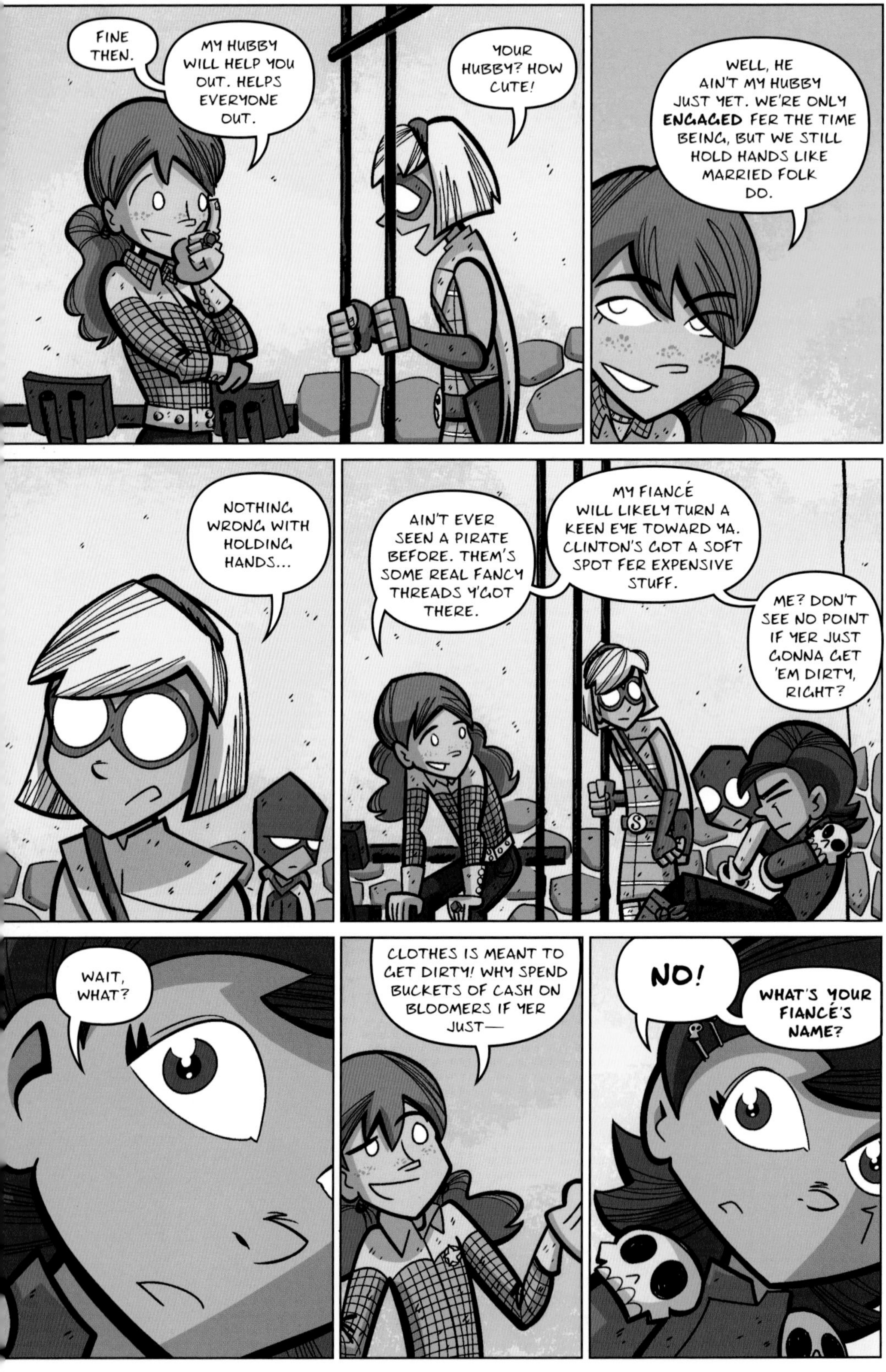
FINE THEN.
MY HUBBY WILL HELP YOU OUT. HELPS EVERYONE OUT.
YOUR HUBBY? HOW CUTE!
WELL, HE AIN'T MY HUBBY JUST YET. WE'RE ONLY ENGAGED FER THE TIME BEING, BUT WE STILL HOLD HANDS LIKE MARRIED FOLK DO.
NOTHING WRONG WITH HOLDING HANDS...
AIN'T EVER SEEN A PIRATE BEFORE. THEM'S SOME REAL FANCY THREADS Y'GOT THERE.
MY FIANCÉ WILL LIKELY TURN A KEEN EYE TOWARD YA. CLINTON'S GOT A SOFT SPOT FER EXPENSIVE STUFF.
ME? DON'T SEE NO POINT IF YER JUST GONNA GET 'EM DIRTY, RIGHT?
WAIT, WHAT?
CLOTHES IS MEANT TO GET DIRTY! WHY SPEND BUCKETS OF CASH ON BLOOMERS IF YER JUST—
NO!
WHAT'S YOUR FIANCÉ'S NAME?

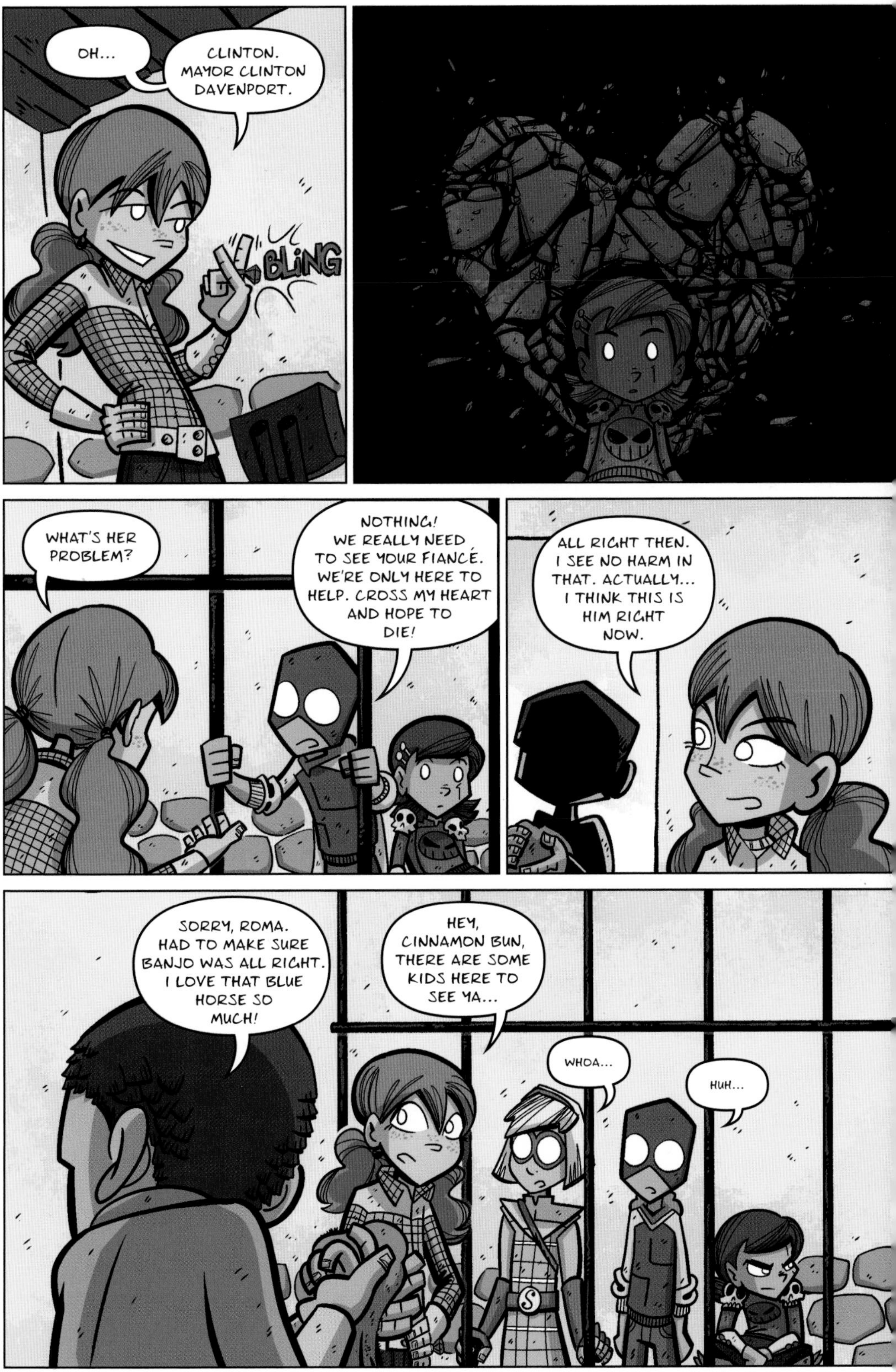
OH...
CLINTON. MAYOR CLINTON DAVENPORT.
BLING
WHAT'S HER PROBLEM?
NOTHING! WE REALLY NEED TO SEE YOUR FIANCÉ. WE'RE ONLY HERE TO HELP. CROSS MY HEART AND HOPE TO DIE!
ALL RIGHT THEN. I SEE NO HARM IN THAT. ACTUALLY... I THINK THIS IS HIM RIGHT NOW.
SORRY, ROMA. HAD TO MAKE SURE BANJO WAS ALL RIGHT. I LOVE THAT BLUE HORSE SO MUCH!
HEY, CINNAMON BUN, THERE ARE SOME KIDS HERE TO SEE YA...
WHOA...
HUH...

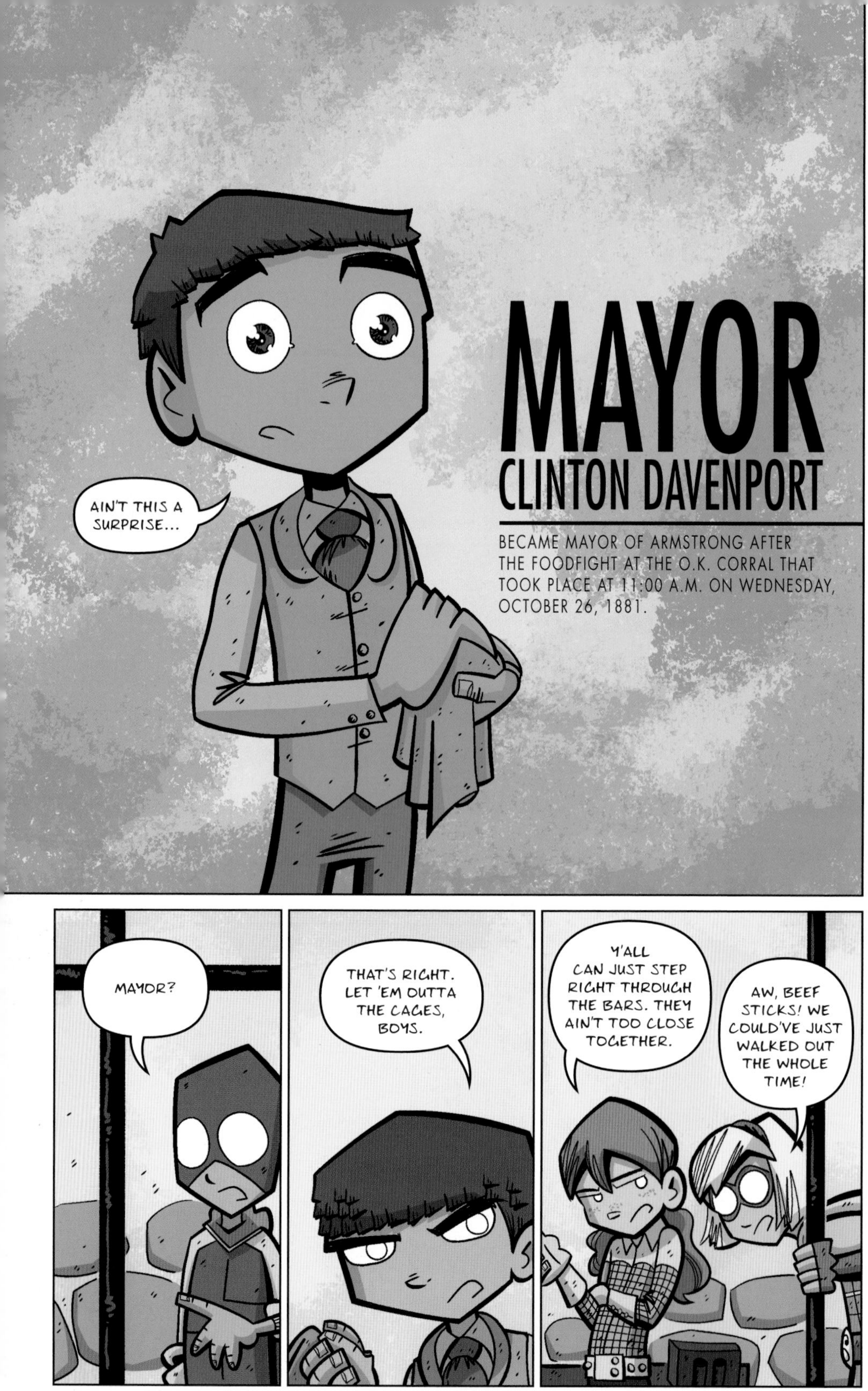
MAYOR
CLINTON DAVENPORT
BECAME MAYOR OF ARMSTRONG AFTER THE FOODFIGHT AT THE O.K. CORRAL THAT TOOK PLACE AT 11:00 A.M. ON WEDNESDAY, OCTOBER 26, 1881.
AIN'T THIS A SURPRISE...
MAYOR?
THAT'S RIGHT. LET 'EM OUTTA THE CAGES, BOYS.
Y'ALL CAN JUST STEP RIGHT THROUGH THE BARS. THEY AIN'T TOO CLOSE TOGETHER.
AW, BEEF STICKS! WE COULD'VE JUST WALKED OUT THE WHOLE TIME!

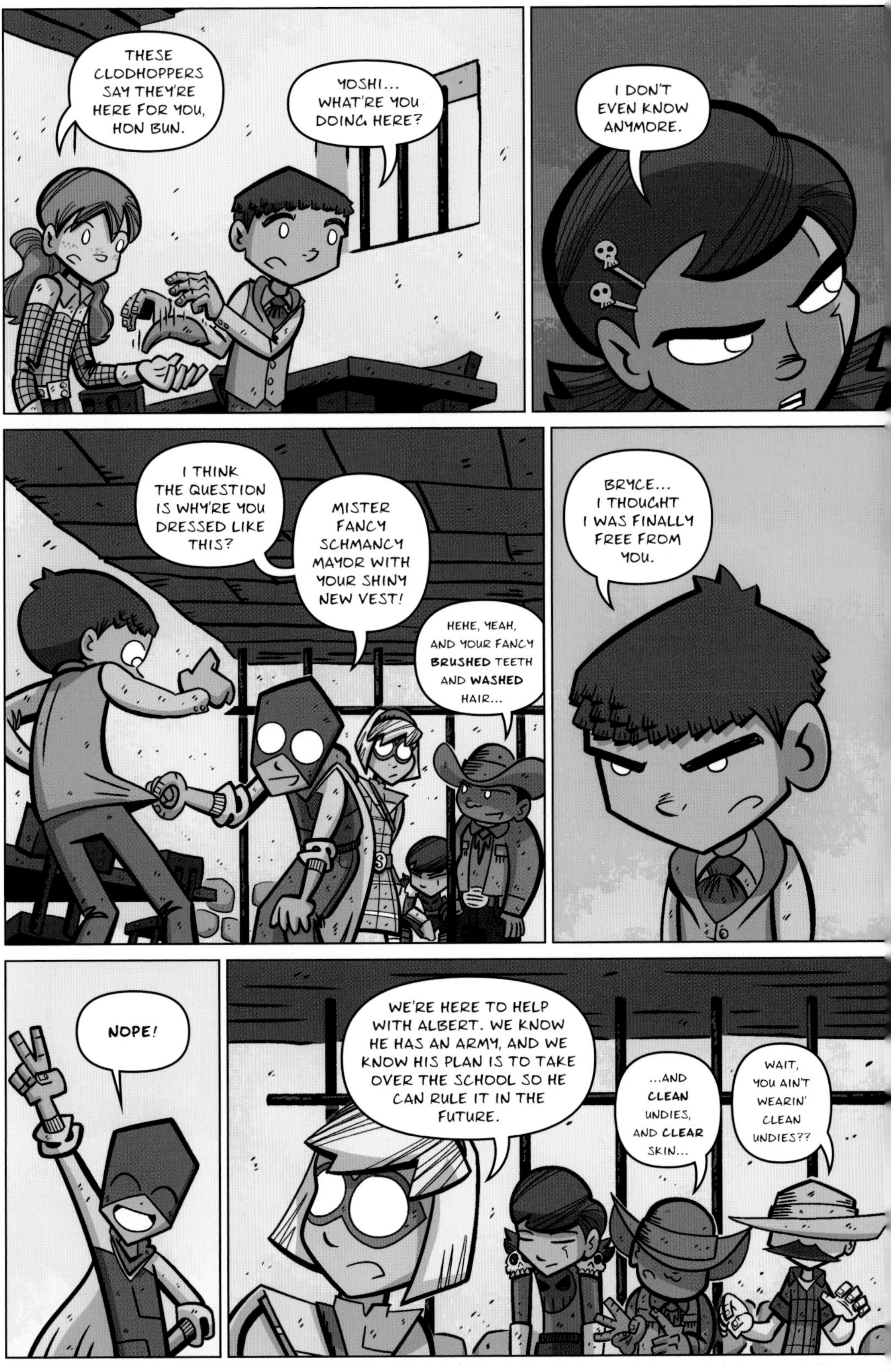

THESE CLODHOPPERS SAY THEY'RE HERE FOR YOU, HON BUN.
YOSHI... WHAT'RE YOU DOING HERE?
I DON'T EVEN KNOW ANYMORE.
I THINK THE QUESTION IS WHY'RE YOU DRESSED LIKE THIS?
MISTER FANCY SCHMANCY MAYOR WITH YOUR SHINY NEW VEST!
HEHE, YEAH, AND YOUR FANCY **BRUSHED** TEETH AND **WASHED** HAIR...
BRYCE... I THOUGHT I WAS FINALLY FREE FROM YOU.
NOPE!
WE'RE HERE TO HELP WITH ALBERT. WE KNOW HE HAS AN ARMY, AND WE KNOW HIS PLAN IS TO TAKE OVER THE SCHOOL SO HE CAN RULE IT IN THE FUTURE.
...AND **CLEAN** UNDIES, AND **CLEAR** SKIN...
WAIT, YOU AIN'T WEARIN' CLEAN UNDIES??

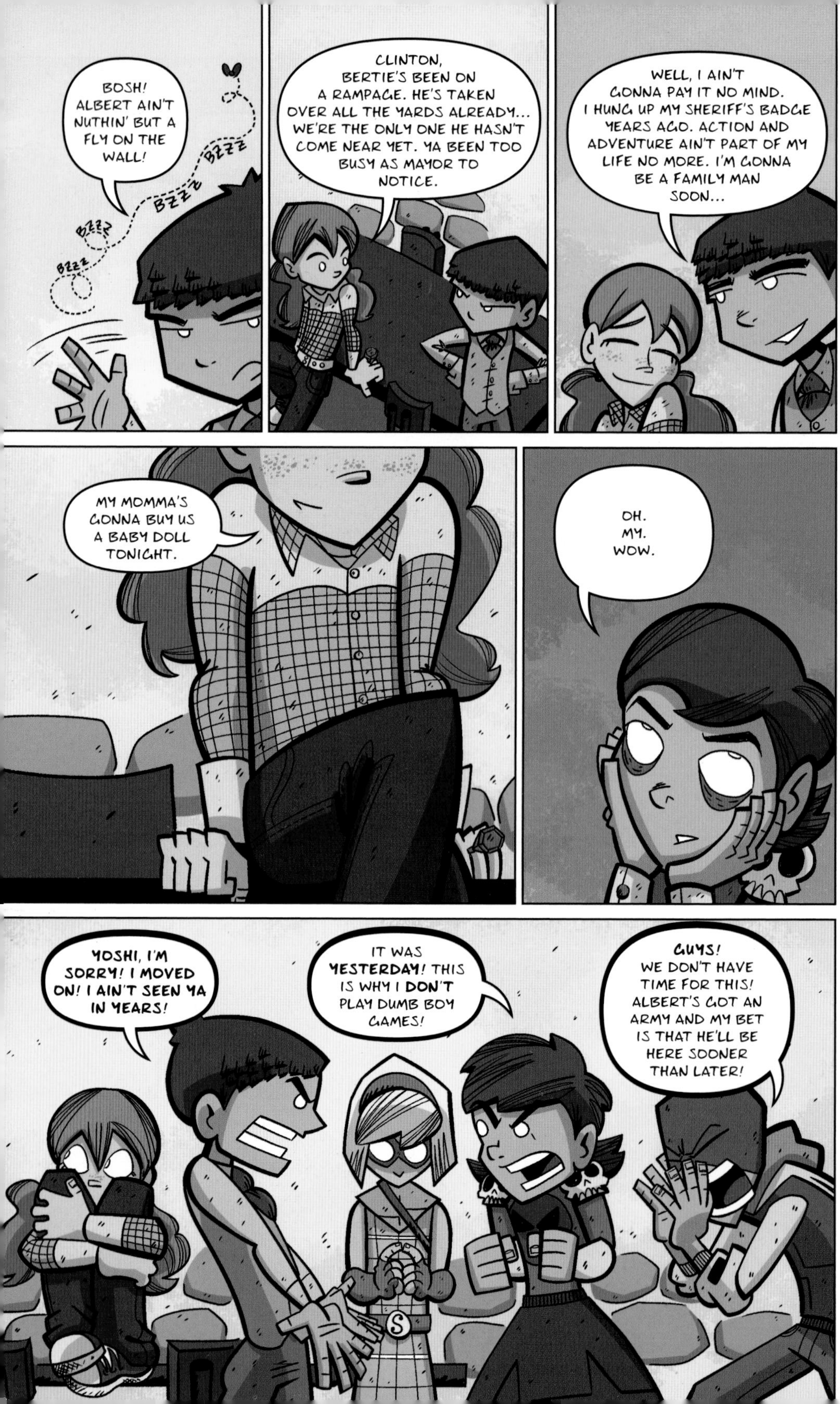
BOSH! ALBERT AIN'T NUTHIN' BUT A FLY ON THE WALL!
BZZZ
BZZZ
BZZZ
BZZZ
CLINTON, BERTIE'S BEEN ON A RAMPAGE. HE'S TAKEN OVER ALL THE YARDS ALREADY... WE'RE THE ONLY ONE HE HASN'T COME NEAR YET. YA BEEN TOO BUSY AS MAYOR TO NOTICE.
WELL, I AIN'T GONNA PAY IT NO MIND. I HUNG UP MY SHERIFF'S BADGE YEARS AGO. ACTION AND ADVENTURE AIN'T PART OF MY LIFE NO MORE. I'M GONNA BE A FAMILY MAN SOON...
MY MOMMA'S GONNA BUY US A BABY DOLL TONIGHT.
OH. MY. WOW.
YOSHI, I'M SORRY! I MOVED ON! I AIN'T SEEN YA IN YEARS!
IT WAS YESTERDAY! THIS IS WHY I DON'T PLAY DUMB BOY GAMES!
GUYS! WE DON'T HAVE TIME FOR THIS! ALBERT'S GOT AN ARMY AND MY BET IS THAT HE'LL BE HERE SOONER THAN LATER!

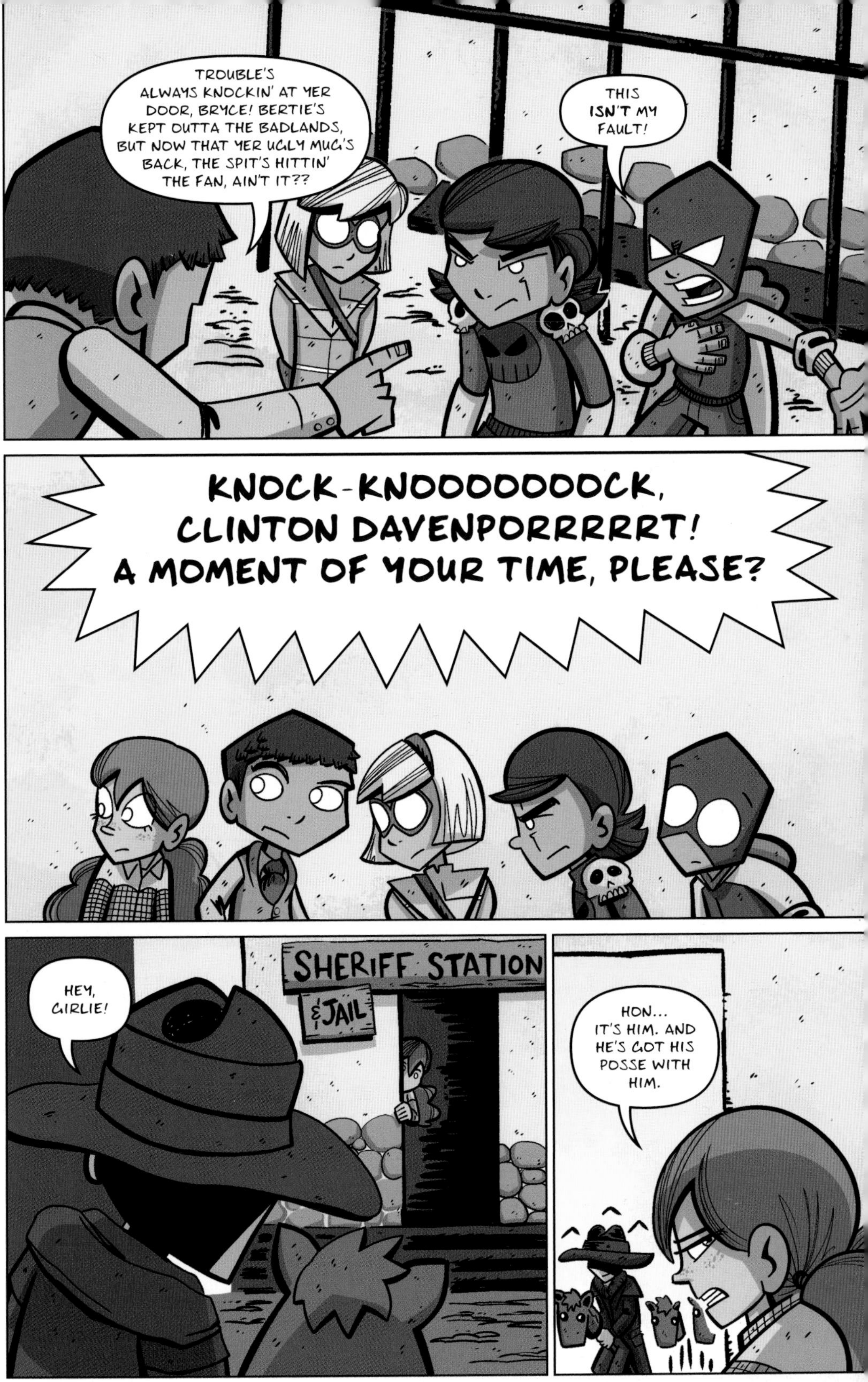
TROUBLE'S ALWAYS KNOCKIN' AT YER DOOR, BRYCE! BERTIE'S KEPT OUTTA THE BADLANDS, BUT NOW THAT YER UGLY MUG'S BACK, THE SPIT'S HITTIN' THE FAN, AIN'T IT??
THIS ISN'T MY FAULT!
KNOCK-KNOOOOOOOCK, CLINTON DAVENPORRRRRT! A MOMENT OF YOUR TIME, PLEASE?
SHERIFF STATION
& JAIL
HEY, GIRLIE!
HON... IT'S HIM. AND HE'S GOT HIS POSSE WITH HIM.

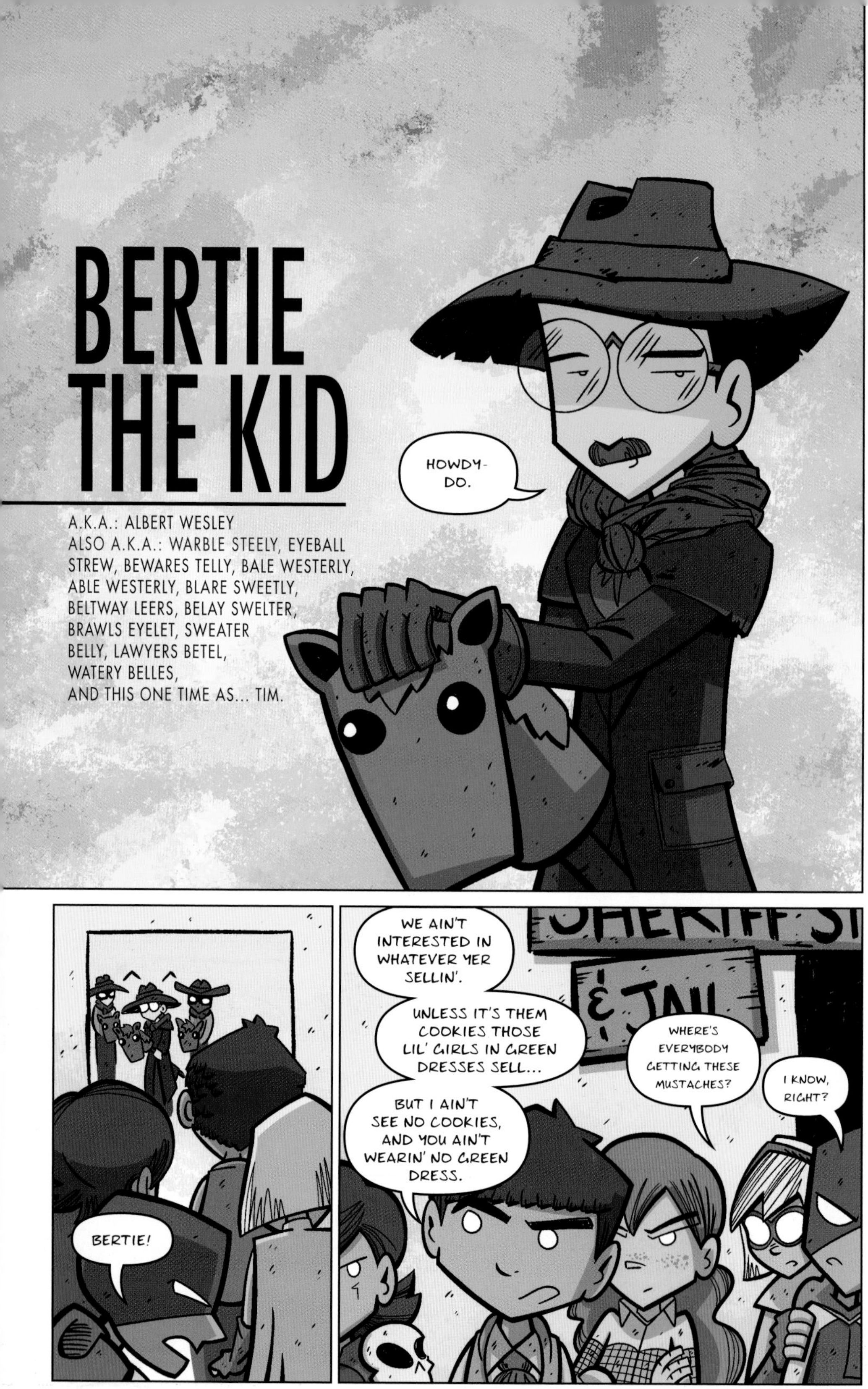
BERTIE THE KID
A.K.A.: ALBERT WESLEY
ALSO A.K.A.: WARBLE STEELY, EYEBALL STREW, BEWARES TELLY, BALE WESTERLY, ABLE WESTERLY, BLARE SWEETLY, BELTWAY LEERS, BELAY SWELTER, BRAWLS EYELET, SWEATER BELLY, LAWYERS BETEL, WATERY BELLES, AND THIS ONE TIME AS... TIM.
HOWDY-DO.
BERTIE!
WE AIN'T INTERESTED IN WHATEVER YER SELLIN'.
UNLESS IT'S THEM COOKIES THOSE LIL' GIRLS IN GREEN DRESSES SELL...
BUT I AIN'T SEE NO COOKIES, AND YOU AIN'T WEARIN' NO GREEN DRESS.
& JAIL
WHERE'S EVERYBODY GETTING THESE MUSTACHES?
I KNOW, RIGHT?

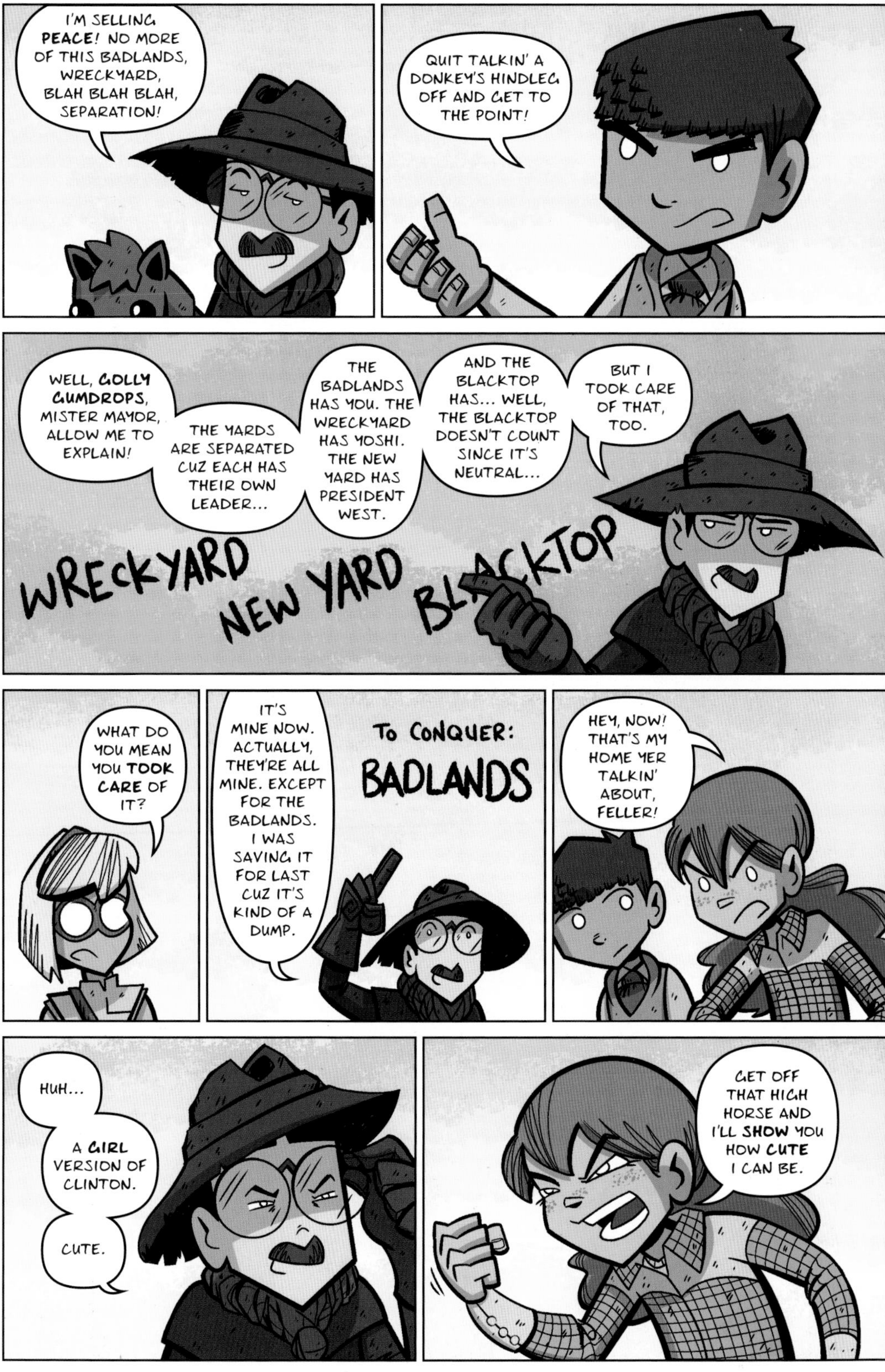
I'M SELLING PEACE! NO MORE OF THIS BADLANDS, WRECKYARD, BLAH BLAH BLAH, SEPARATION!
QUIT TALKIN' A DONKEY'S HINDLEG OFF AND GET TO THE POINT!
WELL, GOLLY GUMDROPS, MISTER MAYOR, ALLOW ME TO EXPLAIN!
THE YARDS ARE SEPARATED CUZ EACH HAS THEIR OWN LEADER...
THE BADLANDS HAS YOU. THE WRECKYARD HAS YOSHI. THE NEW YARD HAS PRESIDENT WEST.
AND THE BLACKTOP HAS... WELL, THE BLACKTOP DOESN'T COUNT SINCE IT'S NEUTRAL...
BUT I TOOK CARE OF THAT, TOO.
WRECKYARD
NEW YARD
BLACKTOP
WHAT DO YOU MEAN YOU TOOK CARE OF IT?
IT'S MINE NOW. ACTUALLY, THEY'RE ALL MINE. EXCEPT FOR THE BADLANDS. I WAS SAVING IT FOR LAST CUZ IT'S KIND OF A DUMP.
To CONQUER:
BADLANDS
HEY, NOW! THAT'S MY HOME YER TALKIN' ABOUT, FELLER!
HUH...
A GIRL VERSION OF CLINTON.
CUTE.
GET OFF THAT HIGH HORSE AND I'LL SHOW YOU HOW CUTE I CAN BE.

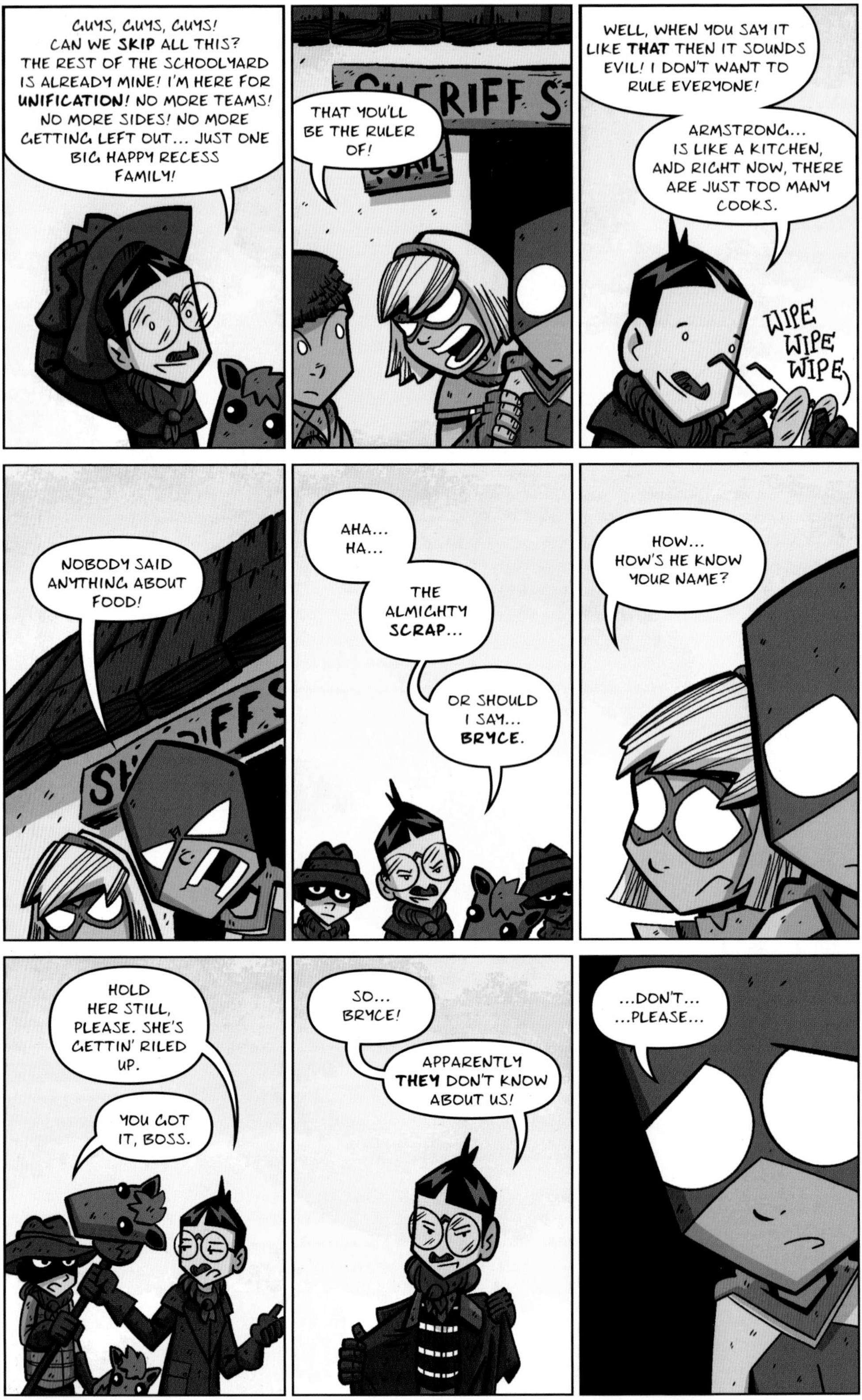
GUYS, GUYS, GUYS! CAN WE SKIP ALL THIS? THE REST OF THE SCHOOLYARD IS ALREADY MINE! I'M HERE FOR UNIFICATION! NO MORE TEAMS! NO MORE SIDES! NO MORE GETTING LEFT OUT... JUST ONE BIG HAPPY RECESS FAMILY!
SHERIFF'S
JAIL
THAT YOU'LL BE THE RULER OF!
WELL, WHEN YOU SAY IT LIKE THAT THEN IT SOUNDS EVIL! I DON'T WANT TO RULE EVERYONE!
ARMSTRONG... IS LIKE A KITCHEN, AND RIGHT NOW, THERE ARE JUST TOO MANY COOKS.
WIPE WIPE WIPE
NOBODY SAID ANYTHING ABOUT FOOD!
AHA... HA...
THE ALMIGHTY SCRAP...
OR SHOULD I SAY... BRYCE.
HOW... HOW'S HE KNOW YOUR NAME?
HOLD HER STILL, PLEASE. SHE'S GETTIN' RILED UP.
YOU GOT IT, BOSS.
SO... BRYCE!
APPARENTLY THEY DON'T KNOW ABOUT US!
...DON'T... ...PLEASE...

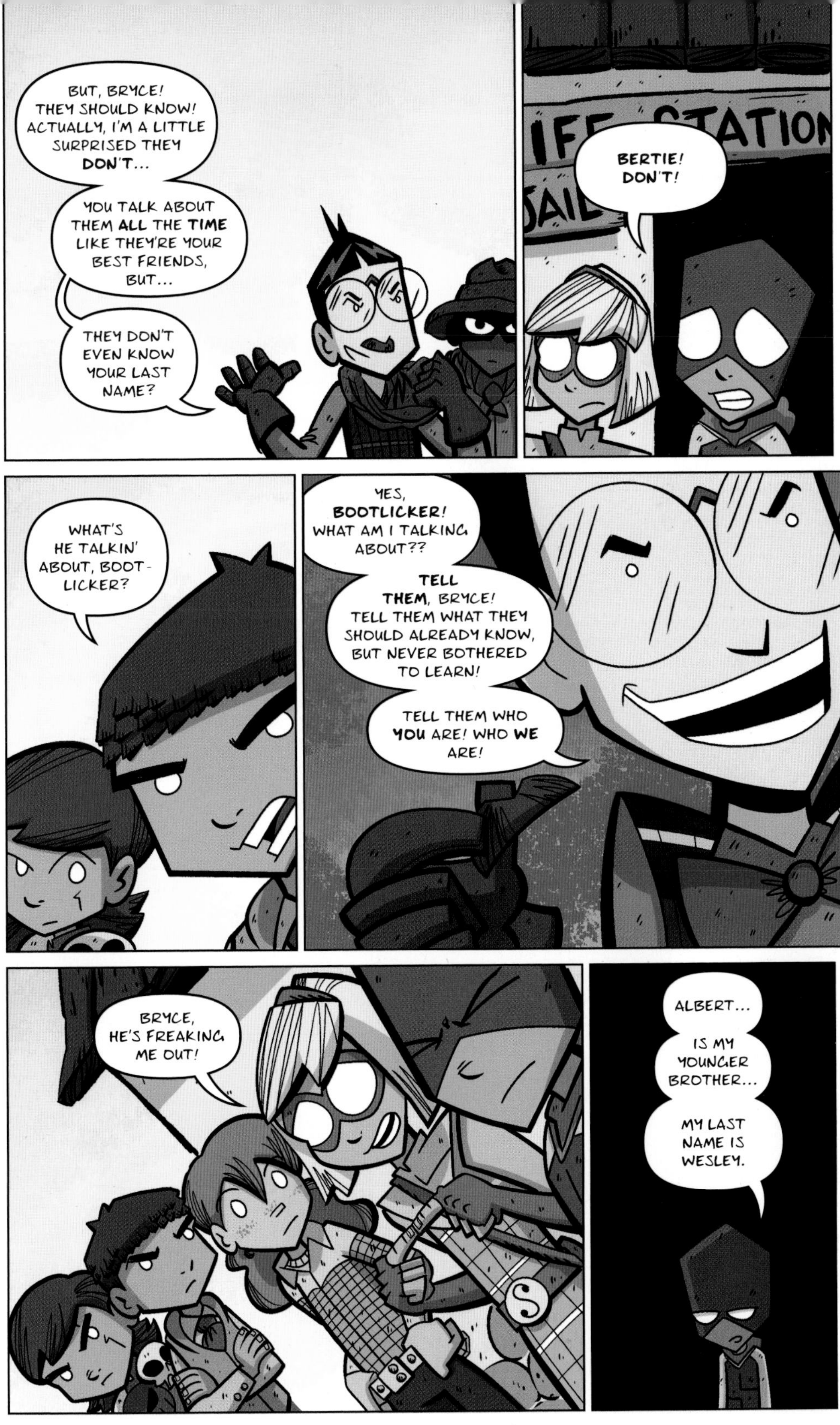
BUT, BRYCE! THEY SHOULD KNOW! ACTUALLY, I'M A LITTLE SURPRISED THEY **DON'T**...
YOU TALK ABOUT THEM **ALL THE TIME** LIKE THEY'RE YOUR BEST FRIENDS, BUT...
THEY DON'T EVEN KNOW YOUR LAST NAME?
LIFE STATION
BERTIE! DON'T!
WHAT'S HE TALKIN' ABOUT, BOOT-LICKER?
YES, **BOOTLICKER**! WHAT AM I TALKING ABOUT??
TELL THEM, BRYCE! TELL THEM WHAT THEY SHOULD ALREADY KNOW, BUT NEVER BOTHERED TO LEARN!
TELL THEM WHO **YOU** ARE! WHO **WE** ARE!
BRYCE, HE'S FREAKING ME OUT!
ALBERT...
IS MY YOUNGER BROTHER...
MY LAST NAME IS WESLEY.

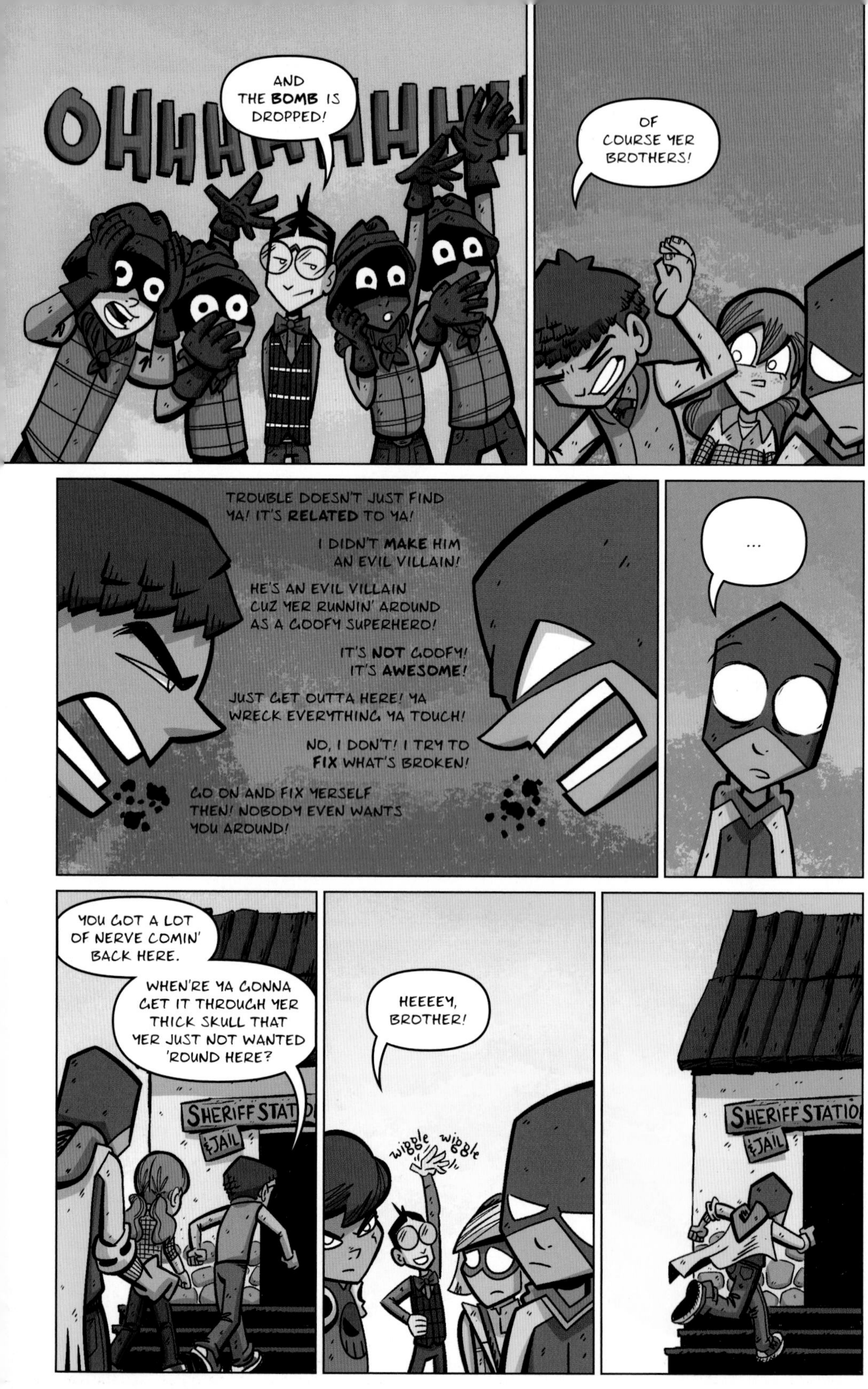
OHHHHHHHHH
AND THE BOMB IS DROPPED!
OF COURSE YER BROTHERS!
TROUBLE DOESN'T JUST FIND YA! IT'S RELATED TO YA!
I DIDN'T MAKE HIM AN EVIL VILLAIN!
HE'S AN EVIL VILLAIN CUZ YER RUNNIN' AROUND AS A GOOFY SUPERHERO!
IT'S NOT GOOFY! IT'S AWESOME!
JUST GET OUTTA HERE! YA WRECK EVERYTHING YA TOUCH!
NO, I DON'T! I TRY TO FIX WHAT'S BROKEN!
GO ON AND FIX YERSELF THEN! NOBODY EVEN WANTS YOU AROUND!
...
YOU GOT A LOT OF NERVE COMIN' BACK HERE.
WHEN'RE YA GONNA GET IT THROUGH YER THICK SKULL THAT YER JUST NOT WANTED 'ROUND HERE?
SHERIFF STATIO
& JAIL
HEEEEY, BROTHER!
wiggle wiggle
SHERIFF STATIO
& JAIL

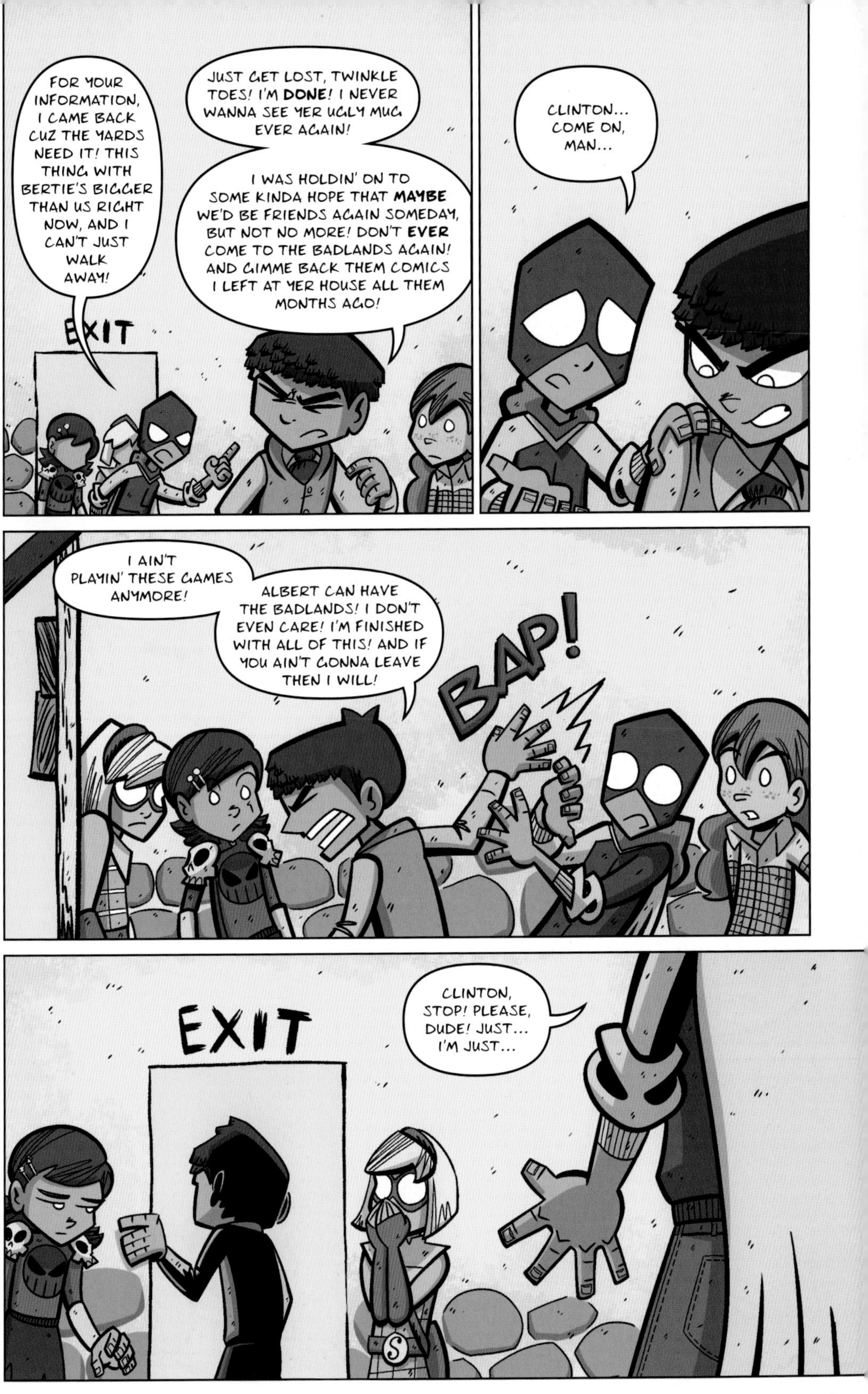

FOR YOUR INFORMATION, I CAME BACK CUZ THE YARDS NEED IT! THIS THING WITH BERTIE'S BIGGER THAN US RIGHT NOW, AND I CAN'T JUST WALK AWAY!
JUST GET LOST, TWINKLE TOES! I'M **DONE**! I NEVER WANNA SEE YER UGLY MUG EVER AGAIN!
I WAS HOLDIN' ON TO SOME KINDA HOPE THAT **MAYBE** WE'D BE FRIENDS AGAIN SOMEDAY, BUT NOT NO MORE! DON'T **EVER** COME TO THE BADLANDS AGAIN! AND GIMME BACK THEM COMICS I LEFT AT YER HOUSE ALL THEM MONTHS AGO!
EXIT
CLINTON... COME ON, MAN...
I AIN'T PLAYIN' THESE GAMES ANYMORE!
ALBERT CAN HAVE THE BADLANDS! I DON'T EVEN CARE! I'M FINISHED WITH ALL OF THIS! AND IF YOU AIN'T GONNA LEAVE THEN I WILL!
BAP!
EXIT
CLINTON, STOP! PLEASE, DUDE! JUST... I'M JUST...

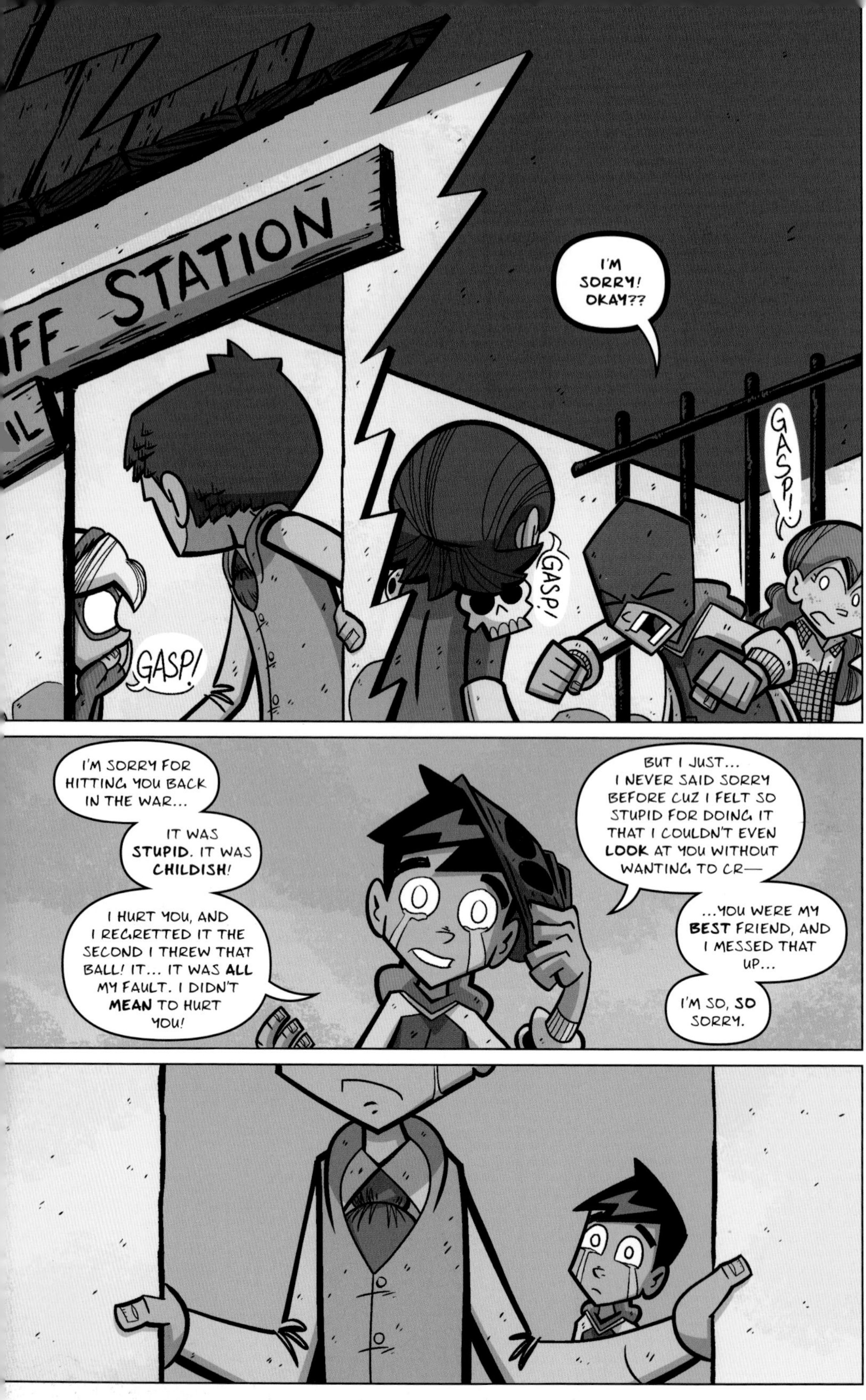

FF STATION
IL
I'M SORRY! OKAY??
GASP!
GASP!
GASP!
I'M SORRY FOR HITTING YOU BACK IN THE WAR...
IT WAS STUPID. IT WAS CHILDISH!
I HURT YOU, AND I REGRETTED IT THE SECOND I THREW THAT BALL! IT... IT WAS ALL MY FAULT. I DIDN'T MEAN TO HURT YOU!
BUT I JUST... I NEVER SAID SORRY BEFORE CUZ I FELT SO STUPID FOR DOING IT THAT I COULDN'T EVEN LOOK AT YOU WITHOUT WANTING TO CR—
...YOU WERE MY BEST FRIEND, AND I MESSED THAT UP...
I'M SO, SO SORRY.

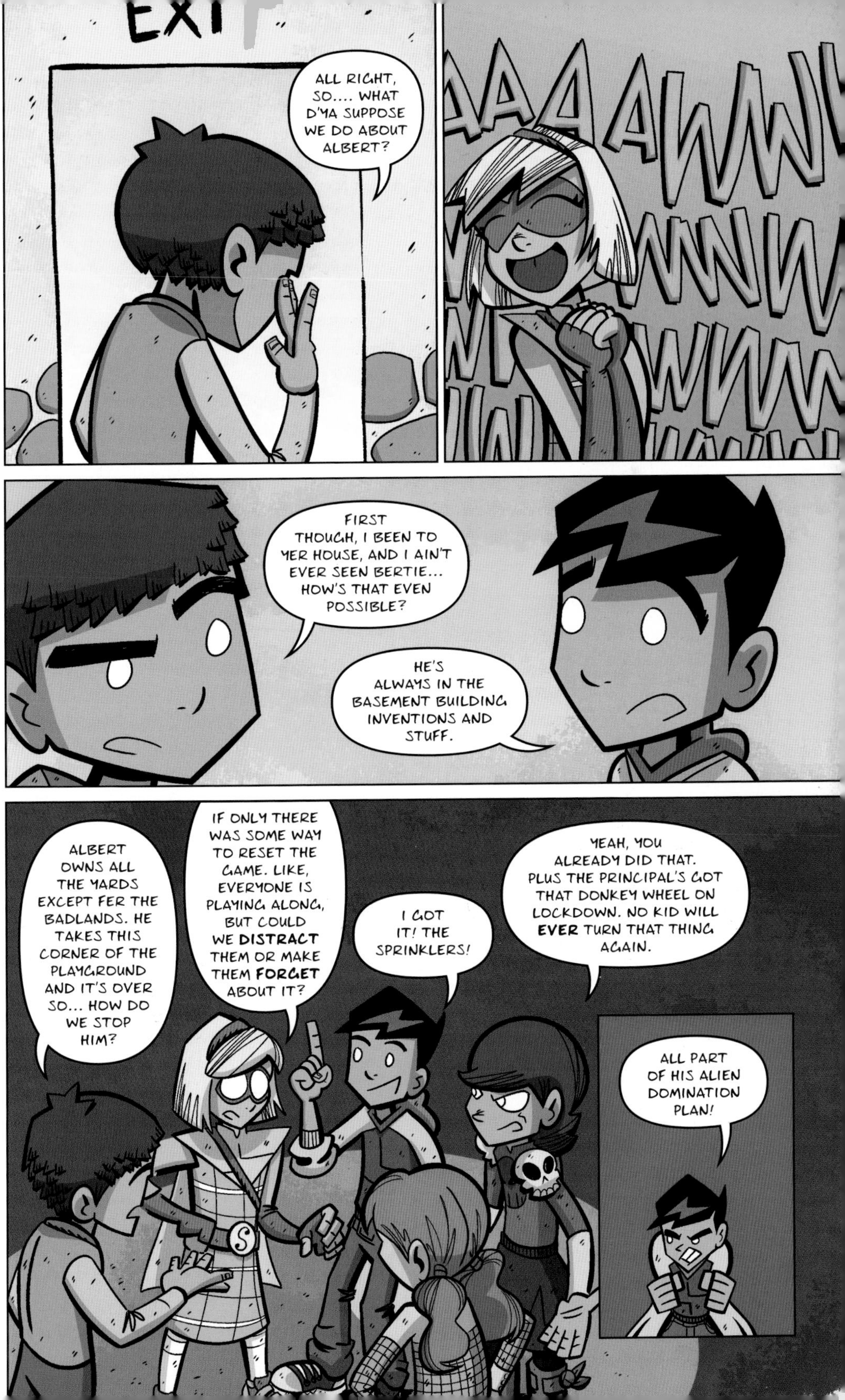
EXI
ALL RIGHT, SO.... WHAT D'YA SUPPOSE WE DO ABOUT ALBERT?
AAAAWWWWWWWWWWWW
FIRST THOUGH, I BEEN TO YER HOUSE, AND I AIN'T EVER SEEN BERTIE... HOW'S THAT EVEN POSSIBLE?
HE'S ALWAYS IN THE BASEMENT BUILDING INVENTIONS AND STUFF.
ALBERT OWNS ALL THE YARDS EXCEPT FER THE BADLANDS. HE TAKES THIS CORNER OF THE PLAYGROUND AND IT'S OVER SO... HOW DO WE STOP HIM?
IF ONLY THERE WAS SOME WAY TO RESET THE GAME. LIKE, EVERYONE IS PLAYING ALONG, BUT COULD WE DISTRACT THEM OR MAKE THEM FORGET ABOUT IT?
I GOT IT! THE SPRINKLERS!
YEAH, YOU ALREADY DID THAT. PLUS THE PRINCIPAL'S GOT THAT DONKEY WHEEL ON LOCKDOWN. NO KID WILL EVER TURN THAT THING AGAIN.
ALL PART OF HIS ALIEN DOMINATION PLAN!

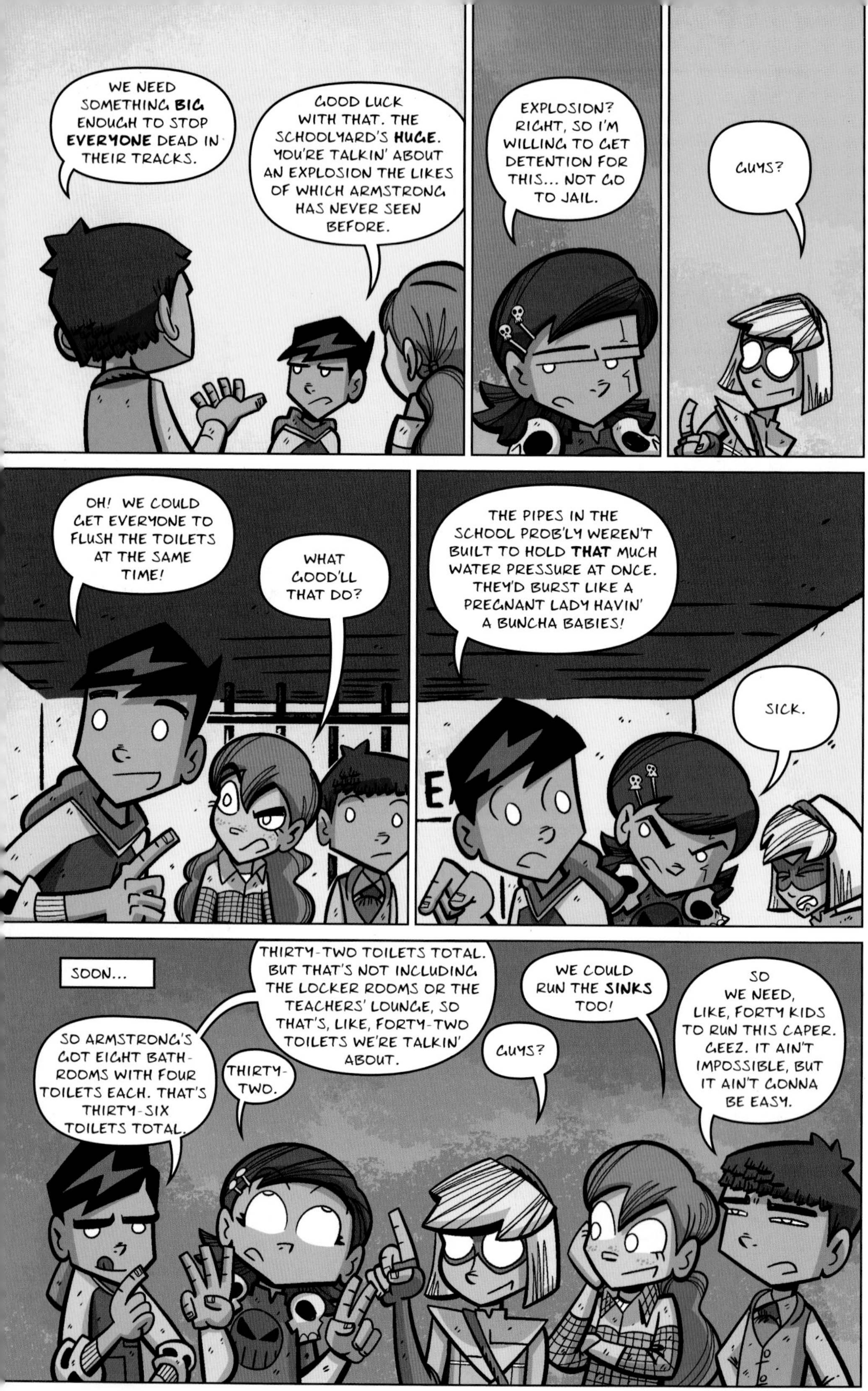
WE NEED SOMETHING BIG ENOUGH TO STOP EVERYONE DEAD IN THEIR TRACKS.
GOOD LUCK WITH THAT. THE SCHOOLYARD'S HUGE. YOU'RE TALKIN' ABOUT AN EXPLOSION THE LIKES OF WHICH ARMSTRONG HAS NEVER SEEN BEFORE.
EXPLOSION? RIGHT, SO I'M WILLING TO GET DETENTION FOR THIS... NOT GO TO JAIL.
GUYS?
OH! WE COULD GET EVERYONE TO FLUSH THE TOILETS AT THE SAME TIME!
WHAT GOOD'LL THAT DO?
THE PIPES IN THE SCHOOL PROB'LY WEREN'T BUILT TO HOLD THAT MUCH WATER PRESSURE AT ONCE. THEY'D BURST LIKE A PREGNANT LADY HAVIN' A BUNCHA BABIES!
SICK.
SOON...
SO ARMSTRONG'S GOT EIGHT BATHROOMS WITH FOUR TOILETS EACH. THAT'S THIRTY-SIX TOILETS TOTAL.
THIRTY-TWO.
THIRTY-TWO TOILETS TOTAL. BUT THAT'S NOT INCLUDING THE LOCKER ROOMS OR THE TEACHERS' LOUNGE, SO THAT'S, LIKE, FORTY-TWO TOILETS WE'RE TALKIN' ABOUT.
GUYS?
WE COULD RUN THE SINKS TOO!
SO WE NEED, LIKE, FORTY KIDS TO RUN THIS CAPER. GEEZ. IT AIN'T IMPOSSIBLE, BUT IT AIN'T GONNA BE EASY.

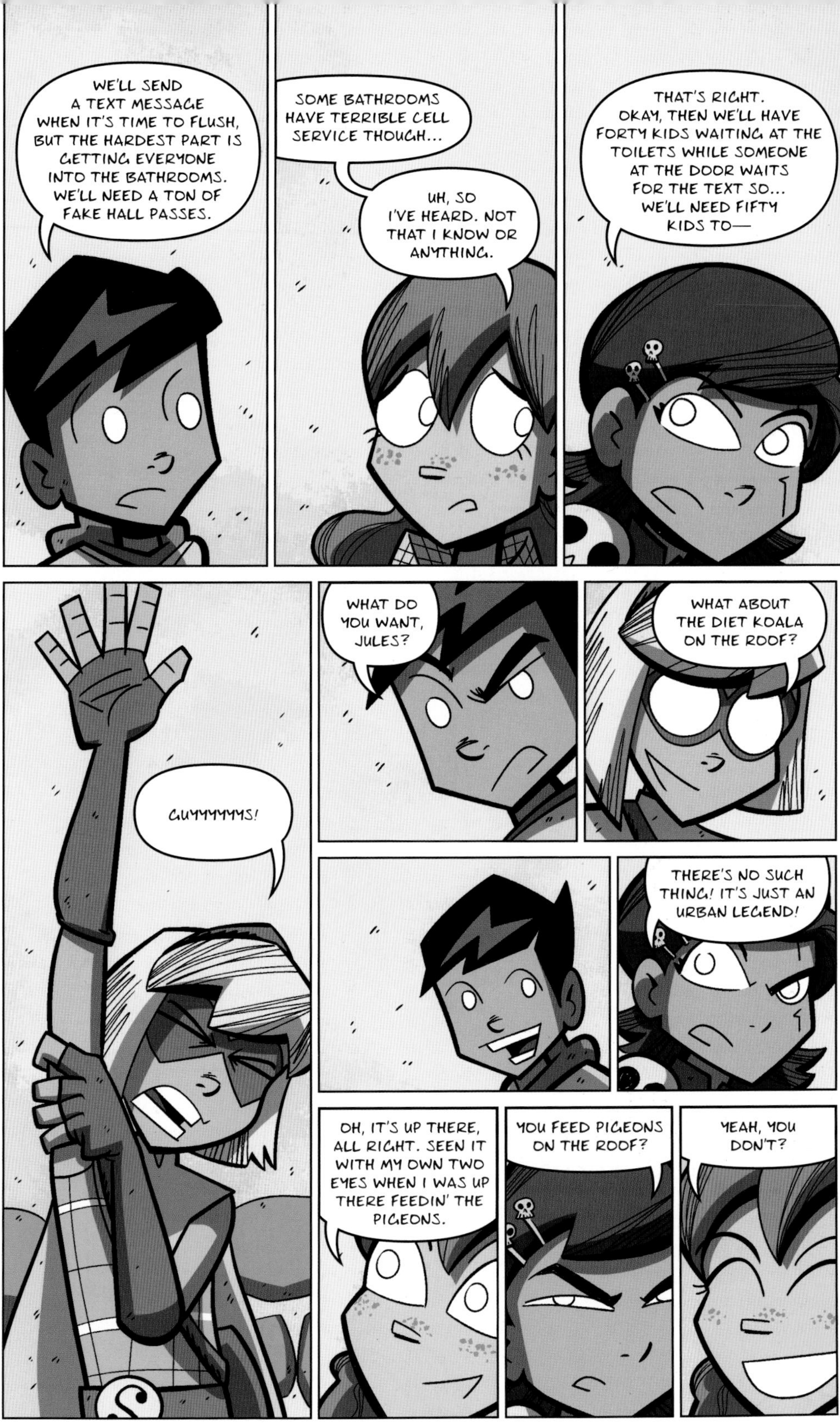
WE'LL SEND A TEXT MESSAGE WHEN IT'S TIME TO FLUSH, BUT THE HARDEST PART IS GETTING EVERYONE INTO THE BATHROOMS. WE'LL NEED A TON OF FAKE HALL PASSES.
SOME BATHROOMS HAVE TERRIBLE CELL SERVICE THOUGH...
UH, SO I'VE HEARD. NOT THAT I KNOW OR ANYTHING.
THAT'S RIGHT. OKAY, THEN WE'LL HAVE FORTY KIDS WAITING AT THE TOILETS WHILE SOMEONE AT THE DOOR WAITS FOR THE TEXT SO... WE'LL NEED FIFTY KIDS TO—
GUYYYYYYS!
WHAT DO YOU WANT, JULES?
WHAT ABOUT THE DIET KOALA ON THE ROOF?
THERE'S NO SUCH THING! IT'S JUST AN URBAN LEGEND!
OH, IT'S UP THERE, ALL RIGHT. SEEN IT WITH MY OWN TWO EYES WHEN I WAS UP THERE FEEDIN' THE PIGEONS.
YOU FEED PIGEONS ON THE ROOF?
YEAH, YOU DON'T?

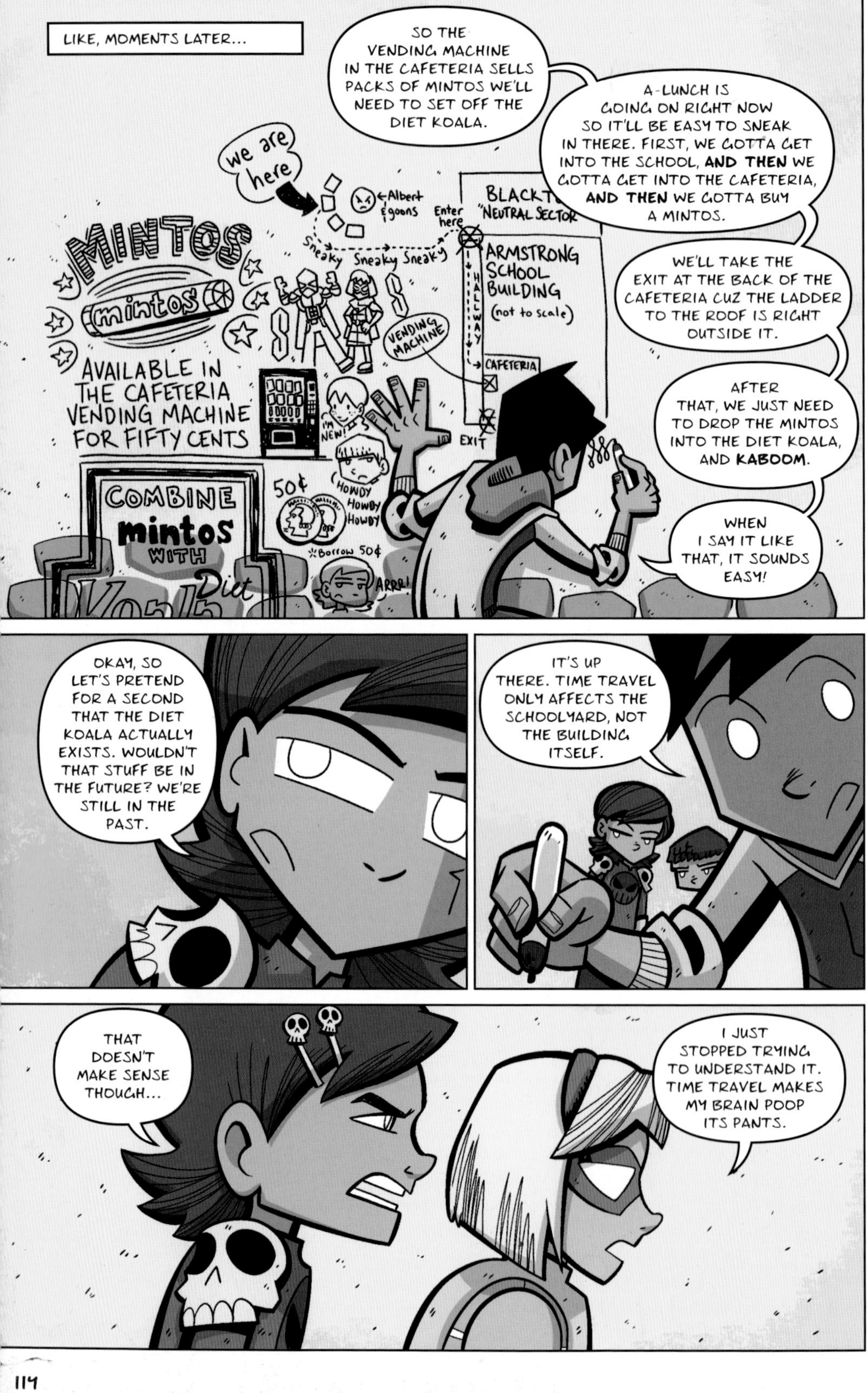

LIKE, MOMENTS LATER...
SO THE VENDING MACHINE IN THE CAFETERIA SELLS PACKS OF MINTOS WE'LL NEED TO SET OFF THE DIET KOALA.
A-LUNCH IS GOING ON RIGHT NOW SO IT'LL BE EASY TO SNEAK IN THERE. FIRST, WE GOTTA GET INTO THE SCHOOL, **AND THEN** WE GOTTA GET INTO THE CAFETERIA, **AND THEN** WE GOTTA BUY A MINTOS.
we are here
Albert & goons
Enter here
Sneaky Sneaky Sneaky
MINTOS
mintos
AVAILABLE IN THE CAFETERIA VENDING MACHINE FOR FIFTY CENTS
VENDING MACHINE
HALLWAY
CAFETERIA
EXIT
ARMSTRONG SCHOOL BUILDING
(not to scale)
I'M NEW!
HOWDY HOWDY HOWDY
50¢
Borrow 50¢
ARRR!
COMBINE mintos WITH Diet
WE'LL TAKE THE EXIT AT THE BACK OF THE CAFETERIA CUZ THE LADDER TO THE ROOF IS RIGHT OUTSIDE IT.
AFTER THAT, WE JUST NEED TO DROP THE MINTOS INTO THE DIET KOALA, AND **KABOOM**.
WHEN I SAY IT LIKE THAT, IT SOUNDS EASY!
OKAY, SO LET'S PRETEND FOR A SECOND THAT THE DIET KOALA ACTUALLY EXISTS. WOULDN'T THAT STUFF BE IN THE FUTURE? WE'RE STILL IN THE PAST.
IT'S UP THERE. TIME TRAVEL ONLY AFFECTS THE SCHOOLYARD, NOT THE BUILDING ITSELF.
THAT DOESN'T MAKE SENSE THOUGH...
I JUST STOPPED TRYING TO UNDERSTAND IT. TIME TRAVEL MAKES MY BRAIN POOP ITS PANTS.

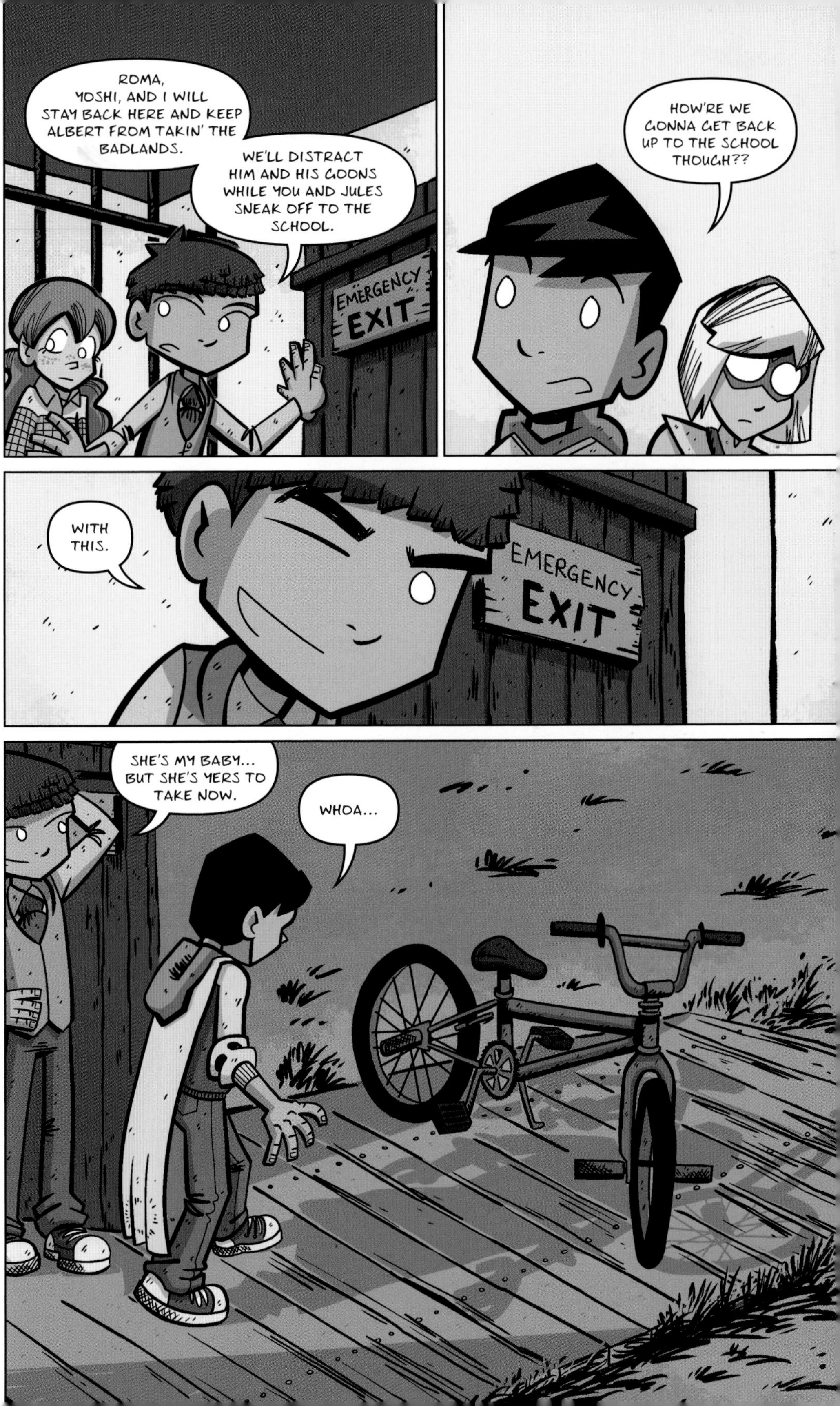
ROMA, YOSHI, AND I WILL STAY BACK HERE AND KEEP ALBERT FROM TAKIN' THE BADLANDS.
WE'LL DISTRACT HIM AND HIS GOONS WHILE YOU AND JULES SNEAK OFF TO THE SCHOOL.
EMERGENCY EXIT
HOW'RE WE GONNA GET BACK UP TO THE SCHOOL THOUGH??
WITH THIS.
EMERGENCY EXIT
SHE'S MY BABY... BUT SHE'S YERS TO TAKE NOW.
WHOA...

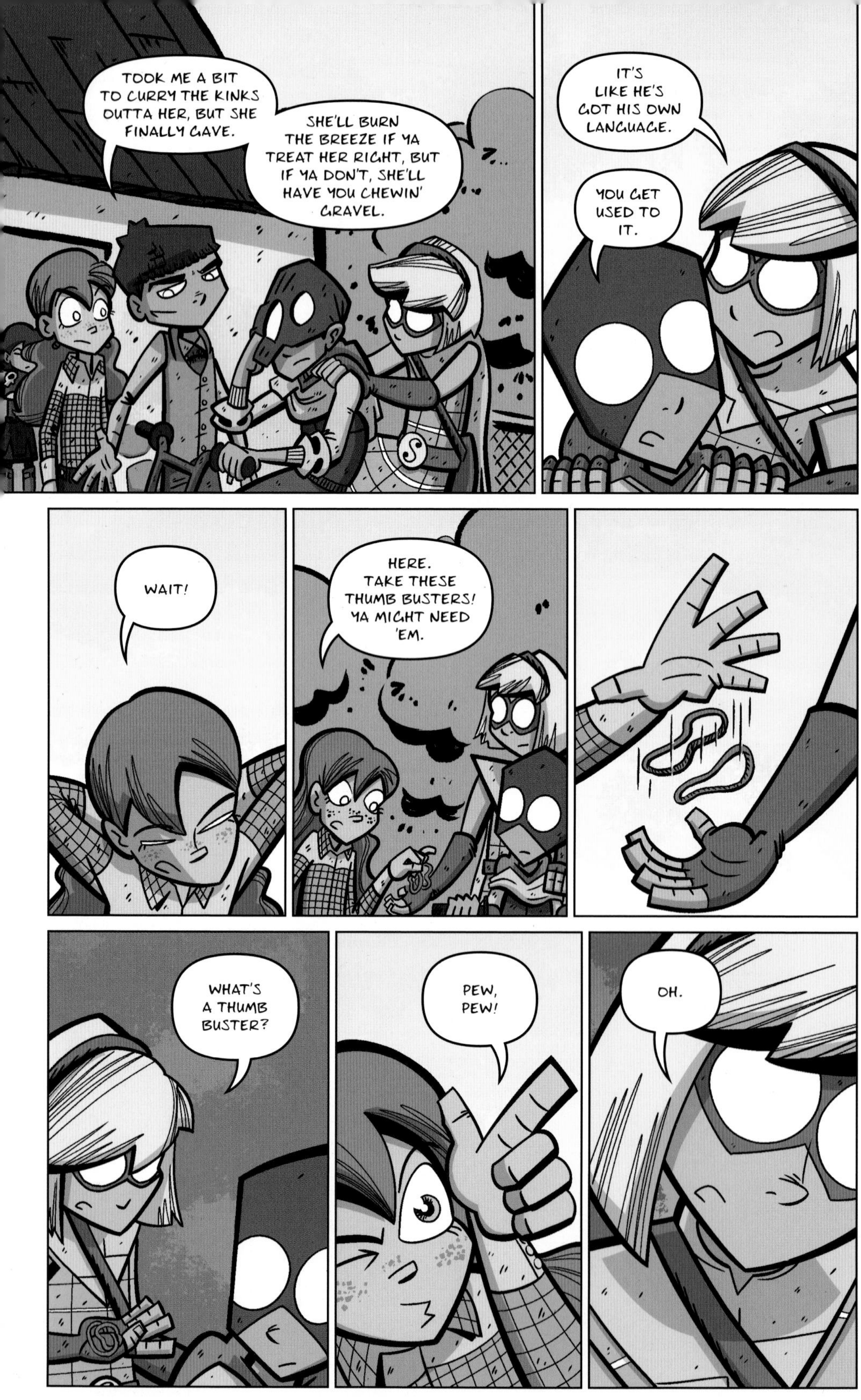
TOOK ME A BIT TO CURRY THE KINKS OUTTA HER, BUT SHE FINALLY GAVE.
SHE'LL BURN THE BREEZE IF YA TREAT HER RIGHT, BUT IF YA DON'T, SHE'LL HAVE YOU CHEWIN' GRAVEL.
IT'S LIKE HE'S GOT HIS OWN LANGUAGE.
YOU GET USED TO IT.
WAIT!
HERE. TAKE THESE THUMB BUSTERS! YA MIGHT NEED 'EM.
WHAT'S A THUMB BUSTER?
PEW, PEW!
OH.

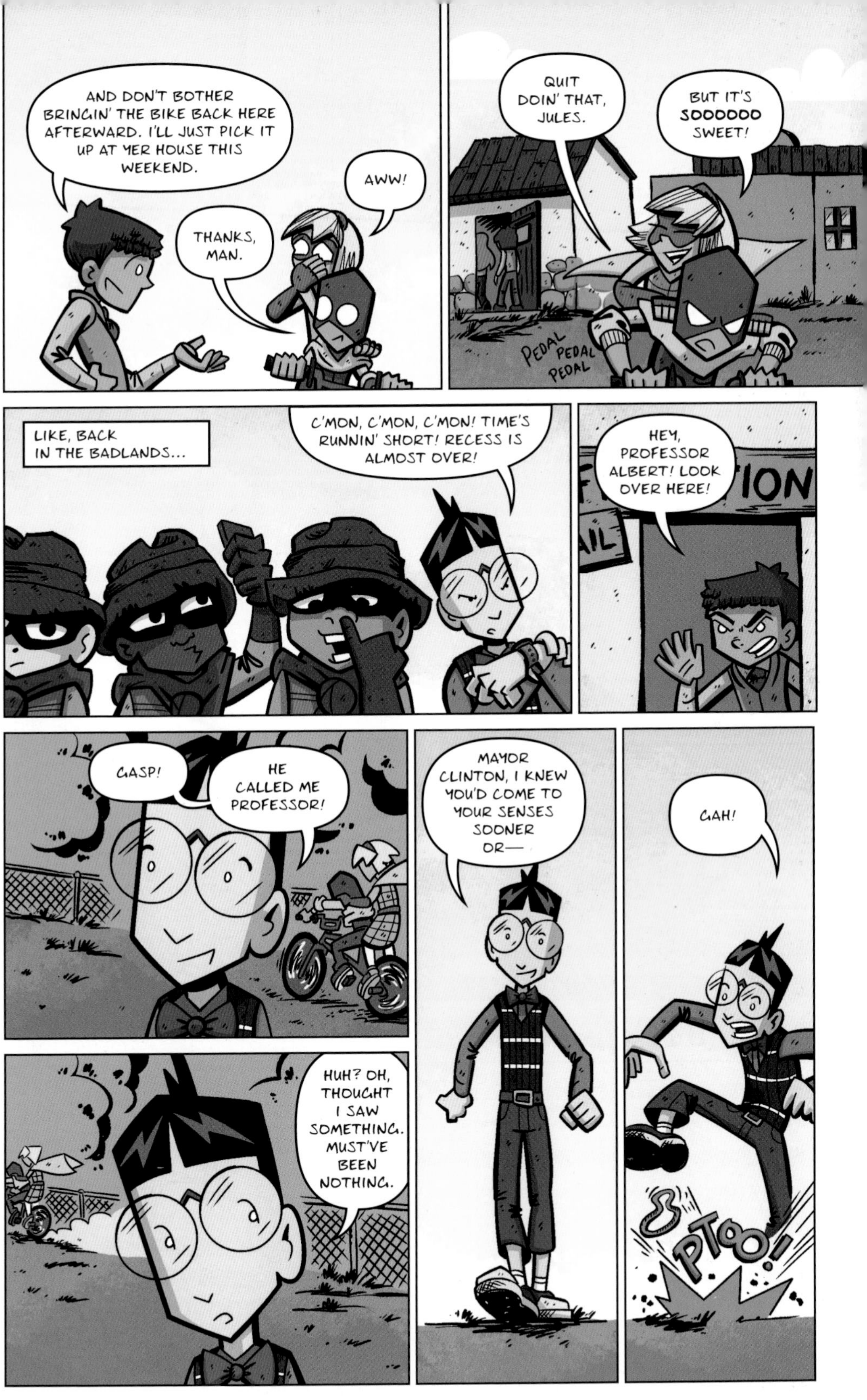
AND DON'T BOTHER BRINGIN' THE BIKE BACK HERE AFTERWARD. I'LL JUST PICK IT UP AT YER HOUSE THIS WEEKEND.
AWW!
THANKS, MAN.
QUIT DOIN' THAT, JULES.
BUT IT'S SOOOOOO SWEET!
PEDAL PEDAL PEDAL
LIKE, BACK IN THE BADLANDS...
C'MON, C'MON, C'MON! TIME'S RUNNIN' SHORT! RECESS IS ALMOST OVER!
HEY, PROFESSOR ALBERT! LOOK OVER HERE!
GASP!
HE CALLED ME PROFESSOR!
HUH? OH, THOUGHT I SAW SOMETHING. MUST'VE BEEN NOTHING.
MAYOR CLINTON, I KNEW YOU'D COME TO YOUR SENSES SOONER OR—
GAH!
PTOO!

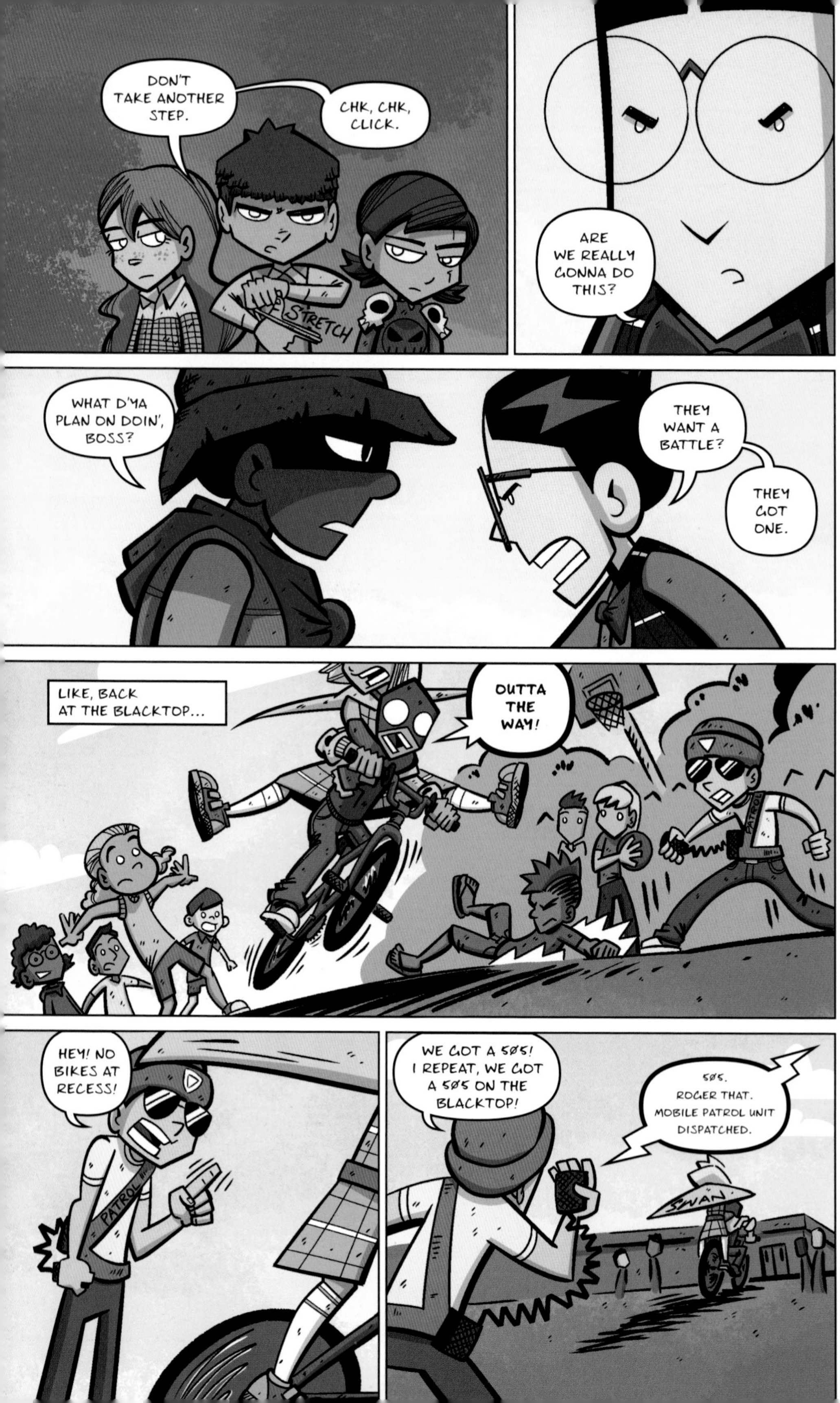
DON'T TAKE ANOTHER STEP.
CHK, CHK, CLICK.
STRETCH
ARE WE REALLY GONNA DO THIS?
WHAT D'YA PLAN ON DOIN', BOSS?
THEY WANT A BATTLE?
THEY GOT ONE.
LIKE, BACK AT THE BLACKTOP...
OUTTA THE WAY!
PATROL
HEY! NO BIKES AT RECESS!
PATROL
WE GOT A 5Ø5! I REPEAT, WE GOT A 5Ø5 ON THE BLACKTOP!
5Ø5. ROGER THAT. MOBILE PATROL UNIT DISPATCHED.
SWAN

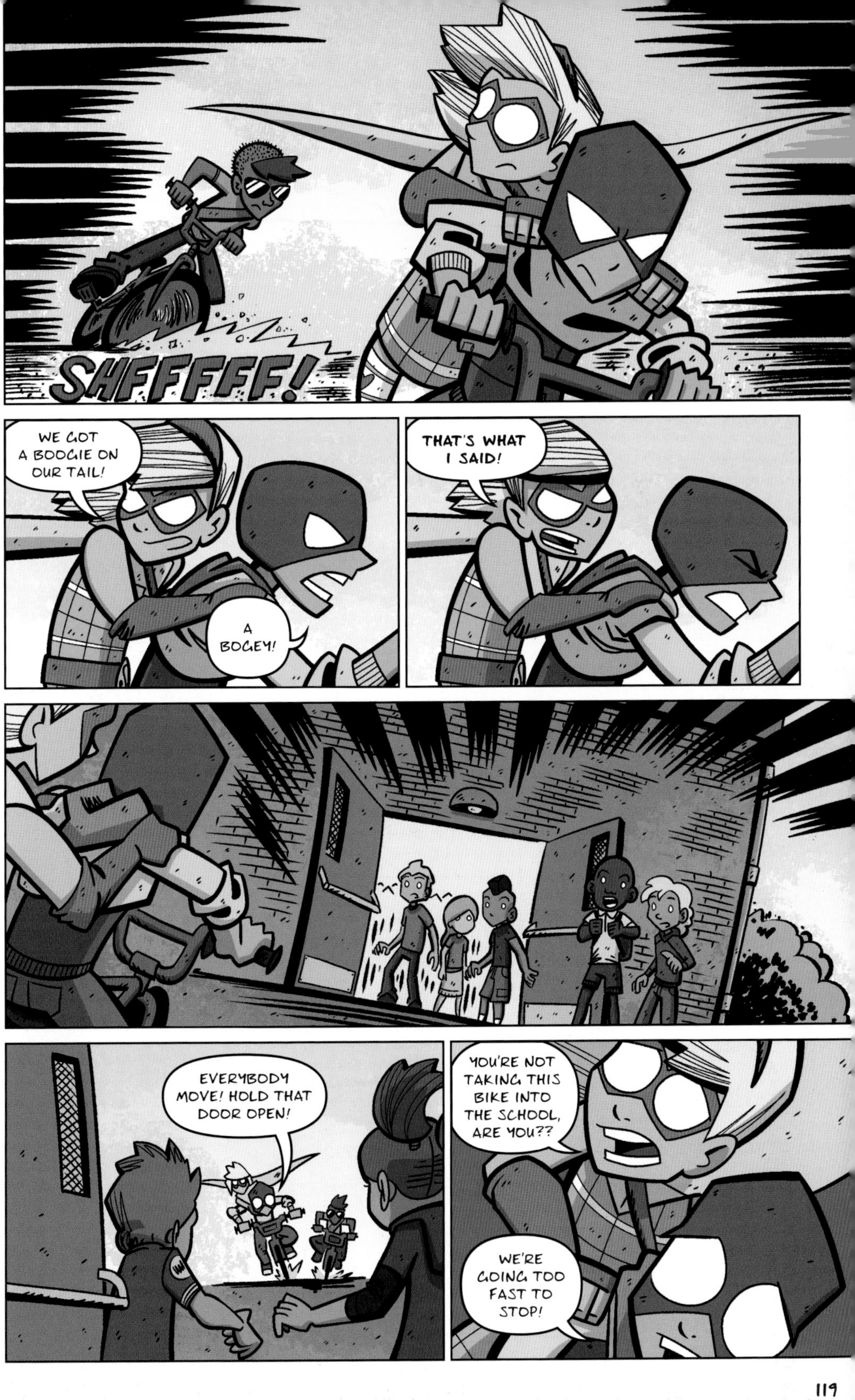
SHFFFFF!
WE GOT A BOOGIE ON OUR TAIL!
A BOGEY!
THAT'S WHAT I SAID!
EVERYBODY MOVE! HOLD THAT DOOR OPEN!
YOU'RE NOT TAKING THIS BIKE INTO THE SCHOOL, ARE YOU??
WE'RE GOING TOO FAST TO STOP!

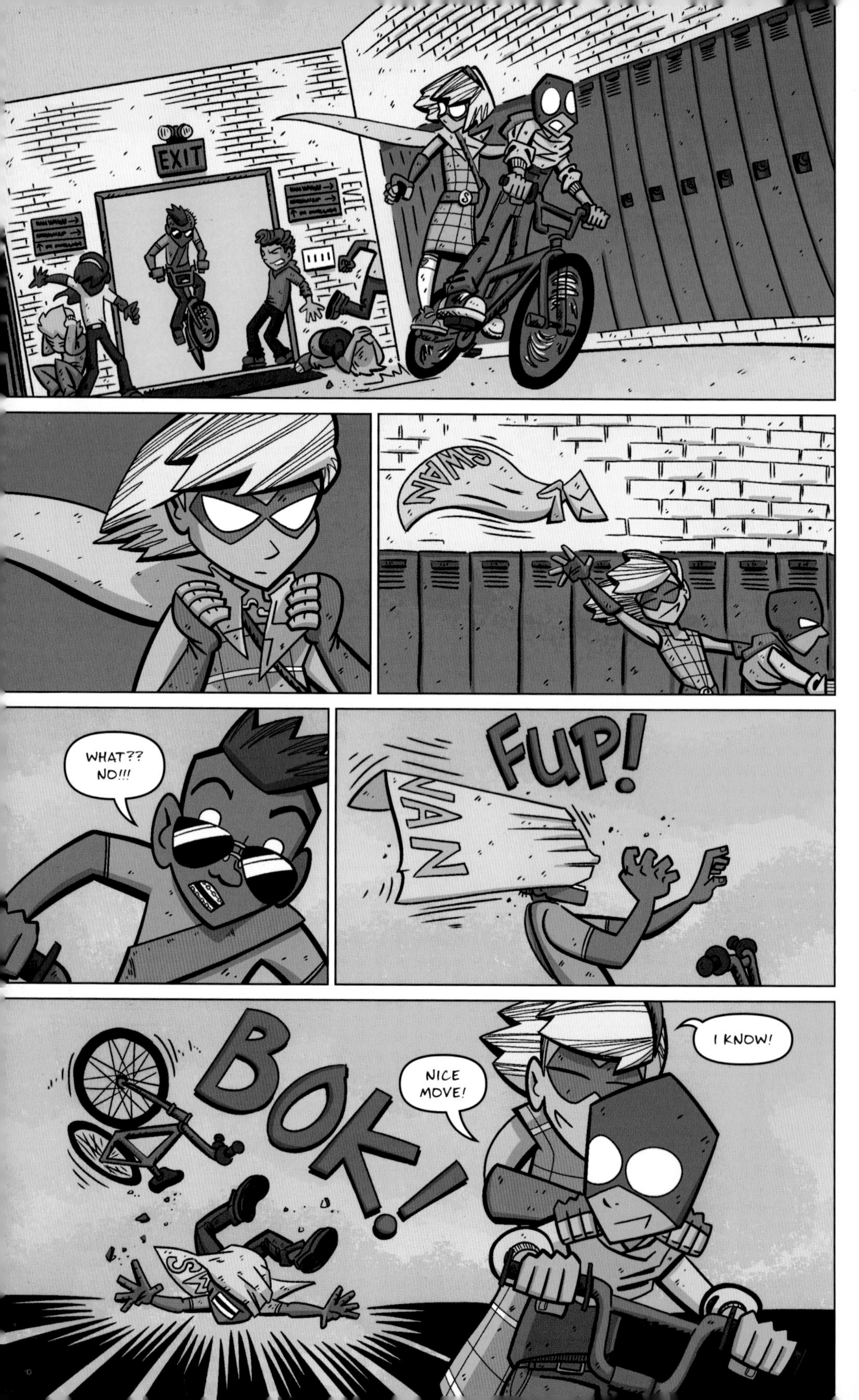
EXIT
SWAN
WHAT?? NO!!!
FUP!
NAN
BOK!
NICE MOVE!
I KNOW!

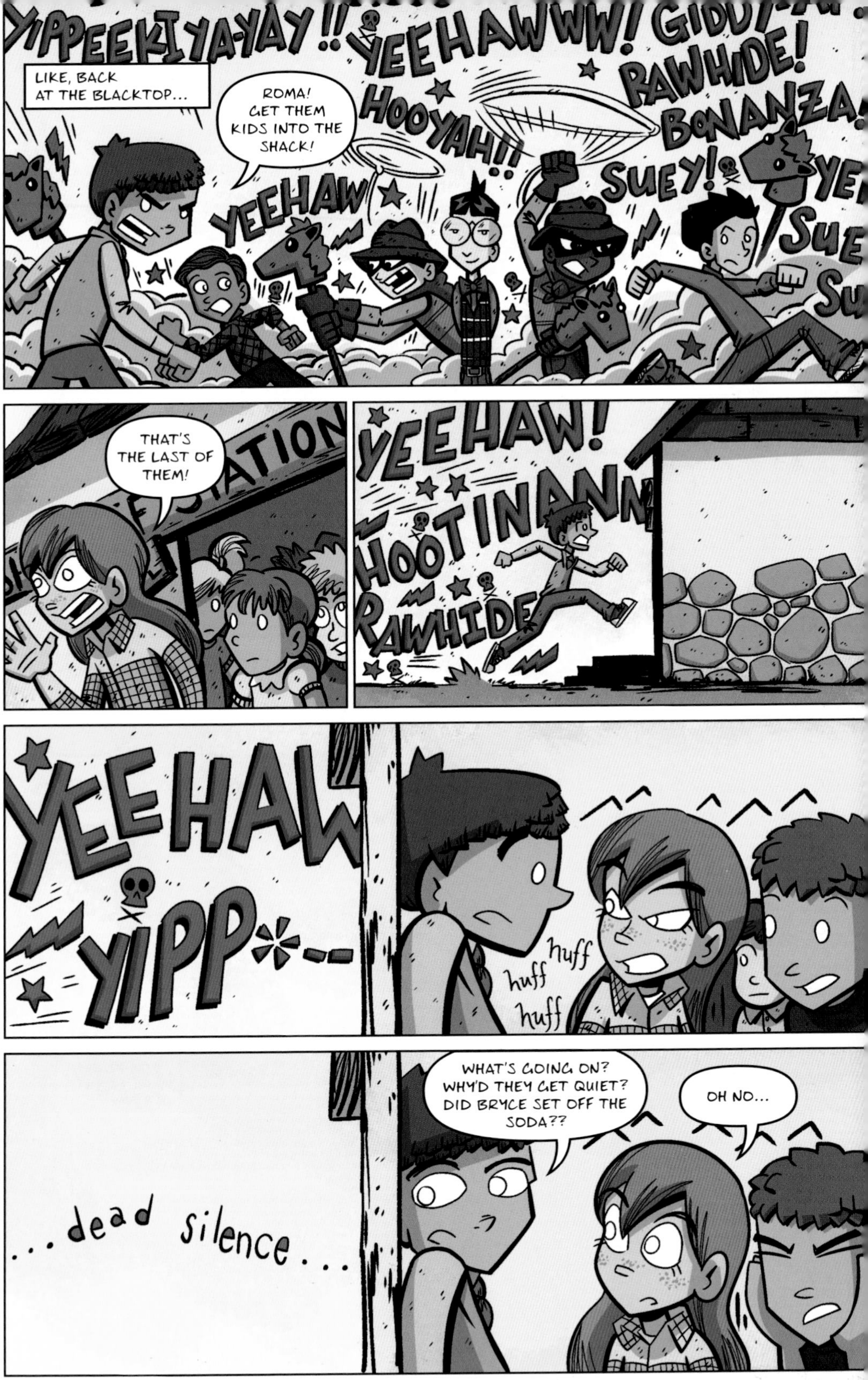
YIPPEEKIYA-YAY!!
YEEHAWWW!
LIKE, BACK AT THE BLACKTOP...
ROMA! GET THEM KIDS INTO THE SHACK!
RAWHIDE!
HOOYAH!!
BONANZA!
YEEHAW
SUEY!
THAT'S THE LAST OF THEM!
STATION
YEEHAW!
HOOTINANN
RAWHIDE
YEEHAW
YIPP
huff huff huff
...dead silence...
WHAT'S GOING ON? WHY'D THEY GET QUIET? DID BRYCE SET OFF THE SODA??
OH NO...

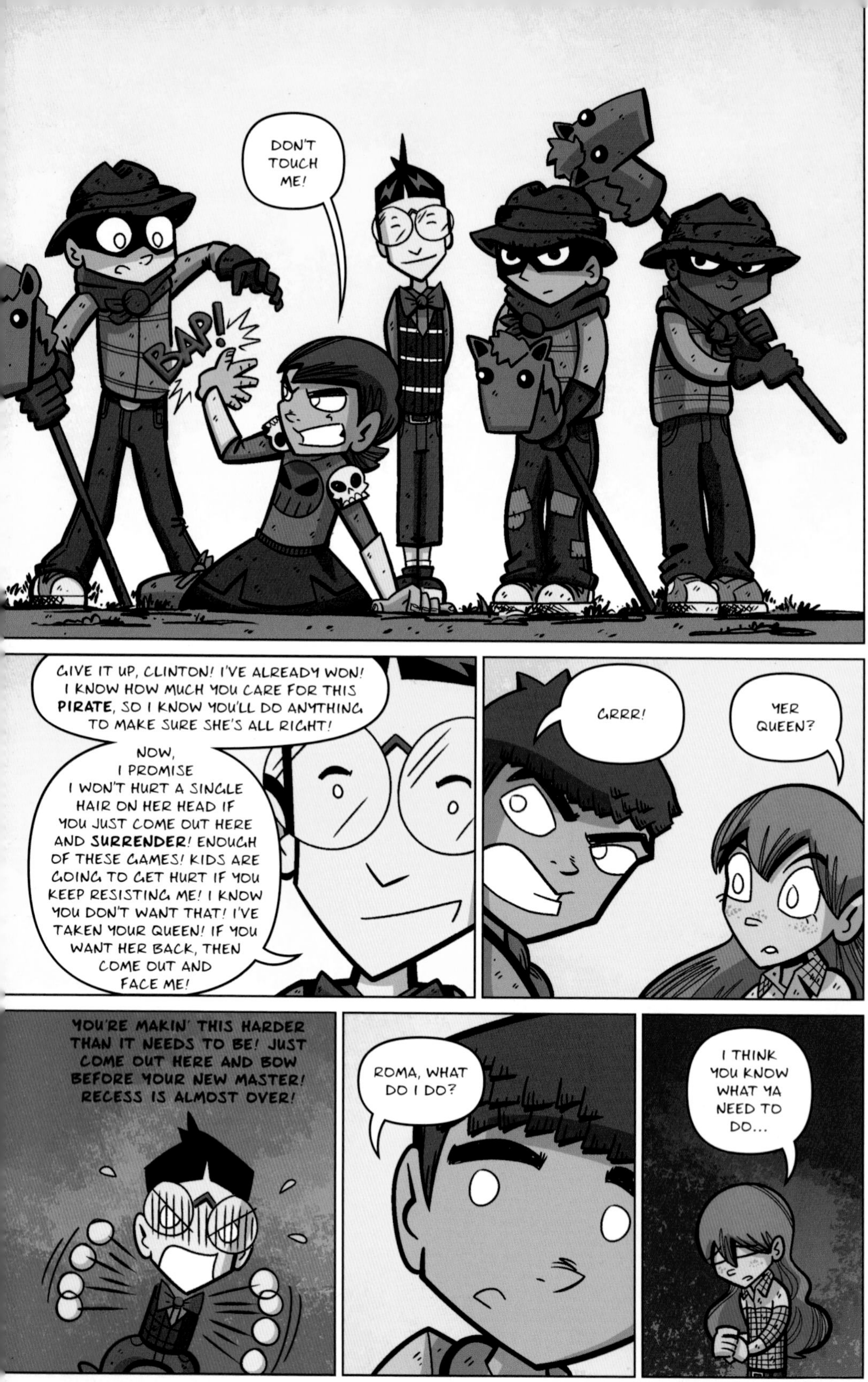
DON'T TOUCH ME!
BAP!
GIVE IT UP, CLINTON! I'VE ALREADY WON! I KNOW HOW MUCH YOU CARE FOR THIS PIRATE, SO I KNOW YOU'LL DO ANYTHING TO MAKE SURE SHE'S ALL RIGHT!
NOW, I PROMISE I WON'T HURT A SINGLE HAIR ON HER HEAD IF YOU JUST COME OUT HERE AND SURRENDER! ENOUGH OF THESE GAMES! KIDS ARE GOING TO GET HURT IF YOU KEEP RESISTING ME! I KNOW YOU DON'T WANT THAT! I'VE TAKEN YOUR QUEEN! IF YOU WANT HER BACK, THEN COME OUT AND FACE ME!
GRRR!
YER QUEEN?
YOU'RE MAKIN' THIS HARDER THAN IT NEEDS TO BE! JUST COME OUT HERE AND BOW BEFORE YOUR NEW MASTER! RECESS IS ALMOST OVER!
ROMA, WHAT DO I DO?
I THINK YOU KNOW WHAT YA NEED TO DO...

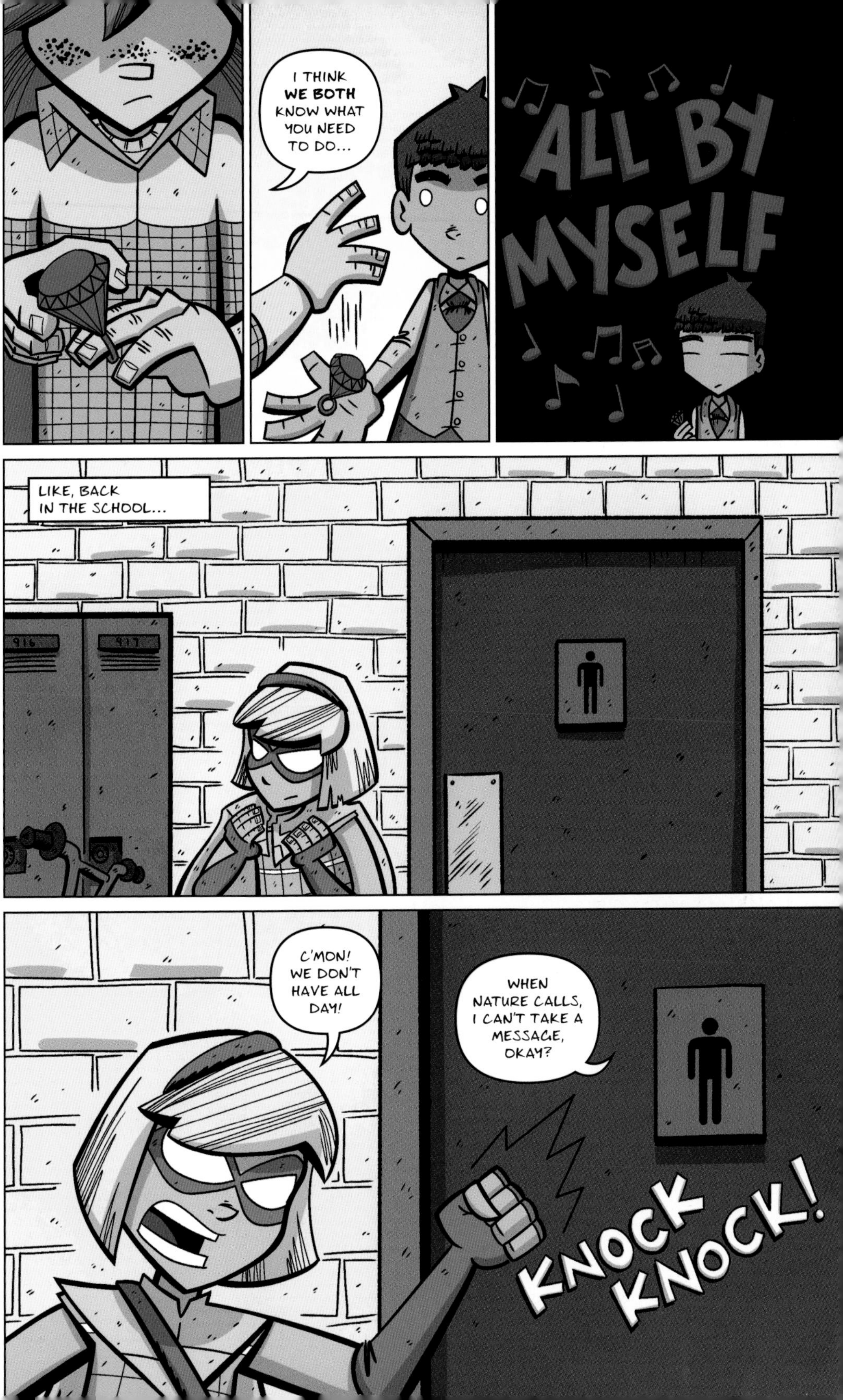
I THINK WE BOTH KNOW WHAT YOU NEED TO DO...
ALL BY MYSELF
LIKE, BACK IN THE SCHOOL...
916
917
C'MON! WE DON'T HAVE ALL DAY!
WHEN NATURE CALLS, I CAN'T TAKE A MESSAGE, OKAY?
KNOCK KNOCK!

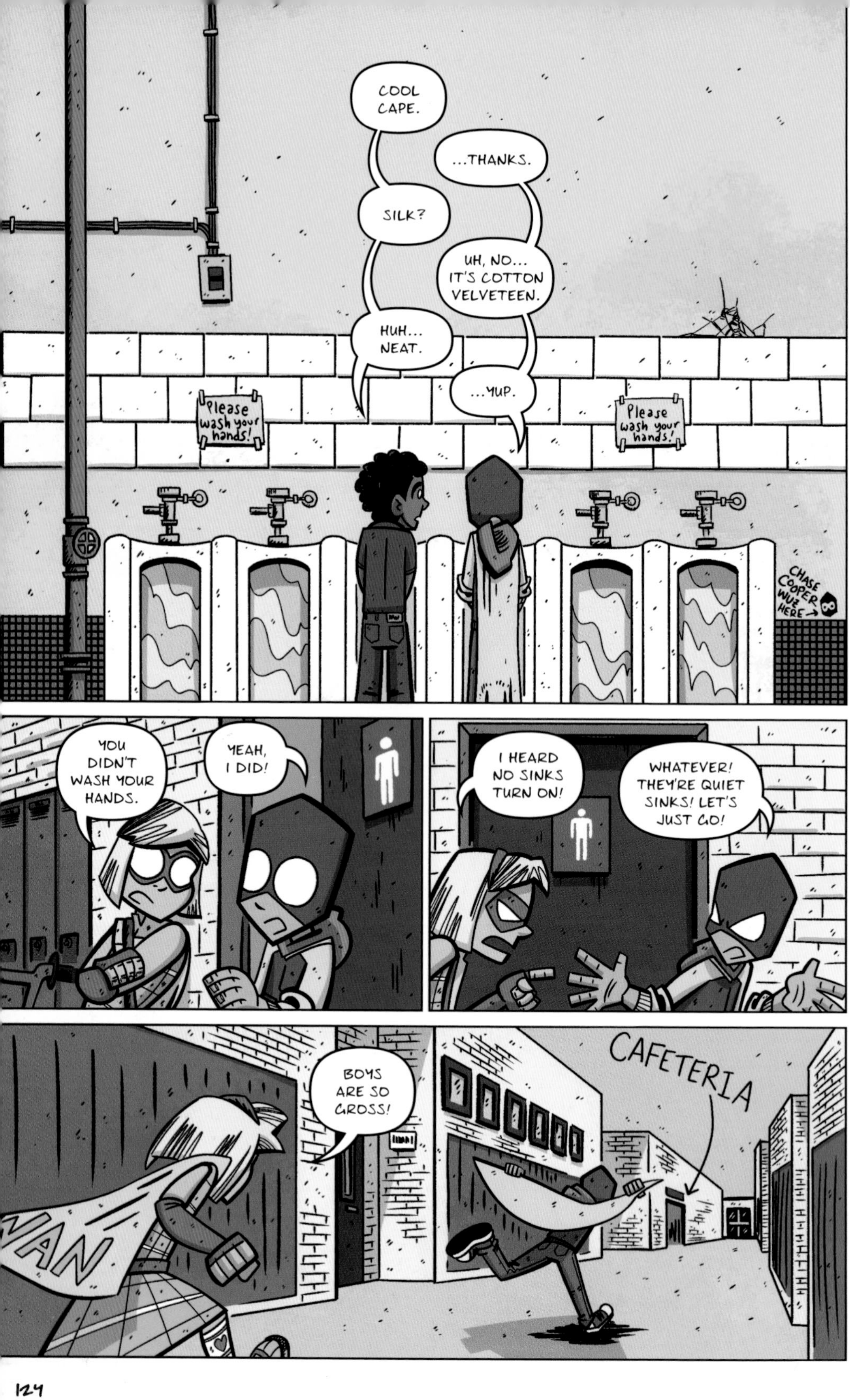
COOL CAPE.
...THANKS.
SILK?
UH, NO... IT'S COTTON VELVETEEN.
HUH... NEAT.
...YUP.
Please wash your hands!
Please wash your hands!
CHASE COOPER WUZ HERE
YOU DIDN'T WASH YOUR HANDS.
YEAH, I DID!
I HEARD NO SINKS TURN ON!
WHATEVER! THEY'RE QUIET SINKS! LET'S JUST GO!
BOYS ARE SO GROSS!
CAFETERIA

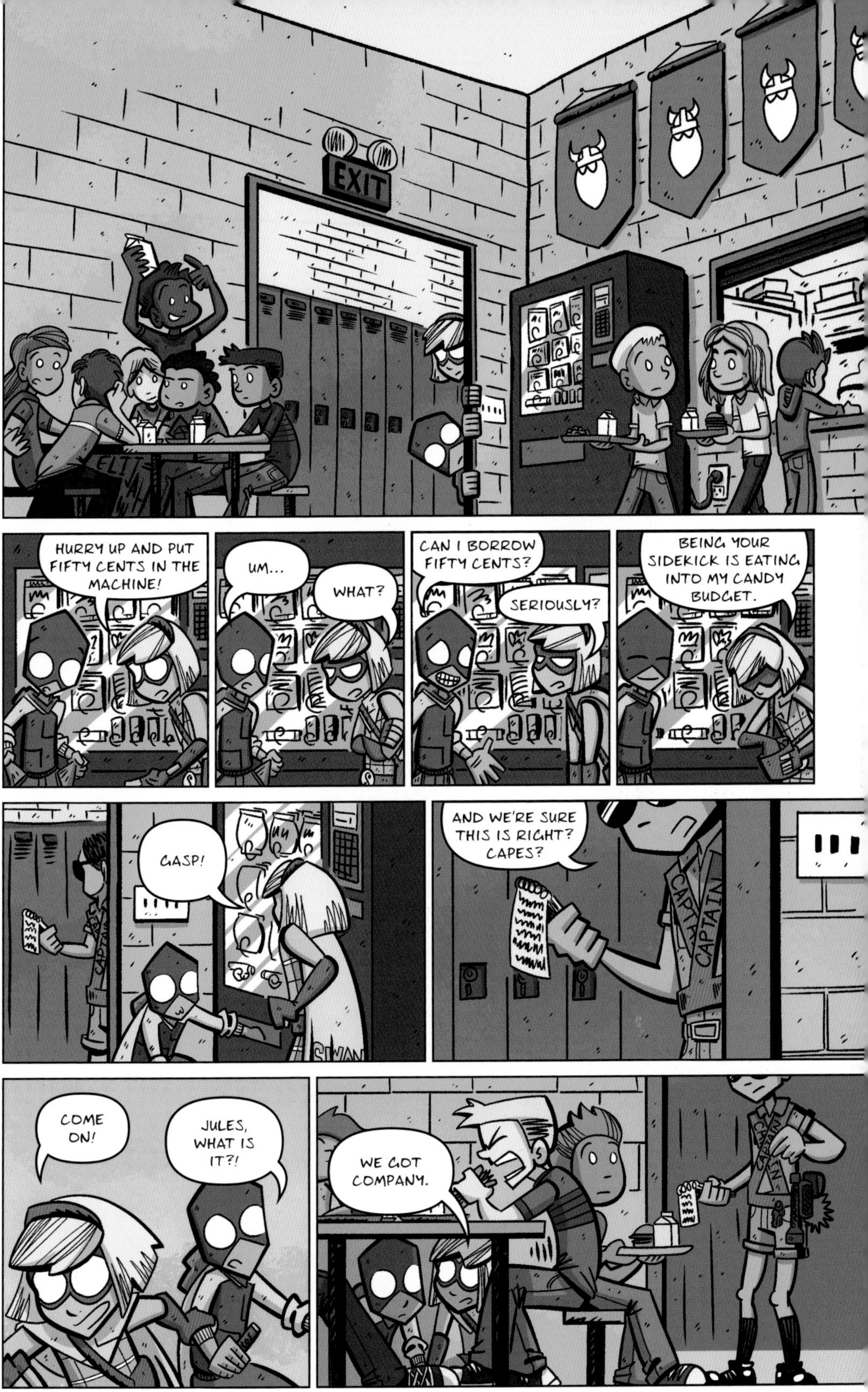

EXIT
HURRY UP AND PUT FIFTY CENTS IN THE MACHINE!
UM...
WHAT?
CAN I BORROW FIFTY CENTS?
SERIOUSLY?
BEING YOUR SIDEKICK IS EATING INTO MY CANDY BUDGET.
GASP!
AND WE'RE SURE THIS IS RIGHT? CAPES?
CAPTAIN
COME ON!
JULES, WHAT IS IT?!
WE GOT COMPANY.

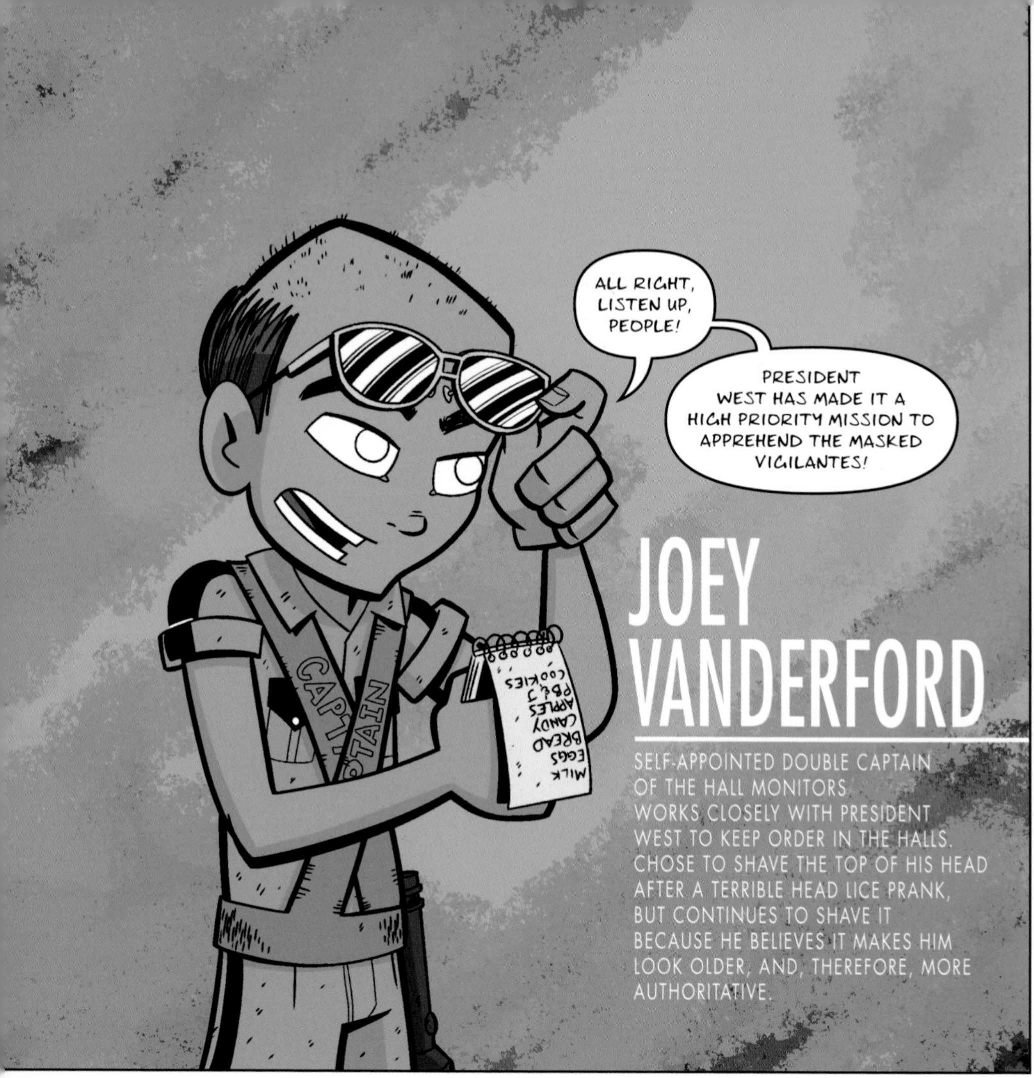
ALL RIGHT, LISTEN UP, PEOPLE!
PRESIDENT WEST HAS MADE IT A HIGH PRIORITY MISSION TO APPREHEND THE MASKED VIGILANTES!
CAPTAIN
MILK EGGS BREAD CANDY APPLES PB&J COOKIES
JOEY VANDERFORD
SELF-APPOINTED DOUBLE CAPTAIN OF THE HALL MONITORS. WORKS CLOSELY WITH PRESIDENT WEST TO KEEP ORDER IN THE HALLS. CHOSE TO SHAVE THE TOP OF HIS HEAD AFTER A TERRIBLE HEAD LICE PRANK, BUT CONTINUES TO SHAVE IT BECAUSE HE BELIEVES IT MAKES HIM LOOK OLDER, AND, THEREFORE, MORE AUTHORITATIVE.

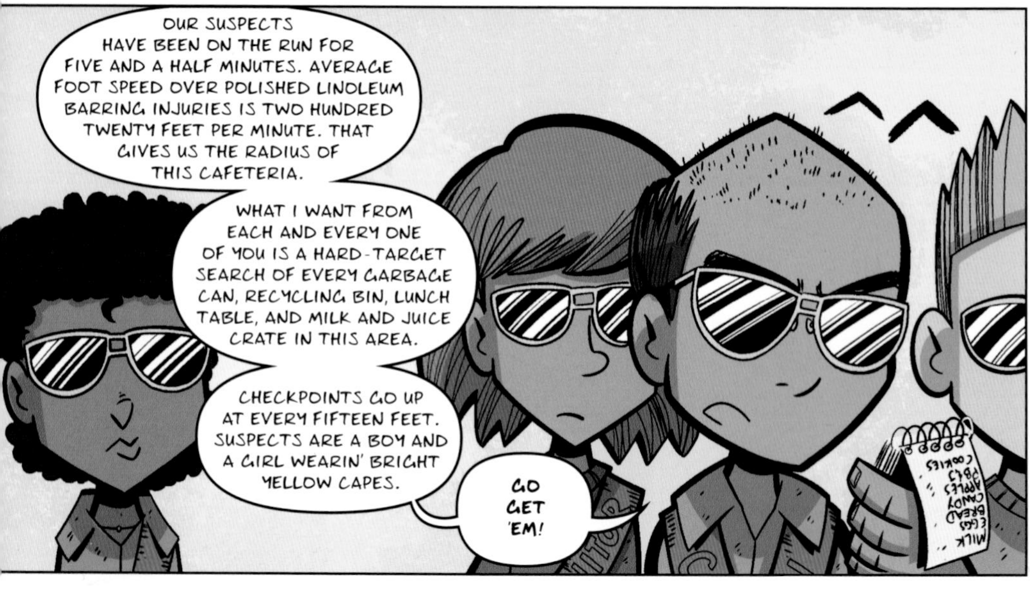
OUR SUSPECTS HAVE BEEN ON THE RUN FOR FIVE AND A HALF MINUTES. AVERAGE FOOT SPEED OVER POLISHED LINOLEUM BARRING INJURIES IS TWO HUNDRED TWENTY FEET PER MINUTE. THAT GIVES US THE RADIUS OF THIS CAFETERIA.
WHAT I WANT FROM EACH AND EVERY ONE OF YOU IS A HARD-TARGET SEARCH OF EVERY GARBAGE CAN, RECYCLING BIN, LUNCH TABLE, AND MILK AND JUICE CRATE IN THIS AREA.
CHECKPOINTS GO UP AT EVERY FIFTEEN FEET. SUSPECTS ARE A BOY AND A GIRL WEARIN' BRIGHT YELLOW CAPES.
GO GET 'EM!

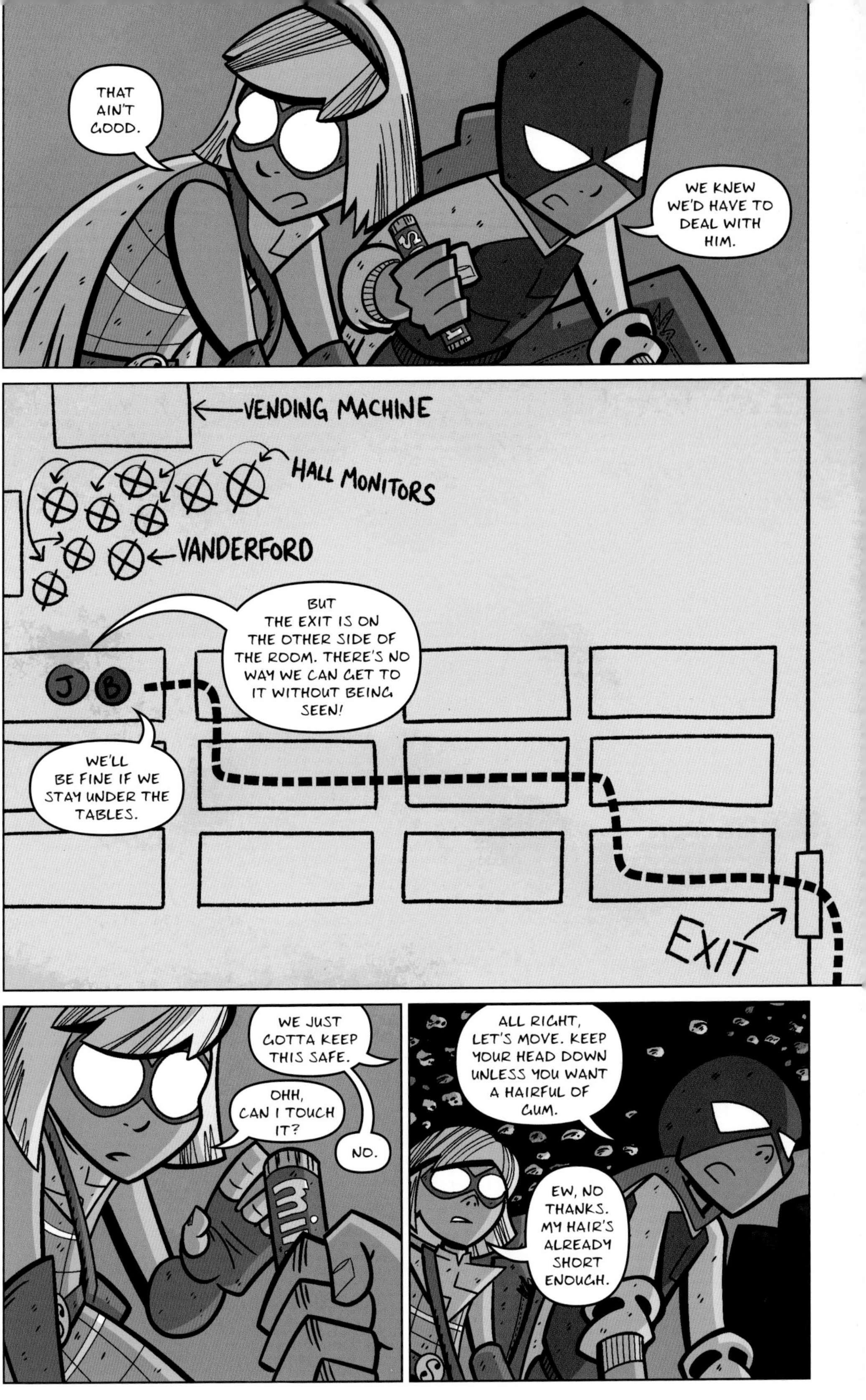

THAT AIN'T GOOD.
WE KNEW WE'D HAVE TO DEAL WITH HIM.
VENDING MACHINE
HALL MONITORS
VANDERFORD
J
B
BUT THE EXIT IS ON THE OTHER SIDE OF THE ROOM. THERE'S NO WAY WE CAN GET TO IT WITHOUT BEING SEEN!
WE'LL BE FINE IF WE STAY UNDER THE TABLES.
EXIT
WE JUST GOTTA KEEP THIS SAFE.
OHH, CAN I TOUCH IT?
NO.
ALL RIGHT, LET'S MOVE. KEEP YOUR HEAD DOWN UNLESS YOU WANT A HAIRFUL OF GUM.
EW, NO THANKS. MY HAIR'S ALREADY SHORT ENOUGH.

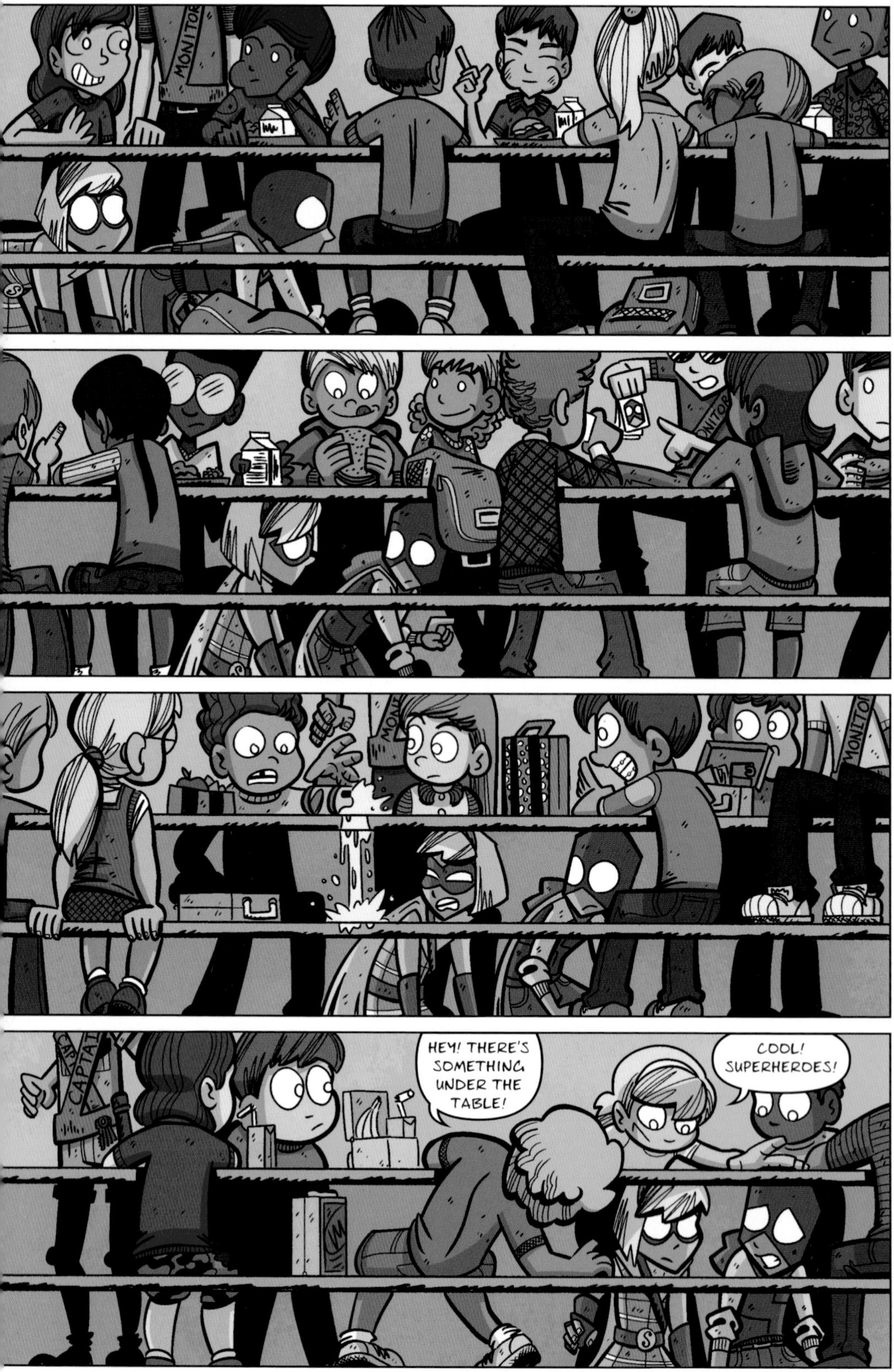
MONITOR
HEY! THERE'S SOMETHING UNDER THE TABLE!
COOL! SUPERHEROES!

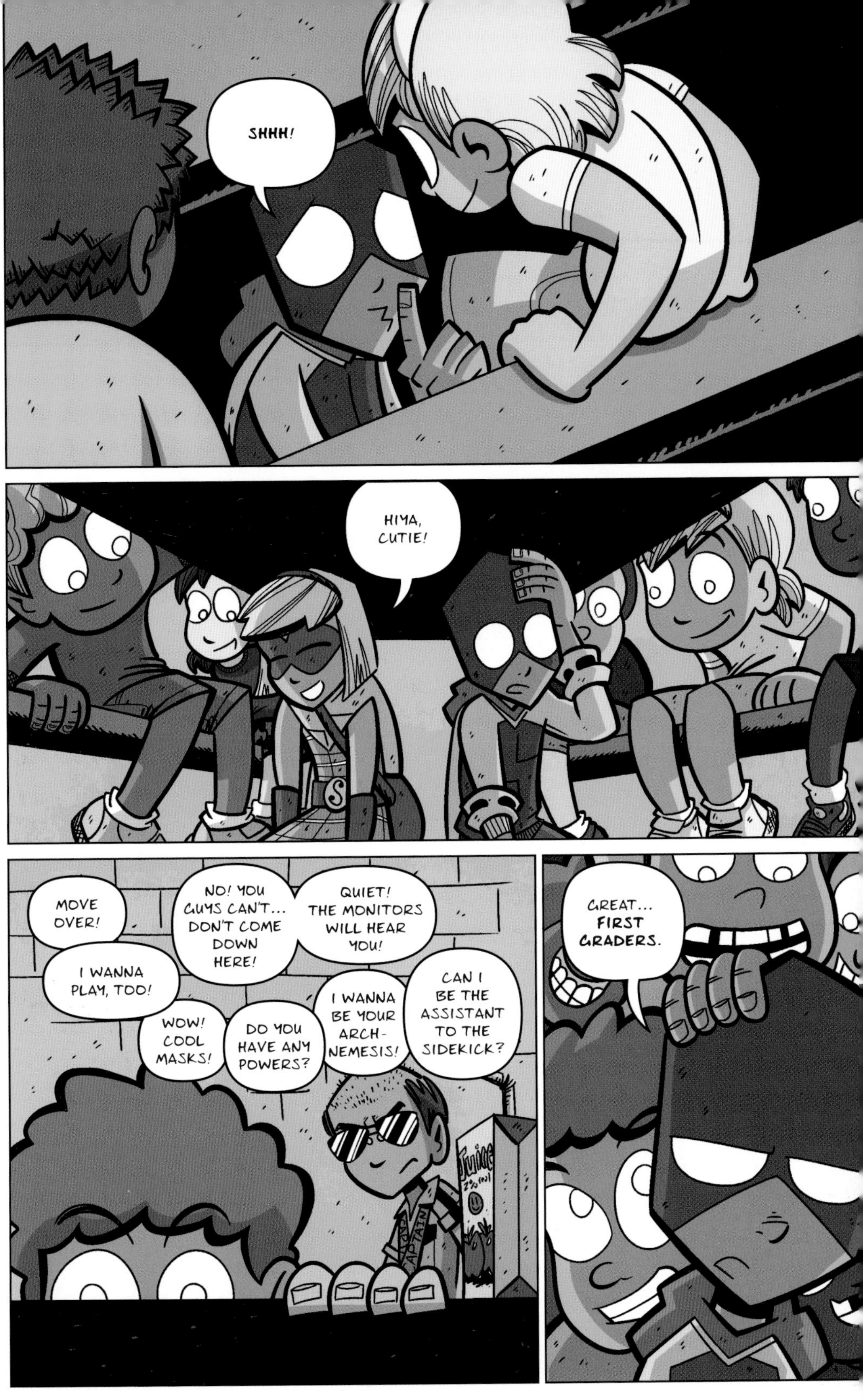
SHHH!
HIYA, CUTIE!
MOVE OVER!
I WANNA PLAY, TOO!
NO! YOU GUYS CAN'T... DON'T COME DOWN HERE!
QUIET! THE MONITORS WILL HEAR YOU!
WOW! COOL MASKS!
DO YOU HAVE ANY POWERS?
I WANNA BE YOUR ARCH-NEMESIS!
CAN I BE THE ASSISTANT TO THE SIDEKICK?
GREAT... FIRST GRADERS.

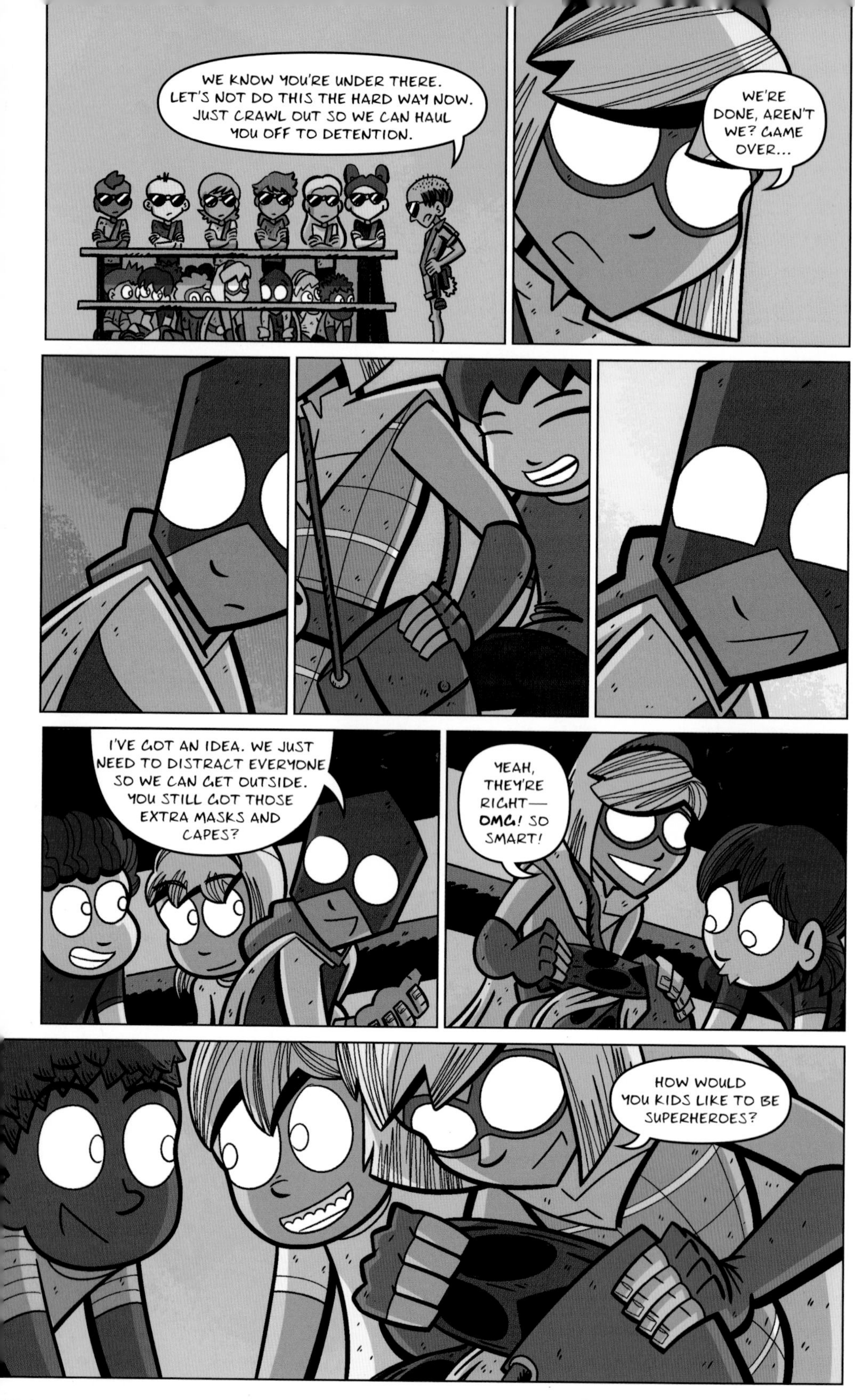
WE KNOW YOU'RE UNDER THERE. LET'S NOT DO THIS THE HARD WAY NOW. JUST CRAWL OUT SO WE CAN HAUL YOU OFF TO DETENTION.
WE'RE DONE, AREN'T WE? GAME OVER...
I'VE GOT AN IDEA. WE JUST NEED TO DISTRACT EVERYONE SO WE CAN GET OUTSIDE. YOU STILL GOT THOSE EXTRA MASKS AND CAPES?
YEAH, THEY'RE RIGHT— **OMG!** SO SMART!
HOW WOULD YOU KIDS LIKE TO BE SUPERHEROES?

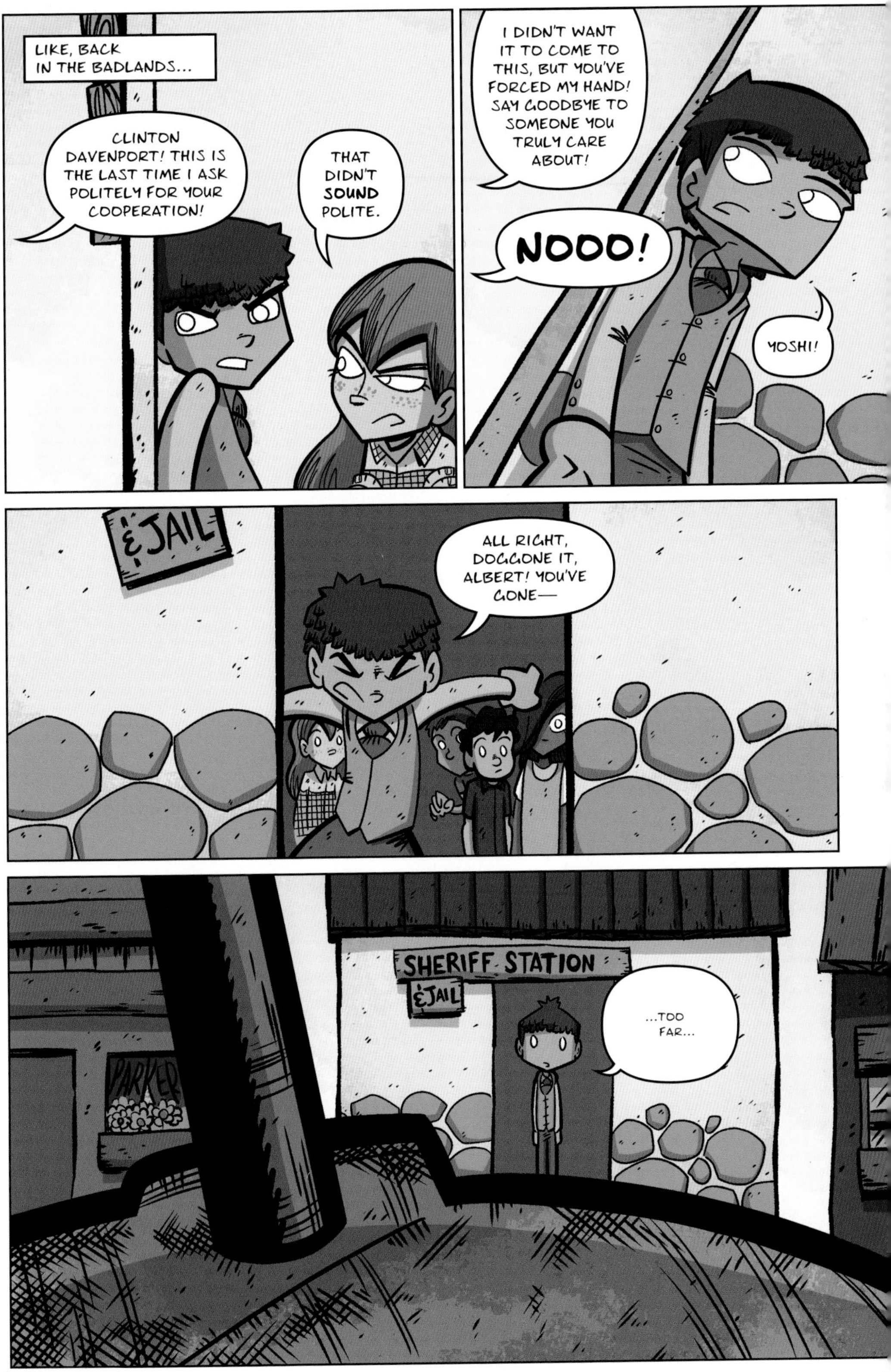

LIKE, BACK IN THE BADLANDS...
CLINTON DAVENPORT! THIS IS THE LAST TIME I ASK POLITELY FOR YOUR COOPERATION!
THAT DIDN'T SOUND POLITE.
I DIDN'T WANT IT TO COME TO THIS, BUT YOU'VE FORCED MY HAND! SAY GOODBYE TO SOMEONE YOU TRULY CARE ABOUT!
NOOO!
YOSHI!
JAIL
ALL RIGHT, DOGGONE IT, ALBERT! YOU'VE GONE—
SHERIFF STATION
JAIL
PARKER
...TOO FAR...

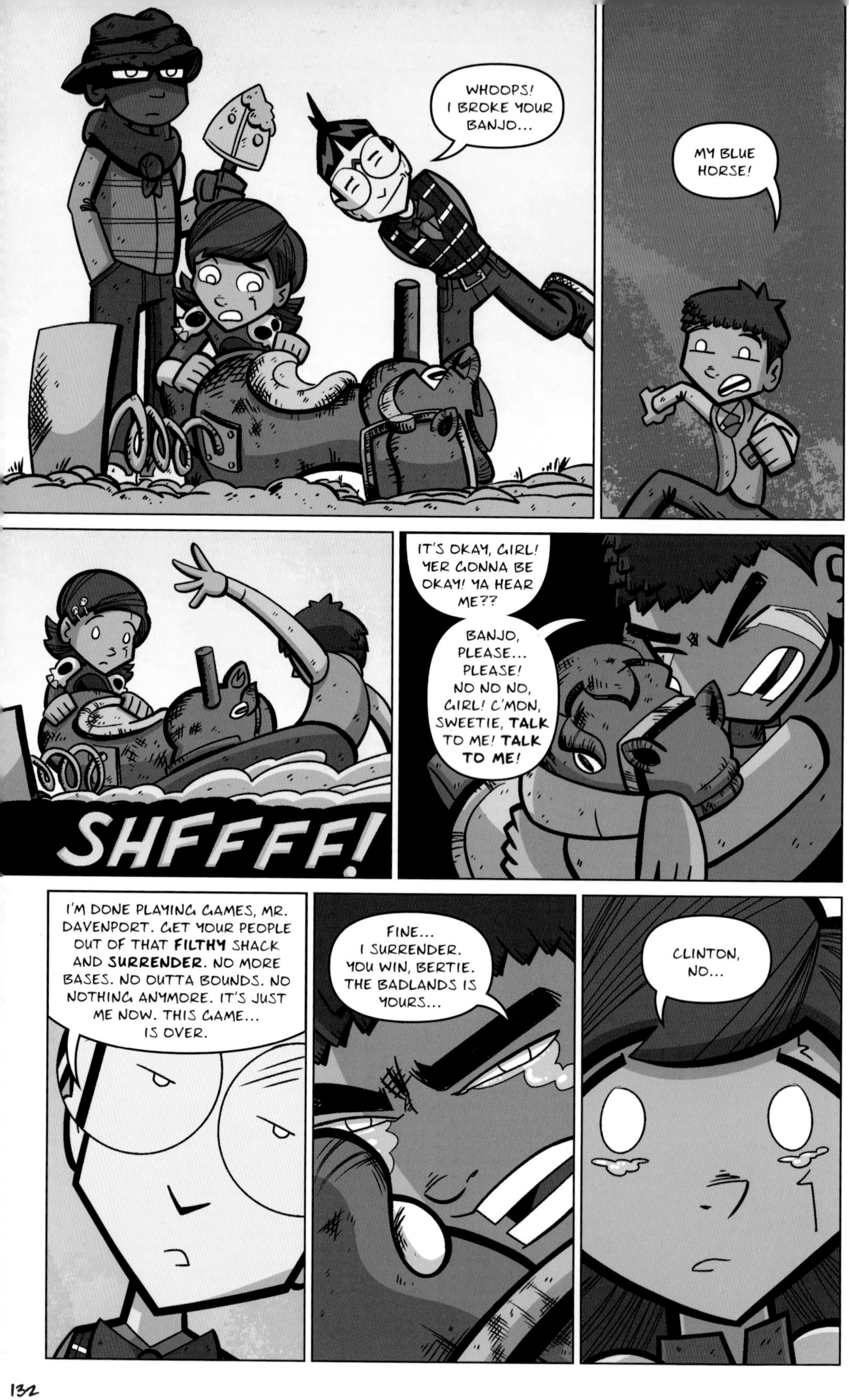
WHOOPS! I BROKE YOUR BANJO...
MY BLUE HORSE!
SHFFFF!
IT'S OKAY, GIRL! YER GONNA BE OKAY! YA HEAR ME??
BANJO, PLEASE... PLEASE! NO NO NO, GIRL! C'MON, SWEETIE, TALK TO ME! TALK TO ME!
I'M DONE PLAYING GAMES, MR. DAVENPORT. GET YOUR PEOPLE OUT OF THAT FILTHY SHACK AND SURRENDER. NO MORE BASES. NO OUTTA BOUNDS. NO NOTHING ANYMORE. IT'S JUST ME NOW. THIS GAME... IS OVER.
FINE... I SURRENDER. YOU WIN, BERTIE. THE BADLANDS IS YOURS...
CLINTON, NO...

LIKE, BACK IN THE CAFETERIA...

YOU GUYS LOOK AWESOME.

MASHED POTATOES?

MASHED POTATOES.

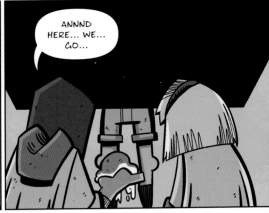

ANNND HERE... WE... GO...

AAAAIIEE!!!

SPLORTCH

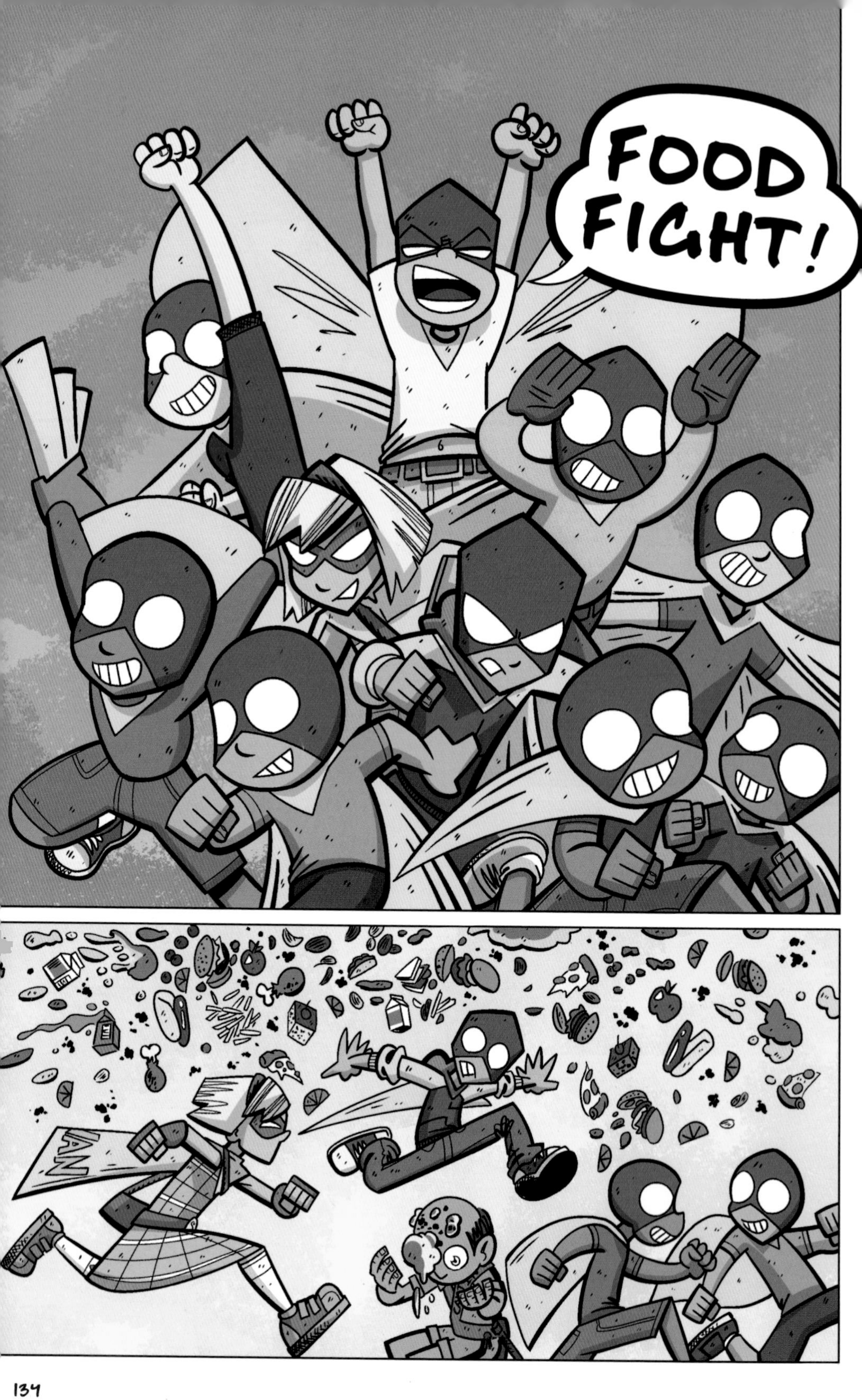
FOOD FIGHT!
IAN

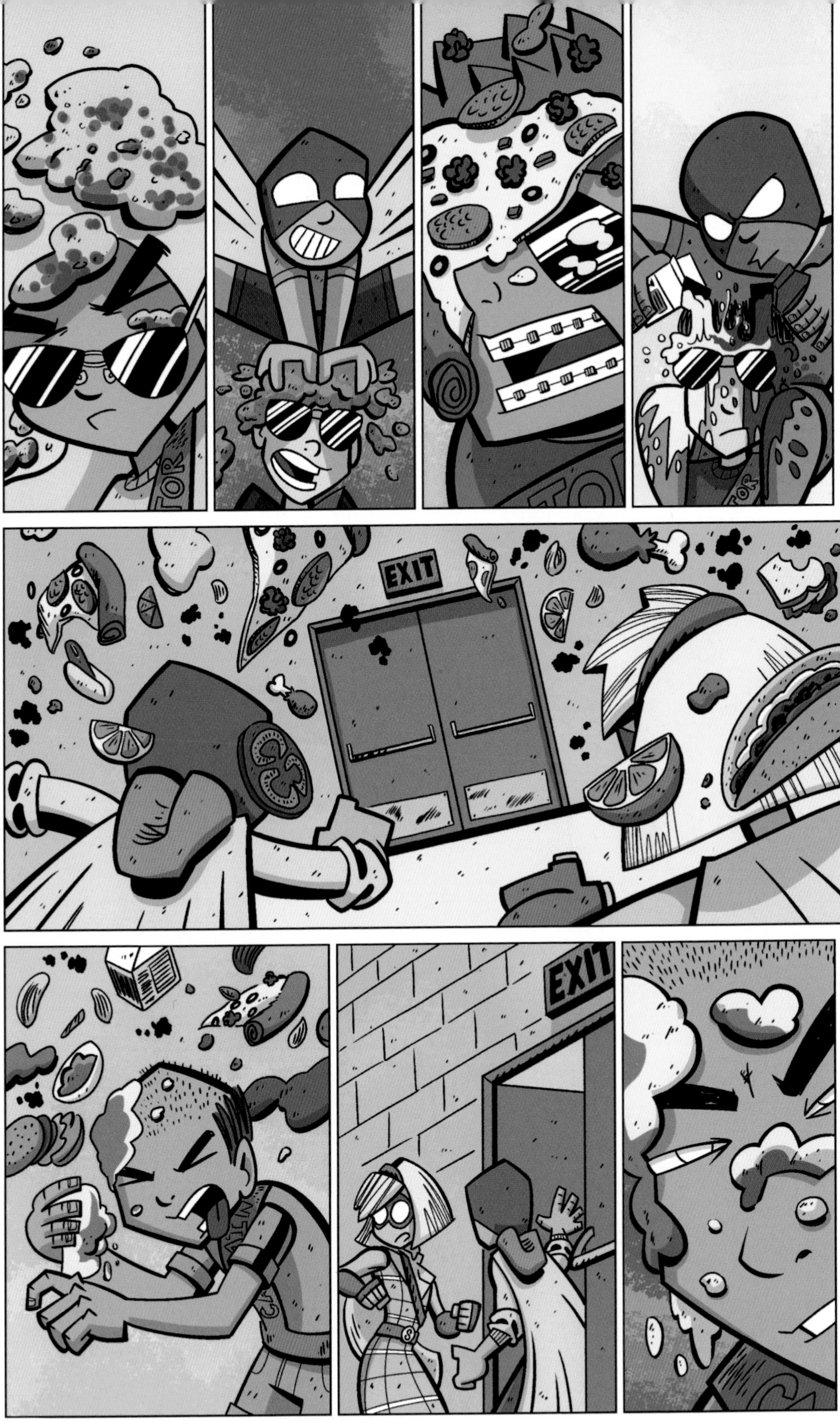
EXIT
EXIT

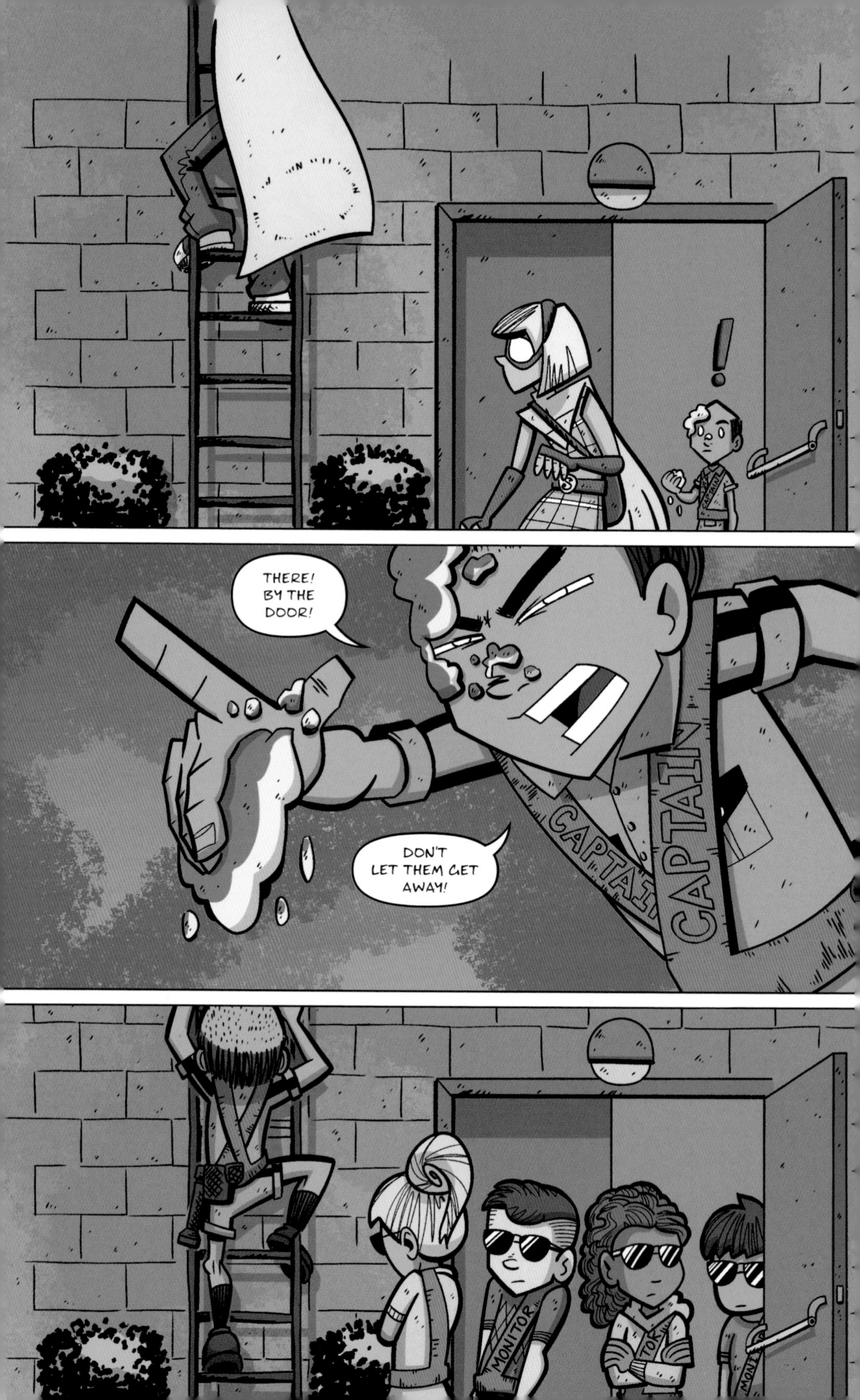
THERE! BY THE DOOR!
DON'T LET THEM GET AWAY!
CAPTAIN
CAPTAIN
MONITOR

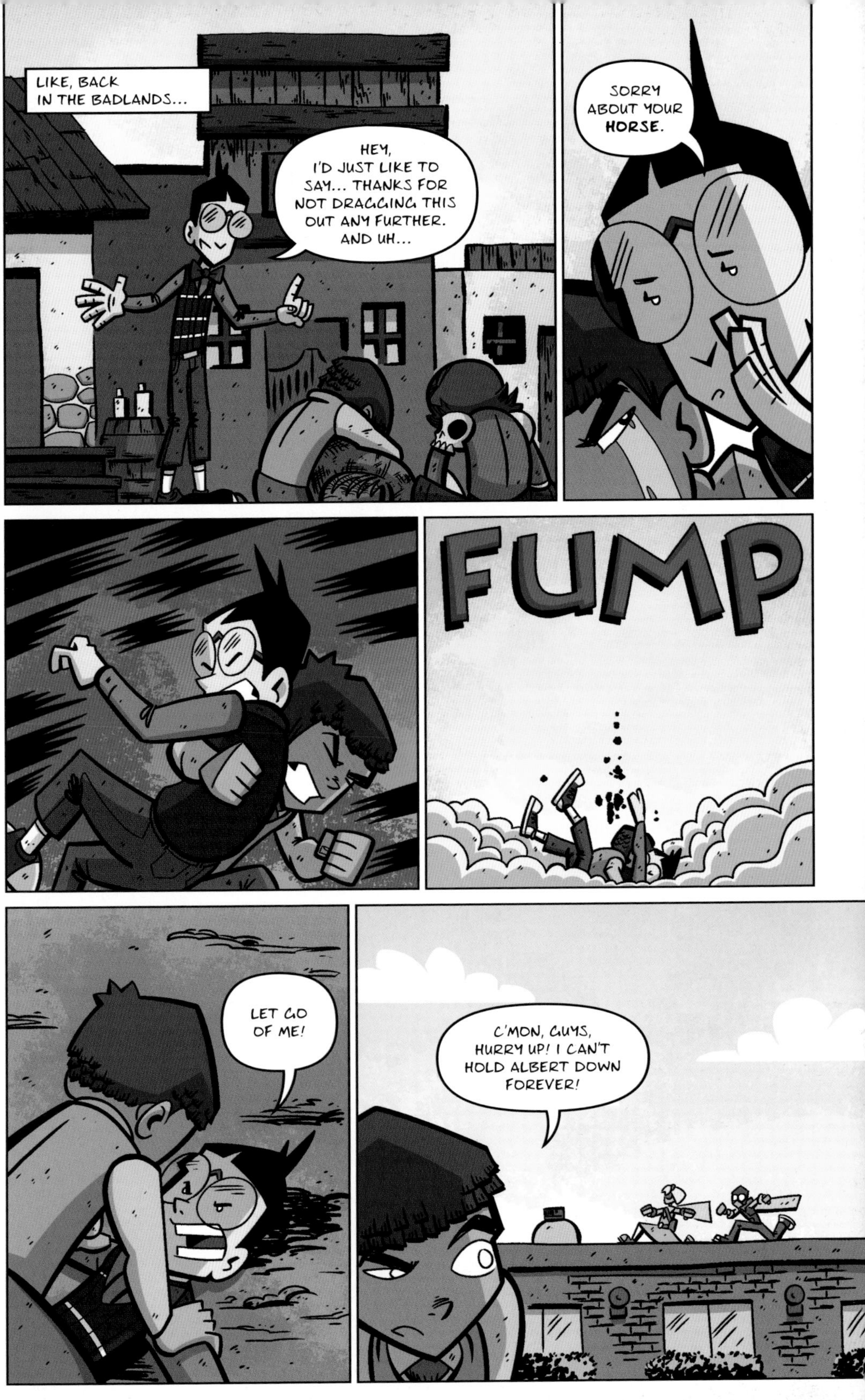
LIKE, BACK
IN THE BADLANDS...
HEY, I'D JUST LIKE TO SAY... THANKS FOR NOT DRAGGING THIS OUT ANY FURTHER. AND UH...
SORRY ABOUT YOUR **HORSE**.
FUMP
LET GO OF ME!
C'MON, GUYS, HURRY UP! I CAN'T HOLD ALBERT DOWN FOREVER!

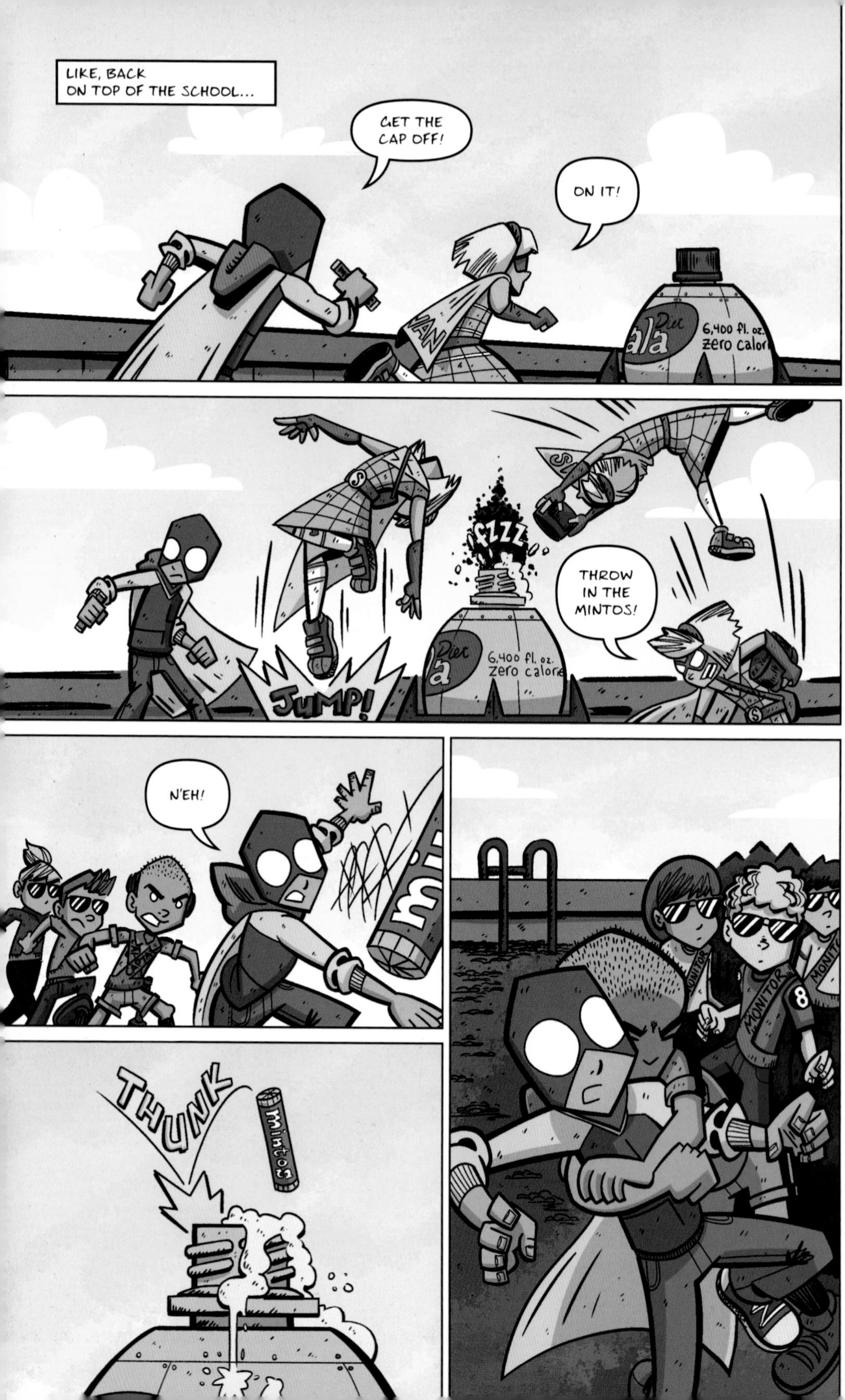
LIKE, BACK ON TOP OF THE SCHOOL...
GET THE CAP OFF!
ON IT!
Diet
6,400 fl. oz.
zero calori
FZZZ
JUMP!
THROW IN THE MINTOS!
Diet
6,400 fl. oz.
zero calorie
N'EH!
MONITOR
MONITOR
MONITOR
THUNK
mintos

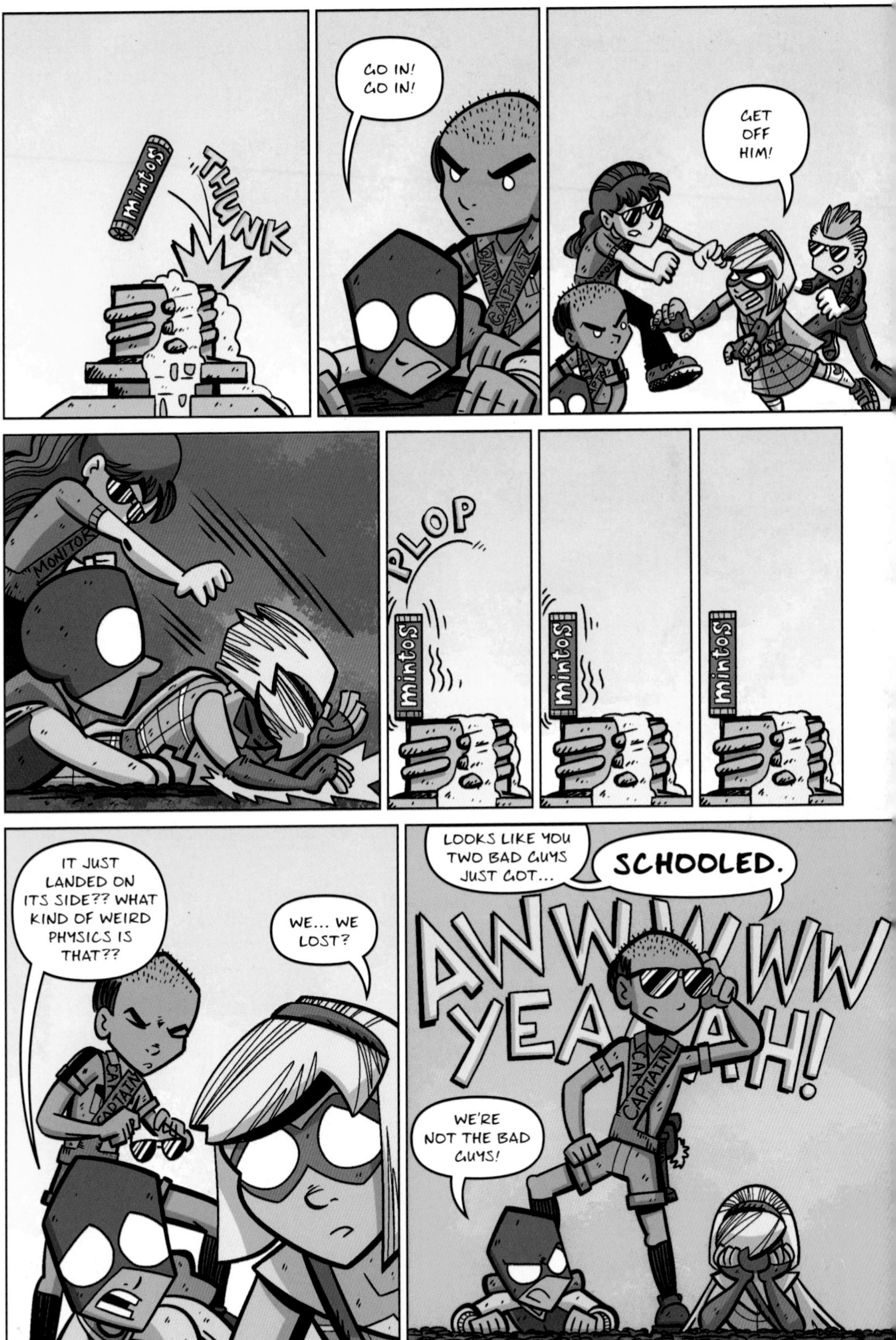
mintos
THUNK
GO IN! GO IN!
GET OFF HIM!
MONITOR
PLOP
mintos
mintos
mintos
IT JUST LANDED ON ITS SIDE?? WHAT KIND OF WEIRD PHYSICS IS THAT??
WE... WE LOST?
LOOKS LIKE YOU TWO BAD GUYS JUST GOT...
SCHOOLED.
AWWWWW YEAAAH!
WE'RE NOT THE BAD GUYS!

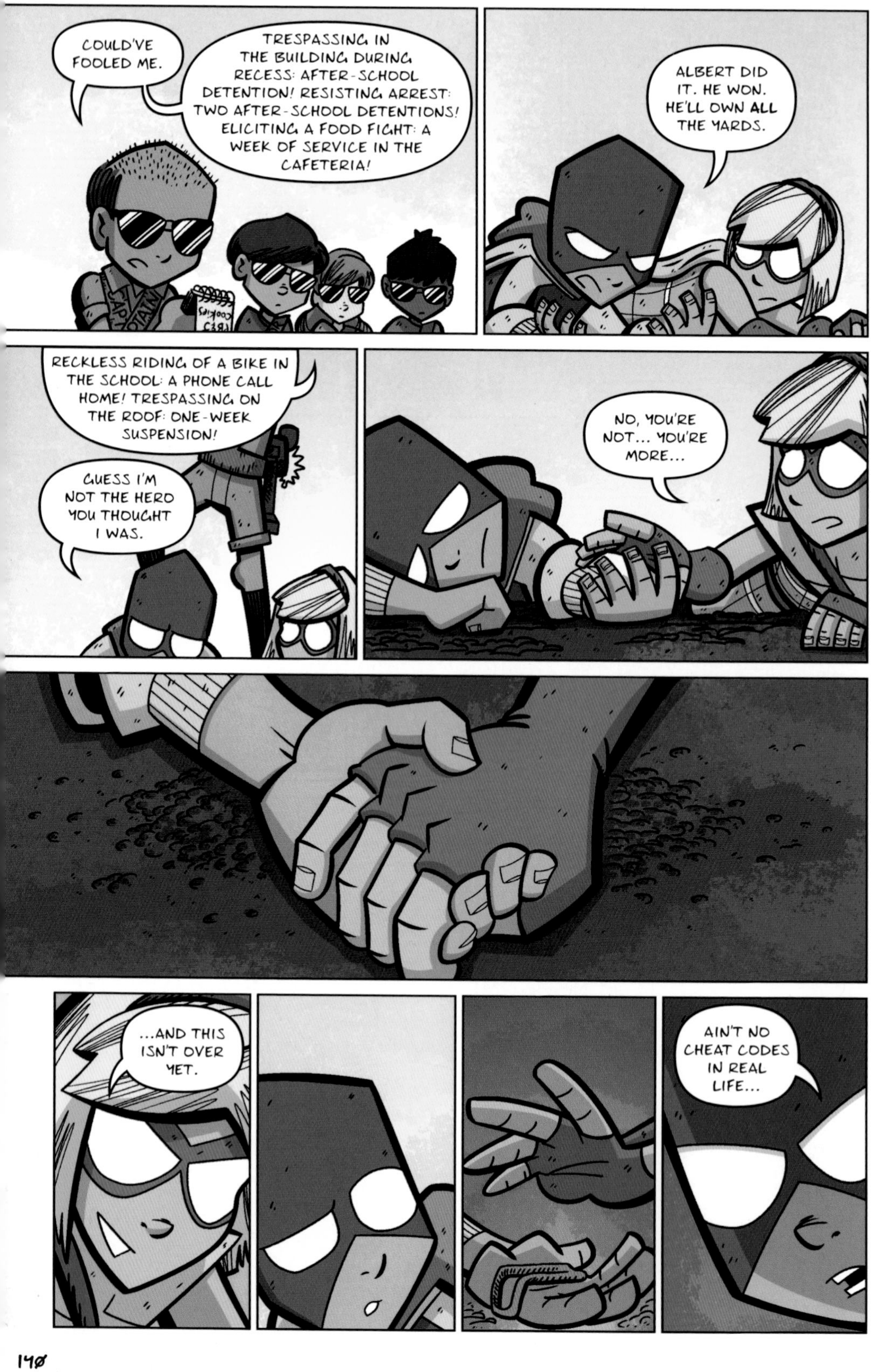
COULD'VE FOOLED ME.
TRESPASSING IN THE BUILDING DURING RECESS: AFTER-SCHOOL DETENTION! RESISTING ARREST: TWO AFTER-SCHOOL DETENTIONS! ELICITING A FOOD FIGHT: A WEEK OF SERVICE IN THE CAFETERIA!
ALBERT DID IT. HE WON. HE'LL OWN **ALL** THE YARDS.
RECKLESS RIDING OF A BIKE IN THE SCHOOL: A PHONE CALL HOME! TRESPASSING ON THE ROOF: ONE-WEEK SUSPENSION!
GUESS I'M NOT THE HERO YOU THOUGHT I WAS.
NO, YOU'RE NOT... YOU'RE MORE...
...AND THIS ISN'T OVER YET.
AIN'T NO CHEAT CODES IN REAL LIFE...

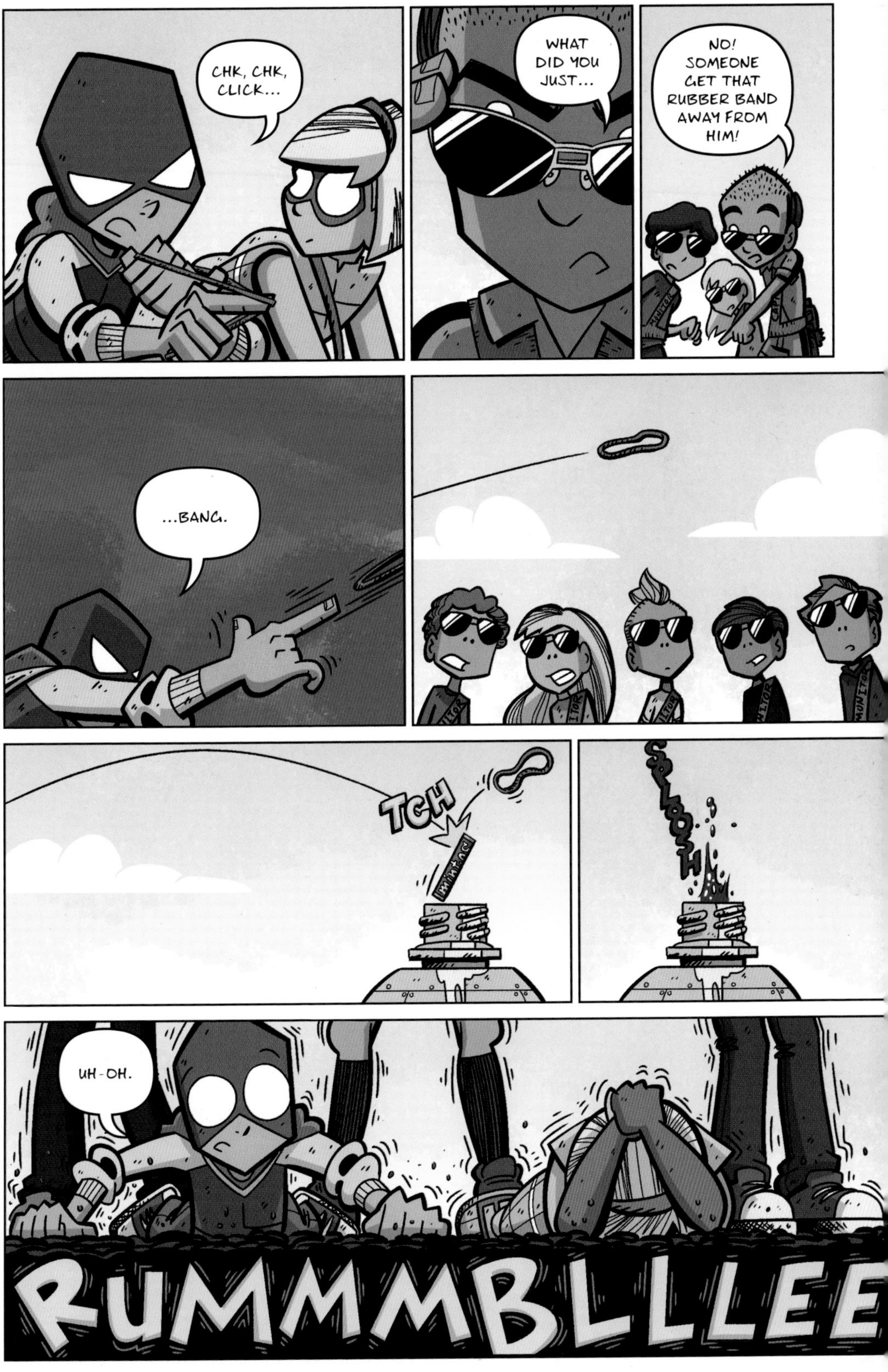
CHK, CHK, CLICK...
WHAT DID YOU JUST...
NO! SOMEONE GET THAT RUBBER BAND AWAY FROM HIM!
...BANG.
TCH
SPLOOSH
UH-OH.
RUMMMBLLLEE

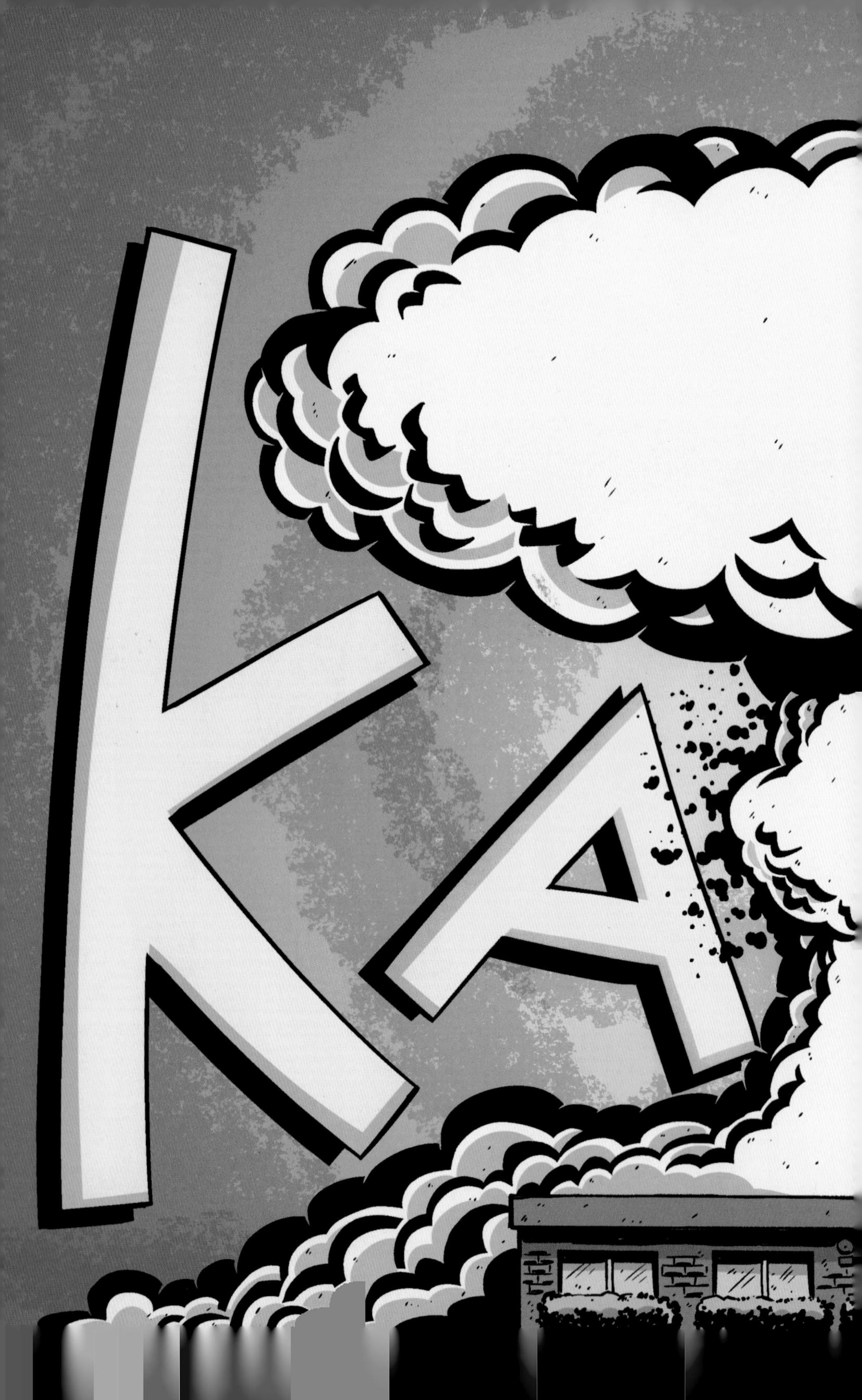
KA

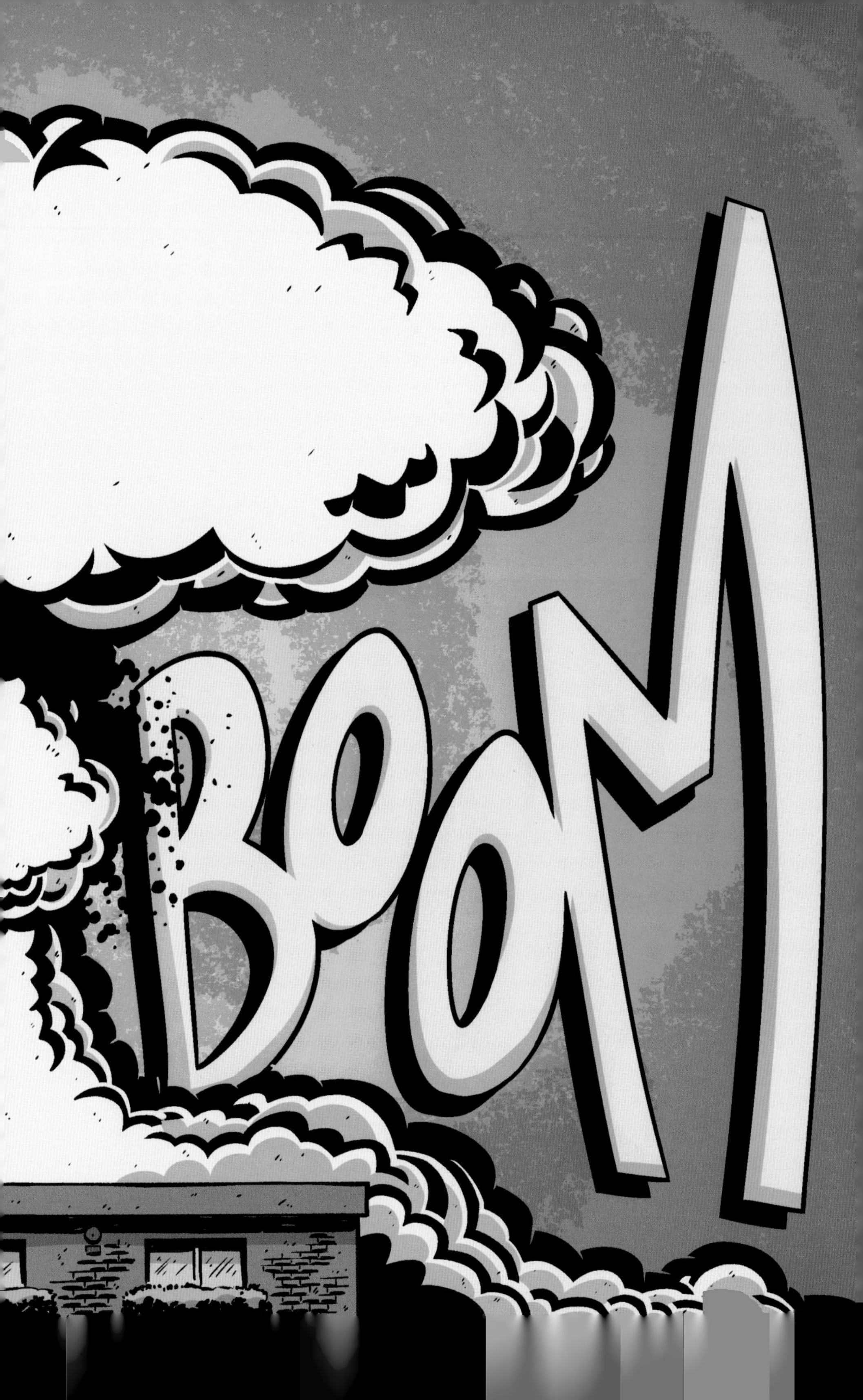
BOOM

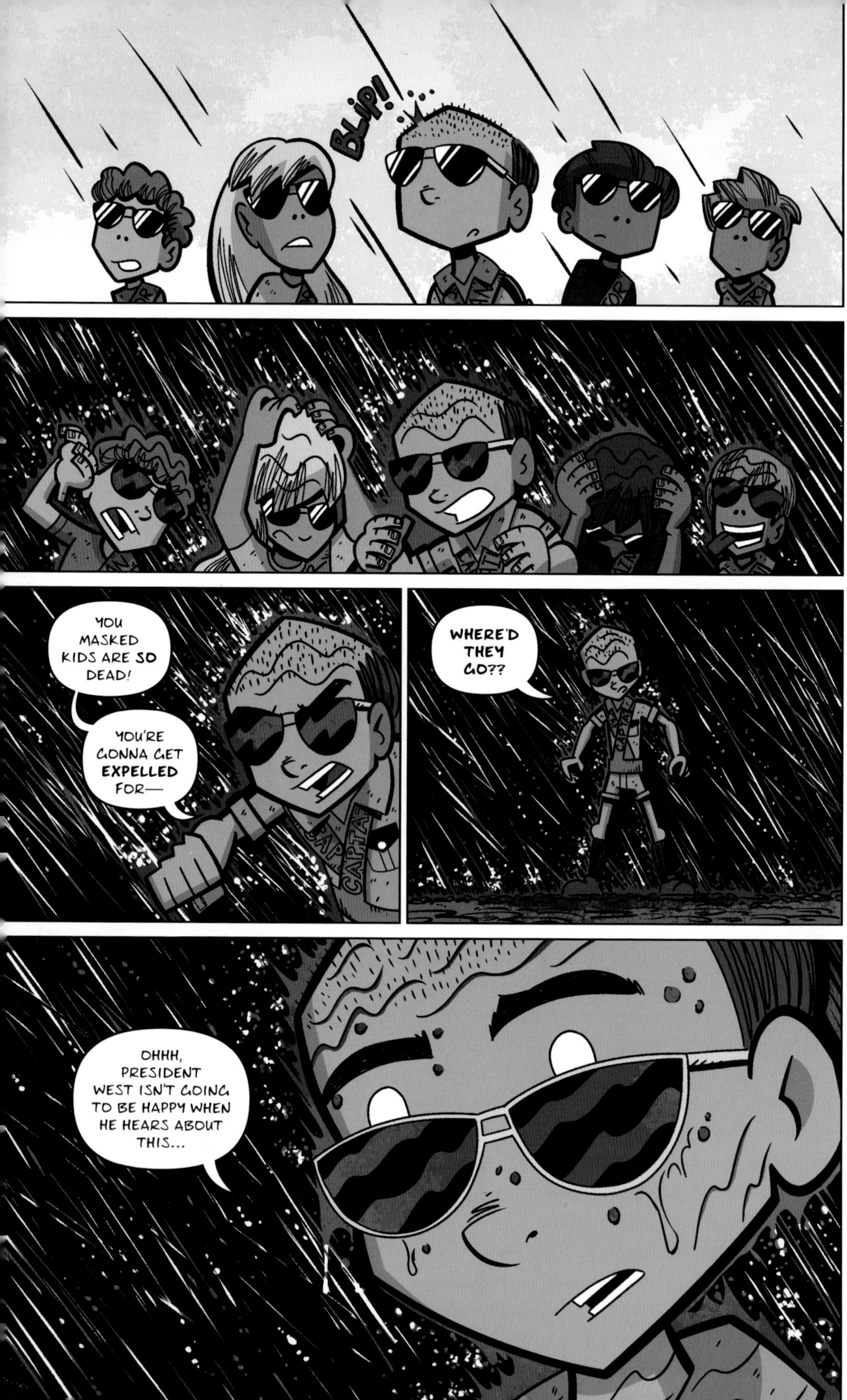
BLIP!
YOU MASKED KIDS ARE SO DEAD!
YOU'RE GONNA GET EXPELLED FOR—
WHERE'D THEY GO??
OHHH, PRESIDENT WEST ISN'T GOING TO BE HAPPY WHEN HE HEARS ABOUT THIS...

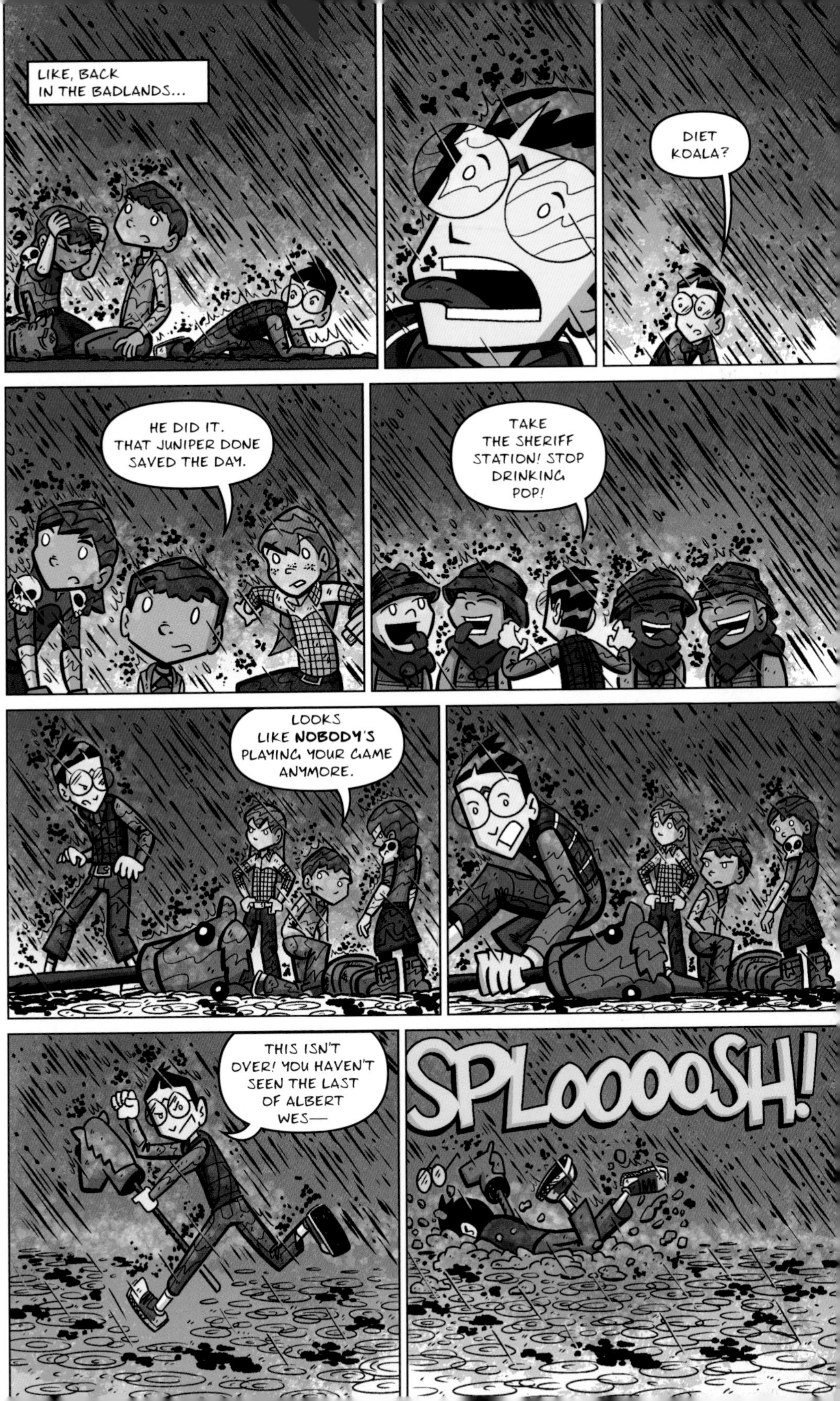
LIKE, BACK IN THE BADLANDS...
DIET KOALA?
HE DID IT. THAT JUNIPER DONE SAVED THE DAY.
TAKE THE SHERIFF STATION! STOP DRINKING POP!
LOOKS LIKE NOBODY'S PLAYING YOUR GAME ANYMORE.
THIS ISN'T OVER! YOU HAVEN'T SEEN THE LAST OF ALBERT WES—
SPLOOOOSH!

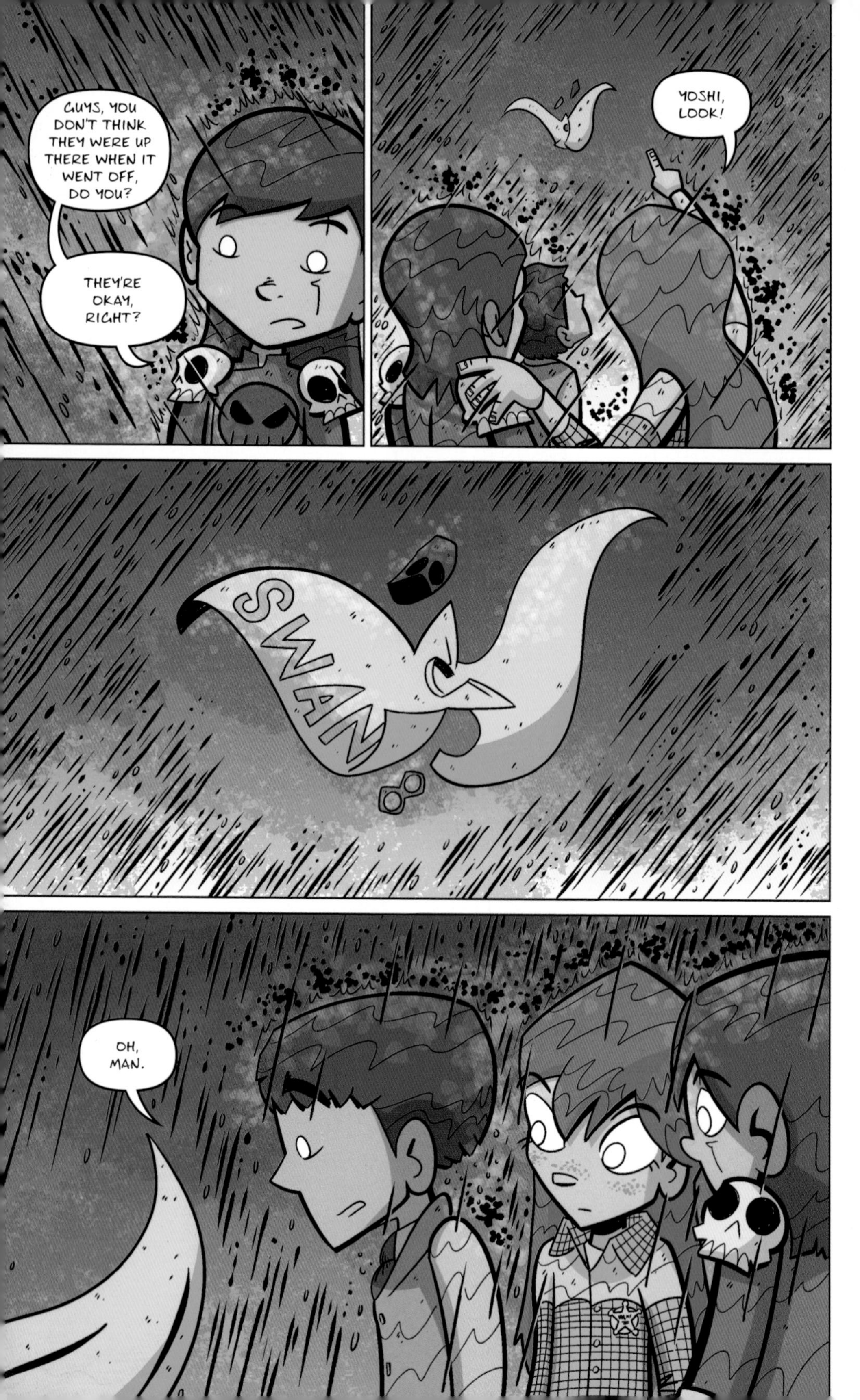
GUYS, YOU DON'T THINK THEY WERE UP THERE WHEN IT WENT OFF, DO YOU?
THEY'RE OKAY, RIGHT?
YOSHI, LOOK!
SWAN
OH, MAN.

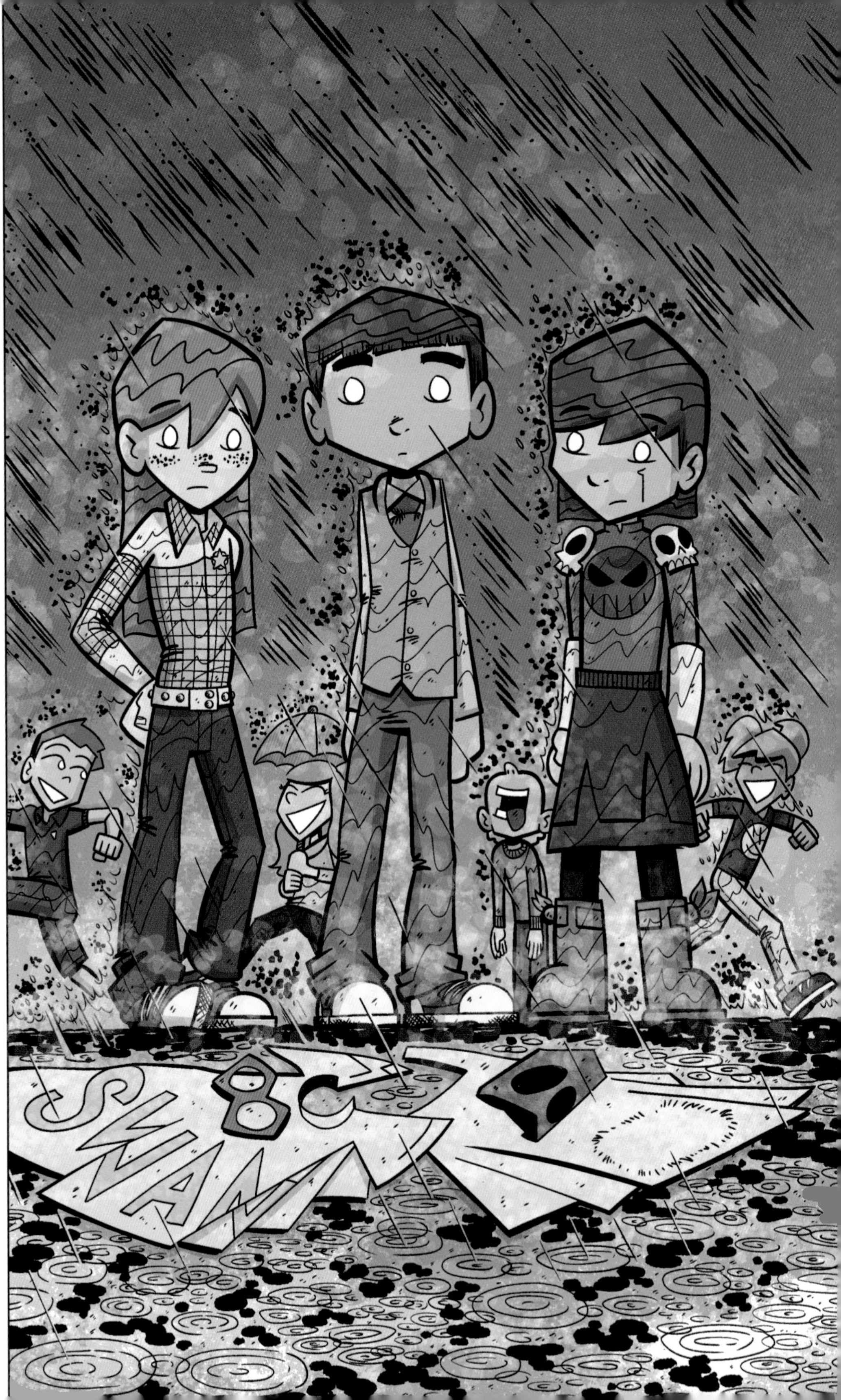
SWAN
8

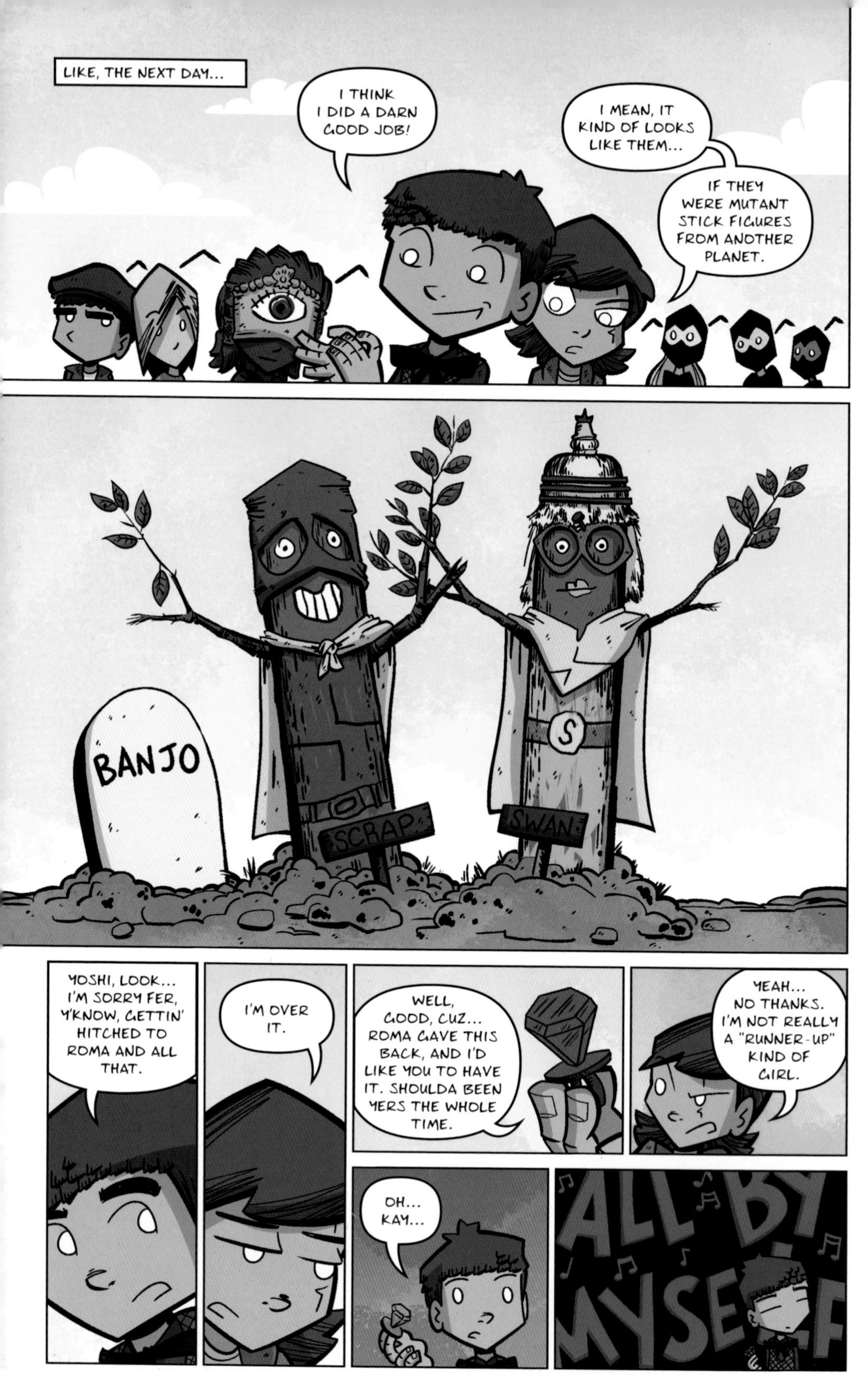
LIKE, THE NEXT DAY...
I THINK I DID A DARN GOOD JOB!
I MEAN, IT KIND OF LOOKS LIKE THEM...
IF THEY WERE MUTANT STICK FIGURES FROM ANOTHER PLANET.
BANJO
SCRAP
SWAN
YOSHI, LOOK... I'M SORRY FER, Y'KNOW, GETTIN' HITCHED TO ROMA AND ALL THAT.
I'M OVER IT.
WELL, GOOD, CUZ... ROMA GAVE THIS BACK, AND I'D LIKE YOU TO HAVE IT. SHOULDA BEEN YERS THE WHOLE TIME.
YEAH... NO THANKS. I'M NOT REALLY A "RUNNER-UP" KIND OF GIRL.
OH... KAY...
ALL BY MYSELF

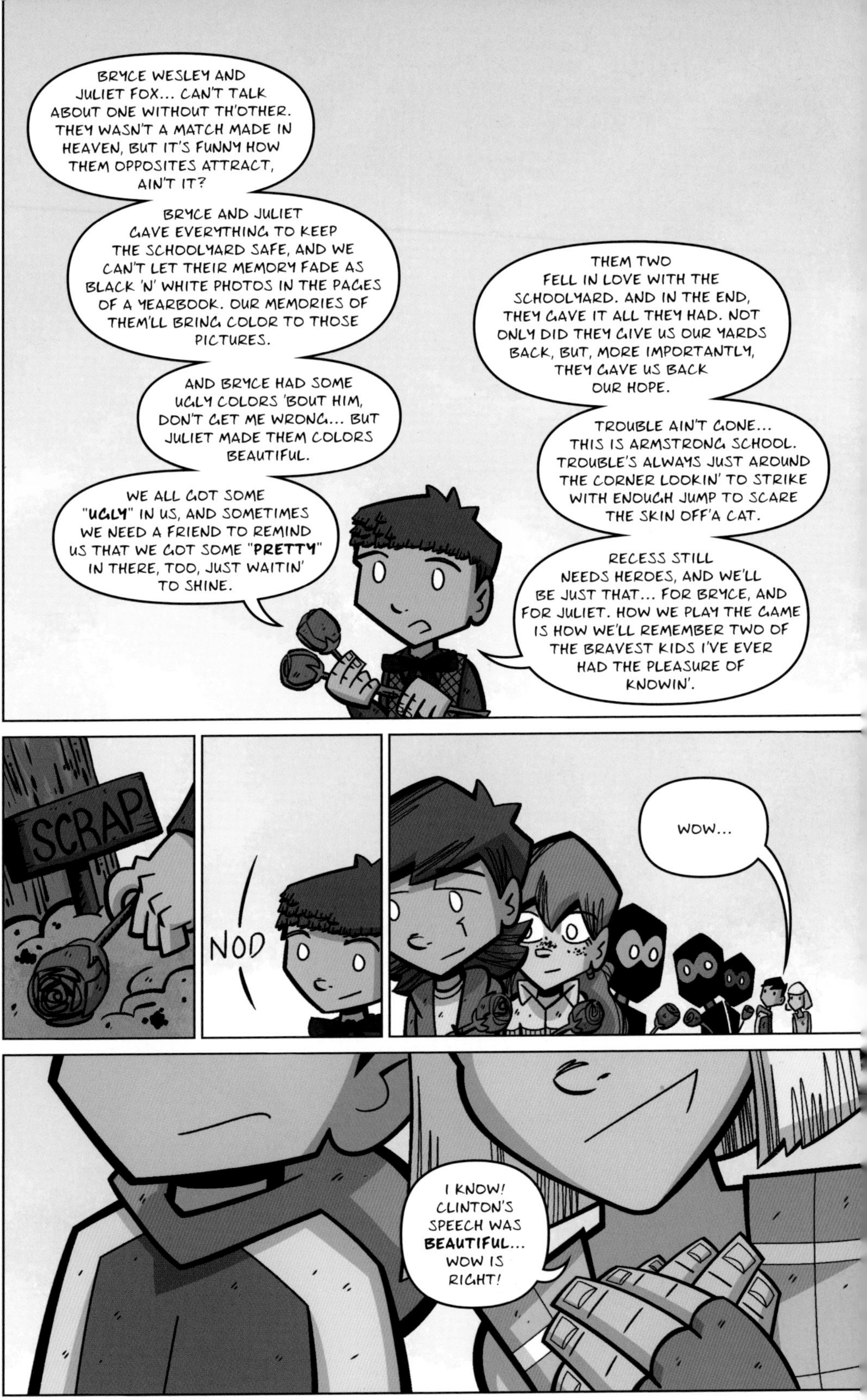
BRYCE WESLEY AND JULIET FOX... CAN'T TALK ABOUT ONE WITHOUT TH'OTHER. THEY WASN'T A MATCH MADE IN HEAVEN, BUT IT'S FUNNY HOW THEM OPPOSITES ATTRACT, AIN'T IT?
BRYCE AND JULIET GAVE EVERYTHING TO KEEP THE SCHOOLYARD SAFE, AND WE CAN'T LET THEIR MEMORY FADE AS BLACK 'N' WHITE PHOTOS IN THE PAGES OF A YEARBOOK. OUR MEMORIES OF THEM'LL BRING COLOR TO THOSE PICTURES.
AND BRYCE HAD SOME UGLY COLORS 'BOUT HIM, DON'T GET ME WRONG... BUT JULIET MADE THEM COLORS BEAUTIFUL.
WE ALL GOT SOME "**UGLY**" IN US, AND SOMETIMES WE NEED A FRIEND TO REMIND US THAT WE GOT SOME "**PRETTY**" IN THERE, TOO, JUST WAITIN' TO SHINE.
THEM TWO FELL IN LOVE WITH THE SCHOOLYARD. AND IN THE END, THEY GAVE IT ALL THEY HAD. NOT ONLY DID THEY GIVE US OUR YARDS BACK, BUT, MORE IMPORTANTLY, THEY GAVE US BACK OUR HOPE.
TROUBLE AIN'T GONE... THIS IS ARMSTRONG SCHOOL. TROUBLE'S ALWAYS JUST AROUND THE CORNER LOOKIN' TO STRIKE WITH ENOUGH JUMP TO SCARE THE SKIN OFF'A CAT.
RECESS STILL NEEDS HEROES, AND WE'LL BE JUST THAT... FOR BRYCE, AND FOR JULIET. HOW WE PLAY THE GAME IS HOW WE'LL REMEMBER TWO OF THE BRAVEST KIDS I'VE EVER HAD THE PLEASURE OF KNOWIN'.
SCRAP
NOD
WOW...
I KNOW! CLINTON'S SPEECH WAS **BEAUTIFUL**... WOW IS RIGHT!

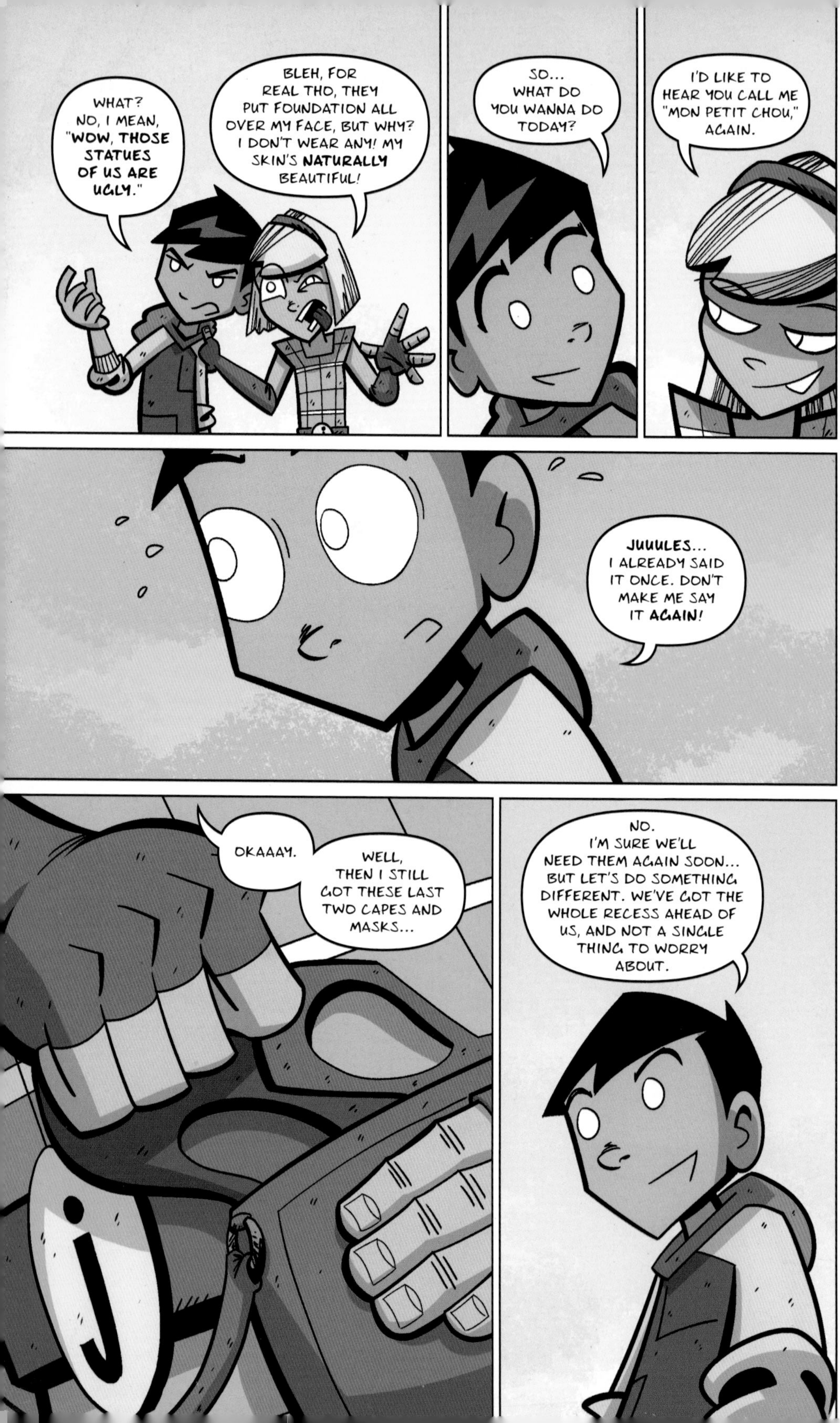
WHAT? NO, I MEAN, "WOW, THOSE STATUES OF US ARE UGLY."
BLEH, FOR REAL THO, THEY PUT FOUNDATION ALL OVER MY FACE, BUT WHY? I DON'T WEAR ANY! MY SKIN'S NATURALLY BEAUTIFUL!
SO... WHAT DO YOU WANNA DO TODAY?
I'D LIKE TO HEAR YOU CALL ME "MON PETIT CHOU," AGAIN.
JUUULES... I ALREADY SAID IT ONCE. DON'T MAKE ME SAY IT AGAIN!
OKAAAY.
WELL, THEN I STILL GOT THESE LAST TWO CAPES AND MASKS...
NO. I'M SURE WE'LL NEED THEM AGAIN SOON... BUT LET'S DO SOMETHING DIFFERENT. WE'VE GOT THE WHOLE RECESS AHEAD OF US, AND NOT A SINGLE THING TO WORRY ABOUT.

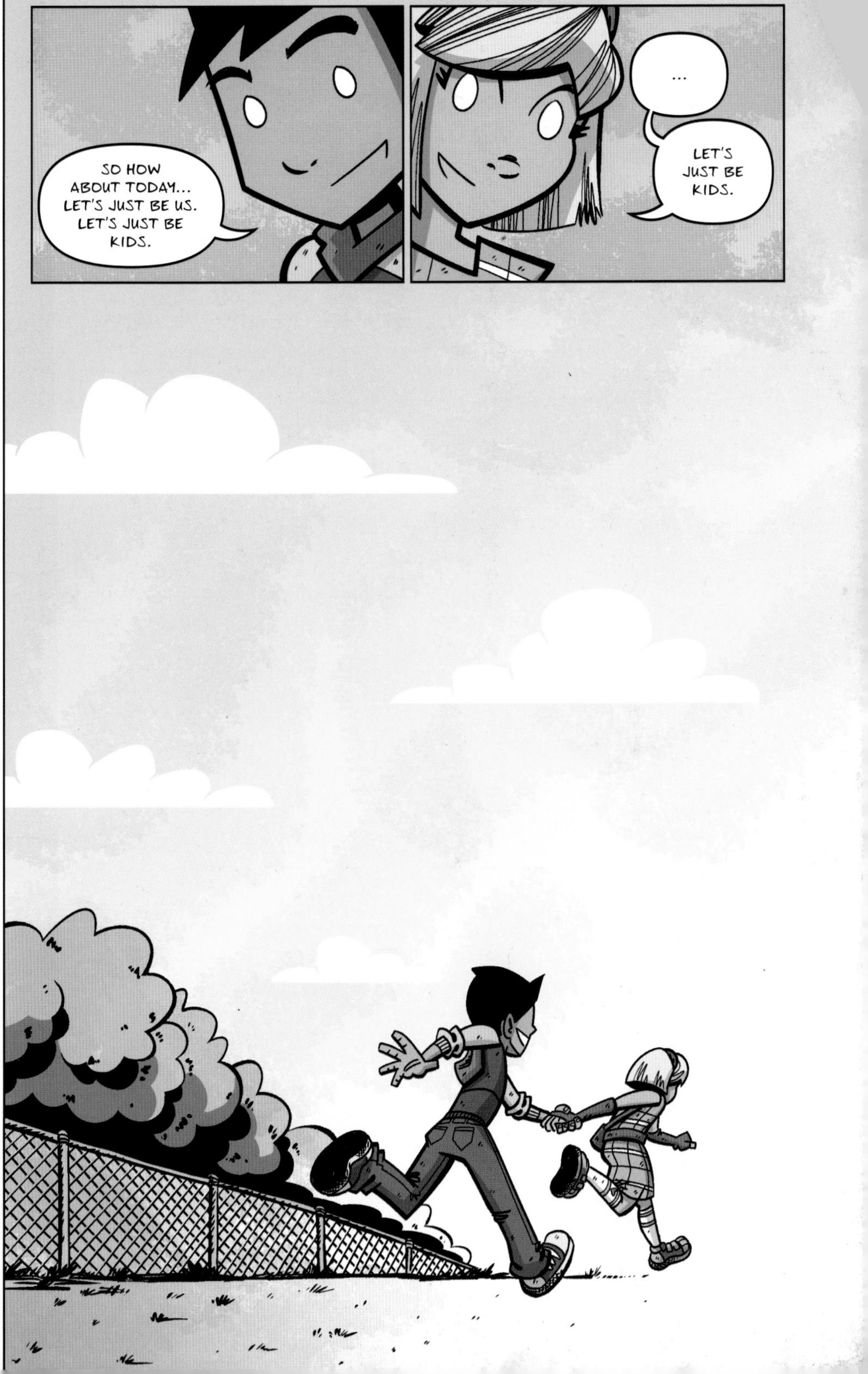
SO HOW ABOUT TODAY... LET'S JUST BE US. LET'S JUST BE KIDS.
...
LET'S JUST BE KIDS.

ABOUT THE AUTHOR

Marcus Emerson is the author of several highly imaginative children's books. His goal is to create children's books that are engaging, funny, and inspirational for kids of all ages—even the adults who secretly never grew up.

Marcus Emerson is currently having the time of his life with his beautiful wife and their four amazing children. He still dreams of becoming an astronaut someday and walking on Mars.

Stories—what an incredible way to open one's mind to a fantastic world of adventure. It's my hope that this story has inspired you in some way, lighting a fire that maybe you didn't know you had. Keep that flame burning no matter what. It represents your sense of adventure and creativity, and that's something nobody can take from you. Thanks for reading!

M.E.

—Marcus Emerson
m@MarcusEmerson.com